Vain & V

VOLUME 2 – VERACITY

JUSTAN AUTOR

Vain & Valour

First Edition 2024

Justan Autor Copyright © 2024

Published by Staten House

Cover illustration by Justan Autor
Cover and interior design by Justan Autor

The right of Justan Autor to be identified as the author of this work has been asserted in accordance with the Copyright, Designs and Patents Act, 1988.

All rights reserved. No part of this publication may be reproduced, stored in or introduced into a retrieval system, or transmitted in any form or by any means (electronic, mechanical, photocopying, recording, or otherwise), without the prior written permission of the copyright owner and the publisher of the book.

This book is a work of fiction. Names, characters, places and incidents are either a product of the author's imagination or are used fictitiously. Any resemblance to actual people, living or dead, events or locales is entirely coincidental.

A CIP catalogue record for this book is available from the British Library

ISBN: 979-8-89496-582-6

Dedication

Again, thank you to Karen, whose words of encouragement & interest in my project have proved a pillar of joy & motivation to keep writing on difficult days; Katerina, who has become an excelling force in my writing journey; Richard & Rosa, their friendship & their support, both bolstering — oh! & the pleasant surprise to know I may have birthed another reader to this world; Steve & Marisa, their companionship invaluable; & the living memory of Lizzie, which continues to spur me on.

Anew, a special thank you to my most generous & kind father, who continues to inspire me in many ways. Again, without his support, I would not, during the most challenging tribulations, have been able to focus on completing this next stage in this project.

Thanks Dad

A note from the author:
do forgive the several typos!

This Author has since been correcting them.

Justan

Table of Contents

PREFACE

Act 1

10 APRIL – 01 MAY 1769	1
01 MAY – 18 JUNE 1792	16
19 – 20 JUNE 1792	30
20 JUNE 1792	43
28 JUNE – 01 JULY 1792	57
02 – 04 JULY 1792	73

Act 2

05 – 07 JULY 1792	87
08 – 16 JULY 1792	103
17 – 19 JULY 1792	119
20 JULY 1792	134
21 – 22 JULY 1792	148
23 – 24 JULY 1792	163

Act 3

24 JULY 1792	183
25 JULY – 05 AUGUST 1792	198
06 – 10 AUGUST 1792	214
11 – 13 AUGUST 1792	229
13 – 19 AUGUST 1792	245
20 – 21 AUGUST 1792	261
ABOUT THE AUTHOR	278

PREFACE

Ah, my most esteemed & faithful readers, it is with the utmost pleasure & gratitude that I welcome you back to this second volume of our humble narrative; a work which I dare to hope shall continue to tantalise & delight your discerning sensibilities.

May you find it a grand feast!

That said, before we embark upon this next course, a word of caution — a gentle nudge to the discerning historian & to those who fancy themselves so:

For you see, the past is a capricious mistress; she delights in dallying with the unwary & inexperienced historian & whispers secrets in one ear, only to shout falsehoods in the other. Hence, while I have striven for an integrity of yore, this poor author, much like a painter struggling with a particularly stubborn canvas, has, on occasion, found it necessary to take certain liberties, to apply a bold stroke in order to capture the general form of so challenging a composition.

I implore you, therefore, O passionate chroniclers & erudite historians, to be gentle in your judgement, & to refrain from pelting this meek author with the sharp stones of pedantic correction.

Once again, as we reach the last page of this volume, I must take my leave of you, my dear readers, abandoning you in a state of delicious suspense. & once more, I must offer the following disclaimer:

None of my dear friends or acquaintances have been made the unwitting subjects of my scrutiny. Any perceived resemblances are but the result of pure coincidence; a trick of Fate's capricious hand.

Rest assured that no animals or children were harmed in this production. Certainly, no poor avian creatures had all their feathers plucked from their rumps for the sake of a quill!

With all of that said, let us now proceed to the next course of our literary repast.

Bon appétit! my dear friends, and may you savour every morsel!

"Some rise by sin, and some by virtue fall." — Shakespeare

Act 1

10 April 1769

—

01 May 1769

&

01 May 1792

—

04 July 1792

10 APRIL – 01 MAY 1769

My esteemed reader, let us now transport ourselves back some score years, to the time when young Valentin's thoughts strayed often to a vision most charming: a red-haired damsel, quite the mistress of the bow and arrow. It must be granted that any youth of the tender age of eight would find such a maiden so utterly enchanting, so wholly unconventional, so unlike the common sort of girl.

Certainly, not even all the decorous daughters of the *wohledelgeboren* (the nobly born) could hold a candle to her. This girl, though but a lowly peasant, eclipsed them all and enrapt the heart of our young lord.

He knew only her name was Elizabeth, and that she resided with her kin near his great-uncle's esteemed Schloss St Andreas, in the Canton of Zug. Their meetings were sparse, yet her vivacious spirit left an indelible mark upon his youthful mind. Her company, he soon grew fond of and sooner found himself disenchanted with the daughters who he was encouraged to court. Indeed, the captivating Elizabeth even stirred in our young hero a desire to take up archery himself — a desire, no doubt, chiefly motivated by a wish to shine in her eyes.

As so oft is the way with children, when they set their minds upon something, they heed not the disapproval of their elders. "But I dislike all other girls!" declared Valentin, twirling the thick bullion-fringing of the heavy, red velvet curtains while he gazed out of the casement at the Aare River, which meandered northwards, leading somewhere to freedom; freedom from the confines of this fortress, Aarburg Castle, and from the sycophants who sought to curry favour with the schultheiss by parading their accomplished yet lacklustre daughters before him, desperate to heap them on our hero as soon as he should come of age.

Alas, the stern hand of duty does oft crush such tender buds of affection and prune such wayward growths. "As this folly commenced with your visits to your great-uncle," — his father sprang from his crimson velvet, high-backed walnut chair, his broad chest draped with many a medallion, glinting in the morning light — "I shall see that he curbs your ramblings about the countryside!"

Across the library, Gustav strode forth and briskly smacked Valentin's hand away from the curtain. "To fraternize with such inferiors is most unpropitious." He had need to adjust his powdered wig, which did accentuate his most stern visage, befitting one charged with administering justice in the canton. "You shall not associate with that girl again!"

How deplorably cruel of his father! The hotheaded young calf could not help but stomp across the cold stone floor and fling himself into his father's chair. "But why is it so improper?"

"I will not have you question my authority!" thundered his father.

"Hmph!" The Frau Schultheissin found no fault with the acquaintance. She had even greeted her warmly. "But Mother didn't mind my playing —"

"She permitted it, too, did she?" interrupted his father, flicking a speck of dust from his dark-red justaucorps-clad shoulders. "I suppose if your mother allowed cow-milking, you would deem that acceptable as well. And remember, it is 'did not', not 'didn't'. Do not contract your speech."

"And why must I one day wed only among the daughters of those stuffy old men who even you claim bore you to distraction?"

"Valentin!" His father's nostrils flared so large that the young lad did believe the gust exuding from them stirred the large tapestry on the far wall. "Have I not cautioned you against indulging such a latitude of tongue?"

With arms crossed, Valentin averted his face. He would not respond; certainly, he would never apologise. This was too unjust. What was the value of being an heir if one could not even choose one's own companion?

Now he faced his father. "But *why*?"

"Because such is the order of the world. Even in youth, power, wealth, and society must be your sole pursuits."

Gustav glided to the many rows of shelves filled with leather-bound tomes and realigned several that he doubtless imagined were not already in so impeccable an order of display. "You are but a child now," continued he, "yet, when you come of age and are ready to consult on selecting your future Frau Schultheissin, you will understand the wherefore."

Why must the world by this way?

Valentin scrunched up his nose. "But I still wish to learn archery." Unable to resist, he just had to disrupt the meticulous arrangement of his father's inkstand and quill. "Shall you also forbid that?"

After a weighty silence, marked by an arched brow, indicating Gustav's irritation at the sight of his desk's defacement, he finally decreed, "I shall commission the banneret to appoint one of his men for your instruction. Yet, expect that I shall require you to acquaint yourself with the musket as well. It remains the armament of modern warfare."

"Then master both I shall, ready for the hunt in three weeks' time!"

"Overconfidence, boy!" His father motioned him to vacate the chair, upon which he promptly reseated himself. "Now, about tomorrow. I hope you have not forgotten the arrival of the Count von Kyburg and his daughter? This alliance promises not just to fortify the strength and unity of our cantons, but to bring considerable wealth and power to our estate..."

***

Come the morrow, this count's daughter — whatever her name, for it had quite slipped our young Valentin's mind — was as distant from his thoughts as the canton whence she hailed. Alone, engrossed was he with the fiery-haired maiden and her skilled archery; alone, he wished to fly to Zug Canton where he might again see her.

Nevertheless, around the ninth hour of morning, he donned his finest blue silk attire and joined his father and the esteemed Vogt, alongside rows of councillors and a resolute garrison — arrayed in glinting cuirasses, with pikes and muskets to the ready. Upon the south-east-facing ramparts, beneath the vibrant red and yellow Bernese banners bearing the black bear snapping proudly overhead in the morning breeze, all intently watched the dirt road, which stretched some five-and-thirty miles to Zürich.

Ere long, clouds of dust and noise heralded the Count von Kyburg's train. Marching vanguard, two stoic rows of four, mounted on spirited steeds, were the Swiss Guard, splendid in their regimentals; their sombre cuirasses, emblazoned with their lord's sigil, gleamed under the sun while crimson plumage fluttered upon their helms. Behind, rode the count alongside his countess and daughter in an ornately carved carriage, which bore the crest of the Kyburg lineage. A retinue of councillors in their own stately coaches trailed behind, with a procession of wagons heavy with baggage bringing up the rear. A robust detachment of guards concluded the grand cavalcade, ensuring the safety of their esteemed charges.

While the adults convened in the Great Hall, our young lord, relegated to the role of castle cicerone for yet another young miss dressed in the latest French fashions, and under the vigilant eye of yet another stiff governess, soon found his ennui unbearable. However, what did momentarily dampen the tedium was the young miss' ringlets — radiant red; just like Elizabeth's!

He did observe her some more. Though not so pretty as Elizabeth, a resemblance showed: the blue eyes, the smile, and even their stature. Easily they could have been sisters. Such similarity naturally gave false hope to the acquaintance. But alas, this girl had no familiarity with a bow; neither did she prefer tree climbing to playing upon the pianoforte — nor did she think it proper for young misses to pursue such adventurous exploits!

A naturally displeased young Valentin, desperate to evade further monotony, instantly quit both the young miss and her governess in the courtyard and slipped into the damp, dark passageways within the thick castle walls. None would think to look for him there.

Why must these negotiations always take place here? mused he. His father had other castles not only more comfortable but nearer to home. Valentin never liked this castle — he never would. It was always cold, gloomy, and lonely. *Little wonder Mother rarely comes here.*

With solely wistful thoughts for company, and a small torch to light the way, he trudged along, melancholy and morose.

Suddenly, a gust rushed through the passage, extinguishing his taper and plunging him into blackness. The harsh grating of stone against stone rumbled through the corridor, suggesting someone had entered an adjacent passage

Next, a red gleam struck the far wall at an intersection, and low voices galloped in hollow echoes towards him:

"We cannot proceed without the documents."

"Fear not; they shall be here before her arrival."

With cautious steps, Valentin crept along the tenebrous corridor; his fingers traced the rough, moist walls as he inched closer towards the junction, straining to better listen.

"And if they do not arrive?" queried a male voice tinged with familiarity.

Scarce daring to breathe, Valentin peered into the neighbouring passage. By the dim lantern light, he perceived two shadowy intruders, their faces obscured, standing beside a shifting wall which, with a last rumble, closed off some section absent from the castle maps.

Who were these men, and how did they know of these secret passages?

"We cannot lose this opportunity," the man went on. "In the morrow, I must return with the others to Zürich."

"Peace, dear brother," came the reply. "All shall unfold according to our design."

Here, indeed, was a scene plucked from the very pages of those thrilling adventure tales our young hero did devour by candlelight.

"Any way," said the other, "let us return, lest our absence be noted."

Their retreating footsteps echoed through the passage until the grinding of stone against stone, followed by the return of unnavigable blackness, signalled the plotters' departure into an adjoining chamber.

If only Valentin could place that voice. If only he could have learned more of this secret plot! A chill crept down his spine. Deep in his bones, settled a sense of indecipherable dread.

When later he recounted these strange events to his father, not until after first enduring a litany of rebukes for his stubbornness, disavowals, and — according to the governess — his want of gentility, did the schultheiss deign to accompany him to the location in question.

Along the stone walls, the servants diligently groped for protrusions, probing for some hidden lever or mechanism. Yet, their efforts yielded no evidence of any secret passage or chamber. Thusly accused of spurning the future alliance and fabricating the whole, Valentin found himself confined to his chamber; his release, and the promised archery lessons, contingent upon his rectifying forthwith his deficient understanding and wilful disobedience.

Though resolute and hardened by so unjust a punishment, when morning came, our young lord's eagerness for the bow did weaken his defiance. Of course, he was no less averse to his duties as an heir; but with feigned compliance, he might at least effect his release. And so, with a convincing — or rather *conniving* — display of acquiescence, he won his freedom and spent the day under a skilled archer's tutelage.

***

Three weeks hence, just shy of a day or two, the much-expected day of the hunt dawned bright and fair. Rich with red fallow, axis, sika deer, and wild boars, the forests of Muhen became the designated hunting grounds.

From the encampment of walled tents, draped with billowing rich fabrics, where sundry servants kindled fires, the hunting party broke forth. Already adept at riding, Valentin — sporting green wool, leather boots, his feathered cap set jauntily atop his head — easily kept abreast of the galloping beasts as they traversed the groves and winding slopes in search of quarry.

Upon reaching a clearing in the dense woods, marked by an ancient circle of weathered monoliths, the schultheiss proposed the party divide into smaller groups. Thus, Valentin rode alongside his father, Arnborg the banneret, and Adolfus the elector and chief bailiff of Aarberg, whose plumed hats waved like standards amidst the trees.

As they obtruded deeper into the woods, a startled herd of deer erupted from the undergrowth, their hooves pounding a hasty retreat through the sun-dappled environs. As swiftly as the hunting party pursued, the deer, most fleet of foot, had the mastery of the grounds, outmanoeuvring their pursuers with ease.

"Father! Look!" Valentin pointed at a red fox which darted across a nearby glade.

They gave chase once more; yet the cunning creature vanished, gliding into the undergrowth. But then:

"There, Father!" Valentin pointed at a flash of red crouching low in the tall, stirring grass.

Quickly, our cocksure young hero reached for his bow and, nocking an arrow, drew back the string. Overconfident in his exemplary skill and already exulting in the glory soon to be his, he took aim and let the arrow fly with seemingly flawless precision and pride.

But lo! Scarce had the deadly shaft sped forth when a shriek rent the air. A man — a mere peasant, clad in a meagre tunic tied with a rope belt — leapt up from among the growth and came bounding, denouncing whoever had near run his daughter's leg through with an arrow. But the red mounted high on his cheeks soon paled. He fell to his woolen-braies knees, begging for forgiveness.

The schultheiss fixed him with a stern gaze. "Why are you on this land?"

Stuttering, and visibly trembling, the peasant raised not his eyes nor answered. Thus, the schultheiss repeated his demand with booming authority. Just then, a young boy called out from the grass for help to bind up his sister's leg.

With permission granted to aid the girl, the peasant retreated and soon returned, carrying her in his arms. Her leg was bound with torn cloth, and her face muddied and tear-stained. The peasant's son trailed warily behind.

Now, imagine, dear reader, the astonishment that seized Valentin when he recognised the injured lass as none other than Elizabeth herself!

"It is you!" exclaimed they in unison, fingers levelled in disbelief.

The schultheiss turned sharply to his son. "You know this thing?"

Scarce had Valentin stammered out an explanation, his words tumbling over one another in his haste to clarify the situation, when his father, outraged to encounter the very brat who had blinded his son to the proper way of the world, noticed the bow and quiver slung over the girl's shoulder.

Notwithstanding Valentin collapsing to his knees, hands clasped in supplication, begging his stone-hearted father for leniency, the schultheiss, with the coldest contempt marring his stern brow, merely ordered for the peasant — Ernest — along with his children to be bound and conveyed forthwith to Aarburg Castle's dungeons, to be tried for poaching on the morrow.

Once more banished to his bedchamber, menaced with indefinite confinement, and castigated for stubbornly pleading for persons far inferior, Valentin grew only more anxious for Elizabeth's safety. And as the long, painful hours passed, not even the knowledge of his mother's imminent arrival diminished his agonies.

***

Meanwhile, the schultheiss was summoned to the Main Hall. There, his retinue — a gaggle of oldish faces scrawled with concern — had gathered round the venerable elector and chief bailiff Adolfus, who imparted a most shocking piece of intelligence regarding the Frau Schultheissin Vivienne.

"Guilty of treason?" echoed Gustav; his sharp voice reverbed high above in the vaulted ceiling. He rose abruptly from his seat and stalked over to the bailiff, snatching the incriminating documents from him. "Preposterous!" Yet powerful emotions soon contorted his suddenly pallid features. "Can my wife truly be guilty of such a heinous act?" His distressed gaze swept across the assembled men, whose eyes darted amongst themselves in silent communication. "Choosing to avenge her family and her faith at the cost of vows, devotion, fidelity, and —? You must thoroughly investigate this matter and spare her —"

"Your Excellency," interrupted Adolfus, devoid of emotion. "Since this treasonous correspondence is clearly penned by the frau schultheissin's own hand, denial is impossible."

"How dare she betray me thus!" Sudden fury reconstructed Gustav's phiz. "Did I not plead for her soul, sparing her from the rebellion that swept away her family?" Papers cast bitterly down, he returned to his chair and collapsed into it.

Adolfus gathered up the scattered pages and distributed them among those gathered. Soon, a noisy deliberation filled the hall. Faces aglow with violent indignation, each councillor called for heaven's wrath while weighing the frau's crimes against cantonal law.

"Your Excellency, forgive my boldness," again spoke Adolfus, "though it invokes great agony within, with her guilt incontrovertibly proven, she deserves capital punishment! I am sure I need not point out how overlooking this most grievous affair would jeopardise your recent ascension to the schultheiss' seat..."

***

'Twas now seven in the afternoon. From the ancient stone corners, shadows, like harbingers of doom, crept across the damp walls as the dungeon was prepared to receive its victim — Vivienne, herself.

No sooner did her carriage pass through the portcullis than her liverymen found themselves at the mercy of pike and blade point, while Vivienne was seized upon with cold efficiency and dragged underground.

Ah, what a heart-wrenching scene! Stripped of her furs and jewels, the noble dame was unceremoniously flung upon the filthy straw of a lightless cell, and the rusted door crashed shut behind her with a deafening finality. In vain she demanded the cause of her arrest, only to be rewarded with hands and feet bound, and a rough gag to silence her protests.

***

The ninth hour was chiming when our hero, ignorant of the fate befalling his mother, was drawn to his window by a disturbance in the courtyard below.

Through the leaded glass, he espied the forms of the Swiss Guard darting back and forth, their shadows shortening and elongating with the movement of passing torches. Gustav's retinue had congregated as well, shouting and demanding answers. Then, the banneret's voice rebounded, ordering detachments to be gathered and to follow him.

Curiosity inflamed, Valentin threw wide the window and leant forth to better descry the confusion.

Soon, the clip-clop of hooves announced a sizeable cavalry's arrival, their numbers swelling until their overlapping voices drowned each other out. Some minutes later, the cavalry and detachments quit the courtyard; the metal portcullis clunked loudly as it rose to facilitate the unknown march.

Was this war? Our young hero could not decide. With so vast a multitude of the schultheiss' guards called away, a sudden realisation struck him — the castle would be left nearly defenceless, and the dungeon, with its meagre complement of prisoners, would most likely be unguarded.

Here was an opportunity; a chance to liberate the captives. But first, he must free himself from his chamber. There was solely one thing to be done. "I must pretend to apologise."

So saying, Valentin did fly across his confinement to the door and set to hammering upon it, calling — nay, yelling — to the guard stationed outside.

Met with only silence, he tried once more.

But again, no reply came.

Hence, he yelled anew, fiercely yanking at the handle; but all was for naught. No doubt, his warden had likewise been called away.

"How am I to get out?"

Just then, the flapping of wings drew his gaze to the open window where a nightjar alighted briefly on the sill before winging into the night.

That's it!

With haste born of desperation, he tied together several bedsheets and fastened one length to the leg of a heavy oak desk beside the window. The other, he tied round his own person in an impromptu harness.

Limb's trembling, heart racing, he climbed onto the sloped roof — the courtyard stories below seeming to spin dizzily beneath him.

I shall break my neck!

Availing his lungs of the air, he told himself again and again that this was no different from climbing those tall trees with Elizabeth. He needed merely to scale the roof and lower himself to the window on the floor below, from where he could —

But ah! Cruel Fortune had other designs in her head, for presently a tile dislodged underfoot and sent him tumbling over the eaves with a cry. Yet, by good luck, the knots held fast, leaving our young hero a-dangling before the window — his heart fit to burst from terror.

With no small effort did our pendulous lad gain the stone sill and, finding the window unlatched, make his entrance.

Along the empty passages he scurried with a rodent-like trepidation, and, descending the stairs and keeping to the shadows, he at last stole across the courtyard towards the dungeons.

Down the bocardo's winding steps he silently hastened, only to freeze in horror. At the bottom stood a guard, back turned, blocking his path.

What should I do?

A mere distraction would not suffice. The man must be overpowered. But how? At last, an idea struck his brain. Recalling the ancient panoply lining the upper passage, he retreated back up the steps, silent like before and, with some difficulty, wrested a heavy helmet from a suit of armour.

Thus armed, he re-descended, creeping as stealthily as a cat towards the oblivious guard. With but four steps soon between them, Valentin did raise the helm and with a mighty leap, and with a tremendous clang, bring it crashing down upon the poor fellow's head!

The stunned guard collapsed in a clattering heap, nigh bleeding from his skull, too addled to resist as our hero did grab the keys.

"Quickly, we must fly!" cried Valentin; he and flung open the dungeon door and led the captives — Ernest cradling his injured Elizabeth with Elias in tow — up the winding steps and back across the moonlit courtyard.

Snatching a flambeau from its sconce, he then ushered the escapees into a chamber. There, he revealed a hidden passage — known only to himself and his parents — concealed behind the wainscot. "You must away, now!" Valentin pressed the torch into Ernest's hand. "Follow the steps and they will bring you to a forest path to the south. Make haste while you can!"

Overcome with gratitude, Ernest thanked him profusely. But Elizabeth grabbed Valentin's wrist. "Why didn't you tell me who you were? And why dress as a peasant whenever we met? You tricked me."

"The deception was not mine. My mother bade me dress so when we visited my great-uncle and swore me to secrecy regarding my rank and —"

Footsteps loudened ever nearer outside.

"There is no time for explanation. Go now! And be careful when you emerge into the woods. I know not what happened, but the Swiss Guard has left the castle as though headed for war."

"Perhaps they've gone in search of the prisoner," replied Elizabeth.

"Prisoner?"

"I overheard whispers in the dungeon. A woman prisoner spoke, and a man replied. Then the door creaked open, and they were gone."

"A woman prisoner?"

"Guards came demanding if we knew anything. I told them what I —"

Footsteps now sounded on the other side of the door.

"Go!" Valentin pushed her into the passage, slid the wainscot panel back into place, and, just as the door burst open, concealed himself beneath a table hung with a heavy cloth.

10 April – 01 May 1769

"Do you see them?" came a gruff voice as feet paced about the room. "The scullery maid swears she spied them headed in this direction."

Our young hero, hidden in his cramped quarters, stifled a horrified gasp as he realised his discovery might betray the escapees' route.

Alas, in that gasp, having inhaled dust, several motes tickling his nose, he could not suppress a thunderous sneeze.

"Over there!" cried the guards.

***

Meantime, the escapees reached the end of the secret tunnel — a cave opening onto a wooded eminence. Ernest stepped warily out, espying the dark environs for any signs of danger. All was quiet, save for the occasional breeze. "Stay close," uttered he.

Down the wooded declivity and past a shimmering lake, our fretful trio fled. Elizabeth, her injured leg throbbing with each step, found herself again carried in her father's arms.

Soon, they came upon a forest break, where a broad moonlit field stretched ahead, beckoning them to freedom. In the distance, another forest loomed, promising shelter and safety.

"Let's cross while we can!" Ernest grabbed Elias' hand tightly in his own, and together they ran with all the speed their weary limbs could muster.

But they had fled scarce halfway across the field, when a shout rang out behind them. "Over there!"

The growing moonlight, before their ally, had betrayed our trio to all.

Glancing back, they spied bobbing torches converging from the far side of the field. "Make haste!" cried Ernest. "We must reach the wood before they capture us!"

***

Back to our young hero: apprehended as he was by two quite astonished guards finding him alone, they dragged him to the Great Hall.

There, his grief-stricken father paced before the many tall windows. Upon seeing his son hauled in, his feet stopped, and his countenance reddened to scarlet hues. "What is the meaning of this?" thundered he at the men.

Before the guards could reply, Valentin, with a burst of courage, broke free from their grasp, ran forward, and fell at his father's feet. "Leave my friend alone!"

Of a sudden, the lofty arched doors burst open; another guard came rushing in, proclaiming he had received word that the frau schultheissin had been spotted.

Truly, this announcement struck Valentin like a thunderbolt. "Mother?" He jumped to his feet and seized his father's sleeve. "What is happening?!"

Even as this took place, again, the doors flew open. In staggered yet another guard, the very one from the dungeon, clutching at his bloodied head. "The prisoners. They're gone — set free!"

"What?" Gustav yanked his sleeve away. "*Who* let them —?" He stopped short and turned on his son, who instantly quailed beneath so venomous a gaze. "Is this *your* doing, boy?"

***

Through the steepening woods, the fugitives continued to flee, their path strewn with gnarled roots, fallen trees, low boughs, bushes, and rocks that oft impeded their desperate steps. Ernest, burdened by the weight of his injured Elizabeth, soon found himself overcome by exhaustion. He implored between laboured breaths for them to leave him behind. "I'll only slow your escape."

But his filial children would not abandon their father to such a cruel fate. Elizabeth, despite her stinging wound, jumped down and joined Elias in pulling him along, knowing not where they were, nor which way they proceeded.

Alas, the galloping horses and loudening voices carried on the chilling breeze, drew their attention back to the peril that pursued them. Again, torches bobbed through the trees, filling our trio's hearts with dread.

"Which way?" The boy tugged at his father's sleeve.

Still gasping for breath, and his body spent and quaking, Ernest stared hopelessly into the dark. "This way," groaned Ernest, at last.

Then it was that cruel Fortune did betray them. For in their haste, poor Elizabeth tripped. Her hand slipping from her father's grasp, she tumbled down a slope, disappearing into a thick briar patch with a cry of pain.

"Lizzie!" Ernest scrambled after her, only to meet the same fate. His legs smashed into a large trunk as he tumbled, eliciting a stifled scream of agony.

"There!" called Elizabeth; her keen eyes espied in the blackness behind her the appearance of a rocky cavity. "We can hide in there!"

Scarce had her brother scrambled to them when, "stay hidden!" said he.

Ernest grabbed his wrist. "What do you mean?"

"I'll draw them off."

"No, my son!" Ernest struggled to his feet. "I'll go..."

"I can outrun them, Father. If they find us here, we'll all be taken. You need to help Lizzie. I promise I'll find my way back home."

And, with a brief, fierce hug, the gallant lad extracted himself from the grasping limbs and vanished into the shadows, deaf to his kins' protests.

***

As midnight tolled, young Valentin, yet again confined to his bedchamber, heard the ominous groan of the portcullis being raised. His heart nigh ready to burst, he rushed to his window, fixing his gaze in the barbican's direction: a host of guards bearing torches entered the castle walls; their measured tread reverbed on the gloomy night air.

Gripped by sickening dread, Valentin could only watch and wait.

At last, from the haze of torchlight thrown across the courtyard, he distinguished the banneret's figure, followed by the first of the detachments.

Something of an ill-boding hung on the air. His breath caught. Where was his mother? Or Elizabeth? He peered forward. *What about Elizabeth's father and — but wait! Who is that?*

"Take the boy back to the dungeon!" came the banneret's deep voice.

Elias, alone? Then they must have —

"Did you capture her?" rang out the schultheiss' desperate words, accompanied by his sharp footsteps as he appeared in the courtyard.

At once, the banneret and the detachment dropped to their knees; the former instructed that a horse be brought forward. The animal appeared, bearing upon its back a sullied and shrouded figure.

Valentin took in the whole with the terror of uncertainty.

As the schultheiss staggered forward and flung back the cloth, his terrible shriek pierced the air; he reeled back, sinking to the ground. "*Vivienne!*"

"Mother!" Quitting his casement, Valentin raced to his door and, banging on it with all his might, demanded his immediate release.

By the time he got below, weeping woman-servants had gathered about. The banneret was explaining the deceased had most likely perished from a bear's mauling.

With quaking steps, Valentin neared the savaged corpse.

Beneath the torn rags — once his mother's white inner gown — horrific gashes rent all visible flesh. Even her once beautiful face was beyond recognition, rendered a pulpy mass of glistening red flesh and white bone.

This abhorrent sight squeezed Valentin's insides. "*No!*"

"You must not look, boy!" Gustav pulled him back, endeavouring to shield his son's eyes from the gruesome sight. "You must not see her this way."

But the few glimpses Valentin stole between his father's fingers were enough to sear the terrible image into his mind.

Presently, a lifeless arm slipped out. Deep red pooled along the torn skin, gathering at the lacerated, once gentle hands — clearly thrown up in self-defense.

From that same mangled hand — blood dripping from torn fingers onto the slabs — the frau schultheissin's golden wedding band glittered in cold testimony to the horror that had befallen her.

Young Valentin sank to the cold stone floor. "Mother, *no!*"

01 MAY – 18 JUNE 1792

Such were the distressing events of that tragic day, some three-and-twenty years past, when our hero, a mere stripling, was visited by a misfortune most cruel. And now, our present Peter — whom we, at long last, unmasked to be Valentin — found himself ambushed by a deluge of memory's agonising echoes, which ultimately surrendered to him his true identity.

So overcome was he by this revelation that he tottered; his legs, conspiring to give way, almost pitched him in a headlong tumble over the bridge wall.

"Peter?" Elizabeth steadied him. "You have turned as pale as death!"

A darkness presently spun the world about him. As he gazed into her eyes, he succumbed to a tide of emotions and slumped heavily onto her shoulder...

Intrusive shrills did rend the misty veil that shrouded his consciousness, beckoning him back to the waking world. Our hero fluttered his eyes open to behold five countenances peering down upon him: Elizabeth, Emil, and Helene (all blinking); Znüni (panting); and the ever theatrical —

"He lives!" shrilled Edmunda. Enfolding his hand within her own, she doused it with a liberal shower of tears. "But, pray, why he's bent on *incessant* swooning and causing us no end of worry is certainly very vexing!"

Bewildered and disoriented, our hero looked about: rustic whitewashed walls; that small crucifix; meagre decorations, and that little window of humble lace furnishing. "What... what... what befell me?"

"What *befell you*?" Edmunda flung off his hand. "You swooned away — near dead, yet again! Inflicting no end of inconvenience upon us all!"

"Yes, thank you, Mother," interjected Elizabeth with some notable asperity before addressing in gentler accents he whom she still believed to be Peter. "How do you fare now?"

Realising he lay in Lizzie's bedchamber, our hero hoisted himself up. "Why am I here?"

"*Why*?" rejoined Edmunda. "What sort of buffoon — nay, racoon — no, buffoon! Shoots arrows at innocents then swoons as if struck dead, still expecting to be borne home?"

"An arrow? — at whom? And who conveyed me here?"

***

In the throes of arduous endeavour, had our injured heroine hauled the senseless hero upon her slender back — where he hung most inelegantly; arms a-dangling over her shoulders — whilst she laboured, most inconveniently so, one slow, limping step at a time across the bridge.

"Why," panted she, "must this vexatious lout..." — she stopped and re-hoisted him up — "... be so monstrously heavy?!" Beads of sweat verily sprang forth upon her brow, stinging her eyes most cruelly as she strained her neck, scanning for any Good Samaritan to aid her.

But alas! Not a single soul was to be seen.

Another exasperated sigh escaped her heaving bosom as she placed one resolute foot doggedly before the other. "He near-skewered my leg!" Irritation did curl her comely lips. "Then he passes out for me to lug his dead weight hither and thither!" How she did resent the wretched unconscious fellow who, unbeknownst to her, had twice now inflicted upon her grievous harm. "If only I could fling the blackguard into the waters below!"

Nevertheless, since our heroine is not of the avenging species, she trudged on, bearing her unwieldy cargo, while groaning and cursing most unmaidenly beneath its mass.

After much tribulation, her legs quite unwilling to take any more, she spied two figures hastening towards her: Emil and Helene.

***

"Don't you even remember a *wit* of happened, but hours ago?" Edmunda threw her hands aloft in vexation. "You near shot Lizzie dead, causing no end of trouble for the poor girl, then strained every muscle of your rescuers who hauled your lifeless carcass here from the forest!"

"The forest?" Around our hero's eyes, his muscles did suddenly tighten as recollection sent a jolt through his chest, blowing away the clouds from his befuddled brain. "Heavens!" He turned to Lizzie. "Your leg?"

She assured him she was quite well.

Though relief swept away the weight of the surrounding air, something felt amiss. He had blacked out. But he last recalled being at a bridge... A peculiar tightness crept over his breast; he clutched at it.

Concern etched upon her features, Lizzie took hold of his hand. "What is it, Peter?"

But lo! This was *not* his name. 'Twas Valentin. "I am not... Peter..."

"*Not* Peter?" exclaimed all.

"Lord in Heaven!" Edmunda leapt up like a startled cat. "The featherbrain has only forgotten who he is all over again!"

Our hero now looked hard upon Elizabeth, the truth plain before him. His heart striking heavier with the weight of this revelation, he shook off her gentle grasp. "I wish to be alone. Remove yourselves at once!"

Not without scolding him roundly for his rudeness and promising to deny the ingrate all care, company, and comestibles, did Edmunda sweep Elizabeth and the others from the room.

Now alone with his thoughts, Peter — I mean, Valentin — found much solace to know himself again. No orphan of destitution was he but a man or rank, noble stock, and superior wealth. Yet how cruel of Fortune to bring him to this strange pass: reunited after so many years with the very innocent lass who once stole his boyish heart, only to find her matured into a woman of guile and deception! *For what cause did she spin her web of lies?* Purely to thwart her parents' wishes? *To evade the farmer's son?* "How wickedly she has used me!"

Had he but known that Lizzie's motives were not entirely selfish, and that she had spared him from eviction in his amnesiac state, his indignation might have been tempered. Still and all, his simmering resentment cooled to melancholy as he pondered his own dire circumstances since that fateful night at Oberhofen: ostracism, a failed mission, hunted as an outlaw, and fleeing annihilation!

Fresh poundings did now beset his skull most grievously.

Whoever incriminated our hero months ago had set in motion machinations too complex to now unravel — even with the corroboration of the Schaffhausen Small Council members who had seen the scroll. Oh, had not that vital evidence been delivered to the flames, he could dare to exonerate himself, dare to hope! But, as matters stood, to ever return home or assume his true name were indeed impossible dreams. And what is more, he was trapped in the insignificant and contemptible role of Peter. *Perhaps I should seek refuge across the borders?*

A knock, soft yet insistent, sounded at the door, and in popped the worthy visage of Pier. His eyes twinkled with good humour and he bore a folded newspaper. "Are you well enough for the energetic enquiries of a concerned friend?"

Despite the many perplexities surrounding this man, Peter (for now, for the sake of clarity and continuity, we shall persist in calling him thus) sensed he was someone he could trust. Hence, a smile forced onto his face, he welcomed the good fellow in.

Though Pier kept his visit brief, our hero noted the eloquent sympathy and affection glowing in his countenance — a man who was still but an entire stranger. Before taking his leave, Pier placed the newspaper on the bedside table and mentioned, with a cryptic air, there was another matter he wished to discuss, but he would do so upon his return from outside the canton.

Left alone once more, Peter wrestled anew with his disconsolate thoughts. How to endure such ruination, he knew not, nor how to safely apprise his former cohorts of his whereabouts. What *was* he to do? Eyeing the newspaper, he snatched it up and hurriedly passed his eyes over the front page.

The headline ran: "Neutrality in Jeopardy. France and Austria Draw Battle Lines." Its subheading declared: "Fear and Uncertainty Grip the Confederacy. Is War Inevitable?"

How did his own struggles matter amidst such widespread turmoil? He had failed his mission. He had sacrificed everything — his family, his reputation, his very life; all for nothing!

He threw the paper down. "And what of Ludwig?" Had his trusty valet given up our hero for lost? Or had he waited for him at Lucerne on each full moon? Surely, in the time passed, it would be the former? However, if by some small miracle... on the coming full moon... oh! 'Twas a fool's hope, yet 'twas all that Peter had to cling to...

***

Five days hence, our hero, donning a fine bushy beard and garbed in the most inconspicuous attire, arrived in Lucerne, where he lodged under a false name at a posthouse.

As the hour neared midnight, he came near the long, red-roofed, wood-trussed Chapel Bridge. With the warmer weather enticing many folks abroad, it was in vain he sought his valet among the throng. At the sight of the old Water Tower, his hairs stood on end. But what of the watchman? Anxiously, Peter studied the bridge entrance, squinting at the metal-clad man's face. It was someone entirely else...

Feeling the prickle of unseen eyes upon him, he cast a nervous glance about yet spied only strangers passing back and forth.

With his cowl shading his face, he ventured onto the bridge and to the agreed meeting place; there, facing Lake Thun, he feigned interest in the moonlit view. Incidentally, there came to his mind the poem: *Oh, Were I the moon...* A shiver vibrated on his nerves. Indeed, its lines seemed to take on a fatalistic prowess, as if that scrap of paper had guided our hero in the wake of that dead man to the very abode of the woman he so clearly adored. *If the poor chap only knew what a snake he had elevated in his affection!*

The twelfth hour tolled on the distant Zytturm clock tower. Peter shook off this visitor to his memory and peered up and down the bridge, seeking among the many faces that of his valet. Perchance he *had* forgotten about him?

A familiar male voice struck our hero's hearing. As he turned to look, a second voice — that of a woman — elicited a gasp. Deep in talk, the very rogues who had played his parents presently strolled past. But gone were the rich raiments. The villain sported a modest, long cloak and broad-brimmed hat. The villainess looked the part of a fortune teller, bright headscarf, dangling earrings, and flowing robes. The both of them in their true villainous colours!

Happenstance — nay, Fortune — had worked the extraordinary. Were it not for the shock benumbing his limbs, Peter would have flown at them in a rage. But what had brought them here? Their glib and serpentine talk answered to Peter's thoughts; the knaves meant to initiate some recruit into their wicked brotherhood on the first hour at their storehouse.

Impossible as it was that such an encounter might happen again; and such was the temptation too strong to withstand; to follow them to their lair was indispensable.

After tailing the rogues for nearly a mile, Peter found himself at the edge of a secluded wood on the city outskirts. The scoundrels pursued a rude path, which led to a moonlit glen and the exterior of a large, abandoned-looking mill: its waterwheel still; its waterway devoid of life.

Again, sensing himself pursued, Peter glanced back: *was that a figure darting into the trees?* Hence, eluding the moonbeams which glided between the leaves, he hid behind a broad oak, from where he watched and listened.

Nothing stirred. No form reappeared. The still air carried naught but the brigands' chatter and the planks creaking underfoot as they ascended an external staircase to an upper floor of the mill.

Anon, a certain rhythm — evidently some secret code — being rapped on the structure's door, and the scoundrels appeared to wait. A hatch opened, revealing the glow of a torch and a silhouette.

"Take what we want," spoke he who had posed as Peter's father.

"What do you leave?" replied the other from inside.

"Leave nothing behind," answered the impostor mother.

The hatch closed; the door creaked open. Laughing in wicked delight, the fraudsters entered the property before the door closed behind them.

It first came to our hero to return to the city to notify the Landjäger. Yet, without proof of the charlatans' crimes and knowing the hazard involved, he decided against this. 'Twas best to apprehend the swindlers himself!

So resolved, now he had only to await the unsuspecting recruit's arrival.

At last, the outline of the man appeared. Scouring the ground, Peter grabbed a fallen branch. Before the poor fool was aware of what hit him, with a mighty swing, our hero felled him to the dirt.

The senseless man being thus dragged into the undergrowth and trussed up to a tree, Peter rummaged through his garments, discovering a document bearing plans, no doubt, of their next target. Not without also taking the fiend's sword and pistol did our hero, cloaked and cowled, climb the stairs to infiltrate the viper's nest.

Admittance gained by employing the same coded knock, Peter was ushered inside to a large chamber, where six miscreants stood about a vast, ornate table in conference with they who had dared feign to be his parents.

Crates, clocks, fine tables and chairs, elegant paintings — several recognisably from Johannes' schloss — and many other rich spoils filled the room all the way up to the wooden ceiling. Nearby, a rail displayed many costumes; doubtless the sundry characters these villains played.

Among the garb was a familiar red military coat.

"Welcome to our little enterprise," oozed the former pretending father, clearly the leader of this mob. "As we are all incognito here, let us dispense with introductions. Come, what intelligence have you of our next exploit?"

With face lowered, our hero stepped forward and offered the stolen document. The knave's eyes did gleam as he snatched it up, only for the woman, her phiz flushing with rapacious excitement, to then greedily rip it away from him.

"This inventory is a rare prize," crowed she. "You'll be well-rewarded. But you are certain you can gain us safe entrance to your master's schloss?"

Peter seethed. For sure, these were the same wily tricks used to enter Johannes' schloss. Nonetheless, he nodded, playing the part.

The wicked woman, as if struck by a moment of distrust, tried to peer into the shade of Peter's cowl. "Show your face, boy."

Confident in that he could overpower all present, he whipped back his hood. Instantly, the colour did retreat from the pretenders' faces.

"But...?" stuttered the man while a-stumbling backwards.

Gasping, the woman levelled a trembling finger. "It's *you*!?"

In a flash, our hero unsheathed his sword and leapt across the table, pressing the metal razor edge to the stunned rogue's throat. "No one move, or your master dies!"

The six fiends stood a-trembling, hands poised to reach for their hilts, while the old rogue, letting out a whimper, begged his comrades to stand down.

"Why torment us so cruelly?" shrilled the woman. Her eyes welled with tears that Peter's heart was as hardened to as callous skin. "We merely do what we can to survive in this harsh world. Please, don't hurt —"

"Enough!" interrupted Peter, pressing deeper the blade's edge into the fiend's now perspiring, gulping throat. "I care not for your excuses. If you esteem this man's soul as much as your wanton greed, you will do precisely —"

Alas! A heavy blow crashed down upon our hero's head.

Disoriented, he turned to see a seventh ruffian he had evidently before failed to observe.

In a trice, the blackguards wrestled Peter to the floor. After delivering several hearty blows about his pericranium, they bound him with ropes and dragged him over to a thick post, tying him half-senseless and bleeding to it.

"See what you've done!" The woman discharged a jug of water in his face. "What business do you have in following us and interfering with our lives?"

Believing their cover blown, the mob roared for his swift execution.

"I'll deal with him *now*!" came a deep, chilling voice.

All eyes swung round to a brute who levelled a pistol at Peter's head.

"What are you doing?" The woman flew at him. "We cannot have blood on our hands!"

But the miscreant merely pushed her away and pulled back on the hammer. Its reverbing click sent waves of terror through our hero as he stared aghast at the barrel.

"If we let him live," said the antagonist, "it'll be at our own demise."

In a moment of almost maternal hysteria, the woman placed herself between Peter and the assailant. This stance merely provoked further hostility, and an altercation broke out. The woman was pulled out of the way, and again, the ruffian pointed the weapon.

Thud-thud-thud!

A tense silence fell like a pall. All eyes shot in the direction of the noise.

Thud-thud-thud-thud-thud!

"'Tis the door!" cried one.

"D'you think we cannot deduce this *ourselves*?" shrilled the woman. "Go and see who comes at this hour!"

Scarce did the ordered brigand fly to the spy hatch and look out of it when he spun round, face awash with alarm. "The Swiss Guard!"

My, oh my, what a scene of utter pandemonium now erupted. The plunderers scrambled about the space like headless chickens and heedless bulls, crashing into furniture and each other. Items were gathered up; papers cast into a flaming log burner, which now raged like the very portal to Hades itself.

The woman did now round fully on our hero with a face that would have awed even Medusa. "Why have you brought them down on our heads?"

Unable to answer her, Peter trembled from a fear tantamount to everyone else still racing wildly about the space. Was this something to do with the man he had sensed following him? Was this the same guards he had before battled? Was it now that he was to be finally captured and —?

A splintering boom — that of the exterior door being broken through by an onslaught — shook the room, sending the knaves into a wilder frenzy.

Heavy footfalls soon reverbed along the outer passage, bringing doom ever nearer. One ruffian, trembling like a cornered rat and looking every bit the part, lifted a trapdoor. Shouting to their leaders, he lowered them down on a rope to safety before following suit.

Just then, while a second reprobate attempted escape, a great crash preceded the detachment bursting in, led a by a colonel shouting, "stop him!"

Half a dozen guards, at least, did do battle with the brigands — swords clashing, furniture crashing, papers scattering like leaves in a gale. Others clawed at the stove — which belched smoke and sparks like a dyspeptic dragon — snatching from its flames the burning and smoking papers.

Outnumbered and out-weaponed as the ruffians were, they snatched up improvised armaments: a chair leg, a poker from the hearth, a half-eaten mutton chop, even a well-worn fiddle, which, when smashed over a guard's head, produced a most discordant twang! A wayward chamber pot, flung by another desperate rogue, narrowly missed our hero's head, shattering against the wall behind him and showering him with its unsavoury contents.

The colonel, having dealt one rascal a mighty fist to his mighty nose, which did produce a bursting red torrent, noticed Peter. He rushed over, causing no little trepidation in his pounding breast. "Valentin! Are you badly hurt?"

Our hero did stare at the man in bewilderment. "You know my name?"

The colonel did stare back the same. "Your memory has returned?"

A missile flew over both their heads.

Our hero did stare at the man some more. "Yes. But how did you —"

A disturbance erupted below, followed by the slamming of doors, of horses in a hard gallop, and of rattling wheels. The colonel ordered several of his men to go after whoever had escaped.

Only the more stunned, Peter scrutinised his face. "Do I know you?"

"No." The colonel untied him. "But I do *you*. Come, let me help you up."

As the six rogues were hauled away to the garrison, the colonel ordered two men to search the premises for the remaining paperwork. "We must away!" now said he to our hero.

"There is something I first need to get." At that, Peter rushed over to the clothing rail and grabbed the regimentals.

***

When our hero awoke the next day, his thoughts swung back and forth between his valet and the enigmatic colonel. Could something have happened to the former? Who, indeed, was the latter? Perhaps the former arrived at the bridge just after our hero quit it? Was it not the latter who had intervened and saved him and Lizzie and Emil at the Liestal garrison — could it be the same person?

The more Peter pondered this, he became only the more distracted. *I need to find Ludwig! I need to know who this colonel is!* But having no information on which to proceed, he could only wait until they meet again: the valet, pray, on the next moon; the colonel, he knew not where or when.

At any rate, since he had returned to Bubendorf battered and bruised, it was to be expected that he would suffer a fusillade of reprimands and troubled questions. But how he resented Elizabeth's cloying sympathies and misplaced solicitudes. Though his coldness and evasiveness deterred neither her curiosity nor concern, it did evidently arouse her suspicion and perplexity. Even so, he cared neither for her worries nor her distrust.

***

Ah, what a trying time it was for our hero. In the days that followed, he found himself thrust into the rigours of martial training — another burden to bear in this faux life of the fabricated Peter. Such an ordeal was disastrous enough, knowing that this looming war, the rupture between the cantons, and the subsequent conscription owed to his failed commission!

Having, however, an opportunity to pore over the garrison's collection of multi-cantonal newspapers, this he eagerly did. France had declared war against Prussia; the consequences of this commandeered almost every page and column. Certainly, this was another catastrophe. But what of the Schaffhausen Small Council members or the scroll? There was not a single word about it. Why, oh why, was this cursed war still in the making? Worse still, France demanded the Swiss confederates to train their military, draining the canton of its men. Such uncertainties only plagued our hero's mind; a constant belligerent commander and companion to the physical exertions of his training.

***

On the following Monday morn, Peter called upon that lofty lord at Schloss Ebenrain to relate his recent trip to Lucerne. But no sooner had Peter set a toe upon the front steps than the haughty footmen — each scowling like two of the three heads of Cerberus guarding the gates to Hades — sought to dismiss him with a stern reminder to never again darken their master's threshold.

"Be gone, you scoundrel!" cried one.

"Indeed," cried the other. "You have no business here! Off with you before we set His Lordship's new dogs upon your sorry hide!"

Undeterred, our hero stated his business, feeding his report directly into the ears of those solemn footmen. With awe most visible, their earlier disdain melted away quicker than snow in the summer; they scurried off, seemingly in competition to relay the news first — their coattails flapping behind them.

Anon, Johannes — accompanied by two new dalmatians; their spots and snouts not less haughty than their predecessors — not only granted our hero entry, but came in *propia persona* to usher him across the sacrosanct doorstep.

"Well, well, you are certainly full of surprises!" exclaimed he with high satisfaction. His countenance glowed with an eagerness that anyone not acquainted with his volatile disposition might have mistaken for congeniality.

"Come," — he performed a high flourish — "you *must* join me for luncheon."

The veranda became the host of the light meal. Jago also joined — though a cold civility permeated all his conversation. Behind every smile, there lurked a character seemingly of distrust, disrelish, even disdain. Peter could not be sure.

At a nearby linen-covered table of their own, the dalmatians devoured some fine repast.

Presently, a servant came out, bearing the delayed day's newspaper, which Johannes, with several glares, snatched from him and flung onto the table. Peter happened to glance at its front page: "Two councillors and their companions found dead under suspicious circumstances." A strange foreboding shuddered within. But perhaps this was merely the sudden chill in the air?

Wishing not to prolong his audience, or the awkward air which accompanied it, Peter provided Johannes with the direction of where he could find his possessions. At that, he took his leave, whereupon that same afternoon, Johannes and Jago set off for Lucerne.

***

About a week later, a grand procession of wagons rolled through Bubendorf, their wheels churning up dust as they trundled towards Schloss Ebenrain. By great fortune, not only had the bulk of Johannes' belongings been recovered, but his beloved former dogs, too. From several segments of paperwork salvaged from the fire, 'twas revealed that had it not been for Peter's fortuitous intervention, most items will have already been spirited away to some distant canton, never to be seen again, while the dalmatians will have been lost to some foppish dandy who resided near Lake Lucerne's shimmering waters.

As his precious valuables rolled into the courtyard, Johannes was as self-satisfied and gloating as to be expected of his character. He strutted about, chest puffed out like a bullfrog in the throes of a mating call, eyes flashing with that sort of avaricious delight which alone the truly covetous can muster.

Ah, here we must spare a moment to observe the capricious nature of canine loyalty. The erstwhile dalmatians, far from being overjoyed at the first sight of their master, reacted with a disdain that would have put the most pompous patrician to shame. Upon seeing Johannes' new acquisitions — brazenly all spots and legs — they turned their snouts skyward as if in a gesture of supreme contempt. And as if to punctuate their haughty displeasure, the spotted hounds kicked up a storm of dust with their hind legs, sending a flurry of grit all over Johannes' finely polished shoes and directly into the faces of his hapless new pets, before sauntering off inside the schloss.

Petulant pooches, indeed!

Yet, what perhaps set Johannes' mind more awhirl was the accompanying despatch from the garrison, praising our hero's heroism, and enjoining Johannes to perform a bestowal of recognition. Where his gratitude — if we may call it that — would have stopped at that earlier luncheon, Johannes' wife, wanting not in discernment or indebtedness, ensured a more apt distinction was to be paid.

And so, to Peter's no small amazement, several days hence, came an invitation to a grand spring ball at Schloss Ebenrain. But my, the prospect of honouring so loathsome a lord with his presence was no less appealing than spending an evening in the company of the noisy barnyard denizens below his bed. Yet, decorum forbade him from refusing such a tribute. And so, he resigned himself to setting aside his distaste for that man for one evening.

From this obligation, Peter turned his mind on matters of greater consequence — the thoroughly destroyed scroll. Though lacking the scroll itself, its concluding lines hung before his mind as though branded by hot iron: "*My last request is to the raven: release the dove...*" What riddles wrapped within riddles! "This dove, and this raven; what figures do they represent?"

So lost to his musings, he noted not Pier lingering below until the good fellow bid him descend from his roost.

Together, as they strolled the environing hills, Pier canvassed the subject he had desired to speak of. "I have pondered this, these several weeks," said he. "Since I am, at present, without the company of my son — he has, for some time, been away volunteering with the Swiss Guard — the void I am now finding insufferable. Moreover, the loss of his daily assistance, even in trivial matters, has proved challenging to this old widower."

Pier smiled, but his eyes communicated a heavy heart. "In point, wishing to assuage this emptiness, I hope to find in you both a friend and helper? I will, of course, reimburse you for the latter, and provide you your own quarters at my house; should you... *accept?*"

"You are offering *me* employment?"

Again, Pier smiled; though his eyes communicated a searching look. "That, and, of course... friendship, yes."

This offer's timing could not have been more propitious. Our hero indeed wished to effect a distance between himself and Elizabeth. "I gladly accept."

Surprise did plainly lift Pier's brows. "You do not need time to consider? My society, you may find tedious."

"My mind is quite resolved. When may I come?"

***

Meantime, at Schloss Ebenrain, as the manservants scurried to and fro busily restoring the last of Johannes' chattels to their venerated locations, several maidservants got to lolling about and idling while perusing the crumpled wrapping papers — mostly old and recent newspapers.

It then occurred that a most girlish squeal rent the air, causing the other maids to flock to their companion's side. The source of the commotion? None other than a most handsome visage, immortalised in print.

Blushing cheeks and dreamy eyes abounded as the ladies giggled and cooed like woodpigeons; their voices rose in a cacophony of admiration for the winning gentleman whom they swore they had seen somewhere before.

Their continued chirping and cooing did, alas, soon draw Jago's unwelcome alert. He chided them most sternly for their want of employment.

Quick-witted, the maids protested they had merely paused to debate a face that bore a striking resemblance to a former, believed they, employee.

Though sceptical of their claims, Jago snatched up the offending page — a front page of the Bürkli-Zeitung.

Instantly, his eyes did stretch wide as one made awestruck.

For there, beneath the damning word WANTED stared the unmistakable visage of Peter himself!

19 – 20 JUNE 1792

At the tenth hour of the next morn, Peter did repeatedly cross and uncross his arms as he waited at the gate, watching the lane which disappeared over the top of the hill. The carriage Master Pier had promised would soon arrive.

Our hero's departure was met with a medley of sentiments: Matron Edmunda and the good Ernest, though saddened to lose his company, were glad to see the once-troublesome lad so well employed. 'Twas no small feat, considering the legions of townsfolk for miles around claimed they would rather suffer the plague than hazard the bringer of trouble and ruination anywhere near their livelihoods! Miss Elizabeth, however, found her joy tempered by a niggling concern for Pier's tranquillity, prompting her to advise Peter on the importance of minding his manners and attending to even the most menial of tasks with diligence.

Though well meaning the advice, Peter could hardly look at her. *Who is she to instruct one on how they ought to behave?* With difficulty, he did hold his tongue against a sharp rebuke.

Presently, the distant rattle of wheels and the hollow thud of hooves drew the group's attention to the cusp of the hill. The carriage was come.

Scarce had the conveyance rolled up than was Peter eager to be off, like the prophet Ezekiel whisked aloft in his fiery chariot. Yet, as he boarded with faithful Znüni at his side, Elizabeth grasped his arm and peered up at him with such warmth and feeling as to instantly disarm him of his indignation. The spell, however, was quickly shattered. For her subsequent importunities to mind propriety, remember his rank, and to bow soon stoked every ember of simmering resentment. Unbidden memories of her conceit and hypocrisy did flame forth; it took every ounce of restraint not to wrench away his arm.

Waved off thus with maternal tears, paternal cheers, and fraternal wishes, he took his leave, barely motioning a wave in return as he turned away to conceal the flush of anger overspreading his taut features.

Propriety and rank? scoffed he inwardly. He could not replay Lizzie's words without enduring the concomitant pangs of contempt and disdain. *The audacity! That duplicitous woman dares to exhort me on decorum? When I am so far above her in rank and education.* Revulsion slivered up his spine. *Finally, I get to quit this sphere of devilry and deception.*

Eager to forget such insults and to dispel his present mood, he looked to the rolling grasslands, rich and verdant, drenched with tall stalks of meadow buttercup that rippled like tendrils of sunshine in the morning breeze.

Soon the sunlit meadows were exchanged for shaded groves — the shadowy air, rich with damp woody fragrances. Spruce, lindens, and sundry broadleafs climbed either side of a steep dirt track, through which the carriage rattled and bumped along. Somewhere aloft, a woodpecker echoed its tympany; a woodpigeon, with a shrill cry, took flight, while faithful Znüni, head hanging from the window, lapped up the breeze and made known his doggy delight with a robust bark.

Anon, the carriage crested a hill, the trees swept back like a curtain, and there came into view a wide sloping meadow. To the right, a tree-lined avenue curved gracefully, leading to the distant sight of several brown hipped roofs peaking above the foliage. Surely this was Schloss Wildenstein, Pier's residence.

How this view reminded him of home, of Landshut Castle: of times happier; of solace. Had only his mother not conspired and plotted... how many blissful days more they might have shared together at that dear summer palace...

Following the avenue of trees, the carriage then passed several outbuildings. A group of carefree children played together while a dozen ruddy-faced workers paused their employment to smile and bow; their happy good-morrows returned by the evidently happy coachman.

Two tall lindens marked the end of the main avenue, where the crunch of gravel announced a driveway which led to a cobbled forecourt.

No sooner had the carriage halted, and the door opened, than Znüni, panting heavily and thrashing his tail about, did burst forth in a flurry of barks before busying his nose to the ground.

As our hero alighted, a sunny-haired youth bounded up to him, bearing in his small, dirty hands a Toliäsler apple — striped red and green. "For you, sir," said he as he extended the offering.

Peter drew back, uneasy at such proximity and familiarity. "For *me*?"

The boy smiled and nodded, tottering on his toes; apple still outstretched.

Loathe to touch the youth's grubby palms, Peter gingerly plucked it from his grasp. The cheerful imp, smile undiminished, spun about and skipped off down the drive.

"How exceedingly peculiar." Prompt at our hero's feet, faithful Znüni sat drooling; his enormous eyes fixed on the apple. "This is *not* for you."

"Peter, welcome!" came Pier's cheerful voice as he emerged from the wicket door of a dark wooden gate. "Merely the thought of you coming has already brought new life to this old man's heart."

Our hero, poised to return the greeting, found his attention rather stolen by a rumbling noise from the sloping ground beyond the lindens. A cacophonous symphony of grunts and squeals heralded the appearance of so vast a drove of oinking swine — two hundred at least — obedient to several nimble-looking swineherds, who led them down from the meadows.

Peter did hastily grab Znüni's lead, for the eager hound was already straining at his harness to hound and harass the locomotive livestock. One herdsman, remarking Pier, tipped his cap, smiled so brightly and bowed before resuming his charge.

This was beyond intriguing. Such sunny countenances everywhere.

"We have mastered here the very essence of self-sufficiency," said Pier. "Our forests and pastures are most productive. The acorns of the former fatten so vast a number of pigs, whilst the latter serve well our three-field system, satiating the appetites of commerce and my deserving estate workers, whom you will have remarked on your approach."

"Indeed." Peter turned from the perplexing sight to Pier, in whom he noted the warmest smile widen his face as his stare lingered so contentedly at his labourers. Already, the contrast of tempers between these servants and those of Johannes gave to our hero's understanding the diametric polarity he would find in Pier's employment.

Pier instructed the coachman to take the afternoon off to spend with his family, at which the happy fellow thanked him before hailing the equally happy stable boy to remove the carriage to the adjacent coach house.

"Come through." Pier beckoned to him. "You must be hungry?"

Peter followed him through the wicket door, stepping, as if, into a bygone era. A weathered five-story keep soared before him, commanding the sky above a cobbled courtyard. Beside it, dominating a small patch of turf, stood a gnarled oak, spreading about the shade of its ivy-strewn boughs as ancient and tall as the tower itself.

The main residential house's interior confirmed the owner's attachment to the estate's history: sturdy, dark oaken furniture bore heavy ornamental carvings, floors of dark planked woods lined with heavy rugs, tapestries and oils adorning the stoned walls.

Before taking his own seat in the breakfast room, Pier courteously pulled out a chair for Peter. No doubt remarking his guest's surprise, Pier smiled. "I see no need to trouble the servants when they are already occupied. Please, sit. Make sure to eat until your heart is content."

This small gesture both delighted and confounded our hero in equal measures. As he breakfasted with his new companion, the more he listened, the more apparent it became how benevolent and charming a character his new employer would be.

Master Pier did soon engross our hero's studying eye.

At first glance, Pier presented the very ideal of a gentleman; from his well-tailored deep-burgundy frock coat, embroidered waistcoat, ivory breeches, to his polished boots. Yet, while attired in the latest mode, here fashion served decorum, not vanity. Discerning taste shone as clearly as the buttons on Pier's coat. And in his pleasing countenance was exhibited an uncommon union of elegance and modesty, coloured with a spirit and dignity that wonderfully contrasted with the sullen tempers Peter had suffered of late.

A grave-looking man-servant presently entered, bearing tea. Pier, noting his aspect, probed its significance. The man's wife had relapsed into some illness. A mere heartbeat later, Pier instructed him to return home directly, where his personal apothecary would call. "Worry not yourself with expenses; I shall take care of everything. Also, I will send the kitchen maid with provisions. And I expect you to remain by your wife's side until she is fully recovered."

The servant's visage, erst clouded with worry, beamed with gratitude.

Incontestably, Pier was a man possessed of the rarest of understanding; one who disregarded the dictates of fashionable society to tend to the human spirit, enriching and elevating the dignity of his fellow humans. Staggering indeed. Peter beheld him with no little conscience arousing shame.

The clatter of hooves broke upon the cobbled outer forecourt. A loud rap then came at the main gate, followed by another servant entering, bearing a letter for Master Pier.

Of a sudden, his benign countenance surrendered to one of anxiousness. "May this bring me news..." Taking the communication, he then wiped off his knife and sliced it open.

Judging by his wrinkling brow, these were not the tidings he had wished for. Peter leant forward. "Is everything well, sir?"

"Forgive me." Pier placed the letter down and stared out of the window, clearly distracted. But at last: "I have been awaiting word of my son," said he. "He went missing last year. You see, like you," — Pier turned his worry-filled eyes to Peter — "he volunteered with the Guard; but against my wishes. A complicated matter; I shall not burden you with it. I wrote the garrison to learn of his whereabouts. They now reply that they know only that he left Paris homeward bound last September."

"Do you... imagine something has happened to him?"

"I should not indulge such forebodings." Pier formed the similitude of a smile. "It is likely he found his next quest and has merely failed to communicate this to me." A heavy sigh shrank his form. "But I cannot help worry. He grew up so headstrong; very much like his older brother." Something of regret trembled in his eyes. But seeming to recollect himself, he folded the letter and placed it inside his waistcoat pocket. "Though I already gage an unlikelihood of your possibly knowing anything, but where were you stationed with the Guard?"

How would Peter answer this question? Feeling the power of intent behind Pier's gaze, and observing a character of hope dilating his pupils, our hero averted his own gaze to Znüni and barely managed to say, "regrettably, I still recollect nothing of those days."

The hope in Pier's eyes fell away to disappointment. But perceivably checking himself, likely wishing not to burden his guest with the duty of sympathy, he cleared his throat; a ghost of a smile lifted the lines of his face. "As I said, an unlikely event. You see, my daughter is due to arrive in a few days, and

I hoped to enjoy the added pleasure of soon introducing to you my youngest son. But it seems we shall both be obliged to wait out that felicity."

'Twas a deplorable contrivance, to deceive a man who, though still a stranger, had already shown such kindness and affinity. Knowing well the pains of separation and uncertainty, and feeling obliged to offer what meagre solace he could, Peter enquired if Pier had a portrait of his missing son, at which the old man quickly rose, insisting our hero follow him.

Led to the library, Peter stood before a large oil. Nothing came to mind at first glance. But the more he studied it, there appeared something of familiarity.

Pier's countenance was hope and dread. "Do you... *recognise* him?"

If only 'twere in our hero's power to ease a burdened heart. Yet altogether loathe to raise the false hopes of a father, Peter answered in the negative.

A heavy sigh stifled, Pier next showed him a portrait of his departed wife.

A true vision of eminent beauty, indeed; even in representation. 'Twas easy to perceive from the air of dignity and sweetness captured in each brush stroke, how her nature must undoubtedly have been so well suited to forming a happiest of unions — which this still-devoted, mournful widower proceeded to recount with a quavering voice.

Like before, the more Peter studied this portrait, the more something of familiarity captured his attention. Peculiar indeed.

Though wonderful and munificent was the life of this woman, alas, a series of misfortunes had so weakened her heart that, when in the throes of childbirth, she gave up her last breath to preserve the life of her newborn, leaving an infant daughter and doting husband bereft.

Here, the poor man turned away to hide his tears.

Made uneasy at this raw emotion, our hero cast his eyes about the room, searching for some means of distraction. His disbelief and awe were not little when he beheld another oil on the opposite wall. "Who is that man?"

Pier dabbed his tears and followed Peter's gaze. "My eldest child, Paulo."

"Your *son*?" As if drawn by a supernatural power, he strode the room towards the canvas. Surely, this was the face of the Bernese schultheiss' own banneret? Though a much younger representation, the features were indisputable. "How... old would your son... be now?"

The age Pier gave did, indeed, correspond with that he knew of the banneret. And our hero, recalling having once seen an oil of his younger years in that man's personal quarters, felt a deep, chilling shiver enter his being.

"Might he..." said Peter, "... visit anytime soon?"

A gloom stole over Pier's countenance. "I think not."

"When did you... see him last?"

"Some thirty years, at least."

"*Thirty years*? Then you must... *write* each other?"

A cool reserve stiffened Pier's bearing. "He went into the mercenary services... after a family feud. Another complicated history. When I finally made enquiries, I could find out only that he was presumed dead." He cleared his throat of what was a palpable discomfiture. "Why do you ask?"

"Forgive me." Peter checked himself, too. "Mere curiosity."

***

We return to Schloss Ebenrain, where we find Jago, seated at his escritoire in his bedchamber, having lost much sleep to the thoughts which tumbled about his head. The more he scrutinised the crumpled depiction, the more convinced he became it depicted none other than Peter. Jago's mind did naturally swirl with questions: who really *was* the mysterious fellow? What was his history? Did Elizabeth *truly* know enough about him? Did she know him *at all*? Was Peter's amnesia merely a pretence to hide his past? What crime had he committed to warrant such notoriety? What potential dangers might Elizabeth be exposed to?

Such suspense and possibility thrilled Jago's every thought.

Certainly, 'twas a must that he explored and substantiated his suspicions. Thus, he set his mind to various modes of expeditiously realising every answer. First, that Elizabeth had given Geneva as Peter's hometown, he would begin with writing the garrison there. Second, that the condemning front page originated from the Zürich press, and that it was June — time for the guilds' biannual assemblies — and that, with the inter-cantonal unrest, Basel was called into mediate, Jago would accompany his father there and make further enquiries.

19 – 20 June 1792

Howsoever satisfied with this scheme, Jago was filled with that sort of impatience that rarely releases its grip until the passion it stirs is realised. "If only I can sooner discover his character!" He drummed his fingers atop his escritoire; his mind shifted from one design to another with each fall of his slender digits. Since it was only natural to suppose that two lovers long separated would exchange letters, Jago hit upon an idea. Thus, it was indispensable that he somehow gained access to Lizzie's bedchamber.

Whilst Jago breakfasted with his parents on the veranda, racking his mind for a means of achieving his aim, a footman brought him a letter. We may recall that in the preceding volume, Jago had recognised in Znüni a striking resemblance to a dog from an inn at Gunten and had written the ostler to come and inspect whether this was the case. It turns out that this letter in Jago's hands was from that very ostler, accepting the invitation.

That there was a delay of about two weeks between the ostler posting the communication and its being delivered, this meant he would now arrive at short notice — tomorrow.

Now, back to the matter of the lovers' letters. At last, concocting a means of effectuating his plan, Jago set off mid-morning for the humble chalet to seize his chance while the tenants were to be gone, as per se, to the farmers' market.

Finding circumstances as predicted, he slipped inside the property, proceeding directly to Elizabeth's chamber.

A thorough search of the wicker baskets beneath the bed yielded neither letters nor tokens of affection. Inspecting beneath the pillows and mattress proved equally fruitless. Undeterred, he investigated the wardrobe — inside, on top, and underneath. Again, to no avail.

As he glanced about the humble, white-washed room of female decor, his eyes fixed on the ornate, rosewood French bombé commode next to the window.

He thus delicately probed its several draws.

Again, nothing.

"Where could she have hidden them?"

Presently, beneath his feet, under the small woven rug, the floorboards creaked. He shifted his weight from one foot to the next. "Hmm?"

Hence, pulling back the rug and inspecting the cracks, he discovered a loose plank. Lifting it revealed to his widening eyes a small wooden travel box.

Nerves exalting in thrills of triumph, he removed the box from its hiding place and, finding it unlocked, opened it. Among its few contents, what first caught his eye was a golden locket: a half-heart locket. He snatched it up and prised it open to find the watercolour of a woman wholly unfamiliar to him adorning one half's inside. On the other, was an inscription:

Equal is my heart shared between you both

He once more regarded the watercolour. "Who might she be?"

The locket itself was, he observed, of the purest gold and of the finest workmanship; a token only someone of eminent rank could have bestowed.

Curiouser and curiouser.

His chief purpose recollected, he placed the locket back inside the box and withdrew several folded papers. As he opened out the first, his astonishment was immediate. For there, in his shaking hands, stared back at him a WANTED poster — the very one Elizabeth had brought back from Lucerne.

For all of Jago's quick wit and ready intellect, he was struck entirely dumb. Indeed, his mind struggled to grasp what his eyes plainly beheld. "She already... knew of this?"

***

Ill-rested, our hero awoke early the following morn. 'Twas still dark outside. Though indeed comfortable was the bedchamber, the probability that Paulo was the banneret was enough to obtrude upon his sleep. For despite Pier and his son having no relationship these thirty years, irrefutably would Fortune, somehow, soon work her next injustice against our hero and bring Paulo home. Moreover, to have been accommodated, according to Pier's instances, in the very chamber of so hostile a man, every item upon which Peter's eye had landed only compounded the dread that each long hour amassed upon his heart.

Now, Paulo was not the name by which the banneret was known, but rather Arnborg. As Peter understood, he had enlisted in the Swiss Guard in its lowest rank. But by uncommon valour, quickly climbing ranks and, along the way, suppressing several insurrections in several cantons, he became the chosen favourite for the coveted position of the Bernese banneret.

That he gave a family name wholly unknown, and that he never spoke of his kin, nor his place of birth, and eluded every enquiry — never disclosing to anybody his personal matters — this indirectly evidenced, perhaps, a resolution to never return home again. Certainly, whatever the nature of the rupture between this father and son, it ran deep enough that Pier believed the other dead. Regardless, this sad truth did at last teach our hero to trust that no filial duty would bring Arnborg home to happen suddenly upon our hero.

Thus unburdened of dreadful expectation, Peter drifted off...

Around the tenth hour, forenoon, he stirred anew. No longer plagued by Morpheus and his troublesome dreams, how better refreshed he felt and rather content with his new dwelling; the bed, it must be said, was a veritable cloud upon which he would gladly have floated all day. But hunger, that ravenous beast within, soon got him up and led him to the breakfast room.

Upon his entry, he found not Pier, but a plate of half-devoured delicacies, abandoned ostensibly. Still and all, hungry as our hero was, he sat down to eat.

Two missives lay beside his plate, vying for attention. One, from Father Francis, spoke of matters matrimonial. The other, a requested audience with Jago at half past the current hour; a less-disagreeable prospect.

As if on cue, the walnut long-case clock chimed its agreement.

Oh, how quickly can even the finest viands turn to ashes upon the tongue! Peter had just embarked on a second foray of the culinary landscape, fork poised like a tiny lance against a battalion of sausages, when Pier's voice echoed in the courtyard, accompanied by new arrivals. Verily, Peter's blood turned to ice as he heard Jago introduce a man who was quite likely Znüni's true owner.

Fork, still clutched in hand, Peter lurched to the window. His eyes widened in horror as he beheld the ostler from Gunten, flanked by Pier and Jago. "Oh, Lord!" He wrang his hands. "What devilish fate is this?"

Gripped by crippling panic, his mind a whirlwind of desperate schemes, he dashed for the door. Though opening onto the main hallway, it provided no egress — for Pier enquired of a servant Peter's whereabouts, at which his approaching footsteps echoed like the knell of doom. Trapped as our hero was, he glanced about the room for some means — any! — of concealment.

Some meagre moments hence, Pier and his little entourage made their entrance. But oh, gentle reader, the scene that greeted their eyes was one that would have confounded even the most seasoned of playwrights. Stare they all did, a-blinking, a-gawping, in manifest bewilderment at the figure before them, who, ever the master of disguise, had conjured a most peculiar of masquerades.

"By all that is holy, Peter," said Pier, his tongue at last unshackled from the chains of stupefaction, "what madness is this?"

There stood our hero, a knight of the most ludicrous order: attired in a modest tunic, waistcoat, lederhosen, and clogs; his noble noggin encased in a gleaming casque of steel, pilfered with great alacrity from the suit of armour that stood sentinel in the corner. The helm — its visor cranked heavenward, affording a glimpse of the thespian's wide, panic-stricken eyes — sat askew upon his brow. His knees did visibly quake and quiver like maracas, while his limbs and corpus were forced into some gangly posture that would have shamed even the ineptest of court jesters. Oh! Let's not forget the breakfast fork still in hand, the *pièce de résistance* of this absurd tableau. But, desperate times, as they say...

"Well," at last replied our hero, the visa clattering down as he fumbled to thrust it back aloft, "would you believe it, my dear Pier, but 'tis the *strangest* thing! I was just admiring your magnificent panoply when this helmet..." — he presently tapped its apex with the fork — TINK-TINK! — "... as if animated by some *mischievous sprite*, it simply *toppled* — nay, *leapt off!* — and... and landed *squarely* on my head, as you see."

Indeed, even the sceptical Jago exchanged a baffled glance with the ostler, as if to say, "what species of lunacy have we stumbled upon here?"

In sooth, so farcical a sight was simply too preposterous to fathom.

"Well, take it off then," said Pier, his cheeks reddening with patent embarrassment, "and let us be done with this tomfoolery!"

19 – 20 June 1792

"Well, would you believe this too?" Down crashed the visor once more, like a portcullis, only to be shoved back up with a grunt of exertion. "But I find I... *cannot...*" lied he with a forced chuckle. "It appears to be... *stuck fast.*"

"Stuck? How could it...?" With an even more abashed glance at their visitors, Pier set about applying all his might to the removal of the ironclad dome, whereupon a mighty struggle did ensue: man and metal grappled in a battle of wills. "I am sure," said he, puffing with exertion, "we shall have you extricated anon." He cast another mortified look at Jago and the ostler. "Be with you momentarily..."

Lo! No need had our hero for telling fibs, after all, nor to resist Pier's efforts. The iron cap was well and truly stuck, as if welded to his very skull!

At any rate, after the scene devolved into a series of flailing limbs, exasperated grunts, and increasingly desperate attempts to dislodge the helmet; after Znüni burst into the room, assailing the ostler in a frenzy of elated reunion; after the Ostler, thus reunited with his dog, took his leave — though not without sundry backward glances at our hero, as if he were some curiosity in a carnival sideshow — along with a visibly suspicious Jago; after our hero, though saddened at this parting, did now endeavour to more forcibly prise the metal prison from his pericranium, only to fail; the entire house staff was summoned to deliberate sundry means by which to extract his skull from the iron vice. Copious slathers of butter were proposed to be applied to Peter's neck and visage.

Thusly anointed and greased like a turkey being readied for the roasting pan, our hero, bruised and swollen, was at last emancipated and finally sat back down to resume his repast.

Though Pier had, as to have been expected, passed quite a few more quizzical looks upon our hero, admonishing him to perhaps never go near the armour again, his face was sooner stained with a prodigious gravity as he studied a newspaper closely.

Such seriousness did now pique our hero's curiosity. "What is it?"

Pier passed the newspaper over and pointed at the front page of the Nouvelles Politiques — the Bernese Gazette.

"The Bernese Schultheiss' firstborn is dead!"

There, in large bold font, were those very words!

Indeed, strange was the feeling this text induced; Peter found much difficulty in dissimulating an ingenuous interest. But when he read the words beneath the headline — the news of the Bernese Schultheiss' failing health — his breath lodged in his throat.

No! My poor father!

20 JUNE 1792

We must, however, depart from our despairing hero and step over into the canton of Bern and visit the grounds of Jegenstorf Castle. There we find the venerable, yet enfeebled Schultheiss Gustav von Villeroy boarding his gilded carriage despite the protestations of his befrilled, taffeta-clad valet.

"But your health, my lord," cried the man through the still open door. "Can you really not despatch a deputant?"

"It is imperative that I attend," replied Gustav between laboured wheezes. "Grief must bow to duty's urgency. The very seat I occupy, I must protect! Though it may cost me every drop of blood in my veins."

"Very well, then." With a sigh, the valet closed the door, bowed, and stepped away.

And so, with a rap of his cane upon the roof, the carriage clattered forth, and a determined Gustav, surrounded fore and aft by a detachment of stern-faced cuirassiers watching his every move, set-off for the austerity of the Rathaus Bern to convene with the Grand Council.

In the months elapsed, and the many chapters of our tale which began in the first volume, manifold woes had beset the Bernese schultheiss: apprehensions for his soul, his station, his purse, and vengeful passions against his traitorous son and they — whoever the shadowy figures were — that conspired with the young serpent to unhinge the stability of the confederacy, itself. But upon word of his first-born's demise at Reichenbach Falls, Gustav had sunk into so immense a sorrow as to baffle his cohorts. Fond memories of better times had rushed in to claim the chief of his thoughts and soften his heart. Whereas once he would have, in a thousand ways, destroyed his own child, now Gustav wished only to raise the unfortunate youth from the grave.

Sat opposite Gustav was his trusted Deütsch Treasurer, Adolfus — whom we met in our opening chapter — a man of penetrating countenance and conscious superiority. Between discussing the Tagsatzung agenda and offering his opinions on the current inter-cantonal affairs, he offered his pointed wisdom, visibly hoping to guide his lordship's strategies.

"Yes, yes, enough!" rasped Gustav with an impatient wave. "You have plagued me sufficiently. Let me collect my thoughts in peace." He turned to the window only to glimpse his own reflection in the glass. The demands of his seat, his advisers, allies; the relentless schultheissin; the unrest of his subjects, and more recently, contending with the death of his child, had indeed taken their toll. 'Twas a most haggard countenance he beheld. Not even his lavish powdered wig could detract from the hollows in his rouged cheeks or the pallidity of his flesh, which sagged from his visage like molten wax.

With hands made unsteady by exhaustion, Gustav dabbed his perspiring brow, eased his high collar, adjusted his cravat, and straightened out the high turned-down collar of his black silk tail coat. A bracing breath taken, he reclined into the seating, and prepared himself for the confrontation ahead.

***

"All rise for the venerable schultheiss," announced the council herald as Gustav entered.

All within — a mass of representatives of the ruling families, soberly clad in robes of black and snide countenances — turned as one towards the grand doors; they rose from their cushioned benches and bowed.

Attention fixed on the throne at the hall's far side, Gustav strode through great plumes of snuff-scented smoke, his guarded footsteps ringing out sharp against the pillared walls. Though watched by every powdered grandee, who peered from beneath periwigs and black tricorn hats, Paris beaus, cocked, clerical, and tall hats, he paid no regard to any; not even a glance at the chancery table directly in front. Only an inclination of his head did he finally bestow to the presiding ministers — their table heaped with latticed letters, bound by satin ribbons — and Albrecht von Mülinen (former schultheiss) as he mounted the dais and seated himself upon the ornate high-backed schultheiss' throne.

Adolfus stationed himself at his right; Arnborg at his left.

"I SWEAR!" proclaimed the assembly, performing the schwurhand — right hands raised high; index and middle finger pivoted heavenwards.

At Gustav's leave, all settled into the rows of carved oaken pews and benches. The doors to the hall closed. Goose quills scratched rapidly across parchment as the land clerks prepared to minute the session, and the Tagsatzung commenced; the topic first broached: King Louis XVIs' declaration of war on Austria, and the resulting tensions for the Republic of Geneva — the ambassadors of which now pleaded for their confederates' help.

"We have already made our stance of neutrality abundantly clear at the federal diet in Frauenfeld," clamoured one side of the hall, opposed to any intervention. "We must first wait upon diplomatic means to stem this uncertainty."

"Neutrality?" echoed a scorning voice from the other side. "Do you not supply the French army with grain, horses, cattle, and swine, as well as the best mercenaries?"

"Yet your canton profits from this arrangement as well, does it not?" rejoined the former as he paraded with excessive swagger back and forth in front of his bench. "Are not your family merchants? Having built their personal fortune on the needs of such powerful neighbours — flinging open their granaries to both sides? More so since the revolution!"

This riposte elicited many awkward coughs amidst the sea of snuff boxes and shuffling feet as the humiliated man looked ready to bolt for the doors.

"And to the detriment of our fatherland!" replied another. "Is it not our collective avarice and recent exploitation of that kingdom's needs which have provided the fertile grounds for revolutionary ideals to infest our own soil?"

"You speak as though we were quite overrun," interjected Adolfus.

"Ha!" cried out the other. "You forget, *Leurs Excellences,* are not you yourself French in fashion, manners, and in language, so much so that you despise using the German tongue?"

Adolfus merely arched his brow. "Not all things French are to be feared."

"Yes, we are, indeed, overrun," firmly replied a fresh voice. "The revolution has indelibly overshadowed our land. I need only mention the reading societies and the so-called peasant enlightenment. Before long, they will march in here, demanding our very seats from under us."

"Hear, hear!" echoed around the hall. "Hear, hear!"

The land clerks did soon struggle to dip their goose quills and minute the mounting quarrels between the guild envoys, cantonal ambassadors, and bailiffs.

"It is time," resumed the Genevan ambassadors, "not solely for our republic but for the entire confederation to curtail its alliance with the French before their revolutionary venom paralyses our nation's already precarious strength. In their haste to restore the Kingdom of France, they will soon meet us with swords rather than bread knives, demanding our land and not our grains."

Naturally, such a threat could not be hazarded. Indignant voices clamoured, reverberating through the hallowed barrel-vaulted hall.

"Enough!" An enervated Gustav motioned for silence. "If we are compelled to rally arms to support Geneva, you may trust in our aid. And I am certain that Zürich will support you with its militia."

"*Zürich*?" rejoined several ambassadors of that canton. "You are bold, indeed, to speak on our behalf! Have you forgotten —"

"Forgotten *what*?!" Gustav sat up rigid.

"That the kinship of our cantons has been deferred by disillusion and distrust?"

Infuriated, Gustav rose unsteadily. "Have I not asseverated my inculpability? Were not these wild claims of my wavering league already contradicted by the Schaffhausen members? Who, might I add, before their sudden and inexplicable deaths had, while in Lucerne, happened upon the very scroll barer who will soon acquit me of your opprobrium?" He sank back into his seat. "And yet you insist on a continuance of this absurd investigation!"

"And yet," echoed the other, "this elusive document, and its equally elusive barer, still arrives not even until this very day. As it stands, we received word only of the treasonous designs of your eldest child and your own sympathising with the French radicals — which undoubtedly incited that King Luis the Last to despatch his forces to the Genevan borders."

By session's end, Gustav, enveloped in a pall of smoke from so many pipes, sat alone in the Great Hall, massaging the bridge of his nose and nursing his wounded pride. Truly, in a temper as black as night, he wanted only to fly to Jegenstorf Castle and request a vat of wine be tapped forthwith to numb the memory of this calamitous council. But, alas, Adolfus now re-entered the hall.

"I have summoned the Small Council to remain behind," declared

Adolfus as the doors slammed shut behind him. "We shall convene directly."

"*Directly?*" A gust of importuned air raced from Gustav's wheezing lungs. "Have I not already spent enough hours tirelessly debating? For what purpose do you haul them back?"

"The unrest among the proletariat. The bourgeois' petitions. And you have yet to appoint the heir presumptive."

"Heir presumptive? I shall not be bullied into any decision!"

"But the council expects your answer," replied Adolfus with a measured, quiet firmness.

"Expects? How dare —"

The doors presently swung open, and the Small Council filtered in, their faces a mix of indifference and disdain.

Indeed, the majority, staunch defenders of the status quo, instantly argued against the several petitions put forward — each scroll sealed with wax: demands for economic opportunities, rights to citizenship, and access to public office.

"This is preposterous!" bellowed one councillor. "The very idea of granting concessions to the common folk is an affront to our noble heritage!"

"These enlightenment ideas must poison no further the minds of our people," cried another. "We, the patricians, have ruled for centuries, and we must continue to do so!"

Such enlightenment-minded patricians, however the minority, being found among those present, one council member countered with equal fervour, "but we cannot forever ignore the changing times. The Landsgemeinden in the surrounding rural cantons are a clear sign the people demand change."

His ally nodded in agreement. "Nor can we bar the gate to parliament forever. We are barely a breath away from the next revolt over rising taxes. Our own people will soon open the gates to the French! Already, colporteur pamphlets spread, challenging the privileges of the *regiments-fähig*... We *must* consider the long-term stability of our society and the wellbeing of *all* our citizens."

Though their faces twisted with contempt, the conservative majority merely scoffed at this argument.

"Nonsense!" spat one of them. "We have quashed these uprisings before, and we shall do so again."

20 June 1792

The debate raged on; the councillors' voices rose to a crescendo as they argued back and forth, neither side willing to yield.

Head about to split with each impassioned speech, Gustav turned to implore Adolfus' response. His brow simply arched a bridge of complacence; he preened the curls of his grey campaign wig, which flowed like waves beneath the broad brim of his burgomaster hat. "Then we shall censor them," said he, "and block all talk of rights. Simple, no?"

After hours of circular debate, the majority granted only still greater privileges to the nobles and their children, while cracking the patrician gate only slightly wider. All protesters would face exile, their voices silenced by the ruling elite, determined to maintain their dominance in the face of growing unrest.

Gustav now brooked the subject of his chosen heir. Many, lambasting their opinions, advocated the third eldest as a successor on the grounds of his boldness of character and willingness to be guided. Lessor voices, not less lambasting, favoured the second eldest on the foundation of his intellect and rights of primogeniture. On this weighty subject, the council entered a lengthy fray — some members toppling goblets of wine in their impassioned gestures.

All the same, importuned, bombarded, and menaced with the instability of the canton, Gustav at last bent to the pressure and hastened his decision. Despite the slanted faces and enunciated disapprobation of the many, he remained determined on his second eldest, whose appointment would need to wait until after another matter of equal weightiness — and not less controversial.

"I have planned," said Gustav, "the mode of committal for my late son."

"You *cannot* be serious?" Adolfus near-choked on his breath. "A traitor deserves neither ceremony nor exequy. Why have you not mentioned this until now? This will make us the laughingstock of the confederacy — no, the world!"

"The world be damned! He was still my child."

"But this shall merely further rupture our alliance with Zürich!" rejoined another voice, tinged with exasperation. "Do you not apprehend the ramifications of such a decision? Exalting the treasonous son, who merely followed in the treacherous strides of the mother?"

A vein throbbed violently upon Gustav's temple; he hissed through bared teeth, ready to strike at the councillor. "Dare not you speak of the former schultheissin! How I wish to inter my disappointment of a son has *nothing* to do with *any other* canton!"

Undeniably intimidated by his outburst, the councillors fell silent.

"Besides," resumed Gustav, "to omit a funeral will invite but greater reproach on the Villeroy name. Any Zürich indignation, I shall countermand in the name of confederate unity. Now, more than ever, we must stand indestructible before every foreign court. Yes, some may scorn this funeral, but it shall rouse compatriot spirit in the many — namely, they who fill our tables with bread."

***

On his return to Jegenstorf Castle, Gustav was silent and brooding. To have been disbelieved — nay, mocked and maligned by that proud ambassador as a radical Francophile — was an insult beyond enduring! Why, every drop of Bernese blood in Gustav's veins burned with flaming disquiet.

The camaraderie between Zürich and Bern had stood strong for centuries. Together they had dispelled the Habsburgs, cementing Swiss autonomy — their fellow cantons looking upon them as leaders, bold and fearsome. But alas, the scandals flung against Gustav's good name saw eager tongues wag dissent from the pastures to the highest steeples. Gazettes fuelled sensationalism while couriers criss-crossed the land, bearing letters bristling with ever greater hostility between cantonal heads. Not merely political chaos beset each city, but economic and social tremors too! Peasant revolts erupted daily over taxes to fund the defence and grain seizures, reminiscent of the unrest that had plagued the confederation in earlier times. Roving mobs drunk on revolutionist notions marauded the rural lanes, accosting all nobles who dared cross their path. Trade routes south lay imperilled by brigands. Whispers of war preparations plagued both cities. And now with the menaces of Austria and Prussia to boot! Thus, with foes snarling beyond walls, defiant peasants within them, and the French clattering swords across Geneva's borders, it seemed the very confederacy teetered atop a knife's edge when strength and unity were most needed against foreign threats.

And yet, as paternal grief governed Gustav's heart, desperate hope directed his hand — a hope that honouring his fallen son would promote enough

20 June 1792

patriot spirit to weather both foreign and civil strife alike.

Concerning Adolfus, his own shifting countenance betrayed an endless succession of thoughts flaring behind his eyes; many of which, judging by his sharp glances, paid towards Gustav, pertained to profound vexation.

Having reached Jegenstorf, Adolfus took leave of Gustav and boarded his own carriage, directing his driver towards an inn on the Aare River. Notwithstanding this day's added disturbances involving the appointment and the funeral, it was not yet revealed who the mystery scroll bearer was from Lucerne.

Soon ensconced in an upper private room, its velvet curtains drawn against the prying eyes of the world, Adolfus bid the innkeeper to bar entry to all but those he specified by name.

Within half an hour, there materialised a dubious-looking fellow: countenance scored from past skirmishes, and garb frayed at the elbows and collars.

Having drummed his impatient fingers onto the ornate marble mantel, Adolfus rounded on him. "Well? Have you located them?"

The young rogue related his fruitless search across several cantons. However, on investigating the last of the names from the guest book at the Lucerne inn, concerning one Peter von Graffenried (we should recall this moniker imposed upon our hero by those pretending parents), a curious revelation came to light. This trail led back to a dusty Bernese gazette wherein they discovered the referenced Peter had shuffled off this mortal coil over two decades prior

"Dead?" Adolfus' left eye gave a violent twitch. "You are quite certain?"

"When we went back to Lucerne, the inn manager said that this... Peter was with a brother and sister — Basel natives. I'll test the lead myself."

Adolfus seized the man's arm, nails digging in. "Yes. Go at once! You must find this impostor before Gustav catches wind. This Peter and his scroll must be destroyed! I cannot have him, whoever he is, thwart my plans!"

With a subservient bow, the dubious fellow vanished, leaving Adolfus to wield his quill like a weapon upon paper. A sharp tug on the bell-pull summoned the innkeeper, who then scurried off to procure a courier.

Presently, a rapping came at the door, announcing a gentleman of a more distinguished bearing.

"Ah! Albrecht." Adolfus turned to the Nachschauer (Inspector). "What tidings do you bring?"

Albrecht reported his successes in amassing a stockpile of grain smuggled into the capital via a network of Catholic contacts abroad. Indeed, this was music to Adolfus' ears. With resources strained and social unrest multiplying, the addition of an acute grain shortage threatened to leave commoners starving.

Adolfus laughed. "This grain, you will, in due course, see, shall elevate you to a more deserving seat. Another seat claimed for our party. Another step closer to achieving our lifelong aspiration... all will go back to its rightful place."

Shortly after, a gaggle of men, as roguish as a den of thieves, appeared in black velvet tails and breeches, their faces peppered with stubble, and their hats donning flamboyant ostrich feathers.

"Bring me Viktor," commanded Adolfus. "You will, I daresay, know where to find him."

***

Elsewhere, within a secure chamber at the city barracks, Arnborg, the banneret, convened with a covert assembly of agents around a sturdy oak table. Their voices glided over the several documents as they spoke of their luck in locating two of the three men. However, the third man, it seemed, had long since departed this mortal realm.

"A dead man taking lodgings?" Arnborg knotted his thick greying brows in bewilderment; his medals of valour glinted in the candlelight. Like Adolfus, he, too, was tracking down the mystery Peter. "Pray, unravel this enigma."

The agent, whose voice was gruffer than gravel underfoot, unfurled the records he had coveted, which gave the history of the von Graffenried nobility, who, some eighty years ago, sailed off to the Americas seeking earthly treasure. It seemed, however, that a wayward heir returned two generations later and, having secured a wife, married — a son born to them. Alas, the boy of ten years of age met a grisly end, struck down by the merciless hand of the pox.

"And yet the ghost of the deceased stays at inns?" Arnborg shifted in his seat. "What devilry is afoot? Who masquerades as this long-buried corpse?"

"I have already despatched men to Bubendorf to track down the siblings with whom him this apparent impostor sojourned at Lucerne."

"Good... Good..." This intelligence seemed to ease Arnborg's concerns.

But then there came tidings of some unknown party who had also arrived in Lucerne, seeking this very same phantom von Graffenried.

"Another group?" Arnborg's eyes darted about in their sockets. "Gustav has withheld this information...? Could these men be his?"

"Unlikely, based on the descriptions provided by the innkeeper."

"Curiouser and curiouser." Arnborg stood up and faced a large map of the city pinned to one wall. "Then, it's that serpent Adolfus' vile hand at work." He spun around, gathering his startled agents with a piercing gaze. "Whatever infernal trickery has resurrected this spectre, we must find him first. Adolfus will not hesitate to damn the fellow's soul to achieve his aims. We must secure the scroll at all costs. Without it, we cannot ever begin to uncover the conspiracy."

***

From Arnborg, we shift our gaze to Viktor — Gustav's third eldest. Having relished the intoxicating nectar of flattery and the unwavering confidence of his supporters, Viktor's ambitions had soared like an eagle, only to be dashed upon the rocks of disappointment. That he had not been appointed as heir, his wounded pride festered within. He sought solace in the sultry embrace of a decadent salon; a haven for misbegotten wenches, desperate merchants, and other purveyors of vice. Here, he liberally partook of tobacco's smoky allure, indulged his penchant for games of chance, and sought to benumb the sting and drown the remembrance of disillusionment with that potent elixir absinthe.

Being a most handsome rake, yet devoid of purpose, this irascible young brooder had no shortage of admirers to fill the vacuum. As he settled down at the gambling table, two eager trollops, darting at each other barbed insults with the subtlety of alley cats, staked their claim upon his sturdy thighs, and much to the petulance of their envious counterparts, who cast longing glances his way.

Anyway, as is common of the many aristocrats of this age, ever indifferent to financial catastrophe when honour is at stake, Viktor — lavishing jewels and kisses on these rival trulls — did wager staggering amounts of money at the altar of his ego; he rained golden coins like hailstones into the pile as the dice clattered, convinced of destiny's favour.

Alas, as the saying goes, "*un coup de des, jamais n'abolira le hazard,"* no matter the new hand of cards, nor the new throw of the dice, these games of chance apportioned him only a losing streak. Yet, blinded by pride, Viktor fanned his cards: the king, queen, and jack of spades huddled alongside the ace of hearts. Surely, no hand could topple such majesty, nor beat his four loftiest courts!

With reckless abandon, and despite his drinking companion's pleas, he tossed onto the ever-growing pile, his pocket watch — a gift from his father. Leering at his rival, he leant across the half-empty bottles, toppled glasses, and trays of cigars coiling pungent fumes. "This game shall be *mine.*"

In his hubris, Viktor did forget that vixen Chance oft smiles upon other rogues, too. Just then, there came a triumphant: "Jass!" His opponent slammed down his cards — the wretched jack of diamonds glinting atop the pile. Diamonds were trumps; the jack's crimson hue conquered all. "Every round to me!"

As one who wears the look of one slain by ambition's folly, Viktor beheld this guild master's heir at play. This flashy fellow, equally handsome and endowed more with wine and women than morals, gloated with his bejewelled trollops. Their eyes sparkling brighter than the chandelier above, they cast taunting kisses from behind their fans as they gathered the spoils of war — glistening piles of coins, precious stones, and Viktor's unfortunate timepiece.

With a vulgar laugh, the victor held aloft the coveted heirloom, its jewels winking in the light as if to mock their former owner. "You really play a shockingly poor game!"

Such was the loser's bitterness; with a roar of fury, he sprang from his chair, sending his shrieking doxies tumbling while overturning the lacquered table in spectacular fashion! Champagne bottles crashed. Snifters smashed. Crystal cruets flew, spewing rivers of ruby port. Cards fluttered like startled birds. Coins sprayed the air, scattering across the Savonnerie carpet in glittery chaos.

"Can I not even claim victory at the table? Curse this wretched day!"

"Viktor." His drinking companion grabbed onto his arm. "Calm down!"

"My, my!" rejoined the winner, still lounging at ease with his mistresses amidst the wreckage. "What a sore loser gapes before us now. I daresay you took the news of your passed-over inheritance with similar grace and aplomb?"

At this last jab, Viktor launched for the man, clear over the debris. His hands seized at the wretch's throat with the fury of a man possessed, toppling him and his ladies from the chair in a tangle of limbs and lace.

What now ensued as each assailed the other made the onlooking floozies squeal in horror. Fine wood splintered. Gilt trim cracked and chipped. Glittering jewels scattered like shooting stars as the duelling foes tumbled across the floor, overturning furniture like rampaging bulls — billiard balls thundering like musket shots, sending fellow rakes darting every which way.

At last, gaining the upper hand, Viktor dealt his gloating foe so sound a compliment with his fist as to unleash a torrent of red from his nostrils. His bleeding adversary, loathe to be outdone, did return the blood-letting gesture.

Let us forget not those four strumpets. Seeing their paramours sprawled in heaps of shredded, blood-soaked silks, they hastened to avenge the blows, unleashing ten talons a piece. Never, I am sure, was there a more hellish spectacle! Flesh and blood flew as they clawed at the men's arms, necks, and cheeks.

But the chaos did not cease there! Drawn by the glittering spoils strewn across the floors, the four jezebels broke from shredding the contending men and flew at each other with greater fury, screeching like banshees, snatching up what fell from rivals' claws, and spewing words too vulgar to record.

Plum bushels of hair were ripped from scalps. Pelted ash and cigar stubs flew. Powdered faces met hearty cuffs in contest for the ill-got treasures. As the screams turned to roars, the onlooker did gasp in horror. Why, the scene these feminine battlers made could scarce be distinguished from an abattoir!

Meantime, as our two male combatants still wrestled, Viktor, his strength waning, seized a champagne bottle and brained his foe senseless, sending a geyser of ruby spraying forth. Silence descended — only to be pierced by crystal-shattering screams. The clashing women, still clutching their lawful spoils and prodigious quantities of their opponents' hair, stood momentarily frozen. But not so the several guild master son's men.

Hitherto cheering at the affray while monopolising on the distraction in good conscience — pocketing their own shares of the plunder, scattered hither and tither across the battlefield — they, seeing their felled general, now launched at Viktor like rabid dogs.

Consequently, Viktor's comrades rallied to his defence, and a full-scale skirmish erupted between the two camps — reinforced with the militia of hellkittens and other unruly damsels of dubious virtue, in whom flattery and fisticuffs were plainly synonymous.

As the bacchanal raged on like some ancient battle brought to life in all its gory glory, a new force burst in, armed with clubs. The rabble was swiftly routed. Viktor was seized and dragged away, kicking and howling vengeance.

Having been flung into an unfamiliar coach and conveyed he knew not where, he was at length hauled up some creaking staircase to an inn's uppermost chamber, and deposited before Adolfus.

Visibly disgusted at the blood-spattered aristocrat who wavered on his feet before him, Adolfus glared at the captors. "What happened to him?"

"Brawling," answered one.

"And made the centrepiece, too," sneered another.

"What?" Adolfus strode forth and delivered a stinging blow to Viktor's bloodied cheek. "What further disgrace have you caused? Do I need to cover over your transgressions again? You *cannot* be seen engaging in such *ruckuses*!"

"Why should my actions even matter now when you failed?"

"*Failed?*" Adolfus seized his throat in a crushing grip. "You think I shall let that whelp's appointment thwart my years of servitude and schemes?!" With a ferocious hiss, he thrust him back. "Get him home," said he to his men. "Get him cleaned up before the servants' gossip spreads his degradation any further!"

***

Dusk had now begun its descent, casting wavering shadows along the austere Bernese guardhouse corridors. Inside a dimly lit office cluttered with scrolls and documents of great import sat an investigator (the lowest rank of the Bernese Landjäger corps) in his mid-thirties, absorbed in his work.

He leant back in his chair, stretching his arms with a weary sigh; the movement tugged at his dark blue, trimmed with gold and embellished with the distinctive Stadtwache crest, uniform, creased from many a long day spent in the pursuit of justice. His countenance, made hard by hours of diligent work, wore the upright nature of a man to whom duty and honour stood paramount.

From a stack of freshly received reports detailing various illicit activities, a disturbing feature emerged. Several witness statements pointed a damning finger at the schultheiss' third son — the afore-introduced Viktor — linking him to the ungentlemanly exploits of smuggling and extortion. Upon such a revelation, this fellow — one of the Stadtwache's few untainted souls — thus found the call of duty echoing loudly in his ears. "I must show this to Meier."

Of a sudden, his office door swung open. In strode the imposing Captain of the Guard, the formidable operations leader — gleaming brass buttons, gold epaulettes, and insignias of his higher rank glinting in the candlelight.

Swiftly, he loomed over the investigator's desk. "Keller," (for this was the investigator's appellation) "what do you have there?"

Incriminating reports held aloft, Keller rose from his seat. "Intelligence concerning Viktor von Villeroy, sir. There have been multiple accounts of his involvement in —"

But alas, his words were cut short. "Leave those with me," interrupted Baumann (for this was the captain's name). His hot breath, reeking of tobacco and brandy, assaulted Keller's senses. "*I* will handle it."

Ever the dutiful servant of justice, the investigator hesitated. "But, sir, it's both my duty and a chain of command to forward this to the corporal's office."

"Do not interfere, Keller!" Baumann leant in; his voice dropped to a minacious whisper. "This is beyond your purview." His hand, adorned with a heavy signet ring of his office, reached out, fingers twitching with the eager anticipation of seizing the documents. "Attend to your other assignments."

With much reluctance, Keller surrendered the reports to Baumann's grasp, watching helplessly as the captain took his leave — the door slamming shut with a finality that echoed throughout the room.

Keller sank back into his chair, the old leather creaking beneath him. His heart burned with chagrin and indignation, and his mind raced with thoughts of the misfeasance that plagued the Stadtwache. "I can't stand idly by whilst this corruption festers and grows..."

28 JUNE – 01 JULY 1792

Back in the familiar surroundings of Basel Canton, for our poor hero, the passage of a single week had been positively unbearable, each day hanging heavier than the last upon his battered spirit. As memories still slowly returned, like shattered fragments, there came naught but a deepening gloom, conjuring the utter wreckage of his situation.

Obsessively, he kept abreast of the tabloids, scouring for information about the events unfolding in Bern. But each headline, each article, only served to amplify his suffering. To his family, friends, and even his enemies, he was nothing more than a ghost, his legacy tarnished by a premature and ignoble demise. And though he indeed still drew breath, 'twas as if Death's icy hand had, in cruel fact, claimed him. He was rendered a mere wanderer amongst the living; a lost spirit, a spectre of the past, inhibiting the life of an equally unfortunate other whose shattered corpse had duped the world...

Casement flung wide; he leant forward, gasping at the morning air.

... The thought of his father, believing he perished in so gruesome a manner, and thus succumbing to infirmity, was a dagger to the heart. A surge of blood rushed to his brain. Oh, how he wished to race to his father's side. He hovered, poised to advance to the door. But to set foot in Bern was to court death and ruin. Groaning from the very depths of his grief, he collapsed against the sill.

"If only I could obtain an interview. Perhaps then I could explain, and, if not help put order to this calamity, I could at least alleviate his afflictions..."

From this perturbed state, he was startled by a prim knock at the chamber door. A bonneted servant bobbed her head inside. "Begging your pardon, sir, but the master requests you to join him in the parlour, if you please."

And so, Peter made his way to the intricate wood-panelled room.

There, before the floor-length damask-curtained window, he espied Master Pier seated on one of the two carved chairs, engaged vis-à-vis with a female seated on the other; her back turned to the door.

"Of course, I am delighted by your early arrival, my dear," was saying Pier. "But I would not have you exhaust yourself, travelling during the night..."

"Let us go to the spring, Papa."

Pier's eyes fell upon our hero. "Ah, Peter!" He rose with a wide smile. "Come through. Allow me the pleasure of introducing my dearest daughter."

As Peter entered, the daughter rose with an air of elegance and turned to face him, her rich purple-striped silk gown rustling across the floral medallion rug's deep woollen pile.

Possibly two or three-and-twenty in years, framed by chestnut hair pinned in elaborate curls, all in the French mode, her young countenance — formerly wreathed in ruby smiles and a refined alabaster complexion — reddened violently, souring at the sight of our hero. "It is you!" The pearls adorning her slender neck rattled with indignation. "The wretched, monstrous Venetian Folletto!"

Verily the blood retracted from our hero's heart as he too recognised her.

Pier's eyes followed the trajectory of the lady's trembling accusatory gloved finger. "You are acquainted?" said he, indubitably confused.

"*Acquainted?*" cried the lady with a hearty gasp. "Yes, I had the misfortune of encountering this *scoundrel* last year. *This* is the very knave" — she glared at Peter with the intensity of a thousand suns — "who affronted me most indecorously during my travels! Surely you recall my letter describing that horrid creature who plagued our party for days on end at the Venice carnival?"

"The Venice carnival?" Pier's wiry eyebrows, having been suspended quite high for some moments, fell back to his sockets with the apparent dawning of recollection. "Phillipina," (for this was his daughter's name) "are you *quite* certain this is the same... *rascal,* who bedevilled you?"

"Incontestably so!" Her lips curled down in palpable distaste at the mere sight of him. "It would be *impossible* to forget such a rude, *monstrous* rake!"

Pier now turned a quizzical eye upon his friend. "Is this... *true*?"

***

Indeed, it was; the particulars of which were recounted in Phillipina's aforementioned epistle, penned in the February 1791. Now, whilst a riotous carnival atmosphere may oft tempt even the best of men to impudent manners — perhaps emboldened by the anonymity of their masks — our hero, in whom we have erenow witnessed on many an occasion a certain want of courtesy, needed no Venetian disguise to exert his native supercilious spirit.

Picture, if you will, the first act of this comedy of errors: Phillipina, seated in one of the Teatro San Benedetto's most desirable boxes, bewitched by an aria common to the opera seria. But then imagine being abruptly torn from the delightful strains by an usher whispering into her ear the shocking injunction: she must remove herself at once.

With a modest, decorous concession — though it burned bitter as gall behind her fluttering fan — she masked her pique from the odious fellow who, by virtue of his wealth, happened to enjoy connections in the Nobile Società di Palchettisti (notably with the theatre manager). Alas for her, our hero, bent on securing that box — not from mere vanity, mind you, but for the strategic advantage of observing his rogue brother through opera glasses — gave no thought to the females' prior claim and effortlessly usurped their position.

Evicted forthwith from the box, Phillipina and her equally nettled companions were forced to ascend to the inappositely termed "paradise" — or "*piccionaia*" in the Italian tongue. Oh, how this celestial appellation cataclysmically fails to represent the bona fide reality of the highest, exposed balcony tier barely tucked beneath the rafters! Here, they had to squeeze themselves onto a backless bench, offering a view best described as "obstructed" and a price tag that speaks more to its affordability than its desirability.

Later that evening, Phillipina suffered the second indignity. After the curtain had fallen, and she and her friends hailed a carriage and were about to embark, alas, the coachman — greedy for greater recompense and perceiving Peter, or rather Valentin, approaching with his wealthy inebriated entourage — unceremoniously discharged his gentle passengers. Certainly, quite a few showers of sulphurous glares potent enough to ignite the very air did escape from behind the ladies' fans. They surrendered the carriage to their tormentor and watched it whisk away the vexing scoundrel, who, unbeknownst to them, desperately needed that carriage for he went in pursuit of that same above-mentioned brother.

Terrible, indeed, for the poor ladies.

But lo! Fate, it seemed, had not yet exhausted its repertoire of misfortunes. The next morn, too, was to bring another affront from the same villain.

28 June – 01 July 1792

Phillipina and her companions had each stepped but a toe into a last gondola to convey them to the parade when the graceless rogue appeared with his comrades by the canal-side. Once more hot in pursuit of his scheming brother, he demanded the very vessel from beneath the gentle ladies' fine shoes.

Since during Carnival, gondolas were no less exclusive than dry ground, deeper pockets prevailed. Thus, despite the infuriated Phillipina and her bosom friends' throbbing temples and sharp cries of protest, they found themselves again unceremoniously jettisoned and their remonstrations entirely unheard.

To be sure, there were plenty more encounters where she and her companions were repeatedly abused in so ungallant a fashion by this spoilt, entitled mob and its ringleader, the designated "Wretched Venetian Folletto!" But we shall spare the reader the particulars of these impudent affronts. For I think we can easily enter into Phillipina's loathe for the dastardly tyrant of Venice, who, though innocent of any true malice, was all the same rendered so with the detailed wrath of a goddess in her most astonishing letter.

***

"Well... I..." stammered Peter, quite bereft of words as a prickling heat crawled up his neck. How could Fortune play such a cruel hand? That the lady so ill-used amidst wine, revelry, an intrigue abroad could, of all women he would cross in the world, be Pier's own daughter! "While I confess our... *introduction...* was, perhaps, less... *decorous* than it ought to have been ... I am sure... it was probably not quite how she described it."

"It was *exactly* how I described it!" refuted Phillipina. "Every drop of my ire-filled blood, forever preserved in the ink that ruined the lines of what should have been solely a delightful correspondence!"

Notwithstanding his daughter's manifest wrath, Pier seemed lost in momentary contemplation. And, at length: "Peter," said he, "this is *wonderful* news!"

"This is?" echoed Peter, naturally confused.

"This *is*?" reverberated Phillipina, naturally appalled.

"Indeed." Pier beamed. "This means you at last remember something."

Err recognised, Peter could only look away to disguise the uncomfortable warmth which crawled over his face, while Phillipina rounded on her father, demanding answers — demanding to know the reason for the vile rake's presence in Bubendorf, and, more importantly, within her father's house.

***

The following morning, the newspaper's arrival cast a pall over the breakfast table. Headlines blared the projected funeral of the Bernese schultheiss' first-born. Peter's eyes alighting on the article, and his appetite instantly vanished.

Sharing the front page, an article reported on some wealthy patrician's mysterious death; another article, more unsettling, reported from Paris: several days prior, on June 20th, a mob had stormed the Tuileries Palace — the very residence of the French King!

"Good heavens..." uttered Peter. Though the king and his family were unharmed, the *sans-culottes'* growing power betrayed the monarchy's vulnerability. And with the Revolution's escalating radicalism, who knew what future instability and violence might yet spill across the border into Switzerland... He lifted his disbelieving eyes towards Pier, whereupon he observed in his countenance a peculiar gravity — seemingly of grief. Before Peter could discover the sentiment it spoke, a manservant entered with a despatch for his master.

This arrival produced in Pier's expression a desperate earnest tantamount to that which accompanied his receipt of the earlier communication pertaining to his youngest son. Indeed, the breakfast room seemed to hold its breath, anticipating the unveiling of yet another misfortune.

***

Meantime, to prepare for the impending ball, Elizabeth was whisked away, mid-afternoon, by Phillipina to Liestal. Their mission: to buy the perfect accessories for the opulent silk sacque gown gifted to Lizzie for such a special occasion.

Soon ensconced in the mercerie, our belles fell to fingering ribbons, beads, and silk flowers. During the light-hearted chatter and the rustling of French lace, Phillipina appeared to observe how Lizzie blushed and stammered whenever Peter's name arose. But such blushings and stammerings befitted not entirely that species of a young woman in love; no, there was something altogether else. And Phillipina, already averse to our hero and dubious of the account provided for his engagement to her friend, and unconvinced by the tale which Lizzie had woven about her enigmatic beau and their supposed history, seemed bent on discovering what it was.

"Think you," now said she, holding aloft a sparkling hair comb, "this is fine enough to turn even a vile Venetian Folletto's head?"

Though Elizabeth tried to conceal her discomfiture, she turned crimson at the implication. "Phillipina, he is not so frightful once you get to know him."

"A life-time in his company could never remove so stained an impression. But come, come, your blushes betray you." She glanced pointedly at the ribbon, which Lizzie unconsciously worried between her trembling fingers. "You are hiding something; of that I am certain! Now relieve my mind, lest it arrive at some dire conjecture."

At this, Elizabeth mumbled denials. Yet the more she fumbled and demurred, the faster suspicions clearly took flight in her auditor's mind. Regardless, the interrogatories at last ceased; several fine accessories were purchased to ornament the forthcoming occasion with and the ladies quit the shop.

But unbeknownst to our heroine, two brutes lurked across the bustling lane, their scowling faces filled with villainous intent. Who were these men? Why, none other than two scoundrels from that wily band of rogues whom we encountered in the bloody incident of Lucerne, recounted in our first tome.

Now healed of their injuries but smouldering for vengeance and more desperate than ever to claim their bounty, these villains had heretofore scoured every wretched corner of Liestal until Fortune, that capricious trickster, did at last reward their vile efforts.

Keeping slyly out of sight, they shadowed Lizzie and her bosom companion's every step through the market and all the way to the carriage, which the ladies clambered within, laughing together merrily, entirely ignorant of the scheming men's gaze.

And so, as the conveyance rattled down the lane and out of town, this cunning pair mounted their horses and kept to a careful distance behind.

For several miles they followed, at last, reaching that cusp of the hill which overlooked the lane leading to the chalet. There, they observed our heroine alight from the carriage and, waving it away, proceed through the gate and make her way to the premises.

Rightly guessing this to be Lizzie's home, they turned about and drove their horses in a hard gallop to their place of meeting, where they would soon plan their method of attack.

***

The following day, as the afternoon sun dappled the forest floor, Peter embarked on a solitary perambulation, his mind burdened with the unsettling revelations of the Venice tale and its potential consequences.

Anon, the young apple-bearing lad, his face presently streaked with tears and mud, rushed to him. Between the sobs — punctuated by hiccups, sniffles, and gasps — Peter learned of the child's transgression: defying his mother's orders, he had ventured into the pigpen to cavort with the piglets. As a result, his beloved Acorn (his porcine companion) had absconded and now roamed, most mischievously somewhere in the woods.

"There, there." Peter patted his heaving little shoulders, uncertain how to calm the inconsolable creature. "No need for such carryings-on, my boy." He glanced about, seeking inspiration. "Look!" He pointed. "We shall gather those acorns there and tempt the truant rascal back. What say you to that?"

Thus, armed with their acorn bounty, they set off in pursuit of the errant piglet, their calls echoing unanswered amidst the ancient oaks and wild garlic.

After some minutes, their quest led them to a small ravine, where the Sormmatt Falls gushed into a pool. The boy skipped across the pool's stepping stones, while Peter's attention was drawn to a hewn stone at the water's edge.

A metal plate affixed to it bore the following inscription:

In fondest memory of my Apollonia.

1727 - 1769

*Dearest wife and most enchanting friend, may you
find in death the harmony you sought in life beside
this gentle spring.
I count the days until we meet again.
Ever and eternally your devoted Otto*

Touched by this eulogy, Peter crossed himself. Yet, as he re-read the inscription, the names stirred a faint sense of familiarity. "Apollonia...? Otto...?"

Of a sudden, a rustling sound caught his hearing. Turning, he found himself face-to-face with a rather portly ginger piglet charging at him with surprising speed. Wholly caught off guard by this porcine stampede, he attempted to flee but succeeded only in stumbling over the mossy rocks and tumbling, with an undignified yelp, headlong into the drink.

"Acorn!" came the young lad's gleeful cry.

The pig, ignoring his caller, merely wagged its teeny corkscrew tail and munched merrily away on the acorns strewn across the ground in Peter's inglorious fall. Sparing no thought for our hero re-surfacing with weeds in his hair, the young keeper seized the piglet by its makeshift lead and merely trotted off into the thick growth.

"Boy!" called out Peter. "Boy?! W-w... where are..?! — The rotten youth abandons me!" Stung thus to the quick, soaked and deserted, he dragged himself ashore, looking, feeling, and smelling much like old King Lear who raged against thankless daughters.

Just then, a stiff breeze swept through the trees, rustling the leaves high above and carrying the strains of a haunting melody. The notes, as if played upon a pianoforte, mingled with the ethereal resonance of a voice and seemingly emanated from the surrounding woods.

Pier's tale of the Kunigunde legend — the vain daughter of Wildenstein's former owner — came to Peter's mind; he imagined her mournful spirit presently lamenting the loss of her beloved mirror.

The breeze shifted, and the strain faded, leaving behind an eerie silence. Hairs rose on his neck. Fearing the apparition might materialise at any moment, he hastened onwards, his sodden boots squelching with each step as he sought to find his way back to the schloss.

As he trudged through the undergrowth, surrounded by the spotted bush-cricket's rasping buzz and the twittering of birds, the haunting melody returned. This time, the plaintive notes stirred within him a distant sorrow that gripped his heart like a half-forgotten dream. Something rang with uncanny familiarity.

Ear inclined in every direction, he chased through the trees the strains that swelled, then ebbed, at times abandoning him again to nature's sounds alone. At length, the melody crescendoed above the tree line as the last quavering note faded into silence — and there loomed Wildenstein upon its rocky height.

Convinced of the emotive strains' inexplicable familiarity and the music had to have originated from Pier's pianoforte, he struggled up a rude path towards the schloss

Yet, upon reaching the library, he found it empty, the instrument silent with its lid closed. From a pile of manuscripts tucked beneath it, he picked one up and read its song title: "'Thy Dove'?"

"You're soaking wet!" came the housemaid's irritated voice. "Get out! Get out! Before you ruin the master's carpet!"

"Ah! Forgive me." Hastily, he retreated from the carpet onto the wooden floors. "But was there any person playing the pianoforte just now?"

"Never mind the piano!" The woman, eyes a-bulging like freshly laid eggs, rushed in and, grabbing his arm, discourteously dragged him out.

Finding the servant impervious to further interrogation, Peter asked Pier's whereabouts. This, the woman answered directly and bade him go to the gardens where the master and his daughter were entertaining a Miss Elizabeth. "And be quick about it, too. For you can water the flowerbeds along the way."

The very notion of seeing Lizzie was enough to drive him directly to his bedchamber, where he spent the day's remaining hours in feigning a headache to avoid all possible encounters. Though he attempted to read, his mind was far from at ease. With his memory returning in full force, he realised he could not forever maintain the charade of amnesia. Yet, anxious as he was to confront Elizabeth about her deception, he loathed to be anywhere near her and lacked the courage and resolution to hazard further complications arising.

Dusk soon spread across the world outside, and the waxing gibbous rose high, its silvery light flooding through the window, drawing Peter's thoughts back to the poem. *Since Elizabeth believes me to be the author of such sentiments, she cannot have known who he was... or perhaps... she did... but was unaware of his romantic interests...?*

How was he ever to discover the connection? With the one dead and the other, evidently ignorant, it was near to an impossibility.

***

Sunday morn's arrival brought with it the dreaded obligation of church attendance. Unwilling, however, to engage in what would undoubtedly be a most excruciating ordeal, our hero irreverently concocted an excuse — feigning being unwell. Freed thus from fiery sermons and instead armed with paper and quill pilfered from Master Pier's desk, he devoted the quiet of morning to composing a letter to a trusted friend in Bern; his pen scratched furtively across the paper as the distant church bells tolled their solemn reproach.

The various uncertainties, coupled with the colonel's continued and disquieting silence, compelled our hero to seek information from behind the scenes. Aware of the risks involved, and to safeguard his companion, he sagely employed their customary coded language, ensuring the message would confound all prying eyes yet be instantly recognisable to his confidante. Leaving only the Liestal posthouse address for a reply, he sealed the missive and gave it to a servant to convey to Liestal the next day.

The morning soon passed, and Peter, yearning for fresh air — and, perhaps, more aptly, an escape from Phillipina and Lizzie, whose voices now wafted from below — stealthily descended the stairs and made for the outside world.

Alas, his newfound freedom was short-lived. As he ventured through the main gate and down the driveway, he spotted, to his utter dismay, Father Francis alighting from a carriage, his black cassock billowing ominously in the breeze.

Divining, with very little difficulty, the guillotine blade poised to fall on his head, our hero's sole recourse was to seek refuge behind the nearest tree.

Incidentally, as he thus crouched behind the thick oak trunk, Fortune, ever fond of vexing our hapless hero, betook it upon herself to smoke the rascal out. Having so vast an arsenal at her disposal, this truly wicked goddess did call upon nature to orchestra a most ignominious assault upon his person. Perchance plucking a feather from some unsuspecting avian's rump, she provoked a startled squawk that drew Peter's eyes skyward to witness the descent of not one, but *two* malodorous missiles. These feculent projectiles, propelled with the force of a thousand angry cherubs, found their marks with uncanny precision. The first, a direct hit between our hero's eyes — SPLAT! — robbed him of sight; the second, in a feat of marksmanship that would have made even Cupid blush, flew straight and true into his gaping maw and right down his gullet. "URGH!"

Sputtering and choking on so unholy an amalgam of excreta and bile, Peter did unleash a muffled, purblind, and veritably poopy tirade against whichever feathered fiend had so brazenly chosen him as the target for its aerial bombardment. Alas, his blind rage and wild gesticulations proved his undoing. He toppled backwards over a retaining wall and landed in an undignified heap amidst Pier's prized roses, their thorny embrace adding insult to injury.

Limbs flailing like an upended dung beetle, our hero lay there, entangled amidst the flattened petals, barbed branches, and broken stems.

Magnifying his mortification, a young voice probed: "What you doing like a fool down there, sir?"

Expunging his sight of the birdly ordure, Peter observed, through one half-cleared eye, the very young lad — who abandoned him at the pool — peering down at him from the wall's edge. "Hush, boy!" Peter winced as he drew with his thorn-splintered finger the sign of silence. "Pray, tell the Father I have left the canton. Tell him you already saw me heading up the avenue yonder."

The boy scrunched his mouth. "But isn't that fibbing?"

As if this was a time for such piety! "But I shall give you a shiny batzen."

Swift as lightning and with greedy zeal, the boy dashed off and spun his little taradiddle, whereupon the Father uttered several unintelligible curses, turned about with a great harrumph, and waddled back up to his Holy carriage, which soon faded into the distance, leaving behind a cloud of dust and a scent of thwarted righteousness.

No sooner had Peter extricated himself from the prickly predicament than the youth returned, extending his grubby flattened-out palm, demanding the afore-promised coin. Oh! But upon learning our hero's pockets were as empty as his excuses, the lad did ball his little fists and stomp his little feet, giving vent to his little lungs a-wailing at the injustice.

Enter the boy's mother. With the efficiency of a seasoned inquisitor, she soon had the whole sordid tale out in the open and promptly scolded both the abettor for his fibbing and then the instigator for his egging her son on to such devilish disgrace.

As if this were not ignominy enough, Elizabeth and Phillipina strode down the driveway, lured by the commotion. Witnessing Peter's sorry state, bedecked in mud, petals, and thorns sticking out every which way, yet discovering what had occurred, they, too, joined the chorus of opprobrium and harangued our scapegrace hero for corrupting innocents for sport.

"Folletto?" Phillipina dragged her friend away. "Nay, the Devil's own godson! I pray fire and brimstone besmirch you next time!"

This Sunday, though scandalised by the above-scene, soon found its focus shifted onto a more auspicious occasion: that of the ball; this very evening.

As Peter fell to bemoaning the lacklustre potential of his green woollen suit, quite at a loss about how to make it dazzle before the looking glass, a knock heralded Master Pier at his door. Bearing a lantern and key, he proceeded directly to an adjacent closet. It soon being unlocked, it revealed several rails laden with garments of evident quality — all of which belonged to Arnborg. As Peter ran his fingers along the garb, his touch sensed succouring silks and velvets.

"I see no wisdom in allowing dust to collect on what can be better put to use," said Pier. "You appear to be of a similar frame and height, and you will find something appropriate for this evening. And I will brook no objections. You may consider this a small reward for your company. When you are finished, come join me in the courtyard. I have something to show you."

With that, Pier quit the chamber, leaving Peter to investigate the closet's best offerings. To his no little ecstasy, he found garb that not only fit his physique perfectly but aligned with his taste. As strange as it was to be donning the attire of an enemy — one who he knew still lived — he selected a fine blue, albeit dusty, satin brocade suit. Satisfied before the looking glass, he made his way to the courtyard to model his new arrayments before his kind benefactor.

There, Master Pier and Phillipina were engaged in talk beneath an arbour; a small beribboned box was placed between them. Upon seeing Peter approach in his new fineries, Pier rose from the bench with a wide smile, while Phillipina remained seated, offering a sly, albeit glowering, glance.

"Hands out, Peter," instructed Pier. "The box, please, Phillipina."

Hands were thus extended, some glowers thus darted, which Peter cared not for, for oh, what delightful new shoes must be secreted within this fair box.

But when the lid was lifted, to his surprise and delight, he beheld, nestled within, not sparkling footwear, but rather, the tiniest Bernese puppy, asleep amidst a bed of hay, its paws dusted with snowy white fur.

"Heavens!" Peter's heart instantly swelled at the sight of the creature, which now blinked up at him with coppery eyes. "For *me*?"

"For you," confirmed Pier.

Peter raised the pup on high; it yawned, unveiling a tiny pink tongue.

"I hope your new friend will, in time, make up for the loss of another," said Pier. "I do not presume to know your heart, but I have observed your melancholy of late, and I can attribute it to no other cause than Znüni's absence."

Though not entirely without merit were Pier's observations, Peter merely nodded as he caressed the pup's downy ears and snuggled it under his chin. "How can I ever thank you?"

Phillipina reached out to pet the puppy. "What shall you name him?"

"Schatzi," declared Peter without hesitation, kissing the creature's velvet-soft crown. "He is, indeed, a little treasure; more precious than jewels."

***

'Twas already gone the eighth hour when our glittering guests began arriving at Ebenrain. Peter had travelled alongside Master Pier, Ernest, and Emil, while the ladies went in a separate coach.

All now alighted into the bustling courtyard — with carriages coming and going, disgorging their bedizened occupants in a riot of colour and ostentation. As they entered the vestibule to relinquish their capes and coats to the overworked footman, Peter's gaze was suddenly arrested: Elizabeth, her fine countenance aglow, her radiant hair pulled high, and resplendent in a flowing French emerald gown, nigh stole his breath.

"Does the Folletto not know," uttered Phillipina, "it is most ungentlemanly to gawk at a lady in such a fashion?" She emphasised this reproach with a sharp prod of her fan at his chin.

Peter's glare could have cut glass. "And does the viper," retorted he, "not know how unpleasant and vexing is the sting of her own venomous tongue?"

Her delicate sensibilities affronted by the verbal riposte, Phillipina flushed a violent hue of scarlet that clashed most unfashionably with her soft pink silk robe à l'anglaise. Just as Pier was about to intervene in this battle of barbs, Johannes' voice stole over the hum of talk and strains of Mozart streaming down from the colonnade balcony above.

"Pier, my good friend." His Lordship stood with his wife and Jago at the doors to the garden room, welcoming their guests. "Come, come."

Johannes beamed at Pier and Phillipina, but upon beholding Elizabeth, his smile vanished. "Well, well..." His lordly gaze darted suspiciously to his son, whose visage had lit up at the charming sight. "What *illusion* is *this* that stands before me?" With feigned gallantry, he extended a gloved finger for her to take hold. "My guests shall have to be careful not to mistake your rank, my dear...."

Edmunda presently bowled forth and brusquely shoved aside the blushing and still curtsying Elizabeth. "Johannes." She seized his gloved hand with the force of a bear trap. Her voluminous layers of thick linen skirts — a homespun affair of sturdy wool dyed in an unfortunate shade of mustard as to sting every appalled eye — gathered up, she attempted a curtsy not unlike a hippopotamus at a pirouette. "How good of you to invite us to your splenetic affair!"

At the mere sight of so monstrous a sartorial misstep before him, conjoined with such undesired sycophancy, and more particularly such clumsy misuse of genteel words (for Edmunda meant to say, "splendid," dear reader, in case it escaped your notice), his lordship's face turned only the sourer. He snatched his hand back with icy incivility.

Visibly discomfited by her husband's sharpness, Johannes' wife quickly intervened and warmly welcomed Edmunda, Ernest, *and* Emil before she whispered into Johanes' ear that she had extended an invitation to them herself.

"Indeed?" He now glared at his wife with an intensity as to melt metal. "Well," resumed he, glancing at Edmunda with poorly disguised repugnance. "Do move it along, then."

While Johannes thus brushed the unwelcome aside to make way for the more pleasing additions to the occasion, Jago swept over to offer his arms to the ladies — Phillipina and Lizzie. "Permit me to escort you within to some refreshments, dear creatures," purred he, "before you faint from the sheer magnitude of your own loveliness."

The occasion soon swirled on in dazzling fashion, lit with candlelight that glittered all about like a spangled sky. Entreated by Johannes' wife to open the ball, Peter finally acquiesced and led Lizzie to the dancefloor, where he soon felt — to his no little unease — all eyes slide from his finery onto his partner's elegant gown.

To the strains and one-two-threes' of the walzer, they floated around at the marque's centre. Hushed whispers galloped about the awed crowd; many a raised brow and approving smile confirmed our heroine had stolen the veneration of all present; much to the chagrin of sundry noble ladies, who seethed with envy behind their fans, their white knuckles betraying their vexation.

Though still guarding his heart, our hero could not help but be sensible of this attention, nor ignore the twinge of admiration which distilled his antipathy towards her. Once more did her beauty capture his mind, and her smiles tease his soul. 'Twas as if Cupid had darted him afresh with his blazing quill, the wound both sweet and agonising. Even as his traitorous eyes drank in her loveliness, feasting on every graceful turn and elegant gesture, he steeled his resolve; he would not be taken in again.

After procuring refreshments for them both, he settled Lizzie with her family and betook himself off outside the marque to avail himself of the night's air. "That siren!" muttered he between impatient sips of champagne. "She still tries to bewitch me of my senses. I must flee; no matter how radiant she is or —" He spat out his drink, the bubbles stinging his nose. *Am I mad?!*

Presently, Peter spied a footman serving nearby; the very one attacked those several months back. Eager to discharge the shame this memory induced, he stole over to him and again offered apologies. The stoic servant bid him to think no more of it, then cocked his head at Peter's mention of the mysterious garden confidant he had once seen him engaged with. Confounded indeed was our hero to learn that not only was this figure unknown to the footman, but had bid the servant to ensure Peter's comfort whilst in Johannes' employment.

"How vastly peculiar." Peter pressed for clarity. "But you truly have no notion who he was?"

"Absolutely none, sir."

Jago appeared as if out of nowhere and requested Peter to join him inside the schloss. Away from the music and candlelight, they proceeded to the dim drawing room. Jago closed the heavy doors, sealing them in stifling silence.

"Found among the possessions returned to us," said he, "was a most curious piece — owing to your... *heroism*... as they so *inappositely* label it." His angular visage, sculpted and manly, loomed as an accusatory spectre in an immaculate black tailcoat. "And I have given this matter significant consideration."

Indeed, our hero felt dread's poison spread through his veins. "Sir?"

From inside his silken waistcoat pocket, Jago produced a folded sheet of newspaper. Unfurling it, he thrust it into Peter's face. "Perhaps you can explain the significance of this?"

All warmth fled Peter's body at beholding the familiar face glaring back beneath the all too familiar and damning WANTED.

"Who really *are* you?"

Tongue-tied by dismay, held under so exquisite a scrutinising glower that seemed to peel back his very skin, our hero knew not where to look.

"Rest assured," resumed the accuser as he tapped a gloved finger on the tattered paper, "I shall discover whatever criminality this manhunt pertains to and indeed unravel every strand of the tapestry with which I suspect you have draped about your questionable past. And if you *are* the rogue sought by the world, no dungeon will be deep enough to hide you from the gallows' kiss! Of that, you have my oath."

02 – 04 JULY 1792

Daybreak saw Peter pacing his chamber, harassed by the greatest consternation imaginable as he replayed in his mind the prior evening's alarming incident — Jago's damning pronouncements echoing in his ears. The confines of Bubendorf, once a refuge, now seemed to close in like the walls of a prison; our hero was perhaps never so unresolved on what next to do.

To be sure, he had refuted so strong a resemblance to the poster, averring his accuser was entirely misguided in his opinion. But his words broke vainly against the rocks of Jago's conviction and incited solely the more unquenchable menaces of investigation. Though Jago had spared Miss Elizabeth any interruptions to her enjoyment at the ball, he vowed with an inexorable determination to speak with her upon his return from Zürich; moreover, he disclosed he had already written off to several garrisons across the cantons.

Fear, cold and clammy, snaked its way around Peter's chest, squeezing tight. Where before Harris had failed, this young noble, possessed of the necessary wealth and connections, Peter feared, may in fact discover his true personage, thus exposing him to the very dangers he sought shelter from.

He sank into a nearby chair. "Where am I to run?" muttered he. "To turn?"

***

At the breakfast table, to our hero's no little consternation, he received word from the garrison. With troubles escalating at the borders, he was ordered to accompany the regiment for Geneva on the morrow. Though he strove to disguise his disturbance, his sudden pale complexion fixed Pier's discerning eyes.

"My dear fellow," said he. "Is something amiss? You have barely touched your food."

Folding the missive and depositing it within his pocket with fingers that threatened to tremble, Peter lifted his gaze and mustered a weak a smile. "Perhaps the grape took a stronger hold than I expected."

Phillipina, delicately sipping her tea, narrowed her eyes at him over the rim of the cup and raised a thin, disapproving brow. Our hero diverted his own gaze. Truly, matters only further deteriorated with every ticking hour. Caught in the crossfire of equally distressing and perilous fates, he knew not what to do. Near suffocating, he, in a bid to steady his nerves and affect a semblance of normalcy, attempted to partake of some tea; but his hand shook so violently that the cup rattled against the saucer like a prisoner's chains, drawing further interrogatories his way.

Thankfully, the arrival of the morning papers soon diverted all attention.

As Pier scanned the headlines, he exclaimed, "good heavens! It appears the Bernese schultheiss has taken a turn for the worse."

"What?" Peter's heart tremored; all heat fled his body. "What else does it say?"

"Have a read for yourself." Pier passed him the paper. "I would imagine that his decline stems from the natural grief of a father. The funeral is tomorrow, it seems."

"*Tomorrow?*" Peter darted his own eyes across the print. Never had so many words communicated so little. What he sought to discover, he found not in this article; barely a few lines touched on his father's ill health. Endeavouring to stay the tumult of his thoughts, Peter reached for his throbbing temple. The focus was all on the funeral. A heavy sigh escaped his lips, unbidden, drawing anew the unwanted attention of his auditors.

"Are you certain there is nothing amiss?" pressed Pier.

"Perfectly fine, thank you." The lie tasted bitter on Peter's tongue, and at that very moment, 'twas as if a phantom from otherworldly realms sprang from the page and pierced his very soul with its ghostly blade.

Every woe, every anxiety raged a battle within. His chest pounded. His temperature fluctuated. At length, the urgency of a heart, fuelled by filial duty, eclipsed every reservation. He would brave the inferno, the tempest, to gaze upon his father's face once more, even if it were to be their last farewell.

"Peter?" Pier's gentle voice broke through. "What troubles you?"

Throat clenched by anguish, scarce able to breathe, Peter feigned a sudden headache — a convenient consequence of his supposed overindulgence — and to the solitude of his chamber he fled. There, shutting himself away for the better part of the morning, he paced and warred within himself.

Despite the thorny and involute history our hero shared with his father, 'twas now he repented of his pride and his stubbornly hating him these many years. After his mother's death, Peter vehemently blamed the schultheiss for bowing to the council's prescriptions. The schultheissin's rash treason, however intended, had sunk Peter's world entirely, leaving him adrift in a sea of grief and confusion. *How could a council be so merciless as to have demanded her immediate end? Surely deposition and exile would have sufficed?* Mayhap, given time, she would have tempered wrath's hot flames? 'Twas inconceivable that so loving a mother could not have surrendered her revenge for the happiness of a most devoted son...

Alas! This was something he would never know.

And what of his father's other failings? Again, bowing to the council's orders to elevate his half-brother who, despite no ill will Peter felt for him, was still the offspring of that cruel, calculating, cold step-mother; a madam who had been welcomed into heart and home so soon — too soon! *Would the council have dared to strip me of my primogeniture if my mother still lived and stood beside my claim?* Would our hero then not have been caught in dissipation's grasp, vainly diminishing the disillusion he felt for his superfluous and stagnant life?

With life being so brief, precious days had slipped between child and parent, unreconciled. Yet, could chance, however frail, mend what bitterness had ravaged?

At length, the tempest of indecision subsided and resolution dawned: he would return to Bern.

Hence, entrusting Schatzi to Pier's "temporary" — Peter promised — care, he offered only a vague explanation about needing to substantiate recovered memories.

But first, before embarking on his journey, there was a visit most necessary to Peter's peace. Having obtained the use of a horse, he set off; his destination: the chalet.

His arrival was met with clear apprehension by Elizabeth *and* Helene. Without a word, he seized Lizzie by her wrist, snatching her away from her companion, and swept her to the confines of the toolshed.

All cries going unheeded as he sealed them both within the weathered timber walls, visibly deepened the trepidation heaving in Lizzie's bosom.

"This charade ends *now*," vowed our hero, utterly indifferent to her bewilderment; he shoved her into a beam of light swirling with dust motes. "I can pretend no more to the ignorance of my true identity, nor can I countenance any longer the deceit with which you have ill-used me."

Deep was the crimson which flushed our heroine's countenance; her eyes fell to the ground.

"Whilst circumstances forbid me from telling you who I truly am," continued Peter, "I most assuredly avow that I am *not* Peter. No more will I play a part in this spectacle. You have spun a piece of fiction, which I still, however, hope is not entirely worthy of your character."

Here, Elizabeth's senses did plainly near-forsake her. She stumbled backwards, barely clinging to a bench. Her eyes darted frantic yet unseeing, no doubt chased by the terrors in her mind; her expression melted into one of condemning horror; her colour drained to a ghostly pallor.

"I see in your shamefaced aspect that I am vindicated in my charges." Peter buried her further with his hate-filled looks. "There is no time at present to discuss your machinations, for I must away to Bern. But know this: your architecture of lies shall crumble. What your hand first laid as its foundations, mine shall raze to the ground!"

***

The midnight hour saw the Bernische Post carriage clatter at last into Bern, with Peter and his humble wardrobe in tow. Though Master Pier had bedecked our hero most fine of late, Peter trusted 'twas better to dress down to avoid the unwanted attentions and conversations of the upper class who, when obliged to travel post, do like to expunge their tedium with idle interrogations.

Despite the hour being well advanced, he secured lodgings at a less-frequented inn in the heart of the city's Innere Neustadt region. There, a plump little innkeeper with a round, overly-rouged, one-eyed face bustled forth to greet him. Her features, though crowded together upon her visage like piglets jostling for a place at a trough, exuded an air of effusive hospitality.

"Oh, my!" exclaimed she, squinting up at him with her one good eye while she adjusted the angled, gaudy embroidered patch covering the other. "Just look at the weariness of travel in that face — but lo, what a handsome face it is. Such looks must be fed."

And nourished he was, with a late-night repast, before being escorted upstairs to the inn's second-best room — only her second-best, mind you, for the finest was already taken. That said, she hastened to assure him that, should his behaviour prove as agreeable as his person, he would be granted the privilege of an upgrading to her best room — which boasted the finest views of the street — as soon as its current inhabitant vacated:

"Which, pray," added she with a conspiratorial wink, "can't come soon enough! For though the gent has coin aplenty, he has the most hideous countenance in all of Christendom! He most vexingly sits at the window all day long, staring out at goodness knows what, as if he were a gargoyle perched upon a cathedral's ledge. He'd verily drive away even the plague from my doorstep! And in these times of uncertainty and civil unrest, I need every coin I can get!"

'Twas at this moment, our hero realised, with a start, that with his thoughts being so consumed by his father, all such other matters had quite eluded his mind.

Peter's room was pleasant enough — for the second-best. The woman, her bulging bosom puffing out with pride, preened that each item was her own special selection. Making quite the to-do, descanting on and on, she fingered the petit point chair covers, adjusted the crewelwork embroidered curtains, smoothed out the hand-tied floral patchwork quilts, fondled the pillows and the bedsheets, all the while, near-eulogising their quality and comfort.

Eager for privacy, Peter curtailed the woman's idle prattle with the subtlety of a sledgehammer and ushered her quite briskly straight out of the door.

At last, settling beneath the bedcovers, he gradually lost every care in the world to the sleep's sweet embrace, which fell heavily upon his eyes.

***

Next morn, bright and early, brought the innkeeper rapping at the door. With cheery good-morrows and a merriment quite unsuited to the hour, she balanced a shiny tray as ample as her own generous proportions. "The very finest fares my pantry holds!" The lashes of her lonely eye clapped like Hermes' wings.

Unable to endure her incessant prattle and such an onslaught of early morning enthusiasm, nor able to suffer her singular fulsome gaze — which did make our hero feel quite the trapped Odysseus beneath the great cyclops' orb — the door Peter could not slam fast enough!

Anyhow, belly soon filled with honey cakes and aromatic coffee, he readied himself for that strangest of spectacles — his own funeral procession.

He was just stepping out onto the landing when the creak of the adjacent room's door caught his attention. From the corner of his eye, he glimpsed a figure emerge and disappear back inside with mouse-like quickness. Assuming the lodger had merely forgotten something, Peter descended the stairs.

Onto the grey and uneven cobbled Bernese streets, he stepped out, keeping to the shaded stone arcades. Despite the inter-cantonal strife and the looming threat of war, the city swelled and hummed, held at bay by Swiss guards as the throngs gathered to catch even a glimpse of the morbid parade soon to file past.

As our hero made his way towards the Münstergasse, every city smell rushed into nostrils: the yeasty tang of fresh-baked rolls and pastries; the earthy aroma of strong-steeped coffee; and the biting, honeyed smell wafting from the alehouses. Such familiar smells brought back to his mind, in an assailing wave, his favourite vending houses and the leisure he enjoyed with past acquaintances.

At last, he reached the Münsterplatz. The soaring Bern Minster's ornate grey façade, dominating the square, seemed to sigh upon the crowds. From here, Peter would best descry his father and adjudge the severity of his condition.

Wedged amidst the crowd beside the Mosesbrunnen statue, he glanced up. Moses' stone face, its stern, wide eyes, seemed to glare reproach upon this prodigal son only now skulking, incognito, back home. The giant tablets, too, loomed over Peter's head; ten numerals etched in gold, symbolising those eternal commandments — including that ever accusing fifth:

"Honour thy father and mother."

Hands wringing anxiously, alternately flexing his fingers, and then clenching his fists, he awaited the prescribed hour. According to the itinerary printed in the newspapers, the procession would soon arrive at the cathedral's west façade. Consulting his timepiece, he flicked open its damaged lid: but five minutes more.

The watch's cracked glass barely shielded its ticking hands; his mother's faded and marred watercolour miniature bore the jagged scarring of the lead ball which, were it not for this timepiece, would have sunk into his chest those many months ago when his present hell had begun.

His eyes he now tore away from the scarred heirloom and scanned the buildings lining the square. From among the many tall windows, each filled with the nobility looking down on the scenes soon to unfold, he noticed one countenance he believed he recognised; but the face withdrew before he could be certain. "Franz?"

Peter had just begun forcing his way through the crowd towards the building when a neighbouring pamphlet in the hands of a bystander snared his attention: a seditious diatribe which condemned the oligarchy, blasted the extravagance of such a funeral in such critical times, and admonished all opposed to the patriciate rule to stay away from this event.

As our hero leant closer to read its content, brass suddenly blared through the square, accompanied by the steady rhythm of percussion.

All eyes turned to behold the approaching Geneva Grenadiers corps drummers — the very best of Geneva's militia: a marching wall of proud blues, pure whites, vibrant crimson, and deep bearskin caps adorned with blood-red plumes, floating high in martial splendour. Behind, followed the hornists, trombonists, and trumpeters, their sombre requiems flowing out of curved brass and filling the air with melancholy tones.

Indubitably, this bold display proclaimed Geneva's impregnability and immortal staunch unity with her sister canton: a message made vivid in so proud a parade to all French, Austrian, and Prussian aggressors — and, consequently, to the world.

Meanwhile, within the tallest of the three soaring cathedral portals, beneath the over-elaborate tableau archway of aureate statues depicting the Last Judgement, there now gathered the ordained ministers in funeral robes of black. Heavenward, they turned their eyes as they uttered silent prayers through quivering lips.

The martial band reached the plaza's far end and took their positions. With flawless synchronicity, bayonets raised, the guardsmen fired the artillery; a roaring volley sent panicked birds erupting into the now smoke-stained skies.

There now came the solemn clopping of coal-black steeds, the rolling of wheels, and there appeared the sleek oaken casket, draped in black and red cantonal colours and laden with wreaths. Certainly, to gaze upon one's own funeral and see one's own name — one's true name, that is — woven through florid garlands with all worldly accolades and titles, was incomprehensible. The coffin, though bearing the corpse of the yet unknown poet, encapsulated his own death-like existence, his former self laid to rest forever in its shadow.

Would our hero ever be able to step into the light? Could he rise as one resurrected from the tomb to reclaim name, and right?

Just then, as if jolted by a thunderbolt, our hero's heart hammered. From behind the cathedral's far side, there emerged his ashen-countenanced father, astride a magnificent black charger ornamented in intricately beaded netting and sweeping raven feathers that caught the morning light.

Flanking the schultheiss, rode Peter's half-brothers: on the left, the worthy Varus, and the unworthy Viktor; on the right, the adored Vitus — the youngest. A fifth steed, riderless, outfitted with an empty dragoon's saddle and sheathed ceremonial sword, served in ode to the departed. Behind them trailed the retinue of councillors, all clad in Death's hues.

Time itself seemed to cease its forward momentum as Peter studied his father's careworn face... Breath shuddered within his chest; his fingers curled into desperate, strengthless fists... A mere sixty paces separated them now; yet it remained an unbreachable distance enough to span worlds. The rupture between father and son and world was one that not even the cruel belief of untimely death could undo to unite them. Truly, no prison was so cruel as a child's exile from a grieved parent's exhausted eyes...

Of a sudden, there came:

BOOM!

Shockwaves tore through the ancient square; windows shattered; the very cobbled earth convulsed, sinking in several places, dragging the brier into an abyss; geysers of smoke and stone erupted, flinging manhole disks into the air, rending past and present asunder.

Horses reared in terror. Screams rent the air. Guards strove to affect order as the panicked crowd surged to the side streets, trampling one another in their desperation to escape.

Seeing his father suddenly toppled from his horse and struggling beneath the churning, iron-shod hooves, Peter, forgetting himself and the dangers entirely, heedlessly rushed forth with a tormented cry.

But no sooner had he gained three strides than several guards seized hold of him with a bruising grip, wrenching him back by both arms.

Peter strained against their vice-like restraint. "Unhand me, this instant!"

It was then, over their mailed shoulders and through the smoky, dust-strewn chaos, that our hero locked gazes with Vitus, whose incredulous and almost fear-stricken eyes narrowed with recognition visibly dawning.

What am I doing?

Brought back to his senses, Peter broke free of the guard's grasp, wheeled about, and bolted into the stampeding mob.

Half-blinded by the tears streaming down his dust-stained cheeks, he stumbled back to the inn. There, brushing past the clucking landlady, ignoring her questions, he staggered upstairs, his mind echoing with the thunderclap realisation of all he had thrown away in one reckless moment.

Several hours had now passed. So distraught was our hero that he sought strong wine to slow his heart's frantic slamming. But alas! Not even intoxication's spell could still the waves of horror.

What if his weakened father had been seriously injured? What if he had died? And what of Vitus — would he spread word of the "ghost" seen risen? Could Peter soon find himself hunted through these old streets and alleys by dogs thirsty for fugitive blood?

Pray, may I not become trapped in this city!

Such thoughts like this hounded his brain for some hours more, stealing reason itself. But then, from amidst the swirling chaos, there broke, like a lightning flash, through the storm: "Was this brazen attack Franz's doing?"

Could *this* explain why he was at the window?

There came fast to Peter's recollection a fullest remembrance of when he was captured by the Swiss Guard in the mountains, only to have then been taken by bandits. Though those brigands had vehemently cursed the patricians and professed their intentions of overthrowing the unjust rule at any cost, this could not be a scheme of theirs, of Franz's, could it?

Presently, the heavy footfalls of boots on the stairs obtruded upon Peter's thoughts.

Then, came the discordant clanking of blades along the corridor... before:

Bang-bang-bang!

"Open up!"

Our hero convulsed within; had his folly seen him at last to the gallows?

Bang-bang-bang!

"Open, this instant!"

Nauseous, Peter rushed to the window; peering down, he noted several troops amassing below. "It cannot be! Not so swiftly..."

Bang-bang-bang!

"This is the Guard! We will force our way in!"

Almost unable to breathe, his very limbs violently shaking, he stumbled across the room to the door separating his chamber from the one adjacent.

Trying the handle, he yanked hard. But to no avail. Frantic, he threw himself against it. Still, the barrier remained impervious to all assault.

Bang-bang-bang!

What am it to do?

Then, there came gently through, "fear not, Brother, for 'tis I, Vitus."

Vitus?

Then, there came the childhood name, soft yet unmistakable. "Val?"

All madness abated at once. Peter flew to the main door and pressed his ear against it. "Vitus, can it t*ruly* be you...?"

"Yes, 'tis I."

Still disbelieving, but impelled by agitated yearning, Peter opened the door just wide enough to permit a glimpse through its slit.

Indeed, the fond Vitus' face smiled at him. "Brother!"

"Vitus!" Peter swung the door wide and flung his arms about him in a crushing embrace. "How beyond joyous to see you..." choked he, tears streaming forth. "I... I..." surging emotion robbed him of his words.

Vitus, too, succumbing to the ardour of his feelings, clung harder to his resurrected kin. For some moments, they stood there, locked in a silent embrace, the months of separation melting away in the warmth of their reunion.

At length, our hero, first to master his tears and compose himself, stepped back and spoke. "How did you trace me here?"

It emerged that after Vitus had seen him and, indeed, recognised him, he despatched two trusted men to tail our hero's panicked flight back to this very inn. No doubt observing the fear in Peter's — or rather, Valentin's — eyes beholding the waiting soldiers, Vitus offered a smile of reassurance. "Fear not, Brother. They shall breathe no word of your presence here. And I have guaranteed the innkeeper's silence. Trust that you are in friendly, shielded hands."

The threshold at last crossed over, and a flurry of fervent questions tumbled forth: our hero, desperate to learn of his father's condition and the events transpired since his disappearance; Vitus, astounded at his brother's miraculous survival and anxious to know what sorry soul — whom he wept over — had welcomed Death's cold embrace in his stead.

Though still drunk on the joy of their reunion, and though there were many things yet to say, Vitus curtailed their meeting. Fearful as he was of arousing suspicion by staying overlong, he sternly dissuaded Peter from leaving his room, before he himself took his leave with a pledge to return on the morrow.

Alone once more, and with hope flickering anew in his heart, Peter settled himself down at the window. Every fibre of his being seemed to soften as the weeks of tension, weeks of uncertainty, weeks of abject horror at last loosened their grip on his wearied soul. As with a man, long-parched, who at last discovers a life-giving spring, he drank deeply the dewy abundance of fortuity's refreshing sweetness.

Like the cleansing wrought by blood-letting, so did the impurities of dread and despondency ebb from his veins. A warmth infused his very soul, a complete, perfect, and unparalleled sense of tranquillity. A long-forgotten harmony returned, a wholeness that seemed to mend his fractured spirit.

As he sat there, lost in newfound reverie, his mind's eye delineating the incomparable joys awaiting him in the morrow, he noticed a faint light bleeding from beneath the adjoining door, accompanied by a lingering shadow.

Curiosity piqued, he squinted hard, focusing his gaze.

Indeed, it was a shadow; it wavered slightly.

Convinced this shadow belonged to some unknown person, he silently rose and crept over the floorboards to the door.

Ear placed against the wood, he listened intently.

Was that not the muffled yet distinguishable sound of someone breathing?

"Hello?" softly called out our hero.

Silence.

"*Hello?*" repeated he.

Again, naught but silence.

Perplexed, Peter stepped back and scrutinised the gap beneath the door.

The light had vanished entirely, and the shadow along with it.

Act 2

05 July 1792

—

24 July 1792

05 – 07 JULY 1792

Scarce any sleep found our hero's eyes that long night. His mind, a tempest of galloping thoughts and anxieties, refused to grant his body the respite it so desperately craved. Soon the devoted Vitus would return, and with him, mayhap the possibility of Peter somehow gaining private admittance to his father. Whatever judgement would be determined by that stoic and grievously deceived man, our hero might still get to plead his case.

As the first rays of morn pierced the chamber's lattice leaded glass, the rosy-cheeked, monocular innkeeper came a-rapping upon his door, bearing a veritable feast of fresh-baked breads, hot and cured meats, and cheeses worthy of the schultheiss himself.

Though curiosity surely burned behind that single orb, 'twas undoubtedly Vitus' influence — or rather, a liberal greasing of the palm — that kept her impertinent queries at bay. Still, this did not forestall the garrulous woman from accosting Peter's poor ears about the most mundane matters of her business.

But with a brusque word of thanks for the victuals, he shut the door upon her and fell readily upon the generous meal.

The morn inched by at a slug's pace: every footfall and voice in the cobbled street below, drawing Peter to the window, parting the lace curtains; each groan of the timbered stairs finding him poised by the door, ears pricked. But where no coded knock or familiar voice came, impatience returned twofold.

With a gusty sigh, he returned to the window and kept an anxious vigil. Below, the scant citadins of Bern went about their quotidian routines: merchants' carts and the occasional carriage mingled amongst the patrols of redcoats who, from door-to-door, made the expected enquiries into suspicious persons or activities around the ancient city as of late. 'Twas a boon indeed that Vitus found our hero and recompensed the innkeeper handsomely for her silence.

What an astonishment now seized Peter, when he spied none other than Franz on the street below, lurking outside the timbered tavern, directly opposite. After casting several furtive-looking glances, he slithered inside the building.

Forsaking entirely his brother's stern counsel, he snatched the glinting breakfast knife, concealing it within his sleeve, tore from the chamber, stormed across the cobbled street, and burst through the weathered oak doors into the tavern — thick with wreaths of smoke and the murmur of conversation.

His eyes, adjusting to the gloomy interior, found their target. Franz lodged in a corner alcove surrounded by a company of roguish men; scoundrels, murderers, and thieves, no doubt!

Peter hurtled across the room — heedless of the patrons' startled cries.

Knife flashing in his clenched fist, he vaulted upon the table, seizing Franz by the neck and pressing the thin blade to his pale throat. "Why?!" bellowed he. "*Why* this betrayal, villain?!"

Franz's eyes widened and his mouth twitched mutely. Three of his brutish companions lurched up to wrestle our hero off, but halted at Franz's raised palm.

"Why?" repeated Peter. Wild with rupturing desperation, he forced the blade deeper. "I saw you at the window."

Eyes fixed on the blade at his throat, Franz replied, "you have gotten this wrong, my friend. If you put the knife down, I will explain everything." He gulped hard against the sharp metal. "Please... for the love of God."

For all the fury blinding our hero to all but revenge, this unexpected show of vulnerability disarmed him momentarily; he withdrew the knife.

Several steadying breaths taken, Franz assured his wide-eyed comrades that this blade-wielding stranger posed no threat. After begging the flustered tavern keeper not to raise the alarm, he explained to our hero his presence in Bern. "We are in pursuit of a splinter group suspected of an indiscriminate attack. These former comrades broke away from us several months ago over ideological differences. We have reason to believe they have since joined a secret radical society within the capital."

"And what proof do you possess to support such a claim?" challenged Peter, closing his grip tighter about the knife's handle.

"By day's end, we shall confirm their involvement. We have already... *apprehended* one of their members. It shall not be long before his resolve wavers, and his tongue, at the... *threat* of removal, confesses the whole."

Peter shuddered at the implied torture.

Vitus' warning now came fast to his mind. Moreover, who knew whether any of the eyes still fixed on him had possibly recognised him? "Where do you lodge whilst in the capital?" Peter covered his lower face with his hand. "Do you remain in Bern for many days more? I have questions."

Franz scribbled a location on a scrap of paper and pressed it into Peter's palm. "Come tomorrow, after nightfall. We shall speak more then."

"Very well." With that, he turned on his heel.

Scarcely had he slipped back inside the inn when a flustered innkeeper bustled forth, ushering him posthaste into the musty confines of her broom cupboard. After darting her single orb nervously about, she closed the door and informed him in anxious whispers that visitors were waiting upstairs.

A claw, as if of ice, gripped Peter's chest. "Visitors?"

"'Tis the same thoughtful young gentleman who came calling yesterday."

"Then, pray, good woman, tell me why you felt such theatrics necessary merely to relay this happy news?"

"Well..." Her lonely eye blinked most rapidly. "Erm..."

Her stammerings waved off, Peter extricated himself from the cramped space and bounded eagerly up the creaking stairs, taking them two at a time.

There in his humble chamber awaited Vitus, plus two unfamiliar men — one posted by the window, keeping vigil upon the streets below, the other, his hand resting upon his hilt, standing as guard at the door.

Having greater liberty than before to speak, the brothers' second reunion was marked by a swell of equanimity and jouissance. What comfort it brought to Peter to learn that their father had escaped his equestrian mishap, needing but a short convalescence to heal from the sprains, scrapes, and bruises he suffered. What elation Peter felt upon hearing the stern schultheiss had, since the corpse's discovery, relinquished all rancour towards his, believed he, dead son.

"He is afflicted solely by the anguish of paternal longing," said Vitus, "which remains steadfastly for you, Brother. To know that you still draw breath will surely lift his grieving spirit and speed up his recovery."

This reassurance, thus voiding the chokehold of apprehensions, increased our hero's determination to gain access to his father behind the heavily guarded ancient walls of Jegenstorf.

"It is far too perilous to attempt," repeatedly insisted Vitus, shaking his head. Yet, seeing Peter would not relent on this score, he at length yielded. "This is sheer madness! But since you are set upon this reckless course, I shall endeavour to think of some way to smuggle you inside."

Peter leant forward. "In fact, a scheme has already formed in my mind."

Vitus drew back, raising a brow. "What cunning Trojan horse have you devised now?"

"Disguise me as one of your own guardsmen. With uniform and helmet, and my head kept low, none shall be the wiser!"

"But what if the ruse should be uncovered," countered Vitus, his voice ladened with concern, "and you are recognised?"

Peter met his agitated gaze unflinchingly. "I am willing to brave the risk. I must see my father, whatever befalls me after."

After some tense moments of contemplative silence, Vitus nodded. "So be it. Allow me a few days to acquire a uniform for this mad endeavour."

Peter reclined back into his chair. The crushing weight of uncertainty lifted from his chest now that a scheme was unhatched.

'Twas now that Vitus disclosed a most astonishing set of revelations:

Several days after the Oberhofen explosion, he had been intended to ride out alongside their father to Burgdorf Castle. However, a pressing personal matter compelled Vitus to delay his own departure by an extra day. Having informed none save the schultheiss of this, and that he kept to his private chambers, writing missives to his most trusted companions, his presence within the ancient stronghold's fractured walls went unmarked.

Come early morn, while Vitus prepared to set off, his ear caught the clipped tones of a tense disagreement in the courtyard below. Upon studying what were two dubious-looking men, he discerned they were neither of the house guard nor the stonemasons who laboured to repair the gaping cavity torn through the southern wing. A wagon rolled into the courtyard, trailed by a dozen more men of equally rough and disreputable countenances, hauling multiple wooden barrels that Vitus observed must have comprised the largely intact stock of explosive gunpowder previously stored in the cellar vaults.

The conversation between the men soon provided Vitus with keen insight into the true orchestrator behind the destructive explosion. But then, adding to his astonishment, a figure garbed conspicuously as a man of God emerged. This supposed cleric, the apparent mastermind — unpriestly malice scrawled across his face — gave explicit instructions to the conspirators. After unfurling a document, evidently pleased with the penmanship it contained, he threw back his head, emitting a caustic laugh that chilled Vitus to the bone. Gleefully, the villain confirmed that incriminating letters had been forged in so fair an approximation of Valentin's hand that, "once discovered, they shall banish the impetuous pup forevermore to the inescapable fires of culpability!"

"You cannot imagine the volcanic fury which overcame me in that moment, dear brother," continued Vitus. "I confess, I yearned to hurl myself from the casement, blade drawn, to run the foul betrayer through! But had I succumbed to such rash impulse and made my presence known prematurely, I realise our paths would likely never have intersected again."

Vitus had then shadowed the conspirators' procession through remote forest paths to a secluded lair. There he lingered out of sight, observing the suspicious figures robed as members of the church coming and going. Rather than hastening to his father, he returned to his own estate from where he despatched loyal men to unmask the remaining vile conspirators whose wickedness had unjustly imperilled his brother.

Within a week, the diligent agents apprehended the lead villain and brought him to Vitus' stronghold for a *persuasive* interrogation. The cur initially refused to confess but broke eventually, admitting that a scribe, protected by powerful yet anonymous allies, had fabricated the entire plot against Valentin. This secret society, the bleeding brigand vowed through cracked teeth, would stop at nothing to achieve their devious ends. With his last ounce of defiance, the villain released a chilling cackle at his master's triumph, and before the armsmen could ply him further about the shadowy society's intentions, the cornered viper abruptly sank his teeth into his own tongue, perishing outright at their feet.

"Good heavens!" Peter's lungs emptied themselves entirely in one great rush. The sheer scale and cunning of this conspiracy overwhelmed his senses.

"Have you managed to apprehend any more of these black-hearted brigands?"

"Alas, my men returned to search out the former lair too late. The rats had already slipped through some unseen bolt-hole and cleared away all telling traces of their prior occupation." Vitus seized our hero's hand. "But this I vow: my men, even now, work to pick up the vanished trail." His eyes blazed with determination. "We shall not rest until this entire network of serpents is smoked from their nests and made to pay tenfold for their villainy!"

***

Whatever dominion optimism held over Peter's waking thoughts, his attention was soon drawn elsewhere. As he dressed for the new day, a subtle yet unmistakable shadow again crept beneath the gap of the adjoining chamber door. The floorboards, too, seemed to groan and sigh. Surely some sly figure persisted in spying upon our hero's movements?

His instincts crying out to him, Peter noiselessly slip from the room and descended the stairs in search of the innkeeper. She was whistling cheerily amongst the pots and pans in her cluttered kitchen.

Peter apprised her of his concerns regarding the stranger quartered in the adjacent chamber. After tugging pensively at her dimpled chin, the woman's face did now light up; she recollected a curious event from the night Peter had arrived. A second fellow came in after. Deaf to her promoting her larger chambers, this man was bent on securing only those very quarters next to our hero.

Since this was impossible to be mere happenstance, our hero and the innkeeper thus conjured a stratagem worthy of any Machiavellian.

With a last nod, the innkeeper flung off her befrilled apron and hustled Peter to the stairs, her buxom bosom heaving with anticipation as she sorted through her tremendous ring of jangling brass keys.

As they crept upwards like a pair of cat burglars, she reviewed in hushed, albeit excited tones, their brilliant plan they would shortly enact to surprise the potential spy off guard. Replete with dramatic pauses and exaggerated gestures, she scripted who should say what cunning lines and in what convincing manner.

Only after one last rehearsal, at the turn in the stairs, being honed to a razor's edge of deception, did she let our hero depart, who silently continued up and stealthily reentered his room.

After allowing some handful of minutes to pass for verisimilitude's sake, she stomped as loudly as she could up the remaining steps and rapped smartly on Peter's door. Pitching her voice loud enough to wake even the dead (or at least the heavily snoring merchant in her best room down the hall), the woman launched into her performance. "I have some mightily extraordinary news for your ears alone." Her voice rang with mock excitement.

As rehearsed, Peter invited her in. As she spoke, winking her one good-eye, giggling and blushing, the unmistakable shadow was again thrown by what was indubitably an eager listener beyond. At our hero's pointed signal, the innkeeper, scarce able to contain her excitement, key in hand, glided across the room in the span of a heartbeat, had the lock sprung, and threw the door wide.

Here came the lurching eavesdropper, tumbling forth like a sack of potatoes, crashing to his face; exposed at last!

"Why you rapscallion!" The innkeeper seized the flattened fellow's ear in her meaty fist and yanked him stumbling to his feet.

What staggering astonishment now struck Peter's brain when the spy's face was fully revealed. "Harris! In heaven's name, what is the meaning of this?"

"You know this shifty rogue?" The innkeeper tightened her grip on the unfortunate Harris' ear, eliciting a yelp.

"I do. Though I cannot account for whatever could bring him here?"

***

Our loyal readers may recollect that curious morn, several days prior, when Peter called unexpectedly upon Miss Elizabeth and dragged her off to the toolshed. Little did they know Helene had stolen after them. Quick-eared as a fox, she gleaned enough phrases from beyond the shed walls to divine something deeply amiss about the newcomer Lizzie so clearly cherished.

Once Peter had ridden swiftly off, Helene, on the pretence of some urgent obligation she had forgotten, hurried home, where she breathlessly implored Harris to hasten after our hero. Armed as Harris was with some shocking new details — which shall be better revealed anon — he believed he might, at last, thwart his rival and reclaim his lost treasure. And spurred by Helene's plea, he eagerly scrambled after Peter, cautiously boarding the same post-carriage, secreting himself on its roof seat, between the luggage.

Conveyed thus to Bern, he then trailed Peter to the same inn without being spotted once. And with the aforementioned determination to lodge directly next to our hero, he lurked in that very chamber, determined to learn what secrets the scoundrel next door surely hid.

Indeed, it takes meagre imagination to delineate the many muffled gasps which must have escaped Harris' lips when, each time, through the conveyance of the keyhole, he sucked into his ears the litany of deflating discoveries, trampling all over his hopes. Why, to have his rival so unexpectedly transmuted before his very eyes — or rather, ears — from an outlaw into a nobleman, no less, Harris' half-formed revenge plots were kicked from his mind more violently than had he himself been bucked from an untamed horse.

***

"Unhand me this instant, my good woman!" whimpered Harris in profound humiliation, still hauled up by his listening appendage like some naughty child.

"Not a chance, you weaselly rat of a man! Not 'til the whole tale of your sneaky business here's been properly aired!"

Once the hangdog Harris had sputtered through his rapidly unravelling scheme to surveil the newly dubbed Valentin, Peter extracted the fellow's solemn vow to conceal his true identity from any other party. Though Harris clung fast to the tatters of his injured pride, he acceded. But when bid to promptly return to Bubendorf, he planted his feet like a stubborn mule and bluntly refused.

Since no grounds would be gained on this point, Peter modified his demand, restricting all of Harris' activities to a vigilant watch at the inn itself. To this request, Harris willingly complied.

The innkeeper, satisfied that an albeit-shaky truce now stood between the men, set about plying them with all her choicest morsels and ales. It early became apparent that her sole orb shifted exclusively onto Harris. Thus, for the remainder of their repast, she diverted her smiles, giggles, and best dishes his way.

***

Let us leave our hero and his fellow repasters sat around the dinner table and join another scene unfolding in the renowned Café Littéraire; a popular haunt for Bern's intellectuals and a haven of discreet nooks for private parley.

'Tis here, bathed in the afternoon sun's warm glow filtering through the lace curtains, that we find our intrepid band of justice seekers. Amidst the hum of low chatter (no doubt plots and schemes of lesser import); scratching of quills (penning either love sonnets or treasonous manifestos; one can never be sure); clinking of mugs, and haze of tobacco wreaths mingling with rich coffee aroma, sat this little party. They comprised Keller, our resolute investigator, drumming his ink-stained fingers onto the table's worn surface; Meier and Aeschlimann, corporals both, their uniforms as crisp as their mettle; Steiner and Bieri, watchmen, constant indulgers of pastries and mischief; and Marta, erstwhile servant (in a simple, well-tailored dirndl) turned informant, presently clasping her hands around a delicate teacup as if it held all the secrets of the universe. Each of them trusted colleagues were bound by a shared commitment to justice.

"Thank you all for coming," began Meier, quietly. His bushy eyebrows, veritable caterpillars of concern, puckered deeply as he glanced around. "We must exercise caution, as I am sure the guardhouse is watching our every move."

No sooner had these words left his lips than Marta's hand shot out to rest atop his. "Look!" She inclined her head towards the entrance.

"Felix!" Meier's eyebrows flew so high as to nearly take flight. He leapt from his seat. "What are *you* doing here?"

Unfazed by the frowns thrown his way, Felix only smiled the wider as he wound his way towards them between the tables, his golden curls bouncing with each step. "I've been thinking a lot about what you said." With his hip, he shoved Meier along the bench and sat himself down, his exuberance out of place in this gathering of grim faces. "I want to help. I want to join the Stadtwache ranks and make a difference in this corrupt world."

Permit me, dear reader, to formally introduce this Felix fellow — Meier's younger brother by two decades. Full of youthful idealism, this aspirant was possessed of an ironclad resolve to follow in his brother's footsteps, much to the latter's vexation, who presently regarded him with a mixture of pride and exasperation that solely siblings can truly understand.

Meier's weathered hand, marked by years of wielding both quill and sword, rested on Felix's shoulder. "Brother, it's not as simple as you think. The rot plaguing our city runs deep. All who oppose it court considerable danger."

Still, Felix, a portrait of determination, merely sat tall, shoulders squared in resolute defiance.

Steiner, lean as a beanpole, and Bieri, stout as a barrel, shrugged their shoulders at each other while engaging in a silent battle with a plate of Berner Rüeblitorte, their fingers sprinkled liberally with ground nuts.

Aeschlimann, his prodigious moustache nigh engulfing his visage and twitching with each sip of coffee, spoke, "so, Meier, what about these reports?"

Turning from his stubborn sibling with a sigh, the corporal replied, "since the captain seized them from Keller, they've vanished. It's plain Baumann is shielding Viktor and his patrician allies."

At this, Marta leant in; a wisp of raven hair escaped her tightly wound bun. "I fear that's not the extent of our troubles." Her dark eyes flickered with passionate intensity. "It's possible that Viktor's smuggling and extortion are but a small part of a larger, more insidious network. They're planning something big, something that could destabilise the entire city."

Shock and determination rippled through the assembled group — Steiner and Bieri stifled their gasps behind crumbed hands, their eyes wide as saucers.

All orbs swivelled to Meier, seeking his guidance and leadership.

His eyebrows presently undulated, rippling and contracting above his dark, ruminative eyes. "We need to gather more evidence," said he. "Our actions must be meticulous. One misstep, and it could be our heads. Baumann and his cronies won't stand by idly if they catch wind of our intentions."

Keller nodded; his resolve-hardened jaw clenched tight. "Agreed. And we must be strategic, too. But is there still no word from your patron?"

Meier shook his head. His expression turned gloomier than a November fog. "I now fear he has most definitely met his end."

"A pity," sighed Keller. "Marta." He turned to her. "Can you uncover more about this network?" Marta pressed her rouged lips into a thin line and nodded. "Steiner, Bieri, let's keep our ears to the ground and document anything that comes our way."

"And what about *me*?" piped in Felix. "What can *I* do?"

***

Nightfall had now arrived. Peter, hood pulled tightly about his head, ventured forth into the city, following the cryptic direction Franz had provided.

As he soon navigated a labyrinth of narrow lanes, memories of Elizabeth came unbidden to his mind. To be sure, he still despised her for having used him so wickedly, yet he could not help but own to a certain regard for her, which not even reason, prejudice, nor determination could obliterate. An ember remained aglow somewhere deep within. He shuddered. "Disgust is all that she deserves!"

Distracted by these musings, he nearly stumbled into a mule cart, its driver cursing him with the eloquence of a drunken sailor.

"Her prettiness was nearly my downfall!" resumed Peter. "Oh, the curse of a handsome face. But I will no longer be the traffic of her loveliness, nor her —" He stopped short. "What *am* I saying?" Try he did to spit from his mouth such foul-tasting, frustrating admissions. "She has even cursed my tongue!"

After one exasperating misstep too many, our hero at last stumbled upon the shabby establishment he sought; a small tavern tucked some way beyond the city's farthest ancient watchtower.

A scan of the gloomy, ale-reeking interior revealed no sign of Franz or his men. The proprietor, a man with a face more like a bulldog, ambled over, asking about Peter's business.

Just then, a rather nobly attired Franz burst through the tavern door, donning a Paris Beau emblazoned with a bright red peony. Two equally well-dressed confederates, each sporting a continental cocked hat, followed close behind.

"Come!" said Franz, taut of voice. "We must speak someplace else. I believe we were followed here."

With a meaningful glance at the barman, Franz intimated some understanding between them. Replying only by jerking his grizzled head, the owner led them to a small pantry. There, lifting a flagstone, he presented a hatch which led down into unfathomable blackness.

Franz gathered his men with a business-like calm Peter could not help but admire. Faced with apparent encroaching danger, this enigmatic companion — dressed no less fine than any showy patrician — evinced layer on layer of yet unchartered depth.

One after the other, the men descended, and Peter followed.

The cramped earthen passage twisted on and on through musty blackness. But blindly trailing the muted footfalls ahead, our hero at last emerged through a storm drain's raised grill onto a grassy river embankment, illumed by the moon's silvery rays high above.

As Peter caught his breath, he glanced about, noting a carriage atop a hill silhouetted against the skies.

"It is here!" Franz gestured. "This way!"

Puzzled, Peter again looked about at the otherwise barren banks, amazed at the seeming deus ex machina. Yet, his amazement only increased as Franz explained that upon first suspecting they were surveilled en route to the tavern, he despatched a third comrade to ready the transport in advance. Indeed, our hero struggled to reconcile his impressions of the inured and inveterate, face-concealed Franz of the swamps and mountain bandits with this other, so well dressed; so well-apprised of the city's hidden landscapes; so seemingly well-connected; so evidently ingenious a facilitator as to affect their present escape from some unknown enemy.

As Peter clambered aboard, he soon found himself blindfolded. The carriage jerked forward and jostled off to some unknown to him location.

Bundled out of the carriage and hauled up a flight of stairs, Peter was seated in a chair. His blindfold finally stripped away, he blinked against the change: a spacious room, red as any cardinal's robe, lit by several ornate gilt lamp stands and fitted out with a heavy round mahogany table surrounded by twelve chairs. Closed shutters concealed whatever views lay beyond the tall, draped windows.

At Franz's brusque bidding, his men took their seats.

Indeed, the more our hero studied his old friend, the more his wonder bordered on admiration. Such extraordinary trials Franz had endured as a youth, having lost his father to the gallows at the schultheiss' decree, who too easily gave ear to accusations of treachery. Despite that, whatever experiences thereafter moulded the younger into the adult, Franz had emerged from adversity with integrity intact, still bearing a flame of optimism for societal change. By rights, such an ordeal should have fuelled at best a corrosive wellspring of resentment. 'Twas easy to sympathise with Franz's hostility towards all patricians.

A dispute now ensued. Manifestly, the bulk of the party opposed any unknown outsider remaining another instant in their midst. But with Franz arguing Peter might prove useful, and that our hero himself swore to spurn not their help and take with him to the grave whatever he might hear, the men gradually softened their looks, and their disgruntled voices lowered to dissatisfied mutters.

Order affected, Franz lambasted how their secret meetings must have been compromised. "One amongst our ranks has likely turned traitor!"

At once, the outraged men quarreled over how to root out the turncoat. As they did so, they glanced repeatedly at our hero; their suspicious eyes glinted with wicked intent. The full gravity of Peter's unwelcome presence descended anew; he shrank back and scarcely drew breath for fear it might remind the men of unused weapons close to hand.

Mercifully, the topic shifted onto other, more pertinent matters: some coded missive intercepted from their former prisoner. This letter, bearing the seal of a faceless foe, seemed, from the few words they had so far deciphered, to allude to some audacious scheme to strike at the very heart of Bernese power — none other than the esteemed schultheiss himself.

"*What*?!" Peter bolted upright in his seat. "I must lay eyes upon this despatch for myself!"

From the several encoded passages shown to him, the evidence became irrefutable; some machination was or had been intended for his father! Further, the seal and the distinctive, elegant script suggested it originated from the hand of a powerful patrician.

Our hero was beyond astounded. "But how can this be?"

Franz eyed him with clear incredulity. "You will come to learn that there are the schultheiss' enemies found mingled even among his own inner circle."

"*Inner circle*? Ha! You toy with me, surely?"

Franz's brow formed a quizzical peak. "Were you not yourself an innocent, falsely branded a traitor, forced to flee for your life, and exiled these long months...?" A mirthless chuckle escaped his lips. "Unless, perchance, you really *are* guilty of said crimes...?"

Peter only murmured a troubled acknowledgement. He sank back down. Long had instinct whispered of politics rooted in the fetid soil of ambition. But never had he suspected such insidious treachery could take hold so close to the seat of power. 'Twas impossible to conceive!

Who then, amongst the familiar sea of fawning faces within courtly circles, hinted at enmity? None came forth to his mind. Naught but obsequious bows and sycophantic words masked whatever breed of vipers evidently circled in wait. "Then..." — Peter gulped hard — "... have you any inkling... *who* this might be, and who the fanatics they serve? Surely, you *must* extract this intelligence from the prisoner!"

"Regretfully, no identifications passed his bloody lips ere he rendered them forever mute. Crazed with desperation, he bit off his tongue over betraying his connections."

"Bit off his tongue?" Peter shuddered. But then, a recollection struck his mind. "Ah! I know not if there is some link, but only yesterday, my brother recounted the interrogation of a captured ringleader of some nefarious gang who did precisely the same. Surely, two such self-savaging mutilations transcend mere grim coincidence?"

The assembled men exchanged looks of darkling portent. The very air crackled with the weight of unspoken realisations.

A gloved hand drove a blade into the tabletop, the steel quivering with the force of the blow. "Did the prisoner bear a telling mark? An inked sigil?"

Startled by the man's sudden intensity, Peter recoiled. "A mark?"

"A tattoo on his wrist? The Tatzelwurm?"

***

Elsewhere, in that dimly lit upper room of a city inn: "You are certain of this intelligence?" demanded Adolfus of the messenger stood before him. "Absolutely, unequivocally so?" Each sharp word was punctuated by the thud of his oaken cane against the warped floorboards.

"I'll stake my life on it, milord!" The scout's curling grin exhibited a vulgar disposition and a consciousness of the guaranteed favour his explosive news would repay him with. "We noticed some strange movements of late, and whenever we trailed Vitus, we lost him each time along the same street in the obscure sections of the old city. But today, we tracked him to a property unlike any establishments he normally frequents."

"*Which* property?"

"The very den from where we often get our own men."

At this, Adolfus fell silent. His eyes narrowed as doubts and suspicions raced through his mind. "So underhand an establishment should hold no interest for him... What *is* he seeking?"

Presently, a rapping at the door interrupted them. Another man entered. Cut from that same rough cloth as the other rogue, this brigand bowed and instantly apprised his master of a fresh piece of intelligence. "We know what he's looking for! Vitus — that is to say, milord, we know *who* he's searching for."

Adolfus struck his cane against the floor. "Well? Out with it!"

"The master forger you retained for *certain* penmanship service, milord."

Adolfus recoiled as one physically struck. "The *copyist*?"

The triumphant rascal nodded solely for his rival operative to spear him with a glare venomous enough to strike dead — no doubt resentment that this glory-hound had managed to deliver so coveted an update first.

Adolfus limped feverish circuits back and forth; his cane struck the boards with each stride. "How came you by this knowledge?"

Full of gloating excitement, the brigand replied, "I spotted Vitus' scout lurking round the abandoned property of that copyist — the one from years ago."

Adolfus stiffened, his posture as rigid as marble. "*That* copyist?"

A curt nod confirmed Adolfus' fears. He blanched, then flushed. His faced bore the marks of the utmost bewilderment as the full weight of revelation struck home. "*Preposterous*! None have disturbed that nest these twenty years!" He raked a hand through his thinning silver locks as he limped anew in frantic circles, his cane tapping out his mounting dread. "Did he find anything there?"

"Methinks not. But my men discovered after that he went to that inn nearby. The keeper told us he'd made very detailed enquiries about the house and its former tenant. Whether anything more remains worth the finding, I don't know. But Vitus clearly suspects some answers lurk within those dusty walls..."

Adolfus could only shake his head dazedly at the report's ominous implications. "It's beyond all possibility that stripling could have uncovered even the faintest whiff of that operation... No one else survived that time to confess their roles... besides, we lost track ourselves of that vanished forger a decade gone..."

"There's more, milord," interjected the other rogue with a look which told he wished to steal back the glory. "As I was saying, we tracked Vitus to that underground property. But we also shadowed one of his men to an inn in the city. Plain is plain, the man didn't want anyone seeing him coming or going from it."

"And did you ascertain his purpose there?"

"We questioned the innkeeper, but she claimed no knowledge of the man. I wished to tear out her single eye!"

"No knowledge...?" With increasing confusion written in his twisted phiz, Adolfus limped to the window and gazed pensively out of it over the city. "This grows increasingly perplexing..." Some new disquiet stirred his turbulent thoughts. "Assign our sharpest-eyed trackers to monitor the old forger's lodgings, and relay back daily of any return made there."

Of a sudden, he whirled around and fixed his piercing look full upon the waiting men. "I want fresh eyes on that inn as well. Scrutinise every visitor there henceforth. This may not be connected, but I sense that something stirring beyond my sight. It leaves me ill at ease, and I disdain to wander blind!"

08 – 16 JULY 1792

The next six days unfolded with the monotony of a thrice-told tale, devoid of both circumstance and event. Franz was called away out of the city, while the normally steadfast Vitus, having sent word only the once, had still not yet made good on his promise. Thus, bereft of both diversion and progress, our hero sought distraction in Harris' tedious company and poring over accounts of Bern's unfolding turmoil since the attack.

But, on the seventh day, around that hallowed hour when all pious townsfolk ought to properly be returning from solemn Sunday worship to their sedate godly lives, who should come a-knocking at Peter's door but the buxom innkeeper herself!

Framed by the oaken portal, she filled the doorway like a galleon in full sail, arrayed from ample bosom to sturdy toe. Why, her prodigious person had been squeezed and stuffed into her best pale blouse — its poor straining seams all but obscured beneath an avalanche of lace, ribbons, and flounces that overwhelmed even her best puffed sleeves. These monstrosities, flourished so ridiculously high as to reach for the heavens like the Tower of Babel, appeared better suited to festooning some grand parliament window. Upon her face, a plentiful palette of powders and paints had been applied as if by a masonry painter. Below this upper spectacle, her paired skirts ballooned outwards like sails caught in a hurricane! And the whole vibrant concoction, a riot of red and black shot through with white edging, threatened to near blind one entirely if stared at overlong. Crowning this copious maypole of fabric and frivolity lolled the braided coronet of her hair, wrestled into submission by what appeared to be a full battalion of her best pins and combs.

Our poor hero did now reel, overpowered by the clashing perfumes exuding from the hyperventilating woman, almost to the point of swooning dead away himself!

"Special delivery for you, good sir." Bobbing in an approximation of a girlish curtsy somewhat hindered by her ample proportions, she presented a sealed message. "Hand-carried here direct from your fine visitor, I'd wager."

From the inscription, Peter understood the letter to be from his brother.

"Speaking of visitors" — the one-eyed matron craned her plump neck to espy the chamber — "though where that knave Harris has gone off to?" Peter hastily interposed himself between her singular roving gaze and the door, behind which crouched an ashen-faced Harris, fearing for the discovery of his trickery. "He promised he'd accompany me to church, but I couldn't find him anywhere!"

"I confess, I have not seen him either," lied Peter.

"Mark my words," huffed she, puffing her overly-rouged cheeks like a blacksmith's bellow, "that scamp will get a piece of my mind!" At that, with injured dignity bristling in every step, she bustled off along the corridor in high dudgeon; her footfalls boomed like thunderclaps as she stomped down the stairs, nigh shaking the inn's very walls.

"Has she *really* gone?" whispered Harris, still clinging to the wall as if his very life depended on it. "She won't leave me be for five minutes. And what devil spawned such floral scent as to choke a bee swarm?"

With a roll of the eyes, Peter closed the door. "I would recommend, dear fellow, that you conjure an excuse worthy of tempering a scorned woman's wrath. And, in the future, I would dissuade you from accepting invitations you have no intention of ever honouring."

The letter, much to our hero's relief, contained an extenuation of the delay in writing and the news he had so eagerly awaited. This very evening, he was to meet with Vitus' men.

***

Night, at last, provided cover for Peter to slip out of the inn, his vision tinted by the wavering glow of oil lamps lining the uneven streets as he glanced warily about. Though people came and went with none seeming to tail him, he soon could not shake off the sensation of unseen eyes observing his every step. He swung his tense gaze behind again, peering hard into the dim shapes, but he found no confirmation of his suspicions.

Heart hitching a frantic beat, he diverted down an alleyway. From there, he quickened his stride to the agreed place of meeting; the ancient Nydeggkirche.

Before long, he approached the Romanesque church. After a last furtive glance cast over his shoulder, he entered a small arched side door and found himself engulfed by the silence within.

Below the flickering light which danced across the stone walls, illuminating the church's interior, Vitus' men were seated along a pew. No sooner had Peter joined them than a nondescript linen sack was pressed into his hands. Within it lay the regimentals he would assume the next day to enter Schloss Jegenstorf. The men leant in close and, keeping their voices low, imparted the critical details of the impending mission.

Satisfied he understood his part to play, Peter passed a billet to them. "For my brother."

Just then, a flicker of movement caught their attention. In a gloomy alcove, a lone male figure stood almost motionless. His face was obscured beneath the brim of a slouched hat. As if sensing discovery, the figure, with a final inscrutable glance in their direction, slipped out of the church, leaving an unsettling void in his wake.

"We should disperse," murmured one man. "Valentin, wait five minutes before returning to the inn. And may Providence guide your steps."

Vitus' agents had just turned a shadowy corner at the street's end when the noise of scuffling feet broke out behind them: a full seven figures, clad in black and built like oxen, hastened towards them.

An ambush! Vitus' men thus fractured in different directions. The hunters likewise split into pairs and trios and gave chase.

Soon, the city transformed into a battlefield as individual skirmishes broke out, steel clanging with steel. But let us rather follow the fortunes of the messenger who clutched Peter's all-important note.

With lungs aflame, he careened around corner after corner, his ears keenly attuned for sounds of gaining pursuit.

Lo, the relentless thud of boots soon gained upon him, and three blackguards launched their attack.

Swords clashed about the deserted street, at which the pursued put up a tremendous display, fending off the repeated sword slashes.

Windows flew open; angry voices rained down curses upon the nocturnal disturbance, shouting for the devilry to desist.

Momentarily distracted, Vitus' agent left his flank unguarded. The lead assassin lunged as quick as a viper, lodging his wicked blade between cracking ribs. Agony exploded from the wound as the guardsman staggered backwards.

Alas, the single misstep proved lethal. Two of the assailants closed in. Through his blood-soaked clothing, they rifled, clutching their singular prize: that message bearing secrets!

As for Peter, his every sense prickling on high-alert, he hastened for the inn, glancing repeatedly over his shoulder. But too soon, a knot of figures stalked him from the gloom. Their synchronised movements and the ominous glint of moonlight on naked steel betrayed their malicious intent.

Abandoning all pretence to stealth, our hero broke into a desperate sprint and pelted headlong into the patchwork of melding shadows.

But the uneven cobblestones conspired against him, sending him sprawling with a strangled cry into the middle of the street.

Hardly had he crashed down before footsteps swarmed his position; a frigid steel whipped the air and kissed his throat.

"Identify yourself!" came a grating voice from above. "What business have you with those men from the church just now?"

Jumbled thoughts clamoured about Peter's terrorised mind. Who were these ruffians?

The villain thrust the steel closer. "Speak, or else die."

Of a sudden, a crack — the sound of a whip — split the sinister night air, ensued by the thunderous roar of hooves on the cobblestones.

Against all self-preservation, our hero wheeled his head towards the disturbance.

A chariot, blacker than night, hauled by six snorting ebony chargers, emerged from the environing shadows — its approach a whirlwind of speed and fury.

A man's voice yelled out; there came the sharp clatter of a pistol shot.

Like startled rats, the assailants scattered.

A masked driver hauled violently on the reins. The conveyance fishtailed, skidding directly abreast of Peter's sprawled, trembling form.

A panicked heartbeat later, a lacquered door was flung wide by its shadowy occupant within. "Get in!" shouted a deep voice.

Pulse roaring, breath ragged, fearful of certain death with his pursuers and the uncertainty of his fate climbing into the carriage, Peter vacillated.

"I am here as friend and not foe," again spoke the voice. "Get in before they return!"

These words broke the spell of confusion. Peter clambered to his feet and hurled himself into the carriage. The door slammed behind him, and the conveyance surged forward with the same speed and racket as with its appearance.

Unease congealed in our hero's stomach as he gazed about the ornate, blood-red interior and at the four figures sat within, garbed in hats and capes in midnight hues. Each face was obscured behind identical and grotesque disguises: lacquered visages which evoked a spine-tingling spectre of the infamous Morbus masks worn by long-dead plague medics of old.

One eerie masked face swivelled towards him and emitted a muffled, "pay our guises no heed. They are a necessity this night. We shall convey you to the safety of another location."

Little reassured by this vague pledge, Peter pressed for who they were and where precisely his feet would soon tread. But the same unreadable speaker merely raised a single black-gloved finger; its inarguable command brooked no further discussion.

At last, after about an hour's jolting journey, the coach lurched almost to a stop and turned sharply right. The grating noise of iron gates gave to our hero's overwhelmed understanding they were possibly entering some estate.

Indeed, the carriage drew up before a sprawling country palace, rising tall and imposing, its five-storied exterior facetted with ornate statuettes of mythical beasts and ancient deities. Abundant urn torches, their flames waving in the evening breeze, flanked broad stone stairs and balustrade terraces, which led up to a lofty carved door.

Prodded mutely inside by his masked couriers, Peter crossed a glittering threshold into a world of unimaginable wealth. Led down marble corridors, their walls lined with magnificent oils illumed by glistening chandeliers, he was finally deposited in a sumptuous, high-ceilinged salon bathed in perfumed warmth. There met his sweeping gaze an ocean of silken velvet, coruscating crystal, fulgurating gilt, and leafed gold twining up white marble pilasters; antiques from various lands and ages long past stood displayed in alcoves and upon inlaid tables; luminous artwork hung from the walls like reigning monarchs.

An exquisitely liveried footman entered and bowed in wait to offer refreshments and viands. The latter Peter waved away; he demanded only water. Likewise, as with the tight-lipped coachmen, this domestic, when pressed on their precise location, kept his own counsel.

Scarce had the footman withdrawn when a familiar figure strode in. Why, before Peter's widening eyes, stood none other than the imposing colonel, his mysterious rescuer from Lucerne. Gone, however, was the decorated military uniform; today the gentleman of fifty-some years appeared resplendent in exquisite midnight velvets, befitting the highest nobility.

As the man approached — the chandelier light glinting along his strong profile and flickering in the silver threading his dark hair — Peter, so stunned by the whole, involuntarily stepped backwards.

"I see," said the man, "I must take a more proactive hand henceforth in preserving your continued safety."

So utterly confounded, Peter scrambled to unwind these tangled threads. "Who are you?" managed he, at last, palms sweating and heart thudding.

"All in good time. But for now, let us say destiny shaped me into your stoutest defender. My appellation of Bernhard will suit our discourse." With easy nobility, he retrieved a decanter from a glossy cabinet and poured two crystal tumblers of absinthe; its licorice fragrance wafted on the warm air. "We must drink to your escaping a dance with death." He raised his glass.

Our hero was indeed too astounded to even take a sip. "Pray, sir, divulge who you are. For I believe that twice now you have saved me."

"Five times, actually." Bernhard clinked their tumblers. "But who counts?"

Peter rather slammed than placed his tumbler down. "*Five* times?"

Indeed, five it was. Sheer incredulity flooded Peter as he learned 'twas Bernhard who orchestrated his escape from the wretched Oberhofen prison-tower and commissioned his couriering the scroll to Zürich — the first intervention. Despite this man then losing Peter's trail after the explosion, the second intervention resulted from that advert our hero had placed in the Basel newspaper. Bernhard — commanding influence across every canton — had positioned guardians all over (one of such guardians being involved in the mysterious incident with the Ebenrain footman) and, infiltrating the Liestal garrison, he thus manipulated events as to dupe the jealous Harris with that counterfeit WANTED poster. The third and fourth, we heretofore observed, had both occurred in Lucerne. The fifth, we are now arrived at.

Peter did scarcely blink before the conclusion of so astonishing an account. Indeed, the whole so heightened his impatient wonder that he flew to the gilded doors, throwing his arms wide across them. "I forbid you from leaving. I can endure not anther moment. Please illuminate precisely why a perfect stranger plies such tremendous effort in intervening in my affairs?"

Bernhard merely smiled. "You ever were the image of beloved Vivienne in looks." He chuckled. "And now, it seems, temper, too..."

Peter's hands slid down the polished wood and fell to his side. "My...? Did my mother's name grace your lips just now?"

***

Upon his return to the inn at dawn, Peter's mind was a kaleidoscope of awe, amazement, disbelief, and sheer, utter, unfathomable incredulity. To think that Bernhard was not solely his constant saviour but also his mother's ally, sworn to watch over him — why, the journey, lost to the stagger of his thoughts, passed like a trance. 'Twas, it seemed, but one moment he had quit the opulent refuge and, in the next, was delivered upon the inn's creaking threshold.

There awaited a mightily disgruntled duo: Harris and the innkeeper. Both assailed him for robbing them of their wits and a night's rest, and, having led a merry chase for the truant across half of sooty Bern, they scolded and cooed in turns, pressing him for an accounting.

Profuse in his apologies yet pleading forgiveness on the most pitifully extenuating circumstances, Peter hastened to his chamber to ready himself for this most monumental of days: stealing into his father's castle.

Now, worthy of mention here, dear readers, is that when our hero confided his audacious designs to the inscrutable Lord Bernhard, try the gentleman did to dissuade him from so dangerous a scheme. But finding his sage appeals vain against deaf ears, he resigned himself to improving the subterfuge's odds. Hence, summoned forthwith was a true artiste who, blessedly versed in elaborate disguises, employed prosthetics and other uncanny contrivances to so skilfully transform our hero's aspect, that even Peter himself doubted the looking glass.

Imagine then, if you will, the profound befuddlement of Harris and the innkeeper when, after our hero's fantastical metamorphosis — replete with imperial, bushelled black moustache, a woolly mane black as a rook's wing, and nose as prodigiously bulbous and beaked as great Genghis himself! — a bizarre stranger tottered down the stairs into their midst.

Likewise, picture the cautious Vitus — now resolved on abandoning the ruse for fear of its certain failure — reeling in ashen horror at the sight of a wholly unfamiliar guardsman, imagining their entire scheme prematurely foiled.

'Twas only Peter's familiar laughter that restored Vitus' senses and assured him Providence herself had surely ordained this fantastic farce.

However, scarce had they embarked on their journey to Jegenstorf when Vitus, fresh ill-ease haunting his tired eyes, related the previous evening's attack and the seized letter. "What intelligence," implored he, sweat pooling at his temples as he leant forward, "fell into hostile hands?"

***

We briefly rewind the clock, some twelve hours hence, and alight upon a scene where Adolfus, chafing with acidic impatience, espied the return of a fellow knave, bearing that afore-pilfered message.

"Give it to me!" Adolfus snatched it from the ruffian and tore it open, near-salivating at the intrigue that surely awaited within. But oh dear, picture the clear dismay that did chase the triumph clean off Adolfus' craggy features, for the note contained but two paltry words: "'*Thank you!*'?!"

Indeed, Adolfus sputtered and fumed, flipped the note several times and held it up to the candlelight, desperate to discover what secrets must undoubtedly be hidden. "Is this sorry scrap all you rogues bring me? '*thank you*'!"

He turned his leer upon the man. "This tells me less than nothing, you impudent cur! Useless imbecile!" At that, he set upon the luckless fiend with his cane, venting his rage across the poor man's back and skull in a symphony of blistering, bruising, and blood-inducing reproach.

***

Back inside the trundling carriage: "Thank heavens!" Vitus sank back into the plush, blue brocade upholstery. "At least the blackguards pilfered nothing tangible to imperil our designs..."

Peter was not so relieved. "Do you have any idea who those men were?"

"I cannot say for certain, but I suspect a connection to that same nefarious group — oh!" He sat upright, eyes alight with sudden realisation. "We may have smoked out the dastardly forger of those damning letters that condemned you."

Peter, too, bolted upright. "Pray tell! I must know the particulars."

"My agents yet strive to confirm the villain's den, but if he is indeed the rascal we seek, he shall find himself snatched away to a most isolated location. There, cold steel to his throat will elicit a full accounting of his misdeeds..."

Peter's mind galloped, connecting the dots. "And that prisoner who bit off his own tongue — did he bear any distinguishing mark on his skin? The sign of a serpent, perchance?"

***

We return again to Bubendorf. Hardly had the diligent Jago concluded his business in Zürich than his impatient zeal goaded him homeward early to confront Lizzie with his discoveries about Peter's past. Breaking his journey first at Ebenrain, he found, among a pile of letters in his closet, a communication from the Geneva garrison. Hastily, he tore into it and scanned its terse contents.

Investigations with local military encampments confirmed no recently unaccounted-for recruit named Peter had ever marched among their ranks.

"I knew it!" He crumpled the letter between trembling fists.

Down the marbled stairs Jago swept, brandishing both the incriminating communiqué and the weathered newspaper sheet, bellowing for his swiftest steed to be made ready at once.

Poor Lizzie, forced to revisit the shame of her duplicity, found this second attack occasioning a worse timidity than the first. She near-choked as Jago, demanding whether she had any prior knowledge of her lover's probable crimes, slapped down upon the kitchen table the tattered newspaper page depicting the all too familiar visage along with the Genevan despatch.

"Heavens above!" The colour drained from her cheeks, only to surge back moments later. "Truly..." faltered she, "I am as astonished as you..." She again flushed painfully under the heat of Jago's intensely probing eyes. "This is the first I know of this..."

Jago's stern expression evinced only his deepening disbelief. "But now that you *are* aware of this, do not you think we ought to notify the authorities?"

Marking his determination, she forced an airy laugh. "Surely... any... similarities here... must be merely some bizarre coincidence..."

Incontestable displeasure hardened Jago's features. If Lizzie had known he saw through the artifice she practised upon him, she might have confessed the whole at once.

"I fear for your safety, dearest Lizzie," said he, softening with what appeared genuine concern. "It is evident your feelings for this... *questionable* man have blinded you to reason. But for your own sake, I beg you to consider disentangling yourself from him — at least until all things have been established."

With what could she answer him? Her mind galloped, searching for words that would not come.

"Trust further investigation to me," continued he. "I will write the Bernese garrison. If he proves to be this infamous outlaw, be assured that I shall protect you from all perils."

At this, Elizabeth, overwhelmed by the weight of her secret, rose abruptly from the table, pleading a sudden headache — which, in earnest, most acutely afflicted her. She begged leave of the wretched subject and insisted that Jago form no hasty conclusions nor act without her wishes or consent.

Before he could respond, she fled to her chamber.

Unaware of her motives for concealment, Jago, not yet able or willing to believe her capable of willful deception, accredited her subterfuge to feminine naivety and the benevolence of her sympathetic though deceived heart. Much disquieted, he thus departed.

Now alone, our heroine buried her face in the pillow, assailed by the many awful probabilities spawned from this interview. As she bemoaned the likelihood of her closely guarded secret now hovering at the precipice of exposure, Helene happened to arrive.

While hoping to find in her lively friend's companionship a respite from her own worries, Lizzie found the opposite. Helene came not with the usual talk but to make an alarming confession and to plead with her friend to act swiftly to protect her peace and happiness.

We now unveil an earlier discovery that spurred Helene to hasten her brother's pursuit of our hero to Bern. As ladies do delight in dress-up, Helene, having been left alone one day while Lizzie attended chores, got to rifling through her friend's jewellery box — only to let drop an earring, which then fell through a gap in the floorboards. In her efforts to retrieve the lost gem, she unearthed both the loose plank and the secret treasures concealed below.

Whereas Jago, stunned by shock, had discovered but half the tale, Helene, probing more assiduously, uncovered the whole — not just the WANTED poster, but that scandalous account of the rakish Peter who abandons brides at altars. Too mortified to confront Lizzie, she had instead unburdened the explosive find to her brother. And this, combined with Helene's later eavesdropping, as we saw, is what had sent Harris in hot pursuit to Bern.

"But it was an innocent discovery." Helene enclasped Elizabeth's hand. "Don't be vexed at me, Lizzie. I was just so overcome with curiosity that, like when Pandora gazed upon the box, I, too, could not resist the temptation."

"And look what calamity *that* unleashed!" Lizzie snatched back her hand. "*Innocence* ought to have stayed your *nosiness* and spared all but the earring."

But seeing the wounded Helene flinch and pale, Lizzie instantly regretted her sharpness. Of course, the loyal girl meant only to shield her from harm... Besides, had not Lizzie herself fallen victim to curiosity's spell on that earlier, fateful morn, when she probed a complete stranger's regimentals and discovered a certain poem...? These considerations clasping at her conscience, Lizzie moderated her tone. "But come," — she gently reclaimed her friend's hand with a tender squeeze — "let us speak no more of what cannot be changed..."

Alas, Helene relented not; she only charged Lizzie to report Peter to the authorities, lest she be dragged into infamy beside him. "Like when Athena understood she had to sacrifice her son Meleager for the greater good," said she, "your mother will *verily* understand. She would never shackle you to someone who, by all accounts, is not only a philanderer of the heart, but a wanton criminal who will most undoubtedly bring about the loss of your honour and virtue."

Of a sudden, Edmunda exploded through the doorway. "Now see here!" squawked she in matronly outrage, her apron swishing furiously. "What's this talk of outlaws and ruined reputations?"

***

Casting our gaze back to our hero, as the carriage bowled steadily nearer Jegenstorf, his heart near pounded clean through his red coat and ribcage alike. There, through the curtained window, floated glimpses of the beloved terrain: beneath the stately oaks, the tranquil carp pond upon which he had cast skipping stones a thousand misty dawns; ducks paddled serenely, their silken feathers barely rippling its glassy waters. Just beyond, the grand, pale exterior'd schloss, its steeply pitched roofs and distinctive tower claiming the blue heavens.

Yet, such cherished vistas quickly stirred disquiet, for they sequestered his father — again bedridden by grief.

Gravel soon crunched beneath the wheels; the carriage passed between the stone gate piers, and the main façade emerged among the low-hanging boughs and greenery. Rows of arched shuttered widows stared blankly down; a stern attention awaited in long lines of blue-coated Swiss guardsmen, flanking the entrance steps in a display of formality and power.

Peter, dry of mouth and palms clenched and damp, alighted from the conveyance onto suddenly shifting grounds.

"Steady yourself," came Vitus' voice as he grasped our hero's arm.

But our hero scarce noted this support, for bitter memories rushed upon him: there, the ornate ironwork balcony hung overhead; there, his father had stood, stoically receiving a son's contempt for denying him of his birthright.

Could tender affections truly be resurrected from ashes of pride and pain?

Composure regathered, and a steadying breath taken, Peter ascended the stone staircase, passing through the entranceway and into the Grand Salon.

Sunlight speared blinding shafts through the tall, red and gold draped rows of French windows, striking the intricate Savonnerie rug and the Versailles-patterned oak floor. Past quarrels' echoes jeered from nearby wings. Unable to venture another step, Peter sought one of the four chairs about the centre table; its centrepiece, a towering monstrosity of lilac and lily extravagance, near choking in excess — irrefutably his stepmother's ostentation.

Pray, may I not see that woman today!

Vitus' men occupied the remaining seats and broke into light conversation. But our hero, heart pounding, only stared at the towering gilt doorway. Would his brother's emergence herald the long-awaited reconciliation he was so assured of, or rather a swift return to the dank embrace of some fetid dungeon?

Ere long, the gilded mantel clock's hands, glinting in the sunlight, crept around their steady cycle to mark the eleventh hour; at last, Vitus' appearance.

When not even halfway up the sprawling staircase, a glacial dread gripped Peter's rigid spine. For there, beside the first landing's balustrades, stood the fearsome Arnborg — the banneret (who forced him into Oberhofen's vault of gunpowder and flames before piercing him with the blade). With him was that contemptible stepmother — the Schultheissin Vincentia, her ample ivory flesh straining against her corset's confines in a most unseemly display.

Engaged in hushed talk with Arnborg, Vincentia suddenly broke into protests at her menacing, fancily robed, brown capuchin monkey, perched on her shoulder. The little ra'scal gleefully stuffed her décolletage with cherries, only to pluck them forth and lob them forthwith at the exasperated servants below, who indeed looked fit for mutiny against the heckling monkey-hellion!

At such an obscenity, Peter's stomach convulsed. Still, he knew not who he loathed the most: the violent and impertinent simian or the voluptuous and immodest woman, who doted on the beast with a fondness nearer to ludicrous.

Vincentia, noting Vitus poised on the stairs, broke off from her remonstrations. "Darling," purred she in her grating French bourgeoise accent, "you did not relay this visit in advance?"

Arnborg bowed and quit her side. He was just descending the stairs when he halted beside Peter, eyeing him full-on. "I do not recognise you?"

Our hero went to speak, but his words became like stones lodged at the back of his throat. Thankfully, Vitus intervened, explaining Peter was newly employed in his service. With a last, somewhat distrustful glance at our near suspense-strangled hero, Arnborg continued his descent.

Vincentia's hand extended, Vitus thus anointed it with a kiss, and voiced his hopes she would pardon his unfilial neglect and unannounced intrusion.

"*Je l'espère certainement,*" replied she while parrying the monkey's next assault — plucking plume after ostrich plume from her preposterous headpiece. "But come, you must pry this imp's greedy paws loose before I am stripped bald as a billiard ball! One can only endure so much — Jacko! Darling! Unhand Mama's ruby necklace this instant, you furry fiend!"

With only a series of impish cackles in reply, she lamented, "heavens, spare me of this diabolical creature! What laudanum-laced wine was I imbibing the hour when I accepted this accursed simian as a house gift? The creature is the spawn of Satan himself! Between clawing tapestries to threads, pillaging larders, upending inkwells, desecrating my lilies, and flinging food everywhere, the beast has single-handedly reduced half my staff to tears daily!"

Vitus frowned. "I did advise you against this creature, Mother."

Alas, the battle between woman and beast raged on. One hand fending off the fluffy rapscallion — now actively divesting her of her gilded hairpins — and the other creating a hurricane with her large ostrich fan, she glided past. Her hand-painted ivory silk robe à la française, as excessive and impracticable a display of vanity and taste for so sultry a season, rustled as she complained about the humidity, of being cooped up in this castle, of tending to her ailing husband, and of the pleasures of society so cruelly denied her.

Hatred's breath held captive in his chest, battling with anxiety's formidable onslaught, Peter unsteadily followed his brother to their father's bedchamber.

With the drapes closed, smothering the space in darkness, two forms appeared to hover near the bed. Their silhouettes barely touched by the hearth's amber glow, they were scarcely discernible amidst the room's shadowy furnishings. A cloying scent of medicines clogged the stifling air; a collapsing log broke upon the silence between the solemn ticking of the clock.

"Father," said Vitus softly, "I am come."

Upon hearing Vitus' voice, Gustav bade his valet raise him upright amongst the plumped pillows and open the curtains a little.

Consequently, a shaft of harsh light rushed in, unmasking the familiar cherrywood herringbone floor, the wood-panelled walls and coffered ceiling, and striking the gild-framed oils lining the far wall, their solemn faces bearing witness to the unfortunate scene unfolding below.

'Twas now that the schultheiss' withered spectre — so waxen a countenance made visible against the embellished headboard and amidst the silken bed drapes and canopy — unnerved our hero; his throat clenched. The pallid, hollowed cheeks, and sunken eyes — a stark contrast to the rich, embroidered bed linens — were a scant resemblance to the towering colossus Peter recollected. He fought within himself not to race forth and clasp the ailing man.

With laboured breaths, Gustav instructed his physician to leave and beckoned Vitus' approach. In low tones they spoke, and Gustav, with a look of much surprise, turned his straining eyes in Peter's direction. "Approach messenger, so I might discern properly who I should question and, I hope, thank."

Inch by inch, Peter drew nearer, yearning to exclaim, *Father, it is I, your son, returned by miracle!* But prudence and Vitus' previously voiced fears of a sudden revealment mayhap occasioning a fatal turn in his father's fragile state clamped tight the plea in his breast.

Tears restrained, our hero hovered awkwardly, bowed, and, in a voice once smooth and refined but now rough and unfamiliar, he repeated the scroll's partial contents and relayed its bitter demise to the flames.

Silence followed. A pensive expression rippled across Gustav's worn features. "Those indeed formed part of its words," said he, at length. "'Tis most inopportune that it no longer exists... Be that as it may, who are you, and how came you to be in possession of it?"

Vitus took his father's hand and beseeched he remained calm that he may be strong enough for what he was about to witness.

Not without the valet first objecting and venturing to advise his lordship otherwise, did they both, at last, give their perplexed accord.

Hence, with a tremulous chest rising and falling, Peter removed his disguise. Piece by piece, the false person fell away, and there emerged Valentin's face, reborn.

Hands flew to mouths as gasps resounded; the schultheiss jolted against the bolsters and the valet against the wall.

"V-V-Valentin...?" stammered Gustav, his hands knotted and shaking. "Can this spectre be mere fantasy? Do my weary eyes speak the truth?"

Unable to any longer contain himself, our hero plunged to his knees. Seizing his father's frail, trembling hands, he bathed them in filial tears. "Father, it is I... I live... I *live*! And I have come to beg forgiveness!"

17 – 19 JULY 1792

"*Nach langem leiden kommt grosse freude*," so goes the old Swiss wisdom: "After long suffering comes great joy." Truly, did no soul under heaven soar from the depths of despair to relief's sweet summit as our hero upon this hopeful dawn. With his waking thoughts, there mingled, like those of a fantastic dream, every wonderful recollection of the day before. For to have weathered such tumults as to near-rival the weight upon ancient Atlas' shoulders, yet to regain in one miraculous stroke nearly all that was lost, scarcely did Peter trust such raptures as lasting and true.

What indescribable transports were found in that reunion of a most grieved father and a most contrite son. Where but Death's spectre had before sucked at so palpable an atmosphere, sweet birdsong danced on the sunbeams, chasing away every lurking shadow. Laughter, once a stranger in Gustav's chambers, had mingled with the soft murmur of conversation. Fresh air replaced the stale odour of illness and despair.

The schultheiss, having heard our hero recount the events that had so overset his life, professed arrant admiration; this accidental crusade had, by all appearances, began to soften his son's arrogance. Vitus, too, having observed in his brother so already favourably altered a person, his heart swelled no less. Eager to make firmer the present joys, he had unfolded his discoveries since Oberhofen, declaring that with the copyist's anticipated arrest, the rupture between Bern and Zürich would be healed, making possible our hero's return to the world.

As for Peter, though never had Fortune smiled so benevolently upon him, his felicity was tempered by an element of the unknown: who, indeed, from among his father's closest advisors was perchance the very sword still possibly aimed at him. Thusly apprised, Gustav assured him he would double his private guards and assign a trusted comrade to investigate the matter further.

Before we depart Jegenstorf Castle, there occurred something this next morning which requires our attendance. Adolfus was just arrived, and, instead of the hushed whispers and mournful faces he expected, a sense of vibrancy permeated the air. Led not upstairs to a still bed-ridden Gustav, he was directed to the breakfast room, where sunlight streamed through the floor-length windows, illuminating a scene that defied belief.

At the head of a table laden with fine linen, silver, and porcelain sat the schultheiss, perusing a newspaper and feasting on sundry victuals. Gone was the gaunt man sunken into the shadows of Death's waiting embrace Adolfus had last encountered. In Gustav's stead sat another, so seemingly rejuvenated.

The schultheiss looked up. "Ah! Adolfus!" said he with greater strength in his voice. "I was not expecting you today. Come through, come through."

Adolfus glided over the marble to make obeisance before Gustav's brocade chair. While the schultheiss made light conversation, Adolfus' thoughts were most otherwise distracted. Why, Gustav looked nigh half a decade younger!

"Our poor French tormentors," said the schultheiss, feeding on a bite of trout. "According to the press, '*la patrie en danger*' declared the *Assemblée législative* six days ago." He swivelled the newspaper towards Adolfus. "Mayhap" — his lips curled into a grin — "in their fears of an invading Austria and Prussia, they will sooner dismiss the vile traduces against our great canton and put faith, once again, in our cooperation as they do our mercenaries..." He folded the newspaper away and locked eyes with his auditor. "So, what news do you bring?"

Adolfus only hesitated in his increasing confusion. "Dare I ask, has some special event occasioned this apparent restoration of your health and voracity?"

"Oh, come, Adolfus, even we aging despots find edacity strangely returns when well-timed tidings align just so..." Unexpected humour danced along his less-strained words, catching Adolfus utterly off guard. No doubt observing this, Gustav waved his bony hand with sudden casual airiness. "Suffice it to say, certain long-frozen affairs of state show signs of thawing at last. I foresee the feud dividing our great canton and Zürich soon settled."

Mind furiously dissecting such odd statements, Adolfus could not help risk the delicate enquiry as Gustav shook open several missives. "My lord hints at *intriguing* prospects upon the horizon and yet provides his humble servant so few *clues* as to divine what changes are afoot?"

A hearty chuckle rumbled from Gustav's chest; his eyes twinkled with newfound vitality. "Come now, friend, what ruler unfurls the entirety of his stratagems before manoeuvres fully play out? Let us simply say I spy potential resolution at last to this infernal alienation damaging the relations of our confederacy..." He trailed off; a private smile played on his lips. "At any rate, pray, you are yet to tell me your business here. Do you bring word from the general at the French frontier? Or more demands from that Austrian ambassador? — that hawk! Forever circling, insisting we crack down on French sympathisers and close our borders... all to ensure our neutrality! But I fear Austria pushes us towards taking sides..." His smile faded. "And the rebel skirmishes? Has this lawless escalation yet ebbed?"

"Well... there are indeed... several fresh incursions across our terrain this week alone..." Adolfus inwardly cursed the uncharacteristic hesitation fogging his reply. Those allusions to cantonal reconciliation had utterly ambushed his faculties. But marshalling his thoughts, he pressed on to summarise the military analyses, the requests for reinforcements from Genevan commanders, concluding with his concerns over Austrian troop movements near Swiss borders. "The Ambassador swears it is merely an exercise, but with the situation intensifying between them and France, it would be wise to prepare for... *provocations*..."

***

Late afternoon sunlight blared through the rows of windows lining the vast Council Hall. Around the expansive table of dark carved wood worn smoothy by centuries of grave discourse determining the republic's future courses, eight grim faces huddled — shadowed by powdered wigs made fierce by falcate profiles, and hardened by haughty scorn.

Seventeen empty chairs echoed the absence of their devout Protestant compatriots — or perhaps, more accurately, deliberate exclusion from these shadowed schemes. For while nominal public servants in title, every man present knew the real lever of cantonal authority rested in the few hands which moved less visibly through the corridors of influence.

And of all those gathered, none was more acutely aware of this hidden machinery of power than Adolfus. Reticent and distracted from his audience with the schultheiss, he sat with steepled fingers below his sharp features now creased in unfamiliar uncertainty, rousing the curiosity and perplexity of his observers. And as expected, once all servants withdrew with bowed silence, enquiries shot his way like arrows expertly aimed.

"Come man," pressed the Venner of Butchers; his rows of rings glinted as he leant forward; "enlighten us as to the cause of such uncharacteristic gloom after visiting the venerable Gustav this morn." The rich fabric of his coat strained against his corpulent frame. "Does the *old lion* rally, even as we speak?"

Adolfus gave a solemn nod, still distracted by the puzzles crowding his baffled mind. "His health, his spirits... *both* remarkably restored. He alludes to soon resolving the simmering feud with Zürich — some potential reconciliation? But beyond that, details lay obscured."

"*Reconciliation*?!" The Venner of Tanners' jowls quivered with scorn from beneath his bristling grey moustache. "Preposterous! Our schemes have been far too meticulously woven to prevent such a possibility!"

"I, too, find the notion improbable," conceded Adolfus; the lace at his cuffs fluttered as he gestured for emphasis. "Yet Gustav's conviction was... *unsettling*. And knowing that Vitus paid him a visit just yesterday," — he shifted uneasily in his seat — "I suspect it connects to that."

"*Vitus*?!" echoed the seven men with a collective resonance of intrigue.

"All will be clearer in due course." Adolfus redirected the conversation to a coarser subject. "But whatever the case, we have our own plans to forestall cantonal harmony, do we not...?" A sinister smile crept over his lips. All present, understanding his meaning, laughed in accord. "Now, what of the woman? Has she acquiesced at last to our proposition?"

"Ah, yes," answered the Young Secretary; his smile flashed like a dagger. "Our little helper had done his job exceedingly well. His fictitious escalation of debts and creditors has quite driven the desperate lady of means to happily comply with framing Varus..." His tongue swept his lips. "It seems the lady has amassed shameful gambling and wardrobe extravagances atop usual household debts. Ten thousand francs! The price of her freedom. And with the debtor's prison looming," — with his handkerchief, he mimed a woman tearfully dabbing eyes — "the anguished lady stands ripe as a plum for plucking."

A humourless laugh escaped the Councillor (Ratsherr) of the

Blacksmiths' Guild; his bushy steel brows lifted high above his hawkish nose in a gesture dismissing the very notion of compassion. "Our tragical lady, finding herself abandoned and carrying proof of Varus' unworthiness. What a prodigious shame for Gustav's charming protégé! It will invoke the cruellest condemnation of the, dare I say it, *reformed*" — he crossed himself — "church. How grand a spectacle shall welcome His Eminent Antiste Bullinger and his wagging tail of synods, theologians, and clerics..."

"Indeed." Adolfus' gaze drifted towards the empty chairs; he already saw the very future he was orchestrating. "Fortune continues to favour our designs, my friends; improbable as the path first appeared. We need only to keep our canton at odds with Zürich — and with the French — and soon, the curtain will rise on a new era for Bern. We have lived the minority for too long. It is time to seize back the power of our purer doctrine! The Reformation's undoing is long overdue." He turned to the Church Steward. "Are all preparations in order for the Minster?" The man nodded. "And you," — he turned to the Nachschauer (Inspector) — "have you secured the marquis' allegiance?"

"Aye," assured he with a tone as steady as the ancient stones that made up the walls of the surrounding hall. "Bound to us by ambition and a thirst for vengeance, he has fiends aplenty bidding to do his will. He will not falter."

"But what of Viktor?" said the Venner of Tanners, his brow sceptical, his lips pleated in sternness. "Have you managed to rein that wild bull in yet?"

***

Ah, the gambling house, that familiar vicinage of iniquity where fortunes are won and lost with the casual flick of a wrist; where the air hangs thick with tobacco clouds and desperation; and where Viktor, bathed in the chandelier light's seductive glow, is installed once more in his preferred gilt seat. Yes, here stood the true siren, her song of chance forever luring the prodigal heir back no matter how often fortunes proved fickle.

Though the perfumed lovelies had wasted no time in reclaiming their wonted perches, eager for their master's overtures, Viktor scarcely noted their coils and caresses. The setbacks at court and playing field alike had solely whetted his appetite for higher stakes and conquests once more.

Alas! The dice, those mischievous little cubes of fate, continually conspired against him. Like before, raucous laughter rang out across the felt as the wealthy guild master's son — current darling of both dice and doting ladies — raked in his latest pile of winnings.

"I see your noble throwing arm is no better than your playing hand," mocked he with theatrical volume, clearly determined to claim audience beyond his painted paramours. "Perchance, you should stick to... breeding horses or... collecting *snuff* boxes? Mayhap, noble blood boasts no more the skill to master chance than to claim the *coveted* seat..."

Viktor slammed his fists down, scattering his doves in alarmed anticipation. But unlike before, and though murderous intent gripped his frame, other notions entered Viktor's head; he rose with forced aplomb. "Laugh while you can, you simpering fop. I call for satisfaction! Name the time and weapons — tomorrow we duel until blood or death wipe that smug leer away for good!"

A stunned hush engulfed the glittering hall; the posturing youths sat locked by twin gazes, blistering with mutually assured destruction.

"A duel, you say?" rejoined the guild master's son. "How very... *dramatic*. Very well, my Lord Viktor." He toasted the daring invitation with his glittering champagne flute. "I shall humour you with this little duel. The morrow it is then, at first light. The choice of blades or bullets will be your own. Let all bear witness here that I grant my opponent his contest. Let us see if your duelling panache is any better than your clumsy waltz with the dice."

***

Blood-red seeped across the horizon, gilding the glassy Aare, serpentining through the mist-shrouded valley. A secluded gravel embankment serves to set the stage of our rival hotheads, stood tense as matched statues. Save for the lap of dark water, the shuffling of feet, and the trill of waking birds, an awful, expectant silence hung over this impromptu battleground.

Viktor rested a gloved hand atop the polished mahogany pistol cases. His contingent of painted doves and bleary-eyed comrades, still bedecked in the evening's fineries, arranged themselves behind.

Across the pebbled ground, the opponent and his elaborate entourage coalesced from the swirling mist. As the guild master's son shrugged off his emerald-satin damask jacket, Viktor noted his features fell as grey as the mists themselves. Fear, that great equaliser, had finally stripped away the facade of arrogance. A strange kinship with his adversary prickled within Viktor's breast, a shared understanding of the terror that lurked beneath the surface of bravado.

Be that as it may, this duel must be paid in blood.

The arbitrator stepped forth in sombre black. "Gentleman, might you not attempt reconciliation ere bloodshed sullies this majestic morn?"

No rote words would engender compliance; each combatant refused to forfeit their precious pride.

"So be it." The arbitrator resigned himself to his role as conductor of this macabre orchestra. "Terms state each man fires until marks are found or weapons are spent. As the challenged party," said he to the guild master's son, "choice of armament goes to you."

A thick-moustached, burly majordomo glided forth, took the weapons from Viktor and, retreating to the opponent, extended the pistol cases on overstretched palms. The guild master's son indicated his preferred weaponry.

Thus, with outward stoicism belying the turmoil within, and gazes locked, the opponents turned back-to-back. The sharp retort to commence shattered all stillness — fear visibly jolting each rigid and nigh breathless observer.

The men began their measured tread towards that intersection centred precisely between opponents and spectators alike. The seconds ticked by with agonising slowness, each footfall crunching on the gravel like a death knell as anxious heartbeats counted six paces... five... four... three... two... one...

The piercing command to turn sliced through the pent-up tension. In a fleeting second, both men whirled around, pistols raised. A deafening roar of gunfire echoed through the valley like a clap of thunder.

Viktor, certain his opponent had already claimed the advantage, recoiled outright, wincing in anticipation of lead smashing through his ribs to shred his organs. But no visceral blow bursting against his breast came.

Ears still ringing from the violent discharges, he opened his eyes, amazed to behold his opponent still likewise perpendicular.

Emotions, too fast to catalogue, flitted across each foe's face — relief, scorn, disappointment, and renewed fear as each fumbled to reload for a second shot's brutal arbitrament.

Twin clicks preceded twin aims, fingers tightening on the triggers.

And then, with explosive fury, the pistols spoke again.

Twin rounds bolted home anew with thunder cracks.

Across the blood-flecked stones, Viktor's opponent staggered back a half-step, clinging to his abdomen; blood already stained his frills where the lead had found its crimson mark.

***

'Twas just gone past ten that same morn when Peter received word from his dear father. The missive instructed him to don his beguiling costume once more and to attend a trusted associated at a certain locale by noon. From there, he was to journey onward by coach to the elegiac Hünigen Castle — the former family seat from happier times when Peter's late mother lived.

A knot of apprehension tightened in Peter's stomach. *Why summon an audience to a place harbouring such bitter memories?*

Another message arrived, bringing news from the esteemed Vitus.

Imagine, dear readers, our hero's collective thrill to learn his steadfast brother's network of agents had finally confirmed the identity and lodgings of the nefarious scribe! To think the elusive black-hearted serpent would soon find himself hogtied and interrogated regarding every last viper in his slithering nest — such a futurity sent shivers coursing through our hero's veins. Like the wrongly accused Hércules, completing his Twelve Labours and emerging triumphant, Peter's — or rather, Valentin's — name must soon emerge from the ashes.

***

Ah, dear reader, Fortune — that wily mistress — ever-weaves threads of misfortune into what fleeting tapestries of joy might be found. We must turn the clock back again some hours to the evening prior, when Vitus met covertly at a location he believed safe from surveillance. As he confirmed the forger's imminent return home in three days' hence, laying plans to snare the elusive prey, his ear detected creaking floorboards outside the meeting room.

He silently stole over to the door and flung it open, but discovered only a female servant arriving up the staircase. Though the young lass confirmed she had seen no person pass her, this disquieting incident would, however, prove merely the first stone which presaged a landslide of troubles ahead...

"Milord! Milord!" A ruffian burst into Adolfus' clandestine upper chamber. "They've found him! The copyist!"

"*What*?!" Adolfus shot up from his desk, overturning the ink pot and staining important papers as black as his heart and schemes. "Are you certain?"

"As I live and breathe, Vitus spoke of the forger. Though I didn't catch everything, 'twas quite a task, I tell you, I got the gist of what's important —"

"To the point!" interrupted Adolfus, spurring the man with his cane.

"They've found his dwelling and mean to capture him three days hence!"

As the awful truth tumbled free, Adolfus, feeling downfall's chill of blades gather at his own throat, sank back into his seat. For should that forger have his tongue loosened, Adolfus' carefully constructed web of deceit would unravel with terrifying speed. No power in Heaven or on Earth could prevent the airing of most dangerous secrets locked away these past two-score years.

***

Meantime, the Bernese Guardhouse buzzed with the usual morning hustle. Guards and officers scurried about, attending to their duties; the air thrummed with shuffling papers and murmured conversations; freshly brewed coffee mingled with the musty odour of old files and well-worn leather.

Into this scene of ordered chaos, a patrolman burst forth, his face pale and anxious, as if he had met with some spectre from the netherworld. In his haste to reach Keller, he careened into the Captain of the Guard, nearly sending the man's wig askew. Begging pardon for his clumsiness, the patrolman rushed along the corridor and flurried into Keller's office, thrusting a sealed envelope into his hands. "This report just came in, sir." He panted and wiped his brow. "A duel took place at sunrise this very morn." The patrolman retreated to the door and closed it. "One duellist is none other than Viktor von Villeroy."

At the mention of this name, Keller's eyebrows shot up. He tore open the envelope and, racing through the report, gleaned that the duel, witnessed by a motley assortment of onlookers, had culminated in the near-fatal injury of a wealthy guild master's son. With practised efficiency, Keller quickly jotted down the witnesses' names — his quill scratching furiously.

Just as he finished the task and shoved the notes into a hidden compartment beneath his desk, the office door burst open, revealing the crimson countenanced Baumann — the Captain of the Guard. "Is that the report about the duel this morning?" His finger darted at the document in Keller's hands.

A calm exterior maintained, Keller answered in the positive and handed it over to him. "Indeed, it is, sir. You'll find all the pertinent details within."

Baumann snatched the report. "Very good, Keller." A flicker of calculation loomed behind his eyes. "I shall take it from here." Report clutched tightly in hand, without another word, he turned full about and exited the office.

After thanking the patrolman, Keller made his way to the corporal's office. Meier was seated at his desk, engrossed in a stack of paperwork. Aeschlimann, his fellow corporal, stood at the window, looking absently out of it.

"Meier," softly uttered Keller, "we have an urgent matter to discuss."

With the door securely closed, the paperwork temporarily forgotten, and all attention commanded, Meier and Aeschlimann gave their ears to Keller's report, which tumbled out in a steady stream.

Whereas Aeschlimann remained silent, seemingly unmoved, Meier's eyes widened. "It won't be an easy task, tracking down the witnesses," said the latter. "And you say the affront began at some gambling house last night?"

Keller nodded, but explained the establishment's name was foreign to him.

"Then," answered Meier, "we shall have to find out its location."

"Though this duel might not directly aid us in our primary investigation," said Keller, "maybe it could prove useful in the future?"

Meier nodded. "Let us convene in the Matte District after sundown." He turned to Aeschlimann. "Will you be joining us?"

The corporal nodded, though an air of uncertainty tainted his enthusiasm.

***

'Twas nearing two in the afternoon. Swathed once more in regimentals, Peter jostled alongside three other guards on the approach to their destination. As the carriage rounded the last bend and crunched up the long driveway, Schloss Allmendingen's charming silhouette came into view, its weathered stone façade, blue shutters and brown hipped roof bathed in the warm July sun.

Despite the tumult necessitating this covert sojourn back amongst boyhood haunts, as our hero stole glances out of the window, a child-like anticipation unfurled in his heavy-beating breast. What forgotten echoes of bygone happiness and heartache might stir beneath these long-shut-off walls?

The carriage swung round in front of the property, and Peter alighted. Notwithstanding his anxious expectation of stealing long-denied moments to converse with his father freely again, the sight of him at the entrance stirred unease within. Moreover, the schultheiss' stern expression whispered to our hero's understanding that peaceful restoration's whole depended still on outmanoeuvring the mysterious forces who strove to sever the reunited family forever.

Guards ordered to stand on duty, Gustav bade Peter follow him inside. "Forgive the theatrics, my boy, but even after these decades past, these old walls still boast secrets."

The tall, heavy entrance door creaked open, and the daylight chased away the shadows which had long-smothered this once glorious vestibule.

Peter's breath caught in his throat; for a fleeting moment, he expected his mother's beloved form to greet him, welcoming him home. But reality, cold and unforgiving, snapped him back. He sighed heavily, his breath clouding the dusty air, and he trailed his father onwards.

"Your mother's spirit woven into every fibre of this place," said Gustav, "more than I ever realised until you were almost..." he trailed off, clearing his throat as if catching himself in sentiments he wished neither to feel nor express.

17 – 19 July 1792

Having proceeded upstairs, they arrived at the door of a remote chamber — a portal too familiar to have ever been forgotten. Key inserted, the double-doors yielded with a groan against the years to unveil so cherished an opening to the past. There, drenched in gloom and light, emerged the graceful sanctum: Vivienne's private suit.

Only after breath returned to his lungs, did Peter master himself and cross the threshold. With each creak of the floorboards, there mingled fresh recollections of his mother, reclining in her favourite window seat; a book in hand; on her face a gently teasing smile...

Love, like the faint trace of lavender, still lingered within these walls.

And lo! Beyond, in a searing column of light, setting every silken web aflame, hung the radiant Vivienne's face; immortalised upon a gilt-framed canvas. Not even time's passage had diminished the warmth which, captured in hues' enchantment and brushstrokes, exuded from those piercing (so like our hero's) yet wistful eyes.

Though a reverential silence reigned, memories of laughter, music, tenderness, and consolation spilled forth from the oil and swelled each onlooking heart. A poignant vibration stirred emotions long dormant, rooting both a husband and a son momentarily amidst time's inexorable current.

Though our hero stayed the tears welling in his eyes, he observed his father's glistening with the same telling dewdrops of grief revived. Each turned away, feigning distraction: Gustav fiddled with various trinkets; Peter regarded the lake and mountains beyond the glass panels, now greyed with neglect.

"Know this, my son," said Gustav, at last breaking the silence, "that for all storms weathered, I see emerging in you the very essence of those finer virtues your sainted mother fought so fiercely to instil against so ungentle and unchivalrous a world." Heaving a sigh, he gazed up anew at his first wife's visage. "Would that I had proven half so noble guarding this family's welfare and been a *better*..." His phiz betrayed unmoored ghosts no tears could lay to rest. "But come," — he emitted a guttural noise of rough dismissal as he stepped away from the oil, his gestures resuming their habitual crisp command — "my purpose in bringing you here pertains to revelations which will *undoubtedly* invoke *profound* shock. Coward that I am, I cannot voice them aloud even before her portrait, but rather must defer to her own testament."

He fumbled in his velvet coat pocket and retrieved a key. The tiny iron teeth clicked home with the late schultheissin's ornate, mahogany escritoire viscosity — once oiled and glossed, now choked in dust. Out slid a slim calfskin volume. With pointed solemnity, Gustav pressed the journal into his son's hands. "Within these passages dwell answers long buried, my boy."

Gustav grasped his shoulder with sudden urgency. "My dearest Val, while your miraculous return has indeed revived my spirits, I sense time's relentless grip steadily leeching the life from my veins, beyond any mortal's trick to reverse." He clutched Peter's wrist as if to bind them together before Fate's final call. "You must forgive a prideful old man his gravest mistake in ever doubting you on those *outrageous* allegations! Know that I fully acknowledge my abject failure as father and guardian both. Rather than wholesome virtues and veracity, I fed you arrogance and artifice with every spoonful of instruction —"

"Father, I —"

"Pray, let me speak, boy. Your rearing, independent of its concomitant luxuries, proved a savage tutor in its own right. Well do I know how every courtly shadow nurtured sinister forces against you. Yet, where I confront life's bleak end, meeting with bitterness and regrets, you, my son, have a chance to still cling to moral courage. And so, I charge you to make your mother's gentle spirit proud. Before my time comes to quit this sublunary realm, you *must* show the world who you truly are — who you can become!"

Though overwhelmed by such words and cognisant of time possibly truncated, our hero pledged, on one condition alone, his forgiveness for every strain that had divided them these long years: "Only once I am first assured of the pardon you will extend to this unworthy, unfilial, and foolish son's actions."

Gustav brusquely waved aside these terms of absolution. "You may rival me in death, but not in life, dear boy."

Much still lay unspoken. But we shall draw a heavy curtain on this rare stolen interlude.

The creaking carriage bore our preoccupied hero away from the beloved Allmendingen, now fading behind into the wooded horizons. Despite the exquisite nostalgia in seeing his mother's depiction, and the amity enjoyed with his father, restlessness stirred afresh within. What burning revelations had Gustav laboured to impart? And why must time always intervene to deny joy's fullest satisfaction? Resigning himself to shatter the mysteries yet to unfold, Peter carefully freed the leather-bound journal from his satchel.

Though scarce able to breach so intimate an artifact nor brave the startling disclosures which must surely fill these yellowed pages in dearest Vivienne's own immaculate hand, he, at length, with trembling hands, opened it out.

Just then, the carriage jolted as a wheel struck a rut. Peter jerked up; the cascading papers fanned wide. Near the crease, a pair of names seemed to leap, as with a life of their own, from the page and knocked the very air from his lungs.

"*Otto and Apollonia?*"

Surely, these were the very names that were memorialised in the unassuming Bubendorf.

***

Shadows, stretching long across the lacquered wood panels, matched Adolfus and his caballers' spirits — all of them nursing brandy glasses in tense silence inside the shuttered Butchers' Guild House salon. The setting sun's reddish glow, which usually lent a serene ambience to this space, now seemed a mocking backdrop to the storm brewing within. Scattered about the space, each man's posture betrayed the weight of the crisis at hand.

None dared meet their leader's blistering gaze as he stalked the windows, his eyes combing the Kramgasse street below for further threats to plans which now seemed to lie in tatters.

Bribed servants had been summarily ejected once each councillor, necessitated by urgency, filed discreetly into this impromptu sanctuary — for rumours carried fangs enough to savage every ambition.

At last, puncturing the uneasy stillness and drawing every gaze from the tapestries of market life and symbols of the butchers' trade, the Venner of Tanners — face mottled, bristles quivering — groaned, "curse that Viktor's impetuosity!" His doublet, rich with the deep hues of prosperity, ill-constrained the wrath exuding from his tensed form. "Does the empty-headed fool not comprehend how severely this scandal tarnishes the many names integral to the court?"

Disgruntled murmurs greeted the blunt assessment; the men shifted uneasily in their plush chairs and shot their rolling eyes up at the heavy oak beams.

The Church Steward, ever the image of ecclesiastical authority with robes embroidered with the symbols of his sacred office, brought down a hand with thunderous finality upon the oak table, rattling the crystal decanter and tray. "You render the tale with undue grace, sir! Why, this is no mere embarrassing spectacle, but a political death sentence *plain as Holy Writ* across his own *empty* skull! Should the guild master's scion be despatched to his eternal judgement, no bishop *or* magistrate can mend this tear in the fabric of our grand design."

"Tread carefully with that hasty tongue of yours!" Adolfus whirled around to fix his compatriot with a dagger-like gaze. "Rather than *raking muck*, exert that loose intellect to scheme how this mess might be *better fertilised* to correct this blite! The boy may yet live. We need to think only of how we may yet silence his father and the great noise this event will have made in the world."

Even as the chastened steward shrank under Adolfus' cold command, his hand retreating to his cross as if to brace himself against the bitter pill of reprimand, quick raps broke heavily upon the strained atmosphere.

The whole viperous coven of plotters froze as one as the Venner of Butchers crossed the room to unlatch the door. It swung open with a tense creak.

Quiet but intense discourse now passed.

"What is it?" demanded Adolfus.

A harried messenger, a young page barely out of boyhood, entered and bowed hastily. Eyes wide, he took in the assembly of formidable personages hanging on the account he was about to divulge. "P-p-p-pardon, me noble lords. Most grave news I bear. For that unfortunate duel I first told you of has exceeded the worst fears." He seemed to draw a bracing breath and, as if knowing not which hateful and exasperated eye to look at, fixed his gaze on the marble floors. "Not an hour ago, the fallen dueller met with the Grim Reaper."

"WHAT?!" erupted the councillors with howls of dismay, drowning all decorum.

20 JULY 1792

"*Was zusammengehört, kommt zusammen,*" (What belongs together will come together) so the venerable Swiss maxim assures in golden brocade script gracing humble hearts. However, when Fortune's errant threads begin to converge too abruptly from all compass points — when long sundered secrets, strangers, and shadows meet, fuelled by their own momentum — oft do stunned minds find reality and reason have likewise taken flight together...

Dawn's first light crept across the creased pages beneath one out-flung arm as a distant rooster crowed unendingly, finally rousing our exhausted hero.

Still half-lost to the endless tunnels of memory's escort through the journal of ghostly whispers, and blinking blearily, Peter shifted his stiff limbs gone numb. The table had served as desk and pillow both through the long brooding hours after the candle guttered low.

Eyes adjusting to the horizon's glow, he glanced afresh upon the journal — the key to separating shadows from truth that would, according to his father's words, illuminate the many winding paths of mystery he presently walked on.

Within its pages lay more than that curious reference to the deceased Otto and Apollonia — none other than his great-uncle and -aunt. Another intriguing item had seized his attention before the heaviness of sleep had finally stolen him away. Folded between the gilt-edged leaves was a paper torn diagonally asunder; a beguiling cryptic poem laid bare yet another lyrical ghost:

Thy dove,
Though art my truest, fairest love.
No cruel hand of fate our bond shall cleave,
When the faithful heart doth always believe.
What force could rend devotion born so pure?
\times erosion could not I endure?
\erode such fervent fire?
\welded by noble desire.

20 July 1792

Though incomplete the verses, and saturated in longing and poetry's language, their delicate imagery whispered of thwarted love. Much like the torn paper itself, 'twas as if two lovers had been cruelly ripped apart.

But why was such a script secreted in his mother's diary? Might some shattered romance explain the frequent sorrow which had dimmed those once regal eyes? Had Vivienne's faithful heart engraved therein some cherished suitor long before, mayhap, callous politics or family greed had sacrificed her happiness to ambition's claws? And who then possessed the sheet's other torn half?

Could this be the "answers long interred" his father had alluded to? No. Such a long-ago mystery seemed hardly relevant to our hero's present uncertainties. What links then were to be found in his mother's diary, tying former shadows to current perils?

He returned to the torn script. "Thy dove, though art my — thy dove..." *thy dove...?* "Was not this the title of that musical air at Pier's pianoforte?"

Breast throbbing afresh, his thoughts raced with this conspicuous parallel. "This cannot be mere happenstance... this surely traces back to some weighty truth buried within my family's past..."

But how was he ever to unravel such uncertain yet enticing threads? There was only one man whose intellect, discretion, and connections might illuminate the way forward: wise Bernhard; once his mother's most trusted confidante, and, outside of all filial bonds, the one soul, apart from Pier, in whom Peter could repose his full and unreserved trust.

After scribbling a missive for Bernhard's attention, Peter sent Harris to the pre-arranged location where a discreet messenger could be procured to safely convey such messages of urgent import.

In this interim, Peter took up an anxious vigil at the window. In the mist-shrouded bustling street below, cast in grey shadows by the rising sun, crowds of rustics and tradesmen all headed with some apparent purpose in a common direction. From the echoes of grievances and determined hope drifting up, it was clear these were citizens bound for some gathering to air their hardships.

Such sights called to his mind the recent reports of additional privation suffered by the rural folks and the lesser guilds across the canton. Even from his modest vantage, 'twas plain to see an alien mood had infected proud Bern. The very atmosphere seemed charged with simmering tension, her once carefree people no longer greeting each other with genial warmth.

Some hour or so later, a modest carriage drew up directly before the inn. 'Twas no gilded conveyance of the noble classes. Out stepped a solitary figure, garbed in a nondescript black cape and a wide-brimmed hat. His face obscured by inscrutable shadows, he glided across the pavement and slipped inside the inn.

Mere minutes hence came a discreet rapping at our hero's door, heralding the arrival of Master Bernhard.

Peter welcomed his champion into his room. "I see you travel in a rather simple fashion today, my friend."

"Indeed." Bernhard doffed his hat. "For when one suspects eyes everywhere, 'tis best to don the cloak of inconspicuousness."

The usual salutations exchanged, the two seated themselves before the window.

"Come, then," — Bernhard steepled his fingers — "apprise me of what revelations summon my presence with such haste?"

Peter thus acquainted him with the contents of his late mother's journal. "These circumstances seem to weave some mystery about past events and personages. But I grasp not their import. Have you any notion of their meaning?"

Bernhard averted his gaze towards the vista of rooftops beyond the nets. From his altered expression, there was evinced some passage of serious rumination. "What," said he, at last, "said your father when he gave you the diary?"

As Peter recounted the exchange as accurately as recollection permitted, and though Bernhard's phiz remained as opaque as the mists thickening outside, Peter sensed he knew something.

"My dear boy." Bernhard again gazed out of the window as if lost in some appendage of grave memory. "While I cannot yet speak overtly of these strands from the past, this verse does call to mind something your mother once showed me. From what I recollect, a poem — perchance this very one — stirred considerable sorrow within her gentle spirit. When I pressed her for the cause, she would only divulge that it belonged to a love forbidden, long ago... sacrificed, as it were, upon ambition's heartless altar, constructed by the ruthless machinations ever-turning the wheels of powerful families."

"Might the forlorn lovers... in question, have been my... mother and some... *unknown* other?"

"Whatever secrets or misfortunes befell those souls immortalised in verse, and who they truly allude to, I cannot surmise. But it is not beyond impossibility." Here, he paused as one gathering the threads of consciousness. "Still, if your gracious mother's heart belonged to another, she nonetheless proved ever a most devoted spouse to your father."

"I see... And what of my great-uncle and -aunt? Did you *know* them? Might they have been connected to Bubendorf? Highly improbable I own, given the date of their untimely demise. I understood that they, along with other kinsmen who fell afoul of some treasonous plotting, perished in flight over the Alps. And yet... there is... *this* composition — also Pier's peculiar manner and his claim I reminded him of someone. Perhaps he knew my family?"

"Schloss Wildenstein is where this gentleman, Pier, lives, you say?"

Peter nodded.

"Let me despatch an agent to probe these delicate veins of the past." Bernhard rose to take his leave. "Meanwhile, as you continue excavating that journal for glimmerings of light, I would advise you to remain indoors all day. Trouble is afoot."

***

Let us forget not that while troubles turned more cogs than Bernese clockwork, storms brewed in cantons far afield. Wherefore, let us stride together several leagues yonder to the rustic haven of Bubendorf, where we find our poor heroine soon to be once more under siege from all quarters, assailed by a raging tempest of accusations and suspicions.

Mid-morn sunlight darted harshly through the warped glass, casting condemnatory shard-like patterns upon Lizzie's face and across the worn kitchen as she gazed at the doorway. Too well, our anguished maiden knew what the new day's relentless hours held in store.

Mere moments later came leaden footsteps, and in barged Edmunda, Ernest, and Emil, with Hans and Helene in tow. This emergency tribunal convened anew to issue ceaseless decree till some satisfactory scrap be produced to acquit or rather condemn, Lizzie's faux-darling Peter of the multiplying crimes alleged.

Ordered onto the accused's perch (that is, the solitary chair on the table's other side), our heroine faced the terrifying inquisition sat opposite — all craning theatrically, with eyes hot enough to boil bone, while matron Edmunda took on the role of self-appointed Grand Inquisitor.

As Lizzie quailed beneath this multitude of castigatory stares, in strutted Edith and her feathered judiciaries, positioning themselves as impromptu court officials. Several took up bailiff posts beneath the table, fettering Lizzie's feet with warning pecks. Others — Edith included — perched tabletop as adjudicators, clerks, and jurors; all of them, clucking a chorus of condemning clucks, eyed the defendant as guilty pending proof of innocence.

Thus did Edmunda commence this farcical trial. "Come child," demanded she, issuing her decree from on high, "let us ring from you, once and for all, the plain truth concerning this nettlesome Peter!"

The assembled inquisition chorused nods of agreement, while the gallinaceous magistrates screeched and squawked their own accord in a bona fide henhouse *cris de cœur*.

"Ba-gawk!" cried Edith, most indignant.

"Cluck-cluck!" lamented another, her dirge.

"Buck-buck-Ba-gawk!" wailed a third.

"Cluck-cluck- cluck!" bemoaned a fourth, her grief all too palpable.

Now, since layman ears comprehend not the idioms of fowl, nor scholarly intellects parse creaturely cries of jurisprudence; and since given readers must beg a glossary for the barnyard lexis; and since these feathered ladies shared a most vexing part in this business involving the villainous Peter who had twice-slain their most-cherished-bosom-plumule'd-sistren, allow this humble narrator to essay a translation of their impassioned buck-bucks:

"That ba-gawking scoundrel still owes justice for our poor Enya!"

"Truly ladies, a heartless rake to so cruelly prey upon so virtuous a fowl!"

"And our dearest Erika, too! Think of those poor motherless chicks!"

20 July 1792

"Dreadful business all around..."

To be sure, the clucking bailiffs echoed similarly below; but I digress...

No dramaturgist, I am sure, could hope to study high drama finer than this scene presented. Why, even the barnyard menagerie of ducks, pigs, the goat, *and* the cow had gathered at the yard door to watch the courtroom spectacle unfold, lending their own sundry exclamations of quacks, oinks, moos and maas to the general din; a veritable orchestra of accusation.

Under the battery of these additional eyes — bovine, porcine, and poultry alike — humiliation's twin crimson banners did unfurl most vibrantly atop poor Lizzie's cheeks.

"There it is!" crowed sharp-eyed Edmunda. She stabbed a damning digit as though the Scarlet Woman herself sat cornered before them. "Your betraying blood condemns you child!"

Culpable as our henpecked heroine was (albeit for crimes her accusers — earthling and animal alike — were yet unaware of) she found her flustered tongue cleave helplessly to the roof of her suddenly arid mouth.

Seeing the defendant's speech fail most utterly, the human judges conferred for several minutes. Concurrently, the crested clerks cluck-clucked and buck-bucked, all with suspicious glares, further tipping lopsided the scales against our trembling ingenue.

When at last the whispers and gabblings winnowed, lo, who should make his appearance but Jago, to pile the proceedings ever steeper against the wobbling defence.

"What further insights have you gleaned about the scoundrel's guilt?" shrilled Magistrate Edmunda as the young lord settled in his cream and crimson silks amidst the humble scrubbed pines and linens.

Steely-eyed authority did clearly war within as displeased irresolution creased his brow. "My investigations have so far proved inconclusive," said he. "That said, a correspondence secured with martial intimates in Bern may soon illuminate what is uncertain. Of one truth alone, I am unreservedly convinced: the shifty rogue is no solider of Geneva, as claimed!"

A momentary hush ensued — heads wobbled and claws tapped — before a mighty uproar of tutting tongues and raucous squawking erupted from all coats and beaks assembled. So too, the humble barnyard beyond once more joined the chorus, raising their voices in universal condemnation. Clearly, no single creature present stood prepared to spare a single grain of charity for the dastardly Peter, who proved no Genevan son.

Visibly vexed, the lead Inquisitrix rounded on Lizzie with renewed fervour. "Enough pussyfooting!" She brandished the poster with theatrical flair. "What shreds vouchsafe that cowardly accused against these manifold allegations? Vanished from Bubendorf only to shirk his duty to the canton — give me but his scruff, I'd drag the cur to face Geneva myself!"

At this, the pinioned defendant only swallowed uneasily.

Indeed, smelling the proverbial rat, Edmunda evinced a look that suggested she was about to change her tactic; she now pivoted her attack on Emil. "And what say you, Son? What make you of Peter's character while you were in Lucerne?"

"W-why..." — he gulped and glanced at Lizzie, who shot him a subtle yet stern warning — "... ask after L-L-Lucerne, Mother?"

"Come, boy, out with it! Your stammering betrays you. And think not you colluding with your sister in the toolshed this morn escaped my notice! I followed you thither and gleaned enough information to divine some secret between you about Lucerne."

'Tis at this juncture that Helene, with all the subtlety of a cannon blast, jabbed Emil's ribs. She paid him a certain look which spoke he ought to spill the proverbial beans posthaste, lest she do it for him.

Ah, the mercurial nature of a lover's tongue when struck by sly Cupid's arrow! And how utterly naïve the enamoured heart when it unbosoms to another, even under the solemnest of oaths; as if love itself could seal the lips. In the days since this madcap trial began, poor, smitten Emil, quite feeling either the pangs of conscience's voice or the siren song of gossip, found the cement holding tight his lips crumble faster than stale bread. And so, into Helene's astonished ears, he warbled saccharine secrets that sent scarlet rising to her discountenanced cheeks.

Witnessing the accused's further-condemning crimson flush and the flustered abettors' stolen glances, our canny chief judge did swiftly deduce a mischief most foul afoot. Seizing Emil's ear, she wrenched it with such ferocity that three seconds was all it took for the lad's backbone to buckle, and for the first treasonous drops to gush forth:

"'Tis possible — Yeowch! — that Peter might — Unnngh! — as guards — Mother! Have mercy! — in Lucerne, they took us hostage —"

"What?!" shrieked Edmunda.

Her cry echoed by all creatures great and small, voices melded with clucks, quacks, oinks, moos and maas; feathers flew amidst the flurry of flapping wings; chaos reigned supreme as the room threatened to implode under secrets too shocking to be contained...

***

My, my! What a tempestuous whirlwind of woes! Faith, how quickly the world turns. Whilst the humble key players of our drama grapple with their respective tribulations, the city of Bern likewise still wrangles in the throes.

Turbulent as her disputes with Zürich and France had been, with French refugees flooding borders, fleeing their wretched revolution, our fair Bernese order began to falter. Sectarian tensions between native Protestants and incoming Catholics fast boiled over; they fought for grain and scripture alike, brawling and rioting, turning the streets into an indubitable battlefield! But lo! To compound these internal struggles, the Austrians *and* the Prussians now breathed their fiery breath down every councillor's neck. Spies skulked hither and thither. Swiss allegiance was demanded in the conflict against France. Threats to cut off vital trade routes and to isolate Switzerland from the rest of Europe multiplied.

Gustav and the Small Council had barely convened in the Rathaus' Small Council Hall to address these matters when the cherrywood-panelled chamber's increasingly taut atmosphere reverberated to the crack of gunfire without.

"Lord, preserve us!" Gustav bolted up from his lofty seat.

Fresh volleys of gunfire sent councillors rushing to the arched windows, straining to assess the commotion unfolding in the shadowy, cobbled, Rathausplatz below. There, rows of guardsmen forced back a teeming malcontent mob of commoners, their voices raised in protest over rationing measures, their collective will bent on storming the councillors' gilded sanctum.

Gustav squeezed among his fellow councilmen. "At this rate, our external fears prove entirely vain! We are near to collapsing from within! How are we to receive the Antistes?"

"Surely, we cannot continue endorsing such brutal suppression," implored one agitated lord, "when our own people cry out for relief!"

All eyes turned to Gustav, who, greatly disturbed, and rather than turning to Albrecht von Mülinen, looked to Adolfus in a wordless plea.

"I concur," said Adolfus, measured and firm. "This situation warrants immediate mediation. Though I confess alarm that our esteemed Venner of Bakers and Councillor of the Bakers' Guild have failed to address this matter ere now!"

Angry orbs by the dozens shot their way.

"Do we possess the power of the Almighty?" retaliated the Venner of Bakers, blanching under the heat of so many glares. "Grain scarcity has decimated our staple crops! And with the war disrupting trade routes, even attempts to secure supplies from abroad have been thwarted."

"Yet, ought not someone of your rank and authority have anticipated this supply chain contagion sooner?" pressed Adolfus. "What of entreating our foreign allies?"

"*Allies?*" scoffed the Councillor of the Bakers' Guild. "Even the countries beyond our walls, while embroiled in petty disputes, ingratiate themselves with the French, sending their supplies thither! Food costs have tripled within weeks."

Adolfus smiled thinly. "So many seats between you, yet so little capability." He diverted his cutting glare to Gustav. "I demand their immediate resignations; neither of them is fit for civil duties!"

At these words, the room blew up in so acrimonious a debate that none spied Adolfus slip coded orders to an aide awaiting beyond the heavy doors. The first of his dominoes now tottered towards cascading chaos...

Barely had Adolfus' aide set about his commission when a frantic rapping upon the doors boomed through the chamber, cutting through the bickering cacophony like a butcher's cleaver. A grieved-looking guard entered, escorting an ashen-faced labourer covered head-to-toe in dust and blood.

Here it was that had the councillors noted Adolfus' aspect, they would have observed a distinct character of wicked expectation.

20 July 1792

News arrived of a dreadful incident. In the city's haste to repair the minster façade to welcome the eminent Antistes, its weakened foundations had buckled, collapsing the frontage and killing dozens of workers beneath the rubble.

"Great God above!" cried Gustav. "At this rate, we shall have to host our Protestant dignitaries in the scullery!"

All eyes swung on the Chief Construction Burgher, who gawped widely.

"Another incompetent," railed Adolfus with a cunning glint. "I had already communicated my concerns over those questionable structural assessments! How are you *ever* to rectify this disaster in the next two-and-seventy hours? You will bring unequivocal reproach on this land of reformation!"

***

We must now depart from a despairing Gustav and his exasperated council to more closely pursue Adolfus. Lips pursed with carefully controlled satisfaction, he took his leave from the dispersing assembly. Each orchestrated outrage, each calamity, had elicited the desired reaction from those gullible nobles. Indeed, one would little suspect the invisible strings binding all events to Adolfus' masterly will, unless privy to the backstage workings of this consummate puppeteer and peerless political maestro. And, indeed, though the aforementioned calamities may, at first glance, appear as disparate and unconnected as stars scattered across the night sky, their interrelation will, in due course, form the wicked constellation of his designs.

'Twas nearing the eighth hour, and the enterprising statesman glided beyond public galleries into a muted antechamber of some to-do dining establishment, opulent in its discretion, where solely the select elite may tread. 'Tis here, according to the coded summons he had earlier bade his whiskered aide to convey, that there awaited Adolfus' next less-than-reputable appointment: a bitter exiled French marquis, who clung to his wealthy justaucorps coattails since tumbling from aristocracy's lofty cradle, and eager as an attack dog for whatever scraps of influence might be tossed his mendicant way.

"I see my robed associates extend the finest Bernese hospitality," said Adolfus, "befitting even foreign nobility of your discerning tastes, *eh,*

Monsieur?" His voice dripped with unctuous timbre as he greeted the continental refugee.

The fallen nobleman, environed by lacquered mahogany panels, rich tapestries, and bathed in amber luminescence, redolent with beeswax and an undercurrent of intrigue, found breath between ravenous bites of a pheasant only to mutter complaints. Why, the ingrate, ensconced most comfortably in one of the venue's best suites, had the gall to ill compare it to the bloated Versailles. Even the overstuffed cushions, their velvet covers emblazoned with the establishment's crest, paled beside the man's fond memories of ancestral plumage, where he preened over tyrannised starving peasants back in the days of true glory. The Swiss cuisine wanted. The salon was not large — not grand enough! The lack of beauties to attend upon him was an insult to his august lineage!

Adolfus studied him keenly. These fools salivating at the potential for renewed power made useful tools indeed; one merely had to steer the rancour smouldering beneath their fractured family escutcheons.

"Come now, my dear Marquis," oozed Adolfus, bowing and scraping so low his protuberant beak nigh impaled itself upon the burnished parquet, "permit us to remedy this lapse posthaste. For your rarefied comfort, an apartment, as magnificent as Versailles' own glittering Galerie des Glaces, shall be prepared. As for *les belles dames*, I need only enlist another sort of expertise..."

Such obsequious genuflections and sycophantic overtures won naught but a noncommittal grunt from the haughty noble. He merely drained another crystal chalice of claret. But Adolfus, quelling his antipathy, resolved to surmount every superlative expectation and to procure the choicest, feminine hors d'oeuvres. He redoubled his feigning assiduities, simulating in every glance and mellifluent word an ardent desire to please his most illustrious patron.

Only after these two species of pride had inflated, preened, and strutted through their ostentatious pavane did the discourse segue into a more delicate minuet. "Now that we have addressed your comfort and ease," said Adolfus, "we must on to matters of business. I trust I may rely on your utmost discretion and unwavering loyalty to this cause?"

Just then, a most fetching maidservant glided in, bearing some belated delicacy on a silver platter. This rekindling the noble refugee's flagging

20 July 1792

enthusiasm, no sooner had his roving orbs espied the azure-eyed Fräulein's well-turned ankles, so demurely concealed beneath her silken hem, than he demanded additional fair company with all possible expedition.

To be sure, it required naught but sufficient bait — a flock of comely attendants with tightly laced bodices, ruby lips curved in beguiling smiles, and flaxen ringlets cascading over ample décolletages — for the puffed-up, ignoble marquis to at last vouchsafe full cooperation.

"Consider it done this night, dear fellow." He trailed a sly finger down a blushing damsel's downy cheek. "And on the morrow, behold your schemes most satisfactorily fulfilled." He now pawed at the hapless strumpet's rosebud mouth. "However," intoned he with sudden gravity, his frivolity discarded, "*n'oubliez jamais, ma chèr — noblesse oblige.*"

"But of course, your Grace."

For the benefit of my readers not acquainted with the Gallic tongue, I shall elucidate the haughty nobleman's pronouncement: "Never forget, my dear — nobility obligates." This maxim conveys that quasi-manipulative sentiment so oft espoused by the wealthy and influential who forever promise aid but always expects even greater recompense for their pains.

"*Vive le futur Empereur!*" resumed Adolfus, perpetuating the courtly dance lest he betray the barbs of contempt now pricking most uncomfortably beneath his silken raiment. "I pledge that your assistance in this matter shall not go unrecognised."

"*Vive le futur Empereur!*" echoed the marquis.

***

Ah, faithful reader, of the myriad perplexities entangling our ragtag troupe upon this humble stage, perhaps few enigmas have so piqued our fancy as those curious ticking contrivances — each emblazoned with the cryptic motto: *Vive le futur Empereur!*

In the mode of a little aide-mémoire, permit me to summon your recollection to the opening act of our inaugural volume, wherein these very devices first revealed themselves in the most unlikely of abodes: a modest rustic cabin.

Not long after, in the third act, a kindred timepiece — or, perchance, its twin — made its discreet appearance within the venerable confines of Johannes' sacred library. Thereafter, our tale led us to Lucerne, where that singularly eccentric horologist of the famed Die Goldene Schlüssel likewise set his seal upon this mysterious refrain: *"Vive le futur Empereur!"*

***

The cuckoo clock heralded the evening's ninth hour with its distinctive call. Peter had endured a day of mounting tension, intermittently watching troops tramping down below. Distant gun blasts had rent the air; jeering echoes, and cries, and loud rumblings had punctuated the innkeeper's screeched reports of multiplying tribulations besieging the city. Into this stream of uncertainty, Vitus, face obscured by the shadows of a low-swept hat, made an appearance.

"Brother." Peter greeted him. "Come through." But in studying Vitus' countenance, he soon discerned this marked no mere social call. "Do you bring some ill-tiding about the prospective arrest of the forger?"

"No. There is, however," — He glanced a wary look at Harris — "another matter of *equal* importance to discuss."

Sure enough, once Peter bade Harris to grant them privacy, Vitus set loose the first syllables of his astonishing revelation. "Intelligence newly gleaned by one of my men links that hellion Viktor to some intrigue with select aristocrats across the cantons. I know not exactly what connects him to these unknown nobles, but there seems to be some mystery pertaining to certain... timepieces."

"*Timepieces*? — You refer to those bearing the emblem of the honeybee?"

Vitus regarded him with surprise. "Then you were already aware of this?"

"Indeed." He motioned to the chairs by the window. "Viktor's clock is but one of six identical dials which —"

"*Six* clocks?" interrupted Vitus as he sat down. "And *identical*, you say?"

"Precisely. I only know of this because I happened upon on one, if not two, of these very timepieces. Furthermore, whilst in Lucerne — Good lord! How could I have forgotten? The secret compartment!"

Peter's mind raced back to his visit to the horologist's store. There, with peculiar tools and magnifying lenses, the horologer had tinkered with a hidden cavity, producing a strange, wax-sealed cargo bearing the emblem of a honeybee.

"Secret compartment?" Curiosity ruled Vitus' every feature and movement. And as Peter relayed his account, comprehension illuminated Vitus' eyes. "So that must explain the cryptic instructions I overheard. There was talk of co-ordinating a... *meeting*... in the months ahead..."

As Vitus trailed off in thought, Peter's mind raced, a-rush with cluttered jigsaw fragments of what now congealed into a coherent picture at last: encrypted timepieces! Honeybee seals! Viktor's clandestine movements! "This must be it!" declared he. "His ploy to seize power!"

Vitus gasped as if thunderstruck. "You know of this as well?"

Peter stared at him. "As did *you*, apparently?"

Though Vitus concurred that some sinister design indeed lurked beneath these dials, the constellation of clues yet stretched leagues beyond his grasp. What they both already knew or guessed at from the past investigations were but the fringes of Viktor's schemes. That said, they had tumbled far enough down the gaping maw of some vast, unseen cabal — whose true architect and intent remained clouded — to know that something was afoot.

"We must thwart his schemes without delay!" urged Vitus. "We need access to one of these clocks."

"Perhaps," said Peter, an idea forming, "Bernhard could assist us in this matter... I have already solicited of him a favour, which needs carrying out in Bubendorf. I shall pen an additional request. And I know he had dealings with one footman at Ebenrain... But giving due heed to this conversation, as soon as I can, I must also return to Wildenstein to retrieve that billet and learn whatever message is inscribed upon it."

"Though these machinations bode ill, Brother, take heart; Viktor's prospects shrink daily, thanks to his latest asinine spectacle. I doubt his present adherents will soon tie themselves or their fortunes to one so volatile."

"Pray, explain yourself, my brother." Peter leant forward. "What fresh disaster has our rascal sibling wrought?"

21 – 22 JULY 1792

Dandelion tufts and thistles blasted free beneath the relentless lashing hooves across the vast open fields. The winds, carrying whispers of impending reproach, seemingly echoed still with the clangour of that fateful loaded barrel which put an end to the life of the guild master's heir — that proud, vexing, and equally vainglorious scion.

In these two-and-seventy hours since the calamitous event, hearsay had multiplied the poisonous gossip, further blighting Bern's genteel salons with sordid reports of the successor's untimely demise. Consequently, a stern summons curtailed the volatile Viktor's next reckless escapade, ordering him forthwith to Adolfus' secluded and lofty estate, Schloss Oberdiessbach.

Perhaps this solitude promised a safe harbour from the schultheiss' avowed retribution, a momentary sidestepping of the debt for blood? Or so the culpable fugitive mused as the slender carriage, bearing his unworthy and disgraced person, rolled through the imposing wrought-iron gates and crested the long sweeping drive to the schloss' entrance. For here, too, the stage was set; there awaited the full tribunal of surly old vultures, decidedly little enthused to greet so prodigal and recalcitrant an offspring.

Scarcely had Viktor alighted the conveyance and been goaded inside the property when foremost-icy Adolfus, emblazoned in the demeanour of a bird of prey, lifted his beak to violently peck at the errant fool; to strip him of his pretences as though plucking the feathers off his various aspects. "You seem hellbent on dragging us all into ruin with your reckless ways!" thundered he.

A chorus of agitated assent rose from the group of councillors and their parliamentary subordinates — each voice layered upon the last.

"Are you so impetuously spawned from Hell itself as to be utterly blinded to the political inferno your disastrous display has ignited?" bellowed the Venner of Butchers, his iron-grey whiskers aquiver, as if shooting out lightning bolts. "Why, the empty seats of our opponents at the council were the single grace which prevented your shame from reaching their ears!"

"Indeed!" rasped the Venner of Tanners. "Your irresponsible antics imperil months of intricate stratagems! You arrogant whelp! You think our scheme will be easier advanced when key families discover whose noble head it is they yearn to see severed and set atop the city gates?"

"When will you grasp the severity, boy?" Adolfus resumed his charge. "Does your noble birth delude you into believing you are above reproach? Beyond the reach of consequence?"

Faced with such searing reproofs, the profligate merely brushed all off with an indifferent shrug and derisive snort. He sauntered to the main parlour to pour himself a drink, leaving his auditors utterly astounded as they trailed behind, sputtering curses, cheeks blowing, eyes darting to and fro between the ingrate and their fellow affronted comrades. Yet the crystal stopper had scarce clinked insouciantly against the tumbler before the verbal barrage erupted afresh.

"By the Almighty, boy!" Adolfus pulled at his own hair. "Can you not perceive the executioner's blade hovering over our collective necks, thanks to your flagrant folly? Had we not swiftly sought out, silenced, and compensated all witnesses, you would have been hauled before the courts to stand trial, and found yourself in some dungeon worthy of your disgraceful nonchalance!"

Adolfus' diatribe was just resuming when a vigilant vice chancellor, stationed at the window, espied an anomaly on the northern road. "Say here! A solitary rider hastens this way, garbed in the livery of House von Villeroy's colours — unless my eyes deceive me?"

Anon, laboured stomps heralded this winded Swiss Guard courier at the parlour door. Still gulping breath between managing dignified nods appropriate to such exalted personages collected, the man declared his purpose. "Gentleman, esteemed lords," said he, "dreadful events only just relayed require your immediate presence in Bern; so decrees His Schultheiss Gustav von Villeroy."

***

Coils of smoke, like writhing serpents, curled upward into the soaring chamber ceiling as the Small Council grappled in stunned disbelief with the fresh atrocities that had piled overnight — an event orchestrated by none other than that wily French marquis.

"This is inconceivable!" clamoured the majority, their voices echoing off the walls. "Mere bands of migrant rioters overrunning the city watch barracks and absconding with a cache of firearms and ammunition? Has our great canton succumbed to mere ineptitude from within?"

Alas, the woes were compounded: the council's own vaults, a tangible trove of precious metal and bullion assets, had apparently been stormed and ransacked by a motley crew of disenfranchised veterans, exiled dissidents, and French Royalist sympathisers.

"This breach is not merely a failure of security," — Gustav's grip on the armrests betrayed his need for its support — "but a visceral affront! A slap to our faces! A symbolic humiliation! And the very day before the Antistes' arrival!"

The chamber erupted in a deafening uproar. Yet amidst this hubbub of shock and abhorrence which clawed at every agitated face, one figure remained an island of composure. Adolfus. His features schooled in a mask of shared outrage, harboured eyes that rather twinkled with a hint of gratification.

Gustav *and* Albrecht, no less overwhelmed by the seismic disarray, called the riotous assembly to order — for such tumult held no precedent in living memory. Twice were the attendants compelled to futilely bang their oaken staffs against the floor. But accusations flew like arrows, soon directed at the beleaguered Venner of Bakers and the Councillor of the Bakers' Guild for their catastrophic neglect in addressing the land's growing hunger. Likewise, the Venner of Blacksmiths and the Arms Master were ridiculed and spurned. And now their lackeys had failed to thwart this fresh disaster, adding insult to already grievous injuries, which seemed to consume the canton with every strained breath.

But lo, as the noble lords bawled and near-brawled, volleying insults and overturning chairs alike, a sudden fanfare sliced through the fray — a merry cavalry of horns blew crisply aloud beyond the chamber's tall windows, halting the most unholy symphony of dispute.

"By the saints!" exclaimed the Lord So-and-So, first to investigate what heralded outside. "Behold this glorious emergence!"

Why, his fellow dogs of war and politics did charge straightaway to the long windows to espy whatever fleshly miracle so approached. There, through the leaded glass, a caravan of salvation met their gaze: a train of carts, each hauled by careworn beasts — a veritable convoy of deliverance, tottering beneath an untold bounty mounded taller than any hayrick at harvest's peak. Such bulging sacks must have held adequate oats, wheats, and sundry staples to feed every grumbling common belly from one corner of the confederacy to the other!

"Faith!" cried the Church Steward. "This outpouring of the sky can only signal the Divine's mercy upon us!"

A wave of jubilation went up from every throat. The lords, momentarily united by this turn of fortune, tripped over stools, chairs, and cushions as they scrambled to laud the venerable Venner of Bakers and the Councillor of the Bakers' Guild, whose perceived ingenuity had seemingly conjured this bounty.

"How came this manna to relieve us of this calamity?" congratulated one.

"What genius or angels orchestrate your swift gesture?" praised another.

Such eager praise was scarcely launched ere goblets were hoisted and clinked in shared camaraderie. But the pair of putative heroes rather stood equally dismayed at the clamour. Indeed, and to the no little dismay of every congratulator, a distinctive clearing of pipes and throats preceded a sheepish admission that this miracle proved none of their invention at all.

Enter Adolfus. "Whilst the Venner of Bakers and the Councillor of the Butchers' Guild indulged their palate for fine wine with the Tax Collector," explained he, "our industrious Nachschauer," — remember, dear reader, that same gentleman who, not long ago, was smuggling grain for precisely this purpose — "here, busied himself in the dead of night, forging alliances. By his own coin he secured emergency concessions from foreign grain merchants, marshalling a relief column for our beleaguered countrymen."

"Is this the truth?" demanded Gustav with a look quite amazed.

The Nachschauer bowed with modest grace. "A mere duty fulfilled."

Sensing the winds of favour shift, the Welsch Treasurer — keeper of the coffers for the French-speaking Vaud and whose gaze bore the chill precision of a seasoned chess master — seized the moment. Eager to safeguard his own coveted seat and to forestall the schultheiss' wrath, he launched a scathing invective against both the Venner of Bakers and the Councillor of the Butchers' Guild. Though these gentlemen were stalwart allies in the political arena, the treasurer, with cunning finesse, called for their swift expulsion. Moreover, pressed by

Adolfus' adherents and several voices from his own camp clamouring the same, the treasurer — after much grumbling and scowling — reluctantly championed the Nachschauer as interim Venner of Bakers and emergency Trade Commissioner; thus poised as Bern's unlikely saviour.

Herein, dear reader, behold the fruition of Adolfus' earlier prophecy: the claiming of yet more seats.

But Adolfus' triumph extended far beyond this single political manoeuvre. The council next turned to the matter of the collapsed Bern Minster façade — where grief-stricken families clamoured for recompense, and builders, architects, and masons refused to proceed without doubled wages and guarantees of safety. Ineffective in quelling the labour unrest, the Building Master cowered beneath the schultheiss' scorching rebukes. Here, Adolfus unveiled the Vice Chancelor's solution — cunning as it was contentious: the importation of slave labour alongside expert craftsmen from abroad. Thusly, names were proposed; votes hastily cast; the cathedral's shattered visage was to be shrouded beneath scaffolds and cloth in solemn preparation for the Antistes' visit; and the Building Master was unceremoniously ejected, with the Vice Chancellor ascending to his newly won pedestal — swelling Adolfus' faction by yet two more seats.

Feeling the threads of power tightening around his fingers, Adolfus savoured the prospect of propelling the heir — more pliable to his designs — into power. With the aid of corrupt guardsmen, Viktor's scandalous escapades had been covered up, leaving the morrow poised for Varus' accuser to wield the blade of justice. Moreover, in but two days' time, the forger would be spirited away from the insufferably inquisitive Vitus' clutches. Each domino fell precisely as foreseen; each pawn moved according to a treacherous ballet of politics...

***

It was now mid-afternoon. Our hero had spent the day's majority suffering the afflictions of suspense in all its intensity. He paced back and forth, sat down, stood up, lingered, reclined, merely to rise again in fevered disquiet, unable to command himself or his thoughts.

But at last, a rapping at his chamber door pulled him from this cycle.

The innkeeper came to deliver an envelope, bound in fine silk ribbon and bearing a curious wax seal, which, being altogether unfamiliar, Peter guessed must be from his newfound guardian, Master Bernhard. He found his assumption confirmed in the positive; Bernhard had the following message to relay:

> Peter,
> It is with great pleasure I report that my swiftest and most capable agent has completed the twin tasks you set. His investigations yielded useful information:
> Regarding your esteemed great-uncle and -aunt, no records or memory place either as having ties to Bubendorf. The Wildenstein estate's current proprietor, one Signor Pier, assumed tenure only decades ago; earlier owners' names are lost to time. To confirm any personal links, I suggest you approach the current occupant once present troubles ease.
> As for the timepiece at Ebenrain, I eagerly await further details. My agent encountered some difficulties in tracking down the footman, who has since retired from Johannes' service. From the man's fading recollections, it appears the clock was never returned to the library.
> While these enquiries may not reveal all obscured truths, I hope this intelligence suffices for now. Should you require further aid, do not hesitate to call upon me.
> Your faithful ally, Bernhard.

With a deep exhale, our disheartened hero sank into his seat. Indeed, herein this correspondence lay little gratifying truths plucked forth; only enigmatic hints strewn too sparingly across the sheet. No divine or mortal agency seemed poised to unravel the knots which constricted family intrigues and ambitions alike. This attempt at loosening the ropes had solely drawn the coils inexorably closer. Still, time yet remained. Fortune may prove herself an ally.

But as for the clock, it must have been at the horologist's store. And as for the message, once sequestered within the timepiece's secret compartment... Peter sensed the insidious interdependencies binding all lives touched by those bedevilled dials and whatever omens they heralded.

Ere long, fresh wraps resounded on the bedchamber door. The innkeeper reappeared, bearing yet another despatch between her plump, diligent fingers.

Hastily tearing it open, Peter read from Vitus:

> *My most esteemed and beloved brother,*
> *Pray, excuse this abruptness. Come to the Münsterplattform tonight at eleven. There is a matter of utmost importance I must show you. Further confidence awaits when we meet. Affectionately, yours in unbreakable fraternal bonds, Vitus.*
> *PS: Instruct the innkeeper to grant you usage of the rear entrance henceforth. Eyes and ears turn from all quarters.*

So ominous a postscript; the very thought that a veil of surveillance might have been cast around his lodgings. But shaking off this thought, he waited until the designated hour, wherein he cloaked himself and departed with haste.

Solemn vesper bells struck the breezy night air; chestnut leaves rustled as Peter stalked past the hedged partiers of lawns (a former graveyard central to the gardens) and hastened along the gravelled walkway. The rendezvous point, a stone pavilion in a secluded corner, touched by the wavering star light, appeared strange and foreboding, mirroring our hero's unease.

There soon emerged from the structure ahead, Vitus' familiar visage, albeit tensed in shadowy concern under a sharp tricorn hat, and garbed in the stark disguise of poverty.

"Hurry," uttered Vitus.

21 – 22 July 1792

With a wary glance around, hoping that no hidden observers had tracked him here, Peter entered the pavilion.

After cursory handclasps and a brief account of the suspected watchers since he despatched his last courier to the inn, Vitus withdrew from his pocket a billet. "This was slipped under my chamber door not two hours past. From who it came or how it found its way to my quarters, I cannot guess..."

Peter's gaze instantly latched onto the note. He attempted to decipher the cryptic script amidst the encroaching gloom:

> *With the new dawn, soon will tables turn. Better*
> *your breath be held than alarms raised...*

"What think you such opacity intends?" said a palpably anxious Vitus.

In the space of three drawn breaths, a myriad of potential arcs diverged upon Peter's brain. A coup by the councillors? A dramatic turn towards a treaty with the French? Perhaps sudden renewed harmony with Zürich...?

"I... I cannot say?" admitted he.

Thoughts swirling with that cryptic message, Peter made his way back to the inn. But in being in such a state of preoccupation, sidestepping a group of drunken louts, he collided with a young man. The impact sent both stumbling backward; the sudden jolt caused Peter's hood to fall away from his face.

"Watch where you are going!" exclaimed our hero.

The youth was equally startled but evidently emboldened by a state of inebriation. "*You*, watch yourself!"

Irritated by the impetuous young man, Peter rounded on him, his face touched by the streetlamp's glow.

'Twas now that the young affronter, eyes narrowing to slits, raised an impertinent finger. "*Wait a minute*... your face... I know it..."

Indeed, Peter's heart shuddered; he edged away from the youth.

But the young man stepped forward, closing the gap. His orbs now rather widened with something akin to full recognition. "Yes, you're that criminal!"

Verily, panic took control. In his desperation to escape, our hero shoved the accuser aside, sending him tumbling to the cobblestones, and charged forth along the street.

Not so easily dissuaded, however, the fellow clambered to his feet. Shouting for help, he gave chase, albeit an unsteady one, his voice echoing through the narrow streets, drawing the unwanted attention of curious onlookers.

Pushing past startled pedestrians and leaping over small obstacles, his cloak billowing behind him, Peter barely got out of sight. Just as he believed himself out of harm's way, his chaser's persistent shouts rang aloud on the air.

Driven to even higher heights of despair, Peter all but threw himself around the last corner and onto the street where stood the inn.

His breath came in ragged gasps, his lungs burned with the exertion of his flight; but with one last burst of energy, he sprinted to the entrance.

Ducking inside just as his stalker's shouts echoed without, Peter, after availing himself of several gulps of the interior air, forced himself upstairs to his room.

Straight for the window he made and peered out from behind the net curtains. Indeed, there below, stumbling from one side of the street to the other, the young man looked around in evident bewilderment. He scanned doorways and alleys, unable to locate his quarry, who had seemingly vanished into thin air.

**

As the morning sun stretched its golden rays above ancient Bern, her cobbled streets, winding alleys, and archaic nooks came alive with fervent anticipation. Throngs of Bernese citizens, surrounding rural folk, and fellow confederates from the neighbouring cantons lined the city thoroughfares, prepared to welcome the Antistital and Synodal visit.

Crimson banners, proudly bearing the Protestant symbols, festooned buildings. Garlands of magnolia blossoms and emerald fir branches bedecked virtually every post and pillar. Even the remnants of the recent devastation stood defiant, its scars cloaked beneath makeshift beautifications as scaffolds, erected overnight with hurried diligence, propped up the venerable minster's wounded face. Adolfus had spared no effort to ensure that the beloved icon, her majestic visage shattered by conspirators, was honoured with the finest draped crimson.

Jubilant hoorays and vivas crescendoed, heralding the eminent Bernese clergymen and assembled dignitaries' imminent arrival. The encroaching crowds, eager to glimpse this historic spectacle about to unfold in the plaza below, swelled with every minute.

But our hero, disguised once more in the striking hues of vermilion and azure regimentals, brass buttons catching the light with a subdued lustre, shared not in the widespread fervour. Beneath the martial facade, his mind waged a relentless battle with enigmas. The honeybee seals, the mysterious clocks, the veiled threats surrounding him and his family — what role did each component play in the shadowy cabal tightening its yet unknown grip? And what of the promised turning of the tables? To what end did it all allude?

"What strange happenings steered by this unseen hand may come to light on this day?" said he to Vitus, who had just ushered him into the grand salon of a sympathetic guildsman, offering our hero an unobstructed view of the plaza.

"Whatever *is* to transpire," responded he, "*especially* if it unfolds amidst this procession, we shall both be witness its effect." He leant closer. "We shall not converse again until the morrow. Should the forger's plan unfold without a hitch, let us toast our success come eventide."

With a parting smile that did not quite reach his eyes, Vitus excused himself to assume his place across the way: an elevated stage, draped in flags and heraldry — front row alongside his family, resplendent in bright ceremonial attire; a stark contrast to the Small Council behind them, jet black satin cloaks bedecked with heavy golden chains.

A distant eruption of cheers announced the Antistital delegation's arrival. Their carriages, passing through the Bernese walls, entered the flower-strewn streets, thick with the promise of spectacle and ceremony.

As the procession slowly but steadily neared the cathedral, Adolfus, poised to strike a decisive blow in the high-stake game of power, leant close to his confidante. "Prepare," whispered he, "to witness the dawn of our new era."

Across the sea of faces, each of them enrapt and oblivious to the impending drama, the woman whose vulnerability Adolfus had so expertly leveraged stood awaiting her cue. Though but an insignificant pawn in his corrupt hand, she was pivotal to assuring Viktor's ascension. For soon, at the strategic moment, when the clergy's gleaming carriages would pull into view, she needed only to rush forth into the eyes of all, where, prostrating herself before the procession, she would publicly decry Varus a scoundrel and adulterer, proclaiming him an unworthy successor and thus destroying his legitimacy.

Adolfus chuckled. Oh, how he had woven his sabotage so very, very exceedingly well... Again, he lent into his comrade's ear. "I trust your agents will suffer no interference in capturing the copyist tomorrow?"

"Rest assured, friend," came the reply. "Our victory over all wayward events shall be complete."

"Excellent." Adolfus withdrew and, reclining full into his seat, congratulated himself on the unquenchable art and genius of his own cunning.

But the fabric of Adolfus' plan was not so unassailable as he believed. Fate, it seemed, had a different narrative in store — a twist with the power to unravel years of scheming.

The arrival of a pageboy, little older than nine summers, presaged the turning point. Amidst the opulence of the dignitaries' platform, where the assembled aristocrats held court like monarchs upon their miniature thrones, the boy nimbly ascended the scarlet-carpeted stairs while balancing a polished salver of crystal flutes. Here, his eyes met those of Adolfus. With a subtle exchange, a tiny scroll bound in black silk made its way into the hands of the latter.

Adolfus, thus clutching the insignificant-looking yet burning paper, feigned a sudden call of nature and retreated to the cathedral's shadowy alcove, away from all prying eyes.

Vestments swirling and not without casting his wary eyes about did he then unravel the diminutive scroll. The revelation contained within was as devastating as it was succinct:

> *Varus is infertile! He has secretly met with expert*
> *physicians, vainly endeavouring to remediate*
> *what is winter's barren soil!*

"Great God above!" Scarce could he believe what his shaking gloved

21 – 22 July 1792

hand held. Verily, Adolfus' brain was set on fire. He hissed several venomous curses, needing to support himself on a nearby pew as the universe itself seemed to collapse around him.

With the coaches steadily approaching, his window for action narrowed with each agonising tick of the massive clock high above — each echoing like the hammering of nails into his own coffin.

Rage consuming his soul, he burst from the cathedral's gloom and despatched his personal guards with explicit orders to intercept the woman at all costs before she aired the now useless yet perilous scandal!

With scarcely minutes to spare as the clergy paraded ever closer, Adolfus scrambled back to his elevated seat. There, choking anxiety strangling him of breath and enfeebling his limbs, he watched his men plunge into the crowds, praying most fervently, though to what malevolent god I know not, that they would without fail intervene. For, indeed, the last grains of proverbial sand were swiftly draining from his hourglass.

There hung in the balance his very destiny. Should the guards silence not the now-useless woman's tongue, the scandal would erupt — though a hollow echo of what was intended, yet potent enough to spell Adolfus' irreparable ruin.

Mouth gone dry, he demanded with rasping agitation the pageboy's return. Alas, the proffered potation was but a brief respite. The liquid within was downed with the same fervour that drove his panicked schemes.

Ready to sink under the weight of uncertainty, eyes wide with the embers of his thwarted ambition, he scanned the heaving throngs. Where were his men? Each face was but a barrier to the resolution he craved.

Indeed, the next moments would seal his increasingly precarious destiny.

Among the throes of chants and cheers, where the crowds erupted into a near idolatrous fervour at the Antistital and Synodals' gilded carriages' arrival, the woman summoned her resolve. Seizing upon the tapestry of distraction, she emboldened her advance. With a forward lurch, she shoved aside all who blocked her approach and cut a path through the masses, her every motion evincing her desperation and the gravity of the task at hand.

Ah, but Fortune had already cast her lot elsewhere!

No sooner had she breached the moving wall than a crushing hand clamped around her arm and wrenched her violently back through the crowds.

"Unhand me this instant!" cried out she, twisting and writhing with all the futility of a lamb in a wolf's jaws.

Her subsequent shrieks, though fierce and filled with the indignation of the wronged, were engulfed by the fanatical cheering crowds.

"Silence, wench!" The black-clad agent's vice-like grip allowed no escape as he dragged her away from the light and out of sight, plunging her into the penumbral labyrinth of an alley.

"What is happening?" She struggled all the more. "Where are you taking me?"

On all sides, cheers crested as the polished carriages, like chariots of the divine, drew to a halt before the cathedral. Resplendent in the finest of ecclesiastical regalia, the clergy descended like celestial beings from parting clouds. Black vestments woven with gold and silver threads shimmered in the morning light. A cascade of precious metals and jewels transformed the sun's gentle rays into a halo that danced upon the gathered faces. Benign smiles warmed the mosaic of sundry care-worn countenances as the holy men raised and flourished gem-encrusted hands, bestowing benedictions upon the ecstatic masses.

Such was the power of the moment that the square seemed to pulse with a shared heartbeat.

Meanwhile, high above on the crimson-draped bleachers, the nobility rose from their cushioned seats to honour the procession. The clergy floated as if on air down the red velvet carpet, flanked by the purity of white lilies. 'Twas clear this marked a pivotal moment for the city's spiritual and commercial future.

Upon reaching the platform, the delegation first exchanged pleasantries with the schultheiss and his consort — a mere prelude to the key moment. But on turning their attention to Varus, the air grew electric with import. All eyes, drawn as if by some magnetic force, settled upon the heir-in-waiting as the clergy, in unspoken acknowledgement, orchestrated a symphony of bows betokening his imminent ascendancy.

Amidst this veneration, none marked the venom smouldering in Viktor's countenance, nor the dagger-like stare he levelled at all who basked in his brother's glory. Seated beside Varus, he could look not upon the whole without envisioning his sword slashing each hypocrite's throat. Today's pageant, a mere prologue to his ambition, filled his soul with envy for the destiny he believed was stolen from him.

All the same, behind the patriotic and pious tableau, an ominous undercurrent swirled. While Adolfus' fateful schemes had faltered into oblivion, scarcely streets away, an altogether different clockwork ticked towards a most startling, most monumental denouement!

Still ensconced behind the upper room's tall leaded glass panes, our hero — the true scion of legacy long cast in shadow — watched the unfolding events with a heart oppressed. That he should be relegated to the role of a spectre in his own life's story, forced into disguise and dissimulation in a city once his childhood playground, and now held captive to a masquerade of his own making, came down heavily upon his weary soul.

His eyes, sharp with the acuity of one who, having already lost much, had still more to lose, caught in his father's countenance the subtle interplay of emotion: a shade of sorrow that not all offspring could sit shoulder-to-shoulder in solidarity. As much as Peter's sympathy was touched, it was diminished by the searing loss of a birthright usurped and the frustration of stolen hopes — a return to society free of veils and shadows.

Again, had only his mother not trodden so treacherous a path, sought revenge, and ensnared herself in treason's iron trap. Peter would likely now stand proud beside his eminently attired father as a cherished heir, looking upon crowds who would one day be his to lead.

But alas, such was not to be!

Notwithstanding this failed futurity, the tapestry was still woven with the threads of further misfortune. Darker designs moved against him, forcing him into exile. Unseen forces caballed to drive him from the very world itself! Moreover, secret societies, mysterious timepieces, and the powers rising beyond the borders... who knew whether these might yet also gather their blades at his neck?

But tomorrow, at least, the forger would be apprehended and brought to face justice. Perhaps the first twisting tunnel of so labyrinthine a puzzle would be lit up to lead the way onto the next, illuminating the identity of whoever — or whatever sinister power — yet concealed itself behind that initial pawn.

A rising sigh suppressed tight within his swelling breast, Peter shifted his focus back to the scenes below. Whatever tables were to turn this day, everything seemed to move forward without interruption or obtrusion.

That said, the crowd's gaze presently shifted skyward — their attention ensnared by some new wonder. Dozens of miniature hot air balloons, graceful in their ascent, crested overhead, dotting the azure heavens.

Whilst the masses "oohed" and "aahed" at the spectacle, bouquets and doves rained down into the outstretched hands, delighting young and old alike.

But the moment of wonder was soon shattered.

A cunning arrow whistled across the skies and pierced a balloon's breast, sending a stream of pamphlets swirling down.

Adolfus, shaking his head in mounting bafflement, wheeled on the master of ceremonies. "Who choreographed such a spectacle without my approval?"

But the official, perspiring heavily and blinking helplessly, offered a feeble shrug in response as more volleys whistled from hidden perches — each arrow finding its mark, rupturing the bright balloons' precious cargoes.

The skies wept red; crimson paper flurries, like blood gushing from an open wound, streamed down upon the upturned faces. Once a canvas of merriment but now blanketed in vermilion pamphlets, every face was soon stamped with the lines and hues of alarm.

Piercing shrieks and vociferous cries of dawning horror cut the procession's convivial atmosphere; some shocking revelation — like a poison more potent than any physical blade — rippled through the multitude.

A stray pamphlet, carried by the wind's caprice, wafted straight in Adolfus' gloved hand.

Indeed, his eyes widened with a sort of sickened awe. For here were laid Viktor's womanising, gambling, extortion, violence, sordid transgressions; his furtive duel, his role in the tragic death of the guild master's heir; all of it now plain as Holy Writ before all!

23 – 24 JULY 1792

Ere the sun had even spread its indifferent gaze over the land, Adolfus' villainous band crouched concealed amongst the silent woods which fringed the copyist's remote country estate. Nerves rang sharply as weapons were held to the ready. Eyes combed the environing fields and groves for any signs of a possible counterstrike.

Several long hours had crawled by, mounting the reeking tension amongst the cursing brigands. But at length, as the dial's hands aligned to mark midday, there came the distant rumbling of wheels; the carriage appeared far down the winding lane. Instinctively, all bodies shrank further into the growth.

"Think you," whispered one ruffian to their leader, "that Vitus' mongrels might be lying in ambush within the house?"

A flicker of concern shadowed the leader's cold countenance as the click of his weapon in readiness broke the taut silence. Two brigands nearby believed something indeed stirred at a window. Signalling hand motions rippled outward through the ranks of men lying in wait, directing attention to the windows. A group crawled forward through the undergrowth and flanked the property's sides, tightening their snare like wolves assured of trapping their prey.

The moment the creaking carriage turned onto the final approach, the bandits erupted from their cover and overtook the conveyance, hurling aside the coachman without mercy. Their iron-muzzled weapons at the ready, they swarmed about the curtain-drawn windows.

The chief's hoarse cry rent the air. "Emerge at once, or be dragged out as a cadaver!"

But nothing more than a soundlessness came that mocked his authority.

With a nod, the leader beckoned the volley; the muskets roared, their fury rending air, glass, and fabric alike.

Face full of anxiety, the chief signalled for his lieutenant to throw wide the door for him to confirm his victory firsthand. Oh, but what shock and rage instantly throttled his incoherent words when he, rifle thrust inside ahead of him, saw no living soul sitting inside at all!

23 – 24 July 1792

***

Where may we ask was the forger? Well, wisely, Vitus, ever the tactician, having sensed that presence of a spy as he laid those plans to capture the forger, deftly changed his strategy. Aware that the copyist had travelled quite some leagues from his country residence in Friborg, Vitus dispersed his operatives throughout the environing towns. Each was tasked to watch the local coach inns, where a tired steed would inevitably need to be exchanged for a fresh one.

As Vitus expected, the moment of exchange arrived. While the coachman was cunningly drawn elsewhere, the most furtive kidnapping unfolded; all noise muffled by sturdy hands and well-placed gags, all eyes-unseeing. In a further twist of cunning, one of Vitus' own slipped into the scribe's garments (for verisimilitude's sake) and took his place within the carriage. Once the coachman returned, oblivious to the switch and blind to the disguised man, a simple knock from inside the coach was all that was needed for the journey to resume.

The charade required only a single opportune moment along the secluded forest paths for the impostor to disembark undetected from the moving carriage; thereafter to be retrieved by his allies, who trailed at a safe distance.

Now, regarding the copyist, two suspenseful hours' jostling over the rugged terrain brought him to Thun Castle's impenetrable and intimidating bulwarks. Looming above on the rocky hill, its walls an omen of dread, struck hard at his conscience. Fortunately, this fiend was all too willing to barter his secrets for the promise of leniency. Not one to bite his own tongue clean off, it became the instrument of his salvation — or so he was led to believe. Vitus monopolised on the man's running mouth and artfully feigned a pledge of mercy in exchange for every scrap of incriminating evidence.

Most astonishing, it emerged that the late Schultheissin Vivienne von Villeroy had also fallen victim to the same machinations.

"What?" exclaimed Vitus. The copyist, bargaining for kindness, offered to expose the mastermind behind it. "Very well," disingenuously intoned Vitus; he presented the captive with several sheets of paper and a quill. "I bid you confess the entire history of your misdeeds."

Though trembling with fear, the forger was not without scruples as to give up the whole truth immediately. Nevertheless, the partial confession extracted sufficed for Vitus to exonerate his father and his stepbrother. With this leverage in hand, he consigned the copyist to the donjon's dank recesses. Next, he sent word to Bern city, notifying Peter of the arrest and instructing him to await further directives. Then, with discreet haste, he made for Schloss Jegenstorf to relay news of this pivotal victory to his father; the full breadth of their scheme had inched ever closer to fruition.

***

As for Viktor, unable as he was to endure the blistering intensity of ten thousand damning eyes fixed upon his person, he had paled as any spectre fleeing the daylight. Hastily, he quit his privileged perch and slipped inside the darkened cathedral to mourn ambitions turned to ash before the world.

Still, this next day brought further woes. Slanted rays of glaring sunlight, like accusatory fingers, cut across the Rathaus Hall of Assembly, striking the far door through which Viktor was ushered by several guards; less a procession than a march to his fate. His every step reverbed against the stone as a dirge to his fallen status.

Though rare was this chamber of councillors — shoulder-to-shoulder, ominous in black satin robes and glowers — ever a sanctuary of glittering promise, 'twas now rendered a den of wolves; a kettle of circling vultures; all hungry for the scent of weakness and salivating for retribution's halberd to be swung about the head of one who had so egregiously brought colossal ignominy on so great a canton.

A makeshift dock became Viktor's stage; the jury-like council, his audience. And among them, his father — whose penetrating gaze seemed to set even his bones rattling — flanked by disembodied faces glaring from the past; life-sized oils of disapproving greybeards, sages, magistrates, guild masters, even a mitred abbot and two prince-bishops, all hovered watchfully.

From such oppressive stares, Viktor turned away, fixing his gaze upon the floor; a facade of shame masking a heart not chastened but solely embittered by the condemnation he faced. His soul was corroded rather than purified by the judgement which had fallen upon him; his thoughts tended solely to the cruelty and injustice Fortune had rained upon him.

Gustav remained rigid as a statue. His flesh and blood appeared to have been replaced by alabaster. This stony aspect was interrupted at intervals only by the profound disillusionment, detestation, horror, and a family's disgrace, flushing crimson beneath his powdered wig.

After three thuds of the bailiff's staff ended the murmured exchanges, a command was given for the accused to render his account. With the bitter tang of anger still thick upon his tongue, Viktor approached the high-backed oaken seat — a seat that had so long stoked proud fires and covetous desires; now more akin to an instrument of torture. How soon ambitions evaporate!

Settled uncomfortably beneath his father's unrelenting gaze and the council's expectant eyes, Viktor commenced his pitiable account: a litany of denials and deflections; a desperate attempt to salvage the remnants of honour from the wreckage of his reputation.

Venomous curses deluged from all sides. Vanguard, the father of the deceased bellowed the loudest for a full investigation to expose the corrupt dealings of the so infamous rake of a man. Restitution demanded the gallows noose, even the swift justice of the guillotine's blade.

Gustav exploded at last like a flash of hot lightning. His palms came crashing down, the crack of which was not unlike a fissuring glacier. "You peck and prod at this useless cockerel, when injustice still stokes the blaze beneath my house and treasonous vipers yet crawl free?"

"Let us not divert the subject," rejoined another guild master. "The young corrupt must be dealt with according to the laws of our land. Should we falter, this will further sully the illustrious name of our canton, and prove an eternal blight on history's annals."

Again, the chamber descended into a stridency of discord with ministers locked in a fierce tug of war over the proposed sentence.

Moving swiftly to check this breach, the bailiff lunged forward, but he was stayed by Adolfus' raised hand.

"Esteemed officials," began Adolfus, pacing with deliberate steps before the assembly, "though no excuse may mitigate this scandal, neither will the culprit's lynching. Wisdom to prevail over wrath. I propose a temporary asylum under vigilant watch beyond our borders, allowing time for a thorough investigation to unearth the truth and guide us towards a just reconciliation."

"*Exile?*" Viktor's face blazed with the inferno of inner *sturm und drang*.

"Yes, exile!" Adolfus struck the floor with his cane in a declaration of irrevocable fate. "And my kinsmen in Austria will happily assist!"

Thus, was the decree of exile cemented by unanimous consent before Viktor could even summon any defence or plea for the paternal affection once bestowed upon him by his father.

As the chamber emptied, Viktor was marshalled through the doors, bound for his temporary confines until the dawn of his banishment. However, his eyes now caught a shocking glimpse through an adjacent doorway. There, Adolfus and his cohorts were already weaving their next web of intrigue; they presently bestowed upon Vitus, what was unmistakably the mantle of favour once worn by Viktor himself.

Indeed, a vengeful conflagration ignited within Viktor's brain. His body convulsed with an urge to unleash his wrath upon the usurper who had so deftly stolen his place. But alas, he was dragged away before he could effect this...

***

The arrival of Vitus' message instantly set Peter's mind and breast overwrought. At the ticking mantel clock, he stole glances and cursed; only the fourth hour had just passed. How was he ever to endure such jittery pangs until he was to next hear from his brother?

Caught in the throes of anxious anticipation, he paced wild circuits about the bedchamber: he sat at the window, flung it open for air; got up, paced back and forth; sat down, got up again; glanced repeatedly at the dial, at the window, at the note — which this whole time left not his trembling grasp.

Into this scene, Harris entered and begged for clues to decipher the cause of his apparent and yet silent distress. But Peter only replied, "ask me not now!" He wiped his fevered brow. "Ask me when this is all over."

23 – 24 July 1792

***

From our hero, we shift our gazes to that scheming devil, Adolfus: "What?!" raged he at the rogues who, having brought word of their ill-success in apprehending the forger, shrank from the wrath which met them like a hurricane.

"Fools! Dolts! Undeserving dogs! To let victory slide through your clumsy fingers!" Each syllable spat was punctuated by thrashing the quailing men with his ebony cane. "Neither pity nor patience await those who fail my edicts!"

Another violent crack announced the cane snapping across a man's hunched back. Noting his broken instrument of vengeance, Adolfus' vehemence only soared to greater heights. Barely had he driven his boot into the cowering men's shins when he, suffering the fatigues of his own violence or the miserable reality of his schemes' demise, stumbled backwards.

Before he fully collapsed, the bloodied and humiliated men hurried to brace their reeling master into a high-backed chair. There, at his feet, they abased themselves and pleaded for undeserved mercy.

But Adolfus sat deafened by calamity's crushing implication; robbed even of the will to rebuke their affronts for striving to mitigate such death-deserving incompetence.

The sudden entrance of Arnborg, however, jolted Adolfus back. "*Where have you been?*" He struggled up. "Do you not know the heavens are about to crash down on us?"

Yet, before Arnborg could reply, in burst another messenger — wild eyed. "They've taken him — the copyist! To Thun! And Vitus rides off with the confession as we speak!"

"C-c-c-confession?" This news struck Adolfus with the force of a fatal blow.

Arnborg, though looking no less overawed by this intelligence, seized upon the informant by his collar. "What precisely did he confess?"

"Naught connecting your noble circle yet. But once Vitus returns..." His words died as Arnborg tightened his stranglehold at the man's throat.

"Returns from where?" hissed Arnborg. "Detail his movements!"

The man only choked out uncertainties. Thus, thrusting the useless informant aside, Arnborg mobilised action. "I will ride this instant with my fastest men to intercept Vitus first. My instincts say we pick up his scent at his private townhouse."

As Arnborg charged out of the room, Adolfus roused his remaining faculties to action. He speared one agent with a smouldering command: "Rally all spies to Vitus' recent haunts and tear that confession from his clutching hands at all costs! Our lives hang by a meagre thread already!" And fixing his cold, determined leer upon the other men: "Make for Thun and silence the prisoner there! Before his tongue unleashes the headsman upon us all! Go now unless you wish to savour slow death by my own hand!"

***

Whilst such storms raged in proud Bern, treacherous gales likewise brewed across the pastoral Bubendorf this day. Forgetting not that mercenary Lucerne band who tracked Lizzie from Liestal and later regrouped with their comrades to plan their attack, the consequence of this was about to unfold.

For weeks, they had lain in wait, observing the comings and goings from a remote refuge. Indeed, their patience frayed with each passing hour. But today, their vigil — carried out through the magnifying gaze of a spyglass — had finally borne fruit, or so they thought.

Mistaking a straw-hatted fellow (face concealed in shadows) for their actual target, working the fields with Ernest and Emil (the latter they recognised from Lucerne), the brigands set into motion a series of events that would lead to grievous outcomes. They had just sent for their fellow ruffians, who now joined them, when the stranger (confused with Peter) retreated alone to the chalet. Fuelled by the anticipation of capture, the relentless mob surged towards what they believed to be the culmination of their pursuit.

Down the hill they galloped to the humble structure and stole inside, flooding the kitchen just as the startled man, preparing refreshments, spun round.

23 – 24 July 1792

Before the fellow could act, six pistols clicked fast round his head, forming a grim halo. A crumpled WANTED poster was thrust beside his bearded face.

But there, to the leader's no little horror and the mutual shock of all involved, stood the wrong man! Though tall and ruggedly built, no similarity was to be found between the faces.

Though outnumbered, this hot-blooded youth, more defiant than wise, gave sudden vent to his indignation. Bellowing such profanities as to make worthy ears tingle, he threw some hearty cuffs indeed at those nearest, his mallet-sized fists cracking noses like nutshells, issuing forth several bloody torrents. Then, snatching a chair — fortunately the ugly seat which Peter erenow repeatedly scorned — he got to smashing it over the invaders' skulls.

Natch, distressed to have been thwarted again in their schemes, and incensed at this defiant uprising, the brigands unleashed their full fury; they rained ruthless blows upon the bold youth now awash in his own crimson tributaries.

Alerted to the racket, Ernest and Emil burst in to the kitchen.

Seeing the assault, they joined the fray and got to heartily wielding kitchenware against the intruders. So, the humble scullery became the battleground — iron pots and pans being smashed viciously into outlawed brains.

For a time, all went remarkably in the favour of our daring trio.

But the tide soon turned.

Ernest was sent hurtling across the trenches into the stove. With a sickening crack, the back of his head bore the impact. He crashed to the ground, convulsing wildly, while dark blood gushed out beneath his matted hair.

Frozen by their unintentional brutality, even these callous souls felt wings of judgement stir the stagnant air. None dared move against the young men crouched over the fallen hero, but all rallied for retreat. Quitting the chalet, they returned to their waiting horses.

As the galloping hooves faded, and Emil screamed for help, pressing rags tight over torn flesh and shattered bone — tears blurring every attempt to assess the damage or slow the scarlet which seeped between his fingers — 'twas into this horrific scene that Lizzie now arrived.

One look at the gruesome tableau unleashed several anguished screams. But commanding her terror and firming her quaking limbs, she flew to the sink.

There, she fetched water, gathered linen, and hastened to her father's aid, striving to staunch the blood flow.

Tears soon fell from her eyes; her vision swam scarlet with dread. Clasping her father's calloused, limp hands close to her bosom, she rocked back and forth. "Father," cried she, sobbing contrition's pangs. "My *dearest* Father. This is all *my fault.*"

At her voice, Ernest's eyes fluttered open and looked into hers. But already the reaper's veil obscured all earthly sight.

One last convulsion preceded a chilling stillness. His eyes fell shut and his chest finally motionless as Death's dark angel swept his gentle soul away...

Lo! Death hungered for a more macabre feast on this ill-fated day. His skeletal finger and sickle now pointed towards the once proud halls of Ebenrain, stilling all birdsong as black dread thickened the mists wreathing its grounds.

We find its first betrayal in the bloodied, trembling, and gasping footman who clambered up the steps onto the pristine rear veranda.

"Merciful heavens!" Johannes's wife recoiled from the sight. "What barbarism has marred your face so?" Sensing something tragic deep within her marrow, she rose from her seat and looked through the rows of opened interior doors that afforded a view out to the front courtyard. "Where is the carriage?" The tightening noose of cold instinct closed round her throat. "And Johannes?"

The footman flung his ravaged body at her feet. "We were attacked, my lady."

"*Attacked?*" shrieked she. But governing her trepidation, she stooped down and raised the footman's blood and dirt-streaked face with her trembling hand. "Explain your meaning."

"It was in the hills..." The man's blackened and bloodied eyes bulged, delirious with fear. "The coachman, my lady — the horses, all of them, they... they went over the — and my... my lord, he, too — I am so sorry, my lady. But only I survived."

"*Only y —?*" Her hands flew to her mouth as a frightened gasp tore from her breast. Overcome by a sudden light-headedness, all strength fled her limbs. Overwhelmed, she fell backwards, the remains of her sanity now lying buried alongside her cherished husband, lost somewhere amongst the craggy rocks.

***

Back in Bern: upon reaching Jegenstorf, Vitus hastened to his father's bedchamber. There, he found Gustav again sallow and feeble beneath the quilted covers; his aged constitution taxed by an endless train of calamities. Beside the ailing patriarch sat his valet and the chancellor, each a silent sentinel in this chamber of intimacies and revelations.

"My dear boy." With the valet's aid, Gustav forced his rigid limbs to sit up to receive his son. "Pray, tell me you bring good news?"

Vitus, his face alight with triumph, unfurled his victories. After reading aloud the apprehended forger's testimony, he declared his intentions of storming this eve into the lair of whoever was, according to the counterfeiter, the backers of this monstrous scheme.

"How you lift this old man's spirits," exclaimed Gustav; a flicker of strength returned to his eyes. "Fortune and family both delivered from the wolves that seek to rip us apart!" He took his son's hand. "This document, along with Valentin's testimony of the scroll's existence, will certainly restore the so long-hindered order of our world."

Vitus' bright mien faded into one of gravity. "I must yet reveal something else, Father." Seeing Gustav steady himself, he, too, took a bracing breath. "The forger informed me that neither you nor Valentin were the first to... have *fallen prey* to the same malignant forces."

The chancellor flushed red, but Gustav paled; a haunting gleam darkened his eyes. He retracted his hand. "If you are burdened with apprising me of the late schultheissin's unfortunate demise, assuage yourself in the knowledge that I am already aware of it."

Vitus started at these words. "But *how*? When —"

"Is Valentin aware of this?" interrupted Gustav, his voice firm despite his weakened state.

Vitus shook his head. "I felt it right that I should come here first and —"

"Then press me no further on this matter, my child. 'Tis a dark moment in this entangled history I would rather forget. Be assured it is my intention to tell Valentin in due time. But until then, please reveal not a word of this to him."

"Of course."

"Now, my son, there is another delicate matter which, when revealed, shall surely roil the court. Pray, say nought of this exchange, but heed my words: would you willingly surrender your claim upon my seat to see our line of succession secured through Valentin?"

"My claim? Father, what...? I am not even — does Varus not stand as heir-apparent?"

Gustav waved aside this comment. "Worry not about that. Simply promise me should I soon fall amidst the chaos, our canton shall not." Seeing Vitus hesitate, torn between confusion and twin loyalties, Gustav pressed on. "My son, dire times necessitate difficult covenants no proud man should demand. Yet demand I must."

For a long, tense moment, Vitus grappled with the weight of his father's request. But kindhearted and ever-devoted to his brother, who, however only a half-brother, was so beloved, fidelity won out. He confessed he could not be happier to do so.

Gustav slumped back, releasing the breath that had paralysed his lungs as he awaited his son's response. "Your noble pledge lifts a vast weight, my son." As if possessed by some portending urgency, he implored his valet to fetch ink and paper. "I would see the future of our canton secured whilst strength endures. For whilst you and Varus prove noble heirs, Fate's tempering has distilled in Valentin the mettle of leadership this era requires."

With writing implements fetched, Gustav shakily penned the fate-sealing words rescinding Varus' claim; sole heirship was assigned to the still-outcast Valentin. "Preserve this epochal order secretly," charged he of the visibly bemused chancellor. "Once our family is fully redeemed from all reproach, I will convene with the Small Council to enforce this change."

Strength near spent, Gustav begged leave to rest his taxed frame.

Bowing obediently, Vitus and the astounded chancellor quit the chamber. The latter set off for home with the edict. The former hastened to his old chamber to pen two vital messages: one for Bern, urgently summoning Peter to some

23 – 24 July 1792

inconspicuous inn; the other, the opposite direction, requesting reinforcements from Burgdorf's leagues.

Vitus had but affixed the wax seals when footfalls hammered, announcing a wild-faced messenger. "Master! Dire tidings! Some strange blackguards have been searching for you at your recent refuges and meeting places. You are certainly marked for ambush!"

"Blast!" Vitus tore his first letter up and scrawled another — his movements feverish with the chase now raised by the jaws which snapped at their very heels — calling Peter again to the Münsterplattform, at the eleventh hour. "Convey this with utmost expedience to my brother."

With the second message despatched to Burgdorf, Vitus himself set off for Bern, the urgency of his mission marked by both destiny and danger.

Alas, Fortune proved fickle once more amidst the perilous mission afoot. For no sooner had the galloping couriers departed than a treacherous servant betrayed their directions to Adolfus' agents, who already massed nearby.

The first outrider, bound for Bern, eluded capture; he disappeared into mist-cloaked forests after a breathless chase, leaving pursuers grasping at shadows. No such providence shone on the second rider spurring urgently towards Burgdorf. Run to the ground like a fox, the valiant courier before long lay slaughtered in a crimson heap; his lifeblood leached into the thirsty soil. Rough hands rifled through his vestments — the marked parchment claimed as rightful spoils.

***

Elsewhere, in the cold halls of power, Adolfus waited with choking expectation as precious time haemorrhaged through his clenching fists. At last, his henchmen returned, bearing aloft a bloodied parchment.

Tearing it from the brigand's grasp, Adolfus ripped it open and read:

> *I have arrested a chief agent and possess a document that will overturn our enemy's treacheries. Despatch the guards to Bern city forthwith. Come*

> *to me at the Münsterplattform. At the eleventh*
> *hour, I meet with the future aid of our confederacy.*
> *Vitus*

In that instant, something ruptured in Adolfus' psyche. His frame shook and contorted — reason overwhelmed by visceral denial warring with visions of gore. Snatching up his quill, he scrawled his next orders. "Take this to the Tatzelwurms!" He shoved it into one ruffian's hands. "Only they can now avert this disaster and retrieve that damning confession! Once delivered, go to that inn and apprehend whoever it was Vitus frequented!"

***

Meantime, Viktor, confined to his opulent yet oppressive quarters in the west wing, he, with armed sentries posted beyond the imposing doors, had seethed all day at the disastrous reversals. Stripped of mobility and influence before impending exile, he shuddered with rage.

Despite his gilded confinement, he kept abreast of all that went on in the city. Through a trusted informant, news reached him of Vitus' wielding proof enough to destroy many people, and some affair set to commence the countdown at the Münsterplattform at eleven.

Action being necessary to stay an aftermath that would undoubtedly sweep him away too, Viktor called for wine solely to test the moustached guard who entered. The man's appetite for status and wealth was soon touched upon. After very little hesitation, and a liberal greasing of his palm, the guard (pondering the lavish possibilities promised for extending a sympathetic understanding to the soon to be exiled noble) released the prisoner.

Till dawn, Viktor was granted his release.

Consequently, freed to stealth down a back stairwell, Viktor flung into the night. Bent on taking matters into his own, blood-thirsty hands, to recover what was ripped away from him, he charged forth.

Neither Heaven nor Hell would deny Viktor his just dues!

23 – 24 July 1792

***

Peter had just received Vitus' message when word arrived also from Franz. Temporarily back in the city, he wished to meet urgently. With the tenth hour barely upon him, our hero set off along the cobbled streets, cutting through the creeping fog and murky night's tension.

Peter was soon at the meeting place. There, he learned Franz had discovered the den of his former, now rogue allies. By means of cruel force, he extracted from them several significant details about the funeral attack. As suspected, the incident was indeed orchestrated by a secret society lurking within Bern's city walls. Few, however, were the details obtained about this society and their goal. But 'twas apparent they were a branch of the infamous Tatzelwurms.

"The devils must pay for their crimes!" Peter's blood proverbially boiled. "But why are you so interested in this society, Franz?"

Franz fell quiet; a sinister expression darkened his eyes.

Peter was about to repeat the question when a nearby clock tolled a quarter hour to the fateful eleven o'clock rendezvous.

"I must go." He sprang to his feet; anticipation thrummed at fever pitch along every nerve. "After tonight, I, too, hope to have good news to report."

***

Cloaked in the ancient cathedral's penumbral veil, Vitus stood poised behind the cold ironwork gates. The Münsterplattform lay before him, bathed in the moon's ghostly luminescence. To know that he and his brother would soon unmask they who had reigned terror upon their family, Vitus' heart swelled like a tumultuous sea.

To confound all who he suspected might seek to thwart his purpose, he sent several decoys to the recently surveilled locations. But had he truly outmanoeuvred all ubiquitous eyes? For if Fortune's scales tipped by even one degree, enemies lurking anywhere could rip this triumph away with violent hands.

At length, seeing no soul present along the gravelled avenues, among the shadows, swirling fog, chestnuts, or hedged lawns, he — his hand hovering near his sword's hilt, ready to parry Fate's cruel jest should it leap from the shadows — quit his shelter and hastened towards the stone pavilion.

At first, naught but his own jarring footfalls crunched sharply against the ill-feeling silence — each step invoking terror and hope in equal measures.

But then something struck his hearing.

Barely had he paused to glance around — his breaths quick and shallow — when, without warning, there came a rush of air; a presence behind him, too real and too late to elude.

Pain — searing, blinding, consuming — exploded through his back, impaling his chest. Vision flashing white, blood — life's essence — betrayed him, flooding his mouth.

With razor-like agony shredding his lungs, the blade was wrenched free.

He collapsed with a wordless cry.

Vicious hands rifled through his clothes, seizing the blood-stained prize.

It was now that Peter arrived. Through the curling fog, he beheld his brother's fallen silhouette. Another sword-bearing faceless form, clad in sable, stood over him.

With a wrathful cry — part roar, part anguished — Peter drew his own blade and charged forward.

The startled villain was driven back as Vitus' strangled gasps fuelled Peter's fury to disarm his opponent.

But the dance of death is ever unpredictable.

For mid-clash with this masked foe, another viper sprang from the shadows. Before Peter could whirl to confront the new threat, a foot smashed into his back, sending him sprawling in pain across the gravel mere inches from Vitus' outstretched hand.

This new assailant, cold and commanding, bade Vitus' slayer to run.

Then, in a blink, a glistening blade-edge was at Peter's taut throat.

In these harrowing moments — held as an agonised witness to his dear brother's shuddering death-throes — Peter traced the blade's line to its hilt, and then to the viper's wrist: there, coiled the sinister Tatzelwurm, erasing all doubt of these monsters' vile sponsorship.

Just then, boots thundered upon the ground, forcing the villains' retreat.

As most gave chase, someone rushed over to our hero — 'twas Vitus' agent. "You must go!"

"I cannot leave him!" He scrambled to clasp Vitus' blood-soaked body. "Please, you must live!"

But already, the light in Vitus' eyes had dimmed. "Brother..." gasped he, still coughing up deep red. "You deserve... it always was..." A smile flickered on his face and then his head fell backwards.

"Vitus?" Peter pulled him closer. "*Vitus*?!"

"You must away, now!" again commanded Vitus' man. "Go!"

***

A couple of hours hence, word reached the schultheiss that his second youngest had met so violent a death, and that his swaddled corpse was borne below stairs. Scarce can any quill convey the depthless grief that convulsed the old man's shattered frame.

Such agonised wailings issued from his soul as to chill blood itself. Deaf to his wife's and his servants' pleas, Gustav commanded they lead him to where he might behold his child's body.

Alas, he had but reached the balustrades beyond his own apartment when mortal catastrophe seized his straining heart. A wheezing gasp escaped his cadaverous lips; he clawed at his breast as strength quit his shaking limbs.

Clinging desperately onto his valet, eyes bulging, the stricken schultheiss then collapsed and crashed in a headlong tumble down the stairs.

Thus, did a devoted heart break irreparably at the loss of a treasured son snatched mercilessly away.

***

In the wake of tragedy, a tavern's muted light and numbing libations offered Peter little refuge from his torment. There, amidst the fug of smoke and the murmur of inconsequential conversation, he sought to drown the pain that gnawed at his soul.

But his meagre solace was short-lived. For even as he imbibed the spirituous anaesthetic, the outside world intruded with a portentous clamour, tearing him from the deepening chasm.

The mighty minster bell cut through a summer storm air, its peals resonating with an ominous finality. These sombre tolls, soon magnified by a chorus of surrounding steeples, blared for one reason alone: for the end of a life — a pillar in Peter's world now crumbled.

Compelled by a force greater than the intoxication that clouded his senses, Peter stumbled out into the tempest.

The heavens wept in torrents. Thunderclaps roared above. Windows, like eyes suddenly wide with shock, lit up in the darkness as crowds gathered in the streets.

Their voices loudening with the swelling numbers, melded with the relentless rain as they bore witness to the tidings that shocked every hearer:

"The schultheiss is dead?" repeated from mouth to mouth, "the schultheiss is dead?" confirming the dread that cleaved our hero's heart.

Still sounding their grim proclamation, the death knells prolonged the tumultuous symphony of the night — flashes of lightning, the reverberating drum of thunder, the relentless downpour.

Our hero's knees, as if severed from the strings of his will, buckled beneath him. He collapsed to the waterlogged cobblestones.

Eyes cast aloft, stinging with the sharp kiss of rain and the bitter salt of tears, he sought an answer, a reprieve, from the indifferent expanse above.

"Father?!" cried he.

But his anguished cries were merely drowned by Nature's own remorseless lament...

23 – 24 July 1792

Act 3

24 July 1792

—

21 August 1792

24 JULY 1792

Having been consigned to the deepest depths of desolation; abandoned to all probabilities; left to Fortune's mercy, and having passed the nocturnal hours in a drunken stupor at the before-mentioned tavern, Peter — under the oppressive morning sun's rays — finally made his staggered return to the inn.

In a twist most unexpected, he barely crossed the rear threshold into the scullery's domain when the innkeeper rushed upon him. Her phiz wrought by consternation and her sole eye awash with sleepless sorrow, she was in a state of such frenzied distress and breathless haste as to render our hero believing some further misfortune had descended.

Alas, 'twas so. Upon his brain, the matron delivered fresh blows, relaying the dire news that scarce after Peter quit the inn the night before, the unfortunate Harris had been spirited away by a band of malefactors most vile.

"'Twas a most sinister crew that beset me," shrilled she. "A blade they brandished, as menacing as the Grim Reaper's own scythe! I stood a mere hair's breadth from death as the scoundrels menaced me about my lodger — about you. Though I managed to keep my counsel, I confess I did let slip in my nerves that someone of worth lodged with me. Up the stairs they stormed, and in less than a minute, poor Harris was hauled down, his hands bound and his head entombed in a sack most foul. I pleaded for mercy, but every word fell on ears as deaf as adders — their gazes were as wicked as Lucifer's, I'll wager! They threatened to despatch me to the hereafter should I dare to involve the Landjäger or pursue them. With that, out into the night, they dragged Harris, tossing him like a corpse into their wagon, which then tore off like a chariot bound for Hades!"

"Good lord!" Peter sought the support of the door frame.

Truly, the vicissitudes of his plight seemed unending. Though his sentiments towards Harris were lukewarm at best, an inexplicable compulsion to assume responsibility for the fellow's fate weighed upon him; another encumbrance, unbidden yet irrefutable, added to the burdens he must bear.

His mind, adrift in the sea of his misfortunes, now clung to the single lifeline of action: to rescue Harris was imperative. But since the captors' identity was a mystery, and to uncover their whereabouts would be a task near to impossible, our hero direly needed assistance.

To beloved Vitus' men, I must appeal for aid!

Meanwhile, the innkeeper, now lost in her own soliloquy, bemoaned the schultheiss' untimely death and the ensuing days of mourning that would put a most unwelcome pause to her commercial endeavours. "Ten days of sackcloth and ashes!" shrilled she. "'Tis the worst inconvenience! Of all the times to pop his clogs, he goes and kicks the bucket in high-summer!"

Though oppressed by a tempest of dread, grief, and incredulity — each vying for dominion — our hero, sudden anger shooting to his brain, rounded on the impertinent and unfeeling wench. "Hold that tongue of yours, woman!"

To be sure, the one-eyed matron cowered and trembled.

But during the ensuing silence, the woman's memory jolted; she remembered two messages delivered at the crack of dawn. With a bustle, she retrieved and handed them over.

Peter eyed the first, and, noting Franz's script, he tore it open.

> *My deepest sympathies. It is not my intent to compound your sorrows, nor can I claim any certainty of a link. However, I am compelled to convey a troubling observation: my men tell me that someone, resembling Viktor was spotted near the Münsterplattform last night. Though he has certainly since been escorted unto his planned exile, for my part, I fear, in this intermission, his involvement in your brother's passing. This information, I hope, will guide your quest for truth and best steer your sword. Franz.*

What words can sufficiently represent the horror, the confusion, the utter dejection which rend our hero's heart and mind alike! For some moments, this report robbed him of all reason. *But how could Viktor have been there? He was held under house arrest...*

Recollecting the other missive in hand, he tore it open with a mixture of trepidation and urgency. The words within read:

> *Come to the Café Littéraire with all the haste you can muster. Our oaths once sworn to Vitus are now bound to you; as are our influence and resources.*

***

Dear, patient reader, lend me now your ear, for 'tis incumbent upon me to convey the gentlest of reminders that the tapestry of our tale is woven with more threads than one. For whilst you have, I hope, followed with rapt attention our hero's perilous journey in the prior act's culmination, other matters, or rather revelations, took place. These events being of consequence to our history must be recounted. It is thus, with a respectful bow to time's inexorable passage, that I beseech you to cast your mind's eye back but a small measure of hours.

If Harris ever had cause for lamenting his dogged pursuance of Peter, it was certainly now he most painfully felt the woebegone circumstance in which he found himself most inextricably mired. To have been carried off in so base a manner by such nefarious fiends — all in the relentless obscurity of his blindfold and sack — to a locality as mysterious to him as the farside of the moon, he rightly attributed the outrage to his being mistaken for Peter.

'Twould be an understatement to inscribe here that the notion had flitted across Harris' mind that upon the removal of his ignoble gag, he should set the record straight with the knaves! But he was not so bereft of sense as to have been ignorant of the consequences such a revelation might provoke. To wit, it might have served rather to expedite his journey from this mortal coil than secure his emancipation. Thus, he counselled himself to hold his tongue once it was liberated. He would feign an abyss of ignorance concerning Peter and, in an act of most refined deception, claim an ill-motive for his intrusion into his chamber. To pretend to such roguish, thieving calibre was his best chance for survival.

Hence, at the behest of a voice, both deep and laden with malevolent undertones, Harris had at last been liberated from darkness' velvety shackles. His

24 July 1792

gaze met with a candle-lit chamber, its shadows pooling like ink in the recesses.

The daunting, conspicuous aspect of a man cloaked in authority — whose malice seemed to writhe in the crevices and shadows of his twitching visage — scrutinised Harris from tousled pate to scuffed boots. "*This* is the specimen in question?" said he.

From behind, an equally austere voice issued, apprising the apparent ring-leader of what the innkeeper had explained to them in her trembling state.

"You assert, upon the shivering declaration of some tavern matron," replied the other, eyeing Harris with increasing contempt, "that *this* is a man of some note? Even without his provincial attire, I discern nothing but the most profound mediocrity even in his deportment."

With a gesture that brooked no dissent, the ring-leader — Adolfus — ordered the captive's gag be removed.

To be sure, Harris took a deep, bracing breath.

"Who are you?" demanded Adolfus. "And what is your connection with Vitus?"

"Who?" Harris feigned as much ignorance and guile as he could muster.

Ere the impatient blood could fully ascend to Adolfus' contorted face, another character burst into the room.

This addition to the mob, countenance twisted with a malignant glee, bore no honourable qualities. There appeared to be blood spattered all over his garb.

"*Viktor?*" Adolfus' hostile mien melted to anxious pallor. "How is it you...?" His voice quavered. "What devilry have you wrought? That sanguine stain — whose blood is —?"

"Our path is now unencumbered of all perils!" Viktor cut across him with a smile of nigh demonic fervour. With a flourish of his blood-stained hand, he produced a similarly stained folded paper and flung it at Adolfus' feet. "Your gratitude can wait."

With marked anxiety and several glowers, Adolfus swooped down, snatched it up, and crossed to the room's far side. As he scanned the stained document, his eyes flashed with the intensity of lightning. Therein were the words that had almost doomed him to certain demise.

Moments passed where he stood like one struck dead through the heart.

Yet, mastering himself, he cleared his throat, marshalled his composure, and shoved the bloodied document into a draw. Slowly, he pivoted round on Viktor. "How did you obtain — no, rather, from *whom* did you obtain this?"

Viktor smirked. "You ask as if you pretend not already to know..."

Adolfus' eyes narrowed. "*Pretend*...? Surely you do not mean —"

"What *else* could I mean?" Viktor embellished these words with an air of cruel complacence. "As I said, all our encumbrances are now no more."

As grey storm clouds steal over a sky, Adolfus' face darkened. In but a few strides, he closed the distance and lashed out, striking Viktor. "When will you *ever* learn?! In your reckless attempts to reverse your own disaster, you have solely spawned another!"

Adolfus went to strike him again, but Viktor grabbed the incoming wrist. "Your fury is misplaced; direct it at your own incompetents who failed to extract this damning evidence in the first instance! I have averted your ruin. You owe me thanks, not censure. Even now, you need me as much as I need you."

"Owe you thanks? *Need you*?" Adolfus hissed at him. "I have no use for impetuous fools who, in their myopia and avarice, threaten to collapse all that I have engineered." His fire and ice gaze swept over to his men. "Remove this pestilence from my sight and ensure his expulsion to Austria is immediate!"

Indeed, Viktor kicked, screamed, vented, spat, and wrestled against the hands which dragged him from the room while Adolfus, turning his back on him, ordered two men to hasten to Schloss Jegenstorf to contain every report of Vitus' passing. To the remaining mob, he ordered them to watch over the captive. At this, Adolfus then stormed out.

Around two hours passed before Adolfus returned. Looking only all the more agitated, he stalked back and forth across the space, all the while his cane striking his ire and fears into the boards; all the while Harris' dread-filled eyes fixed on his erratic movements.

Of a sudden, several other ruffians rushed in. After bowing nervously to their lord, they bore news of their return from Basel, and their discovery that the sought-after scroll bearer was, in fact, to be found somewhere in Bern city.

"What?!" Adolfus staggered backwards. "*Here*? In *Bern*?" Struck with

24 July 1792

palpable terror and violent tremblings, he glanced wildly about. "If Gustav learns of this... we... we are *doomed*! Locate that man and —" Stopping short, he rounded on Harris with dawning realisation.

He levelled a finger. "*You!*" At that, he snatched a sword from the nearest rogue's hilt and swung it at Harris' neck. "You are he, are you not?!"

"M-m-*me*...?" Harris' eyes alighted on the glinting blade.

"Yes, *you!*"

'Twas at this moment, however — sword in hand, poised to slice Harris' throat — as the loud rumblings of a storm burst overhead and bells blared with incessant tolls, that Adolfus' fiery rage dampened, supplanted by a sudden, icy chill. Indeed, his mind foresaw, like a prophecy, a spectre most horrific.

"Great God above!" Blade cast aside, he flew to the casement and flung it wide — the flashing, clattering, booming, and knelling instantly flooding in. Indeed, the bells indeed betokened something more dooming: that of Gustav's passing. "This *cannot* be?!"

***

Resuming with the present timeline: in a discreet cellar in the Matte District, our righteous Bernese Stadtwache fellows had gathered around a rough-hewn wooden table to deliberate on key events related in the preceding chapter.

"With the schultheiss' passing," said Meier, gnawing on his knuckle, "we face a fresh wave of uncertainty. Vigilance, my friends, is more vital than ever."

The atmosphere was taut with apprehension; each countenance betrayed an acute unease. None seemed willing to raise their eyes, as if the very act of meeting another's gaze might invite the spectre of doubt to take hold.

Keller, drumming his fingers into the worn oak, at length looked up. "And now, with Viktor's sudden exile, how are we to proceed?"

"But there remains the network," replied Marta, lifting her gaze, her calloused hands clasped tightly before her. "They will still be active. We should focus our efforts on securing more evidence against Viktor's connections."

Meier nodded in agreement. "And let us not forget the corrupt officials we must still expose."

Marta's dark eyes glinted with resolve. "Viktor's exile may actually prove to be an *advantage* to our cause..." Her words hung in the air like a prophecy.

All eyes shifted to the corporal. "I suppose," said he, "by this 'advantage'" — his large hand mauled his square jaw — "you mean without Viktor's presence, his protection and bribes are removed?"

Bieri and Steiner (the patrolmen), silent until now — stuffing their maws with Berner Honiglebkuchen, its spicy gingerbread aroma marrying the cellar's musty scent — suddenly piped up, only to set about speaking simultaneously. Their words, echoing each other's, tumbled out in a rush of excited rapidity, causing naught but confusion and sundry headaches among their auditors.

"Gentlemen!" Meier's eyebrows crashed. "One at a time, *please*."

What followed was a bout of petty sparring and squabbling; a display of childish rivalry that defied the meeting's gravity. But at last, the two men resorted to a time-honoured method of settling disputes:

"*Lass uns eine Entscheidung treffen. Bär oder Kreuz?*" cried they.

For the benefit of our English readers, this translates to:

"Let's make a decision. Bear or Cross?"

Thus, a half-batzen coin was flipped into the air. It arced through space nigh as momentous as the tosses that determined criminality, property, and marriage of ancient Rome... But anyhow, the coin landed squarely on the back of Bieri's hand; it revealed the cross, granting Steiner the privilege of speech.

"As I was saying," began he, only to be echoed by Bieri, insisting he had before said the same. Steiner rolled his eyes. "Very well. We were *both* saying if we gather enough evidence in this case against Viktor, we can oust that corrupt captain who's been stealing away evidence and accepting bribes this past year."

"Yes." Meier got up and paced back and forth. "And with the political turmoil soon to unfold, we might identify potential allies among any new leadership who can strengthen our position. If we obtain fresh testimonies from the witnesses whose statements were destroyed and present this to Secret Council, we can at least begin the cleanup of our own house. But we will also need to get hold of any ledgers and correspondence..." He returned to the table and ground his knuckles into its worn wood. "The captain will most probably communicate with whoever was paying him off. We *must* intercept that route."

24 July 1792

All present chorused in accord.

"But *who* is behind Viktor's undoing?" said Keller. "That stunt with the balloons has to have been the invention of some well-connected mastermind!"

All concurred this was likely so.

Bieri and Steiner resumed filling their mouths.

"By the way," — Marta snatched the food bag off them — "where is Felix?"

Mier looked at her with a smile. "He claims to have some mission to complete; one which will apparently convince us of our need for his help..."

***

From the cellar, we turn our attention to another location. Our hero, having been taken to a safe house, convened with the deceased Vitus' agents to deliberate on tackling the secret society and their unforgivable crimes.

Peter crashed his fist down on the table. "We must apprehend every last one of these accursed Tatzelwurms!"

The twenty men, garbed in blue coats, white sashes, and glinting Bernese medals — seated about a large round mahogany table that dominated the vermilion-walled room — showed unwavering attention. The atmosphere crackled with a tension born of urgency and a shared appetency for vengeance. Though grief scarred each countenance, an attestation to the loss endured, it was tempered by the fierce resolve of men trained in the art of war.

"My sole comfort," continued Peter, gazing at each man, "is found in knowing you seized one of those villains. But can you truly not take me to him?"

Again, our hero met with a uniform refusal. With the villain's comrades potentially seeking to liberate their fellow manslayer, it was deemed too perilous.

"Very well," answered Peter. "But you are certain you will extract from him what we need to know? And you have ensured he cannot prematurely and immutably silence himself?"

A confident yet silent nod corroborated every certainty in this matter.

This was something, at least.

"Left unrestrained," resumed our hero as he fought back his emotions, "they are a most dangerous sword, bound to be wielded anew by so unscrupulous and minacious a..." the heartache of such profound personal loss momentarily choked off his words. How was he ever to endure such filial and fraternal loss?

But now was *not* the time to grieve. "If Viktor *is* behind this attack," resumed Peter, "no matter the distance of exile, he will give no consideration to honour or scruple... *Varus* will surely be the object of his next assault."

But with Viktor now en route to Austria, how were they to confirm or nullify their suspicions? How were they ever to explain why Vitus had to perish?

"I" — Peter raised a hand — "will pursue justice until I have avenged my kin!"

The gathered men responded in unison: "Nor shall we rest until we have avenged our leader's blood!"

Thus, in their quest for truth and retribution, our hero and his newfound allies set about devising plans. Some, with allegiances to Vitus yet unknown to their potential foes, were sent to infiltrate the ranks in Jegenstorf. Others were tasked with breaching Viktor's dwelling. With the need for additional support, Peter assigned several men to recruit more allies. Two guards would remain at our hero's side within the safety of Neues Schloss Bümpliz, their current haven.

"What of the fellow Harris?" probed one guard. "Do you suppose his abduction is the work of the Tatzelwurms?"

"I cannot say." Peter sighed. "But if it was not, then it would appear our adversaries are more numerous than I care to admit. You must try to find him."

The guard nodded.

"Also, tomorrow, we visit Thun to re-interrogate the forger. Without his testimony, we are but blindly prodding the dark. Whatever confession my brother possessed, its cost him his life. Doubtless, that same fiend who drove him through with the blade is the very one took the damning document."

The guard at Peter's right advised him against retrieving his belongings from the inn. He would undertake the task himself. "Your safety and seclusion are our utmost concern," emphasised he. "Not only for your protection but also to ensure our council goes unnoticed. Meantime, do not leave these premises."

"You have my word." Peter took a sip of water to moisten his arid mouth. "Ah! Might anyone here know anything about the incident at the Antistital visit?

Did Vitus show any of you the message he received the night before?"

Two guards confirmed they had personally seen the note. But as to who sent it, none had yet gleaned any details. Whoever had coordinated the spectacle, they had left no trace as to their presence that day.

As the guards broke off into sundry deliberation, Peter's thoughts drifted elsewhere. In so calamitous a time, having both his father *and* his brother snatched from him, he had again lost the sweet promise of liberty to move freely in the world. From this moment forth, Peter's life only took on a new, dangerous purpose; one that would either restore or inearth him.

A servant entered and made his way to the guard on Peter's right, presenting a letter. Seal broken, the guard hurried his eyes over the lines. "Adolfus will, in the next days, convene with the Small Council," his voice carried a weight that silenced the room, "to enforce Gustav's decree regarding Varus."

"And it will be carnage, I daresay," answered a guard. "The Small Council are so envenomed with discord, even between themselves. Adolfus must have brought this forward in order to..." he abruptly trailed off; his gaze fell to the table as if the weight of his unspoken words were too heavy to bear.

Every gaze slowly shifted from him, gravitating towards Peter, who, though still absorbing the gravity of the man's words, could not help but perceive the presage found therein. "In order to what?" said he, leaning across the table.

All eyes shot back to the guard.

"Forgive me," said he, "but with Viktor's exile, and the... the *grievous* loss of your *significant* family, and with the world believing only Varus remains, the schultheiss' seat will surely draw out the covetous poison that runs through every vein of they who will strive to wield this tragedy to their own advantage..."

***

"Indeed," uttered Adolfus' attendant, his every breath oozing conspiracy, "this may be our opportunity. Now that Gustav is out of the equation, and that rotten little snoop, Vitus, is forever silenced, the council is ripe for the plucking."

Though draped in the finery of his own self-assurance, Adolfus favoured his attendant only with a look of disdain. "I am many things," rasped he, removing his ear from the inelegant counsellor's sibilant lips, "but foolhardy, I am not! And even less so, considering we now contend with some additional inscrutable force that rains down red disruption from the heavens!"

From the bay window, Adolfus withdrew. Verily his indignant hues matched the crimson-damask wall-panels framed in gold. His agitation echoed in the sharp clicks of his cane against the Versailles-patterned flooring.

"Even without this additional, *unknown hinderance* to our schemes," said he, "if we precipitate action in grasping power, it may sooner slip like sand through our fingers — more so, with this unforeseen cry of war between our neighbours! We can no longer manipulate France to our advantage. For now — and until I have received further orders — to maintain the illusion of fealty, we must appear to honour Gustav's legacy. Albrecht will advocate for this as well. As for Varus, he will be removed at *my* choosing! But we must bring forward our plan concerning the mint master. *He* is the one who vexes me the most."

Just then, a distant scream erupted, followed by a footman's curses directed at the troublesome capuchin monkey. Up to its usual tricks and mayhem, the furry fiend had apparently purloined the man's wig and was now scampering about the halls, doffing and donning the toupee as if it were a jester's cap.

"But what of the *other* matter?" resumed the attendant. Like a fly about to alight on a choice morsel, he rubbed his hands together. "With Viktor being dragged off to Austria, I *assume* you will have already found a replacement?"

"I am yet to decide," admitted Adolfus. "To whom I should entrust the timepiece and so delicate a commission is not to be determined lightly..." Halting before the red marble fireplace, he cast an impatient glance at the golden mantel clock: its hands indicated half past three. "What delays that woman?!"

As he met his reflection in the trumeau mirror, he caught sight of the schultheissin approaching from the adjoining Grand Salon. "Vincentia!" Shifting seamlessly his demeanour into one of charm and deference, he offered a bow.

"Oh!" exclaimed she. "*Je suis content que tu sois venu!*"

Perched upon one outstretched hand, elevated like a queen's sceptre, a blue macaw screamed with all its might. In her other hand, she clutched a lead, from which a pug — a diminutive dictator on four legs — dragged her along, barking with all its brawn.

24 July 1792

The schultheissin's menagerie procession, however, came to an abrupt halt; her eyes darted behind. "What *are you* playing at?!" demanded she of a maid presently engaged in a floral arrangement on the centre table. "I stipulated sunflowers; not these dull lilies! Remove them instantly!"

With a puerile huff of annoyance, Vincentia glanced at her reflection in the room's large mirror. Vain as she was, she adjusted the tilt of her red leghorn silk hat — its red and white ostrich plumes rolling like waves — and bestowed upon her reflection an air-kiss.

Adolfus studied her comportment and more particularly her attire — a white petticoat edged with twin laurel bands; a regal red silk redingote cinched at the waist by a corset of white and blue silk ribbon; the very embodiment of French patriotism and extravagance. "Pray tell, why are you *not* in *black*?"

Caught mid-parade in her shuffle, she drew up with an expression of much dramatic surprise. "Darling!" Her drawn-on brows gathered into a sardonic display. "Far too dreary!" And waving him out of her way, she promenaded about the room with her still screeching macaw and still barking mutt. "Would you *truly* have me robed in the colour of quietus, when it is lamentable enough that my countenance must wear so *monstrous* a sorrowful character? Black so *ill suits* my complexion and makes me look *such* a fright."

Adolfus stood quite speechless, struggling to reconcile her frivolous demeanour with the situation's gravity. "But you are *supposed* to be in *mourning*!"

"Pooh!" She let out a jejune huff. The macaw squawked, and the dog growled — a miniature army defending their mistress' folly. "Must I forgo my fashions *and* my smiles? Besides, it is high summer; all eyes are elsewhere, distracted by the manifold delights of the city!"

"Manifold delights of the city?" scoffed Adolfus. "The city is *shut down*!"

"You would have me *expire* of *ennui*, I suppose! Then I shall be in black for all eternity!" In her gaze fluctuated a volatile mixture of inanity and indignation, which only blowing more kisses to her reflection seemed to palliate. "Constrain me further, and I shall soon be no better than a lifeless bird myself in this *ghastly* gilded cage!"

"Indeed, if you continue to shriek so!" muttered Adolfus under his breath.

"*Pardon?*" The schultheissin's blood rouge lips gathered into a pout; her overdrawn eyebrows folded together in a contemptuous frown.

Adolfus stood tall. "I am come to convey that in the next days, in accordance with Gustav's edict, we shall elevate Varus to the —"

"*Varus?!*" The name fell from Vincentia's red lips as if like a drop of acid. In a flurry of silk and indignation, she advanced to him. "But what of my *darling* Viktor? Surely, he —"

"Silence!" Adolfus seized her by the waist and dragged her to an alcove. "Have you forgotten what his escapades have caused? Even without Viktor, I will *still* accomplish it! Your role to play is of even greater importance now."

Her dignity visibly affronted, Vincentia flung off his grip and gave a disdainful toss of her head, causing her hat to slide most unfashionably off it. "See what tumult you have wrought!"

The dog barked and the macaw screamed in defence of their mistress' ire.

Vincentia retreated to the mirror. "I fail to grasp why you trouble yourself to come here to deliver so *outrageous* a decision, when you ought to have done us both the favour of writing — along with your note about Vitus! A letter, I might add, I could have satisfyingly tossed into the flames!"

Adolfus took a deep breath. "*Patience,* Vincentia."

"*Patience?!*" She whirled around so fast — her movements a whirlpool of jewels, silk, and feathers — that the dog's lead wove a chaotic dance around her ankles and the macaw nigh teetered from its perch, screeching in alarm. "Have I not been the very *paragon* of patience, wedded to that *decrepit prune husk* these two-and-twenty years?! And all at *your* behest, no less!"

Not without giving vent to a cascade of hearty curses in French — a language, it seemed, uniquely suited to the task of expelling one's spleen — did she at last readjust her temper as she did her hat. "If you have no further bombshells to drop, then you may take your leave. Oh! And regarding Vitus, I am *more* than capable of pretending to all ignorance of the matter! I will not risk losing my sole comforts — my darling macaw and my precious pug — for the sake of a few tears! Now depart from me, *you brute,* before I set my babies upon you!"

***

24 July 1792

Since the grievous day Elizabeth witnessed her father's passing, and since Edmunda was too terror-stricken to remain at the chalet, they found a temporary asylum at Hans' farm. Hence, we find Edmunda confined to Helene's bed chamber, propped up by a prodigious mountain of pillows, with the curtains drawn against the intrusive sun light.

"Oh, Lizzie!" wailed she with every token of despair; her blotchy, swollen face was streaked with unending hours of tears. "How shall we ever endure? My dear, *dear* Ernest, so cruelly snatched from the world..."

Eventually, the tempest and tears abated, only for Edmunda to fix Lizzie with a flash of resentment. "I'll *never* forgive that Peter — or whoever the fiend truly is! That demon — no, the Devil himself! And it was *you!* my *own daughter*, who brought him into our lives!"

To be sure, the shocking revelation of her faux-amour sent horror rippling through all who heard of it. 'Twas only that the magnitude of Ernest's death cast a shadow so dark and vast that Elizabeth escaped the severest of reproaches.

'Tis appropriate I now acquaint our readers with several details of that ill-fated day. Firstly, just before Elizabeth had hastened into the chalet to behold her dying father, she recognised amongst the strangers thundering past on horseback, a former captor from Lucerne. Secondly, while Edmunda had been at the market, she encountered Swiss guards — loyal to Gustav — searching for Peter. Naturally, she condemned our hero before scorning the guards' fruitless quest in Bubendorf, bidding them seek success instead in Bern. Thirdly, and most calamitous was Fortune's relentless rain: no sooner did Edmunda return home to upbraid her daughter afresh, she beheld a sight to haunt her till death. Even as she reeled, Arnborg's agents battered the door, seeking Peter. Amidst grief and wails, Edmunda drove them hence, bidding them to Bern to apprehend the villain. Scarcely had these men gone when Adolfus' band burst in like the hounds of Hell. Yet Edmunda, propelled by anguish and wielding a frying pan, charged forth, proclaiming with a shrill defiance that Peter's head awaited them in Bern.

"Ernest..." wailed Edmunda afresh while beating her chest with a fervour that boarded on the manic. "My *dearest* Ernest..."

Notwithstanding her own heart-rending grief, it was on seeing her mother so beset by affliction that Elizabeth grappled with a remorse so profound. In passing off a total stranger for her lover, it had led solely to an array of consequences far beyond her worst imaginations.

A knock on the door heralded Jago, bearing a most prodigious hamper filled with Edmunda's favourite delicacies. With regrets expressed of the deepest sensibility, he swore to employ every resource at his disposal to track down the mob who deserved the fire and wrath of the heavens, and went on to explain he had sent soldiers to Bern in hot pursuit. Further, if Peter would dare to set foot in Bubendorf, he would be dragged off to the Liestal garrison at once.

Not until after every effort at comforting Edmunda had been exhausted, and she, spent from her grief, succumbed to a fitful rest, did those gathered retreat to the kitchen, where they quickly fell upon their individual, silent contemplations.

At length, gathering her composure, Lizzie addressed Jago. "Your presence here brings much comfort. But how are *you* faring?" She gazed at him with genuine concern, searching the expression in his eyes. "And your mother? Easily, I can sympathise with the anguish you must both suffer. And yet you are here at such a time to offer *us* solace."

Jago shifted in his seat, as though discomforted by some private thought. "You and your family's comfort is my utmost priority." He extended a hand and took hers; his touch was warm and assuring. "My mother has sought comfort in her sister and has gone out of the canton to grieve in private. Therefore, my time is *entirely* at *your* disposal."

A charged silence entered between them; a silence that shared no trace of unease but was filled with a mutual recognition of each other's pain. There was something unspoken, but profound, in the silence; something of that affinity that often blooms in the wake of shared loss.

Grief is a strange and powerful force, capable of altering the very essence of relationships. In the depths of their shared loss, a new bond was forming; one that was neither fully defined by friendship nor the potential for something deeper.

25 JULY – 05 AUGUST 1792

The following day, our hero, though bereft of appetite, at last yielded to the house staff and his appointed guardians' relentless entreaties, and took his place at the breakfast table upon the east-facing patio. The morning sun, that great restorative of the soul, did little, however, to assuage his apprehensions. He listlessly shifted the viands about his plate, his stomach still in so crippling a tumult. The shock of such loss was felt with every strained heartbeat. With his father gone, the vultures of ambition would soon descend with their talons outstretched to seize power. Indeed, Peter's hopes of reclaiming his rightful place were now more distant than ever. Even with the forger's confession, who could predict the chaos that lay ahead? What new authority might usurp the von Villeroy dynasty, rendering all his efforts futile?

A capricious breeze swept past, setting the white tablecloth to rippling like wind-tossed waves. A vase toppled, spilling forth a cascade of scarlet dianthus blossoms that stained the ground like drops of freshly spilled blood.

Unbidden, there came the awful recollection of dear Vitus' last agonising gasps, drowned by blood. The world suddenly span; Peter gripped his armrests.

A manservant appeared, bearing a missive.

Availing himself of several deep breaths, Peter, with trembling hands, broke the seal. Three lines told that in an inconspicuous quarter at the city's edges, a place frequented by sundry men of questionable aspect, there might be found the unfortunate captive Harris. Confirmation of this suspicion was promised in a few days' time.

This was something, at least. A glimmer of light amidst the tenebrosity.

His gaze now fell upon the Gazette de Berne —

No.59 NOUVELLES POLITIQUES
du Mercredi, 25 Julliet 1792.

— folded atop a silver platter. Beneath these words, the bold font proclaimed: "Les Tragédie du 24 Juillet."

Note tossed aside, he snatched up the paper and raced his eyes over the print. While the article eulogised the schultheiss, painting him as a pillar of the canton, it omitted Vitus' passing. Disbelieving it possible his brother's tragic demise could have been overlooked, he re-read the columns. The focus remained solely on his father and the frantic efforts to repair the minster's damage in time for the funeral. A second headline reported a recent train of powerful patricians' inexplicable deaths. A third article criticised the mint master for a recent trade deal having fallen through and the financial repercussions to be expected. There was nothing reporting on Vitus.

How could such an atrocity be overlooked? How could Vitus' unjust and barbaric death be met with such silence? Surely, an investigation should already be underway, its progress reported for all to see? Yet perhaps this very silence was a strategy? A means of protecting the investigation and ensuring the perpetrators were brought to justice...? That had to be it...

***

Later that day, to the clatter of hooves and jingling harnesses, our hero and his comrades approached Thun Castle's imposing iron gates. Word had been sent to a guard within; a man acquainted with the forger's capture and imprisonment. They were expected at this precise hour. Yet, as they entered the courtyard and dismounted, a grave-looking steward was waiting to receive them.

The steward, darting his gaze at the surrounding windows and walkways, as if fearing unseen eyes, rushed towards them. "We must hurry inside."

A chill settled upon Peter as he and his cohorts followed the steward through a series of cold, echoing corridors. The deeper they preceded into the castle, the more the atmosphere grew potent with ill-boding, as though even the very stones whispered of dark secrets.

At length, they arrived at a small chamber. Its door was ajar.

"He's..." — the steward gulped — "... in there, my lord."

Already driven to the heights of anxious expectation, Peter pushed past and entered the cell. An eerie silence, broken only by the rafter's faint creaking, clung to his skin. There, suspended from a wooden beam by a length of rope, the forger dangled lifelessly; he swayed, ever so slightly, above an overturned chair.

"*Suicide?*" voiced our hero, though the very impossibility of the word was felt the moment that it left his lips.

Still stood in the doorway, the steward shifted with palpable unease. "It appears so, my lord. He... he was found just before sundown."

A tipped ink bottled was spilt over a wooden table. A quill lay atop a blank sheet of paper. The stool lay on its side as if kicked away in desperation. But the noose's meticulous knot, the scene's unsettling precision, hinted at something more sinister than a desperate soul's ultimate act.

Peter rounded on the steward. "And the guards?"

"They've not been accounted for all day," mumbled he.

"Vanished, you mean? I want them found at once. I will know what transpired here. I shall remain the night in this very fortress!"

"Sir," interceded one of Peter's agents, "the steward's evasiveness; the guards' absence... something's amiss. We should seek lodgings elsewhere."

Another agent stepped forward, his own distrust cast in the torch's light and shadows. "We should retire to a nearby inn, sir. This place reeks of deceit."

Peter nodded. Safety, for now, outweighed the need for immediate answers. "But the trail must *not* go cold. I want those guards found. We need to know if they are simply negligent... or something... worse."

As they emerged into the courtyard, Peter's first group of agents dispersed into the encroaching dusk; their shadows melted into the gathering evenfall. Watching them go, Peter felt the weight of command heavier than ever upon his shoulders. With a last glance at the steward, he made his way to a nearby inn; a humble establishment with a roof and walls that had seen better days.

Soon settled in the best room, he despatched his remaining men to Bern.

Now alone, Peter sat on the bed, lost in contemplation. The forger — the man he had hoped would unlock the secrets of his mother's past — was dead. The guards — entrusted with his safety — had vanished. Certainly, something was amiss. Certainly, his already dwindling hopes of returning to the world had again been thwarted.

The hours swiftly crept by; the candle at his bedside flickered and waned; the heavy effects of frustration and a heavy drowsiness were just setting in on our hero's brain when there came the creaking of a floorboard outside his door.

Peter's eyes snapped open.

The creak came again, then the rattling of the door handle being tried.

Heart soon thumping in his ears, Peter reached for his sword. Drawing it silently from its scabbard, he crept to the door. Deep breath taken, he turned the key, flung the door open, and thrust the blade into the blackness.

A figure, hands raised in surrender, jumped back. "My lord, it's *me*..."

The voice, though a fearful whisper, was instantly known. "*Ludwig?*"

***

Barely had Peter returned to his temporary residence the next morn, when he realised his cherished pocket watch was absent from among his meagre possessions. Oh, how this discovery struck him with the force of Jove's own thunderbolts! With his agents dispersed on various duties, Ludwig not set to join him for a couple of days, and the house staff possessing the cunning of a flock of startled geese, it fell upon Peter to retrieve the precious heirloom himself.

Thus, with commands of utmost caution to be met, he bade the coachman to convey him, posthaste, to the city.

Happily, Fortune, fickle as she is, smiled on our hero! For upon his entering the inn, the gloomy one-eyed keeper — after subjecting him to a litany of woes and lamentations — suddenly brightened. With a triumphant flourish, she presented him with the pocket watch itself!

It seemed that, in the whirlwind of Peter's agents packing up his and Harris' belongings, the timepiece had taken a tumble down the side of a chair.

Overjoyed as Peter was to be reunited with his possession, the need to quit the city compelled him to offer the good woman his sincere yet swift thanks. With a spring in his step and a lightness in his heart, he thus exited the premises.

Oh, but as he was about to step into the waiting carriage, a sharp blow, as if from Fate's own cudgel, struck the back of his head, and everything went black...

"Confound it!" came a muffled voice as Peter's senses began their gradual return. "I didn't mean to knock the scoundrel out."

"Who cares even if his skull is cracked?" said another. "We've got him!"

Indeed, from within the confines of pitch blackness, Peter's head verily throbbed as if it were split open. As he struggled to gain his bearings, he soon perceived his hands were tied behind his back. And his tongue was denied all liberty of speech by some rough gag.

The volatile motion beneath him and the clattering all around indicated he was being conveyed in a carriage driven by demons, or at least some coachman with a similar disposition.

At any rate, the carriage eventually screeched to a halt, and Peter, unceremoniously hauled from it, found himself dragged down a flight of steps that seemed to lead into the earth's musty bowels.

The reverberating clang of a door closing behind him signalled his arrival at the mystery destination; he was forced into a rough seat.

"Behold!" proclaimed a triumphant voice as the sack was ripped away from Peter's head. "I bring you the notorious outlaw!"

Blinking back his confusion, our hero regarded some dimly lit cellar. He was surrounded by a group of men whose stern visages and official-looking uniforms marked them as members of the Bernese Landjäger.

"*Valentin?*" came another voice, tinged with surprise.

A figure rushed forward and instantly removed Peter's gag.

Gasping at the musty air, which smelled no less of a certain abductor's disappointed hopes, Peter focused on the man now stood over him. "*Meier?*"

"Thank heavens! *You're alive!*" He set about untethering Peter's hands.

With a face of utter bemusement, the ringleader of our hero's abductors — none other than Felix — stumbled forward. "You...? You two" — he pointed first at Meier and then our hero before his index fingers touched in final gesticulation — "know each other?"

"Indeed!" Meier helped Peter to his feet. "You've only gone and brought me the very informant who was aiding me in our investigations into Viktor's nefarious activities."

***

Who, pray tell, could have foreseen so fortuitous a turn of event as those in the preceding scene? Even our hero, no stranger to Fortune's whims, found himself utterly astounded at being thrown into the path of one so essential to his earlier endeavours! These endeavours, I might add, which had begun long before we had the pleasure of meeting our hero. At any rate, there was much discourse upon matters both past and yet to come, and Peter was finally conveyed from the den of, shall we say, *legal enthusiasm*, in a manner considerably more conducive to the preservation of his dignity than had been his journey thither.

Two days, those relentless twins of anxiety and anticipation had marched by, leaving Peter to pace his chamber like one driven half mad. His reunion with Ludwig and their ensuing discussion — Ludwig revealing his knowledge of other forgers who, despite Adolfus' attempts to wipe them out, in fact lived, and who might help in the cause — offered at least a glimmer of hope. To boot, Ludwig possessed a list of names and locations of said forgers employed at the time of his mother's downfall. Thus, though one forger's voice had been silenced, others yet lived who might be bargained with. Notwithstanding this boon, the silence from his covert network of agents gnawed at our hero. Still and all, word finally arrived; not from Ludwig about the forger's hidden lair, but rather Peter's men confirming Harris' whereabouts. Indeed, the locale matched precisely that of what they had formerly written about.

Advised as Peter was to wait out the day within the schloss' safe stone-clad confines, wisdom prevailed. He entrusted the task of rescuing Harris with his men. Consequently, under the veil of night's darkest hours, these agents, swollen by the ranks of newfound allies, would descend upon and storm the den of vice, liberating the hostage.

***

The hours rolled by and the cloak of nightfall hence mirrored the customary colour of nighttime raiders. United by a singular purpose, they needed no leader to ignite their fervour. Failure was a foreign concept. This rescue was not solely about Harris; 'twas about uncovering secrets, however little, of the shadowy society that had orchestrated their former leader's unjust demise.

With a silent nod of shared intent, they mounted carriages and vanished, via separate gates, into the city's heart.

Their approach to the stronghold of vice was as cunning as it was undetected. There, the manager, oblivious to the impending storm, welcomed them across his threshold, unaware that he was ushering wolves into his den.

In point, the clash was fleeting, the outcome inevitable — a swift defeat of the enemy and liberty granted to the hostage.

As it was unanimously accorded that Harris should be conveyed back to Bubendorf with utmost haste, a carriage was procured at dawn's first light. With all the subtlety common to several pairs of sturdy hands, a bewildered and somewhat battered Harris was bundled within. Before the carriage rolled away, a stern warning was issued: silence was paramount; all recent tribulations were to be harboured within the vault of his breast; and not a shadow of Peter's true identity was to be cast upon the curiosity of any soul.

With a nod, taut with the gravity of his promise, Harris did thus depart, his heart filled with less satisfaction than when Fortune had first swept him into Bern's tumultuous clutch.

As he settled into the carriage's comforting embrace, overcome by fatigue, his eyes fell shut, only to be torn wide. Phantoms of his ordeal jolted him awake with a gasp. The mere whisper of a breeze or the louder creak of the carriage interior would send his heart racing. Visions of his captivity, of chains and shadows, of masked figures bursting in, bearing the chilling visages of death, flooded his mind. However, mostly unscathed, his flesh, deep within, were wounds inflicted; the price of meddling in affairs best left undisturbed.

***

Meantime, history, yet about to be made, whispered through the Bernese Rathaus' cool, stony halls. Beneath the arched council hall ceiling, the stone-faced Small Council, lining the table, hummed and harred as they struggled beneath the weight of the city's future.

Despite the cloud of grief and uncertainty, opportunity's insinuations were plainly manifest in many an ambitious face. Gustav's sudden demise, while a tragedy to be mourned, had created a power vacuum; a void that vibrated on every nerve with unspoken possibilities.

Adolfus, the man of the hour, entered with a presence that seemed to gather the hall's light and shadows about him. As he took his position at the table, each council member watched him with eyes sharpened by recent events, their minds no doubt calculating the next hours.

"My friends," began Adolfus, "though we find ourselves unmoored in the wake of Gustav's untimely departure, we must not allow grief to paralyse us. I have summoned you here to discuss a matter of utmost consequence."

He paused, allowing the silence to swell before continuing. "Gustav's decree was clear." He held aloft the document; its wax seal glinted in the light shafts. "Varus is to succeed him. In these turbulent times, we must strive for continuity. Placing Varus upon the schultheiss' seat will serve as the keystone to uphold our canton's stability. Albrecht" — Adolfus gestured to him — "has already vowed his support of this decision."

Whispers rose and fell. Some council members nodded with thoughtful expressions; others wore thinly veiled scowls of dissent.

The Welsch Treasurer, whose girth and sticky fingers declared his fondness for earthly pleasures, cleared his throat. "Whilst none here can dispute the late Gustav's wishes, his unexpected passing and the escalating difficulties facing our canton give us pause. Furthermore, knowing Varus'... shall we say... *limited* experience and political acumen, I — and many others here — believe that elevating him to the seat would be imprudent, if not downright disastrous!"

"Hear, hear!" echoed several staunch, concerned voices, thinly veiling their ambition.

"As unfortunate as it is," continued the Welsch Treasurer, "with Varus lacking the aptitude and acquaintance necessary to navigating these treacherous waters, we need a leader of greater mettle." He paused; his gaze swept across the assembly. "Therefore, I propose we select a new family from amongst ourselves to assume the schultheiss' mantle."

At once, the murmurs grew, and a debate broke out. Albrecht went to speak; but Adolfus slammed down his cane, silencing the room, and introduced a new element to the deliberations — a French marquis' support. "This most puissant figure has pledged to bolster Varus' claim. And considering the given climate between our nations, such an alliance could prove... *beneficial,* to say the least."

Despite their individual ambitions, the council could not but otherwise be intrigued. The French Revolution, with its bloody upheaval and radical ideals, had sent shockwaves through Europe. Owing to the conspiracy already chronicled in our history, Switzerland contended with France's growing anger. And now, with the added menaces of Austria and Prussia, the possibility of any return to peaceful conditions with such a powerful neighbour, however unlikely, was not to be taken for granted.

Again, Adolfus, the sly strategist, seemed to hold all cards in his hand. Who else, among each powerful family present — even if they ascended to the desired seat — had established such a solution?

"Despite our internal fractures," decreed he, "Bern must project strength and unity. A contested succession would only weaken our position, making us vulnerable to internal and external threats alike. Besides, to disregard our late schultheiss' wishes" — he crossed himself and raised his eyes so loftily to the heavens — "would not solely be a disservice to his memory, but would mar our legitimacy in the eyes of those we govern."

Though at this critical juncture, ambition would surely fracture the canton's already fragile unity, this stayed not the raging debate of those who vied for power. The council chamber became a battleground of words and wills, with Adolfus steering the chaos, countering objections, and reinforcing his points — the stakes higher with each spoken word.

Such ferocity did the gathering reach, and there being a tie of votes concerning Varus' appointment, that the council was adjourned until after the funeral. As the majority quit the hall, Adolfus' closest allies turned the subject on the real heir-presumptive, Vitus.

"Ought not we have rather hurried through discussions of Vitus' ascension?" said one. "Surely, our debate would have been much quicker resolved today?"

Adolfus remained silent. Vitus' brutal demise was a truth too dangerous to reveal, even to his most trusted confidantes.

"Where *is* he, anyway?" pressed another. "To abandon the canton at this critical hour, to indulge in private his grief, is not of the common order. He needs to be *here*!"

Adolfus rounded on the man. "Do you presume to question my judgement? Do you truly believe Vitus is unaware of the gravity of this situation?"

This stern rebuke silenced the man.

After a moment, another councillor hesitantly spoke. "But where is he staying? We should at least offer our condolences..."

"Vitus has requested his privacy be respected *without* obtrusion. He has entrusted me with all political matters. So, I suggest you all the do the same." With a final severe frown cast upon the men, Adolfus quit the hall, with his attendant hurrying after him.

"Have you managed to the secure the meeting for tomorrow?" whispered Adolfus as he boarded the waiting carriage.

Not without first glancing around for listening ears, did his attendant reply. "Yes. He will meet you at the agreed location."

"And you are certain he boasts the necessary connections?"

"Without a doubt, my lord. Though I know of neither his history nor his present station, I hear he is a man of many walks of life. For certain, he is the perfect choice for this task."

***

The late hours of the following night were now arrived. It was time for Adolfus to convene in his usually clandestine manner with the aforementioned character. Indeed, Adolfus had already placed vast hopes in this man to effect a most pivotal circumstance attendant to the successes of his grand scheme.

Hence, in the underbelly of Bern city, tucked down a dark alley where whispers of rebellion and corruption stir among the stagnant drafts, there stood a most, I would say, grim tavern. Its façade, no less appealing than the intention of every rogue and strumpet concealed within its walls, offered little inducement to cross its threshold. But since the meeting poised to take place was of such a delicate and, dare we say, *unscrupulous* nature, no better establishment was needed. Thus, we shall enter its most secluded room — a space seldom acknowledged by the common patron — and observe what is about to go forward.

Adolfus entered first. His immediate impressions indeed coincided with the natural state of his environs. The room, but a trove of stench and shadows, proffered merely the dim glow of a single candle — its light dying a slow death against the oppressive darkness. A heavy, moth-eaten tapestry served to divide the chamber. Within its weave lay a concealed hatch, dormant, awaiting the commencement of such covert discourses as this room surely hosted.

Adolfus' men, cloaked and silent as wraiths — their faces obscured by deep hoods, their eyes sharp and scanning the environing gloom — took their places in the room's corners.

Just then, a sound was heard coming from the tapestry's other side. Unperceivable to Adolfus, his appointment had arrived, accompanied by a retinue of equally shadowy figures.

The two men positioned themselves at a table on either side of the tapestry. A moment passed, thick with anticipation. The hatch slid open with the sliver of wood against wood, revealing only the eyes of each party; each shrouded in distrust and veiled intentions.

Adolfus was the first to speak. "I understand that you are possessed of connections within all levels of society?"

"Your understanding is correct," replied the other. Though his air, a stark contrast to the aristocratic Adolfus, spoke of the streets, of struggle and strife, there was an undeniable trace of nobility. "But let's dispense with the introductions and get down to business."

Quite taken aback by this man's bluntness, and piqued by such an informal address, Adolfus cleared his throat of the resentment which clawed at it. "Tell me," said he, feigning his usual smoothness, "precisely how much persuasion do you possess, and how quickly can you direct public opinion?"

"Your presence here suggests you are already well acquainted with my capabilities... for what else could have drawn you to this less than glorious establishment?" Their gazes locked through the wooden slit; each strove to divine the other's fuller features. "The price you are willing to pay will determine how swift the tide shall turn."

Unused to such audacity, Adolfus wanted to reach through the slit and throttle the impertinent rogue. But being in need of this indecorous fiend's services, he suppressed his indignation and calmly said, "the city bleeds under the weight of the mint master's avarice; this is the first rumour that must spread faster than any contagion. The city's ailing economy must be the next; all pinned upon the mint master's incompetency. Can you manage this?"

Through the slit, the man's gaze narrowed; the candlelight flickered in the whites of his eyes. "Easily," replied he with indubitable sharpness. "For the people are *already* primed for rebellion. Their cries for relief fill the streets."

Pleased but wary, Adolfus allowed himself a thin smile. "Your price?"

"How easily such suffering could be alleviated with the right... *redistribution* of *certain people's* wealth..." His words hung in the air.

Such speech, both alluring and provoking, Adolfus could not allow the latter sentiment to escape into his next words. "Hmm." He chuckled, concealing his unease. "You would lead me to believe you have your own agenda?" The man remained silent, neither blinking nor faltering in his stare. "Regardless," resumed Adolfus, "an alliance between us could ensure that the wealth you covet finds its way to more... *deserving* hands."

"Do we have an agreement, then?"

"That depends entirely on you. Three days I will give you to promulgate the rumours. If you succeed, we shall speak again. Perhaps then you will reveal the true object of your desires?"

***

Ten days of mourning being now passed, the day of the schultheiss' funeral had dawned. Upon the chiming of the eighth hour, Peter arose from his bed, wearied by the spectral terrors which had intermittently tormented and obstructed his nocturnal repose. His stomach churned with a grief that defied even the most tempting breakfast. Despair and rage sparred at him in turns. For even without the agony of losing his father, there was still made no mention anywhere of his brother's death; neither his body nor memory was to be found in this day's wake. How was his absence ever to be justified? What fiction had been contrived to somehow conceal the truth? Thus, this day, as much as Peter dearly wished to fully partake of, he equally wished to consign to the annals of the past.

So lost to his ruminations, the next two hours hurtled by, leaving our hero but a scant hour to attire himself in the sombre vestments of woe. But hastily dressing, he then hurried to the city. There, with a small retinue, he would, from that same lavishly appointed townhouse parlour window, witness the solemn procession's arrival.

Again, the cobbled streets thronged with sombre city nobles and townsfolk — a mixture of devotees to the departed, wailing so great a loss; and countless angered souls, cursing the oligarchs' extravagance, demanding the mint master's ousting and a reformation of the rule. A formidable array of Swiss Guard stood sentinel along the route; their eyes vigilant; their hands fixed on their hilts.

The funeral cortège was expected at the stroke of noon. Peter glanced at a nearby clock, noting it lacked but fifteen minutes of the hour. His gaze shifted to the plaza below, where a clutch of men busied themselves with last-minute security measures; a pair inspected the drains while another emerged from the sewer's bowels, his grimy countenance confirming the security of the depths.

Alas, for the cathedral façade, its adornment was still but the draperies which disguised the wounds inflicted by its recent collapse.

Presently, the dulcet tinkering tones of a pianoforte drifted through the room and stole over Peter's abstraction. He was just turning around to identify who ran their fingers along the ivories when:

"Sir!" boomed the disapproving, rotund-shaped butler as he advanced across the marble flooring with the alacrity of a jungle cat. "If you will be so good as to remove yourself from this instrument, this instant!" Barely had these words left his curled lips before he slammed shut the piano lid, catching the hapless musician's fingers in its unforgiving maw.

Wholly indifferent to the offender's ensuing whimpers, scowls, and curses, the butler merely waved him away with the concomitant "shoo, shoo, shoo!", pirouetted full about with a self-satisfied smirk and, resuming that pompous air typical of such sycophantic retainers who idolise their patrons and their chattels with equal zeal, proffered tea.

25 July – 05 August 1792

The funeral procession was as solemnly splendid and meticulously managed as befitting a man of such eminence. Every warmer hue found in the sundry regimentals — blues, reds, whites, and golds — banners, and insignia, however, became but a monochrome tide backdrop to Peter's swelling despondency. Tears surged forth, and the anguish within drove him from the window to seek refuge in a small, adjacent antechamber.

There, collapsing against a wall, he yielded to the burden of so incalculable a loss dilating so inconsolable a heart. Never had such emotions raged in his soul as to drag him one moment down to the hell of despair and, at another, to the height of vengeance. One day, his enemies would pay!

***

The schultheiss was consigned to his eternal rest within an ornate crypt, marked by a plaque as elaborate as the tales spun at his wake. And the next day, the city, like a slumbering giant, began to stir, its heartbeat returning to its customary tempo, rhythm, noise, and bustle of commerce.

With the quotidian mode resuming, Fortune, having but feigned a respectful silence during the period of grief, now grew restless from idleness. Resolved to spin her wheel anew and cast poor Peter into fresh disarray, she thusly determined how to unfurl her latest scheme.

Our hero, having remained an extra night in the city, settled in the window which overlooked the plaza. His eyes wistfully fixed upon the cathedral as though it might bring his father back, he endeavoured to partake of his first viands in days. But whatever semblance of an appetite he enjoyed, it was soon obtruded upon by the crescendo of voices beyond the room — one of them most reminiscent of a squealing pig.

"I am instructed to admit no one today," came the butler's firm avowal.

"But I must speak with him!" insisted the other; an agent.

"Permit his entrance," ordered Peter, his curiosity piqued.

Consequently, this man — whose phiz was so drastically marred by whatever agitation had set his mind on the brink of lunacy as to unnerve even Peter — flustered into view. His words tumbled forth in the same high-pitched and frenetic staccato: "The city — oh, the city! What are we to do? Such confusion! Such shock! — I mean, the art! It's so uncanny — I can scarce believe it!" Every swishing limb, overbearing gesticulation, and facial twitch were equally dramatic. "And the chattering, sir — the patricians, they're all a-twitter —"

"Pray!" interrupted our hero, his head about to split, "will you desist these wild and theatrical ramblings and speak to the point!"

"An exhibition. The painting — oh, the likeness, sir! Your likeness!"

"*My* likeness? Unless you wish to breathe your last breath, tell me of what are you talking?"

"The oil at the exhibition, sir, by all accounts, depicting you!"

"Depicting *me*...?" Some moments it took for the man's words to coalesce into coherence. And then, with a start, realisation descended upon Peter's brain like a hailstorm. "Good heavens!"

***

So, dear readers, this next twist in our narrative, a convergence of art and intrigue that would shake Bern's very foundation, is to be found with that certain likeness, wrought by the hands of that bohemian artist of Liestal, introduced to you in our inaugural volume.

Bound as the oil was, if you recall, to be exhibited in the summer — now unfurling in all its glory — the halls of the Museum of Fine Arts had thrown open its portals to society's refined and cultured echelons. There, amidst a jubilee of distinguished works that annually festoon the gallery walls, was unveiled the canvas bearing our hero's most handsome visage.

Found among the slow-moving pageant of esteemed patrons were several members of the Small Council — those loyal dogs of Adolfus. Drawn solely to the event by their wives' vanity — a parading of sartorial artistry of silks, taffetas, and the like — soon, did these men stare mouths agape as they beheld a likeness so akin to Peter, adorning the chief masterpiece, accoutred in hues of blue. Verily, our hero gazed out from the canvas with an air of quiet confidence; his eyes appeared to twinkle with a gleeful cunning.

Such was the shock and bewilderment that seized the councilmen; they trembled, gasped, and stuttered. Their carefully cultivated composure shattered along with the crystal tumblers that fell from their grasps. And in their hurried disarray, they collided with each other, their wives, and other genteel onlookers, before scurrying off to summon their lord.

To be sure, no sooner did Adolfus arrive in a whirlwind of impatience than, as if by the same wild, unrestrained artist's brush strokes, the glaring colours which overspread his complexion, a canvas of his inner turmoil, delineated the storm of his agitated soul. In fine, his lips parted merely to emit a hissing command for the artist's immediate attendance, at which his minions dispersed and returned with the bohemian fellow in tow.

"Pray tell, sir," — Adolfus seized the artist's wrist with a grip that could crush bone — "when did you commit this piece to canvas?"

Only after prising off Adolfus' fingers did the fellow, with a most displeased countenance, deign to answer him. "Whilst I am no stranger to the fervent embrace of those who hold my work in high regard, I am unaccustomed to such boorish treatment. Temper, sir, your enthusiasm for my craft, lest you frighten off my muse." Oblivious to Adolfus' ominous glares, the artist went on. "This fine portrait I brought into being earlier this very year, and —"

"Earlier this year?" interrupted Adolfus. "And pray, where — where was this scene captured?"

"Bubendorf," replied he, visibly nettled by the interruption.

"*Bubendorf?*" echoed Adolfus.

In the moments that followed, and the subsequent vacuum of silence, the artist, the councillors *and* their wives, all stood visibly confused; painted eyelashes fluttered; mouths pursed and chins scrunched whilst every set of orbs darted back and forth, seeking deliverance from the mystery.

But for Adolfus, as his mind raced through the realms of conjecture, connecting every clue and recent occurrence with terrifying quality, his eyes soon widened with a look of horror-stricken epiphany.

"Great God, above!" He shuddered violently and his complexion frosted over. "The devil breathes! Valentin..." He gathered the attention of his still bewildered men with his awe-filled gaze. "Do you hear me?! Valentin lives!"

06 – 10 AUGUST 1792

"*Das Unglück reist zu Pferd und geht zu Fuss weg,*" so laments the melancholic Swiss saying, which reminds us that, "misfortune travels on horseback and departs on foot." And such, of course, is the case for our beleaguered hero: adversity thundering into his life swift and sudden as a charging stallion, yet lingering long, determined to outstay its unwelcome, obstinate as a stubborn mule.

Chaos, oh, the chaos that now reigned, surging through the city, threatening to engulf our Peter whole. As we earlier saw, with the canvas' unveiling, Adolfus, like a master weaver, sifted through the mystery: the elusive guard and scroll bearer from Lucerne; his absence from Bubendorf; his purported presence in Bern; Vitus' covert activities, and his patronage of a nondescript inn; the forger's capture, and the intercepted message alluding to a figure of great import. Too easily, Adolfus snatched the thread of truth from the web of intrigue, which threatened to topple his own decade-long schemes.

Though thunderstruck as Adolfus was, and ablaze with menacing delirium, he steered his raging impulses into a cold, calculating determination. Upon learning from the artist that Peter — an alias so ill-suited to Valentin — was bereft of memory, Adolfus rightly surmised he must have been somewhere in Bern city, in search of his past. 'Twas a peril most fraught with grave eventualities should our hero have already enjoyed any restoration to his recollection, and unearthed even the smallest relic of his former life or the schemes which coveted it! And so, with the urgency of a huntsman on the scent, Adolfus contrived how to best ensnare him.

The capital's arteries were constricted at once. Every city gate, entrance, and bridge throbbed with vigilance as guards assiduously probed carriage, crate, wagon, and each passerby with an intensity that betrayed their singular aim. All movement in and out of the city was restricted to the most pressing of needs; exclusive to those who dwelt within its walls — contingent on permission being granted by an official appointed by the council, and a signed document verifying the wayfarer's identification.

WANTED placards again plastered every notice board, lamppost, and public square, flapping in the breeze with ominous significance. The press, far and wide, trumpeted the narrative of the man in the portrait who, whether a mere doppelgänger or, in fact, a bona fide Lazarus in the flesh, stirred a frenzy that rippled through every echelon of society. This spectacle, deemed either a work of the Devil or a miracle of Providence, so captured the public imagination that from tavern to washhouse, from marketplace to grand hall and humble habitat alike, the tale of the man robed in azure danced on the lips of all.

The venerable city thus transformed into the hunting ground, all day long, every hovel, every lofty abode, every street, and alley fell under the inquisitorial inspection of innumerable detachments. Finding himself thus an unwilling captive within Bern's walls, Peter could only pray that his presence would go unheeded. But gradually, as the sun relinquished its hold upon the horizon and the city donned her mantle of dusk with a peculiar trepidation, the prowling emissaries, with canines at the vanguard, came a-knocking at the residence sequestering our hero within.

Since Peter's valet and comrades had, on the day of the funeral, already ventured beyond the city walls, there remained just himself and the property's butler as sole occupants. All our hero could now do was trust that his letter to Meier at the Stadtwache would somehow procure the means to his freedom.

Hence, within a small chamber, Peter pressed himself into a recess beneath the hollowed planks of an ancient armoire; a crevice so cunningly devised that it mocked the very notion of space.

Here, awaiting what fate he knew not, he lay in breathless stillness as the muffled thud of martial feet grew ominously beyond his dusty enclosure, and the probing snouts of hounds came perilously close to his place of concealment.

The stifling, dusty air, thick with musty aged oak and now the trace of his own fear-sweat, natch drew the dogs within mere inches. With olfactory prowess, they pawed relentlessly at the armoire's base, their whines rising into a crescendo of suspicion. The searchers' voices converged into a racket of command and response — but a prelude to the detection that, with every thunderous panic-ridden heartbeat, threatened to culminate in calamity.

But lo, amidst the impending discovery, there erupted a clatter from the kitchen, metallic clangs and shattering porcelain; the butler's voice, tremulous with feigned distress, cried out in agony. For a moment, our hero's heart ceased its frantic rhythm, caught in anxious anticipation's cruel grip. The butler's ploy, if a ploy it was, was desperate — the hope slender: that the clamour would draw the hounds' attention and the searchers' priority from the potential prize lurking within the armoire's shadowy recess.

After what felt an age of suffocating and unendurable agony, the soldiers' creaking boots thudded upon the floorboards, and the hounds were, thankfully, lured away by the chaos without.

By and by, the searchers at length departed, and within an hour, Meier, Keller, and their fellow Stadtwache comrades arrived. Triumphant in arranging a means by which Peter might escape the walls' restrictions, they escorted him forthwith.

Night's clear sky being now descended, with it, the curfew bell's iron clang tolled signalling the cessation of all honest toil and the commencement of vigilant watchfulness. Our hero and his escorts stalked along the humid streets, which now lay in enforced silence, save for the sound of regimented boots and hounds' ominous baying.

Providence being on Peter's side, he arrived, without concern or impediment, at the pre-arranged location — a five-story town house built into the ancient fortifications which abutted the Aare.

Here, preparations were afoot for an escapade most daring.

The plan was to exit the city via a window. The apparatus of our hero's descent was not unlike that used by the ancients — a remembrance of biblical lore, where Rahab, the harlot, with a faith as crimson as the cord she cast, had lowered the spies from Jericho's walls. 'Twas a rudimentary in its construction yet ingenious in its conception: a sturdy basket, borne by hands loyal and true.

Accordingly, the basket stood ready to serve as the chariot of deliverance; the ropes, steadfast and strong, were secured around a parapet. Our hero stared down at the mist-blanketed Aare, its waters whispering promises of freedom; several huddled figures, masquerading as fishermen, waited upon a boat.

Alas, Fortune, that capricious jester, would not grant passage without at least a little difficulty.

A glint of light, the lantern of a patrolling boat, chanced upon the conspirators. These guards, their curiosity piqued by the low utterances which echoed across the waters, began their approach, their lanterns bobbing like fireflies in the growing murk.

A diversion was needed, and thus it was on the far side of the river that a clamour arose — a din most cacophonous, contrived by comrades' unseen.

The patrollers were drawn thence; their investigation diverted.

Seizing the providential moment, our hero clambered within the basket's womb. The pulley creaked its assent, and down he was lowered.

From the waiting vessel, hands reached out for the precious cargo, and into their midst, our hero safely descended as Icarus might have had the sea rather been his ally, and the boat pushed off into the Aare's misty embrace.

***

Meantime, the Welsch Treasurer held counsel with his closest allies at his residence. "The audacity of that man!" cried he. "Even with Gustav gone to rest, Adolfus still believes his own influence will continue uninterrupted. And why does Albrecht not step forward again? Surely, it would have been better had he reprised his seat and not simply ratified a dead man's wishes?"

All ears present could not help but soak in this denunciation. The gathered men all agreed on how presumptuously Adolfus had behaved and how something had to be done in order to shift the balance back to where it ought to belong.

"Do we know who this French marquis is?" continued he. But each man only looked back at him, blank as cows. "We must find out. Perchance, if he indeed holds such persuasion across the borders, we should entice him to our side. Whatever the case, leaving Adolfus unchecked in his parade of heroism will result entirely in more seats falling under his control."

A silence entered among the men as all ruminated on these words. To be sure, even in times of order, power was an ever-fluctuating tide. Now, more so than ever, none could be pococurante about their positions or authority.

"And does nobody still know anything more of Vitus?" resumed the Welsch Treasurer. All shook their heads. "Now that Viktor is exiled, doubtless, Adolfus will have already diverted his overtures to Vitus. It would be most prudent for us to swiftly align him with our party. That Adolfus now so eagerly advocates Varus leads me to suspect he is merely wishing to buy time. A leopard does not change its spots. Though discreet Adolfus may be, I sense he is hungrier for power than ever. But for what nefarious purpose is yet to be manifest..."

A general murmur of assent went through the room, and another spoke. "But is it not most peculiar — Vitus' conspicuous absence from his father's funeral? No word received from him during such pivotal times? Adolfus claiming him to be too unwell for visitors? And yet no physician has been seen to visit his residence these past days."

The Welsch Treasurer nodded gravely. "Even the house staff refuse entrance and obdurately evade all interrogations. If Vitus is truly as indisposed as we expect, we should be permitted to offer our offices. I wonder, is Adolfus shielding him for other reasons?"

"Perhaps this is the very reason Adolfus pushed so fervently for Varus' instalment?" suggested another. "Should we not despatch a few discreet men to ascertain the truth? Whatever illness this may be, mayhap Vitus is being manipulated or held against his will? Why look at me so? There have occurred stranger things before! We ought to know for his sake as well as ours."

"Yes," accorded the Welsch Treasurer. "See that it is done. But take great care to ensure Adolfus does not find out, lest he thwart our efforts."

***

Going back to Harris, for the first leg of his journey back home those several days ago, he had indulged the luxury of brooding solely over those tribulations which so unwelcomely entangled him in a web of peril. But, as the carriage trundled along, he tired himself of these preoccupations; his contemplations gave way to a matter of equally pressing merit: that of Peter's true identity.

Indeed, often we find the human condition is generally afflicted by the same sort of malediction. Such that when we find ourselves custodians of a titillating secret, especially one having annexed to it an edict of silence, how torturous the burden is; how it seems to grow in proportion to its required concealment. Thus, our kind readers will, I am sure, extend their sympathies to Harris, who, despite his earnest pledge of silence, soon felt the yoke of this commitment growing ever more oppressive as he neared the hearth of his home. This internal struggle did sap at his fortitude, and he fancied the singular salve to cure him of the contagion was to be found in dispensing its symptoms.

Thus resolved, Harris alighted from the carriage, flew across the yard and burst into the farmhouse in a cloud of dust, finding Helene, the very picture of domestic diligence, attending to the stove.

"Sister!" exclaimed he, depositing his travel-worn luggage upon the flagstones with a thud. "I return with tidings most astonishing!"

Helene wheeled about to face him; she countered that she, too, was possessed of news most astonishing. Harris, quickening his steps, protested his news was vastly superior, brooking no delay. Kettle placed upon its fiery throne, Helene commanded his advance to halt, promising that her report would eclipse his own. After an interplay of eager retorts and spirited parries, Harris relinquished the floor to his sister. She unfolded a narrative so interwoven with the threads of tragedy and discord concerning Lizzie, Emil, and Edmunda — particularly their severing of ties with the infamous and worthless scoundrel Peter — that Harris indeed found himself not merely utterly astonished, but verily struck dumb.

"I can hardly believe it," murmured he, anchored to a chair by her words.

"Believe it, you soon will, for they lodge here under our very roof."

Hot water poured, and tea, that most civil of comforts brewed, Helene served Harris a cup. "Now, my brother, unfurl your own prodigious news."

About to unload his burden, Harris rather paused — a man at the precipice of confession. Possessed still of those little jealousies which men of narrow souls too easily indulge, he found a spark of ungentlemanly opportunism did seize upon his heart. Apprised of Peter's ignominious descent in Bubendorf, he pondered if fair Elizabeth's affections might once again be unclaimed, free to be captured by his own designs. Thus did this ignoble thought stay his tongue.

Turning full about within himself, Harris dismissed the import of his own news as trifling and hardly mention worthy.

After giving so very bare an account of his stay in Bern and his observations of Peter — equally scant and uncommitted as they were — Harris exerted his every effort at affecting an air of disinterested civility. To fair Lizzie, he offered attentions both deferential and discreet. To the still-lamenting Edmunda, he lent the full measure of his sympathetic ear, never failing to align his silence with her tirades against Peter as tacit endorsement.

In like measure, Hans, his eye ever-turned towards the pragmatic union of his offspring, was not tardy in drawing his son aside to whisper into his ear of the fortuitous prospects borne by Peter's disgrace.

Alas, all for Hans' contrivances, Lizzie's affections were perhaps never so far beyond his reach. As our heroine and the young noble lord Jago were more thrown together of late, Elizabeth had much increased exposure to the leading assiduities of his disposition.

Notwithstanding her grief, she spent time sufficient in the fondness, solicitudes, and merits of one man, to find the passion she felt for the other swiftly driven from her breast. Though she did not all at once withdraw her affections from Peter, nor confer them entirely upon Jago, the heart wounds caused by the recent tragedy could not but otherwise reveal to her, in the most glaring colours, the handsome, dignified, and discreet perfections of the latter gentleman. Jago's sangfroid, affability, and benevolence — testified in all his words and actions — stood in stark contrast with the turbulence, irascibility, pride, and showy pretence found in much of Peter's behaviour. This dissimilitude served only to increase her admiration for the one and disapprobation for the other.

Now, to permit the reader into a little secret — in case it had gone unobserved erenow — let us not forget the sundry occasions where vibrant blushes would rise to her fair cheeks, or the spark of light that would illumine her eyes upon this noble lord's appearance. Speaking plainly: although she might outwardly eschew the prospect of unsuitable matches pressed upon her by her meddlesome mother; and though she might generally disavow any inclination towards matrimony, her heart had, in truth, already begun to harbour the tenderest inclinations towards a man who, despite the disparities in their stations, appeared to embody every quality she deemed perfect.

And where vulnerability has any say on that score, so we oft find even the most insurmountable of hearts do yield. How terrible a pity it is, therefore, for our hero: so well fashioned by the Divine; so favourably nurtured by so kind a mother as to render him the most promising among his contemporaries; only for Fortune to have so worked against him from infancy, contriving all manner of tragedies and duplicities to his disadvantage.

***

With a hesitant hand, Peter drew his mother's diary from his coat pocket. Seeking comfort in her memory through the night's long and distressing hours, he had thumbed through the timeworn pages filled with the faded ink of her elegant script. As he roamed through the text, a particular entry caught his eye: a passage where she spoke of an encroaching shadow. An omen perhaps of her own peril; a belief in mortal danger.

Again, his father's allusive words, "herein dwells answers long buried," gnawed at his thoughts. Surely this passage in his mother's diary must have been what his father referred to?

Again, Bernhard's presence was indispensable.

Ludwig entered the parlour bearing a message.

The note, from Peter's agents, bore chiefly their ill successes: the captured Tatzelwurm agent remained inscrutable; he withheld secrets even in the face of starvation's cruel kiss. Neither had they still tracked down the phantoms of yesteryear's atrocities, whose names and locations Ludwig so fervently guarded these past decades. Some had already slipped beyond mortality's veil; others had dissolved as if into the ether, leaving no trace behind.

"Something will soon prove auspicious," assured Ludwig. "I am convinced that the net will close around one of these rogues, and from his lips, we shall glean enough to illuminate the path ahead."

Disillusioned as Peter was, he could scarce muster a sigh. The nefarious society again eluded him; each line of interrogation led to a labyrinthine dead end. Yet perchance Bernhard might possess a fragment of this enigmatic puzzle?

"Thank you, Ludwig," replied our hero at last. "Your restored presence is a balm to my vexed soul. Pray, fetch me paper and quill; there is someone I must summon."

Later that afternoon, Bernhard arrived and was led to the parlour.

"My deepest sympathies for your father," said he with much gravitas as he approached our hero at a window. "And for you brother's passing, also accept my heartfelt condolences."

"Thank you." Peter motioned towards two nearby chairs. "The days have indeed been heavy with — *My brother?* How came you to know of his demise? For I have not penned a word of it to you, and neither has the press, for whatever inconceivable reason, publicised it."

Visibly discomfited, Bernhard cast his eyes about the room as if seeking some distraction. The butler's entrance with tea offered a brief interlude; but the silence was filled solely with that tension common to words left unsaid.

Once the servant retreated, Peter once more put the question to Bernhard.

"My words are never without weight," replied Bernhard, assuming a sudden air of cool reserve. "As I earlier stated, my vigil over you has been unceasing, my men your shadow, reporting back to me daily of your movements."

"Then, *on the night of the attack*, were they my sentinels even then?"

Bernhard's gaze anchored on a corner of the room, where shadows held court.

"Were they following me, *even then?*" persisted Peter.

"*Your* welfare alone is my concern," at last replied he, meeting Peter's gaze. "And it is exclusively this with which I have charged my men, and —"

"Enough!" interrupted Peter, stung to the quick by this ostensibly unfeeling response. "Do you mean to say they witnessed what horrors took place and yet failed to intervene? That my brother, whose life could have been saved — spared the blade which tore him through — was so little esteemed?"

Bernhard, whose countenance had been a citadel of composure on every occasion prior, surrendered to a vermilion hue. "Your affection for your half-brother is not lost on me. But he was *not* birthed by the same mother and —"

"Not birthed by the same mother? Though but a *half-brother*, he was kin all the same! And to me, more akin than the closest confidant!" Able not to look at Bernhard without exhibiting his detestation, Peter removed himself to the window. "You profess to hold my welfare as your cardinal charge, and yet you would so easily disregard that which lies closest to my heart?"

"Your present state of agitation," rejoined Bernhard with measured cadence, "will only disfavour us both if we canvass this subject any further. Now, I am also come at your invitation for a matter of pressing nature — one of grave import, which I trust you will discern."

"That is?" Peter barely glanced at him.

"It was at your mother's behest that, only after your father's passing, I reveal a certain truth pertaining to the tragedy that overtook her."

Peter wheeled about. "For this very same reason, I summoned you here. But what do you mean by 'only after my father has passed'?"

Bernhard first related the details of adversaries and the treasonous narrative contrived against Viviene by agents of dubious repute — much of which Peter had already surmised. That these conspirators, or rather, the clandestine society they represented, bore a sinister connection to our hero's recent perils was also known to him. And that poor Vitus, having entangled himself within their web, met his untimely end as a result, was a truth Peter still struggled to reckon with. But what our hero had not fathomed was the reason for Bernhard's oath and guardianship — that Peter might fulfil his destiny.

"*Destiny?*" Curiosity momentarily softened our hero's fury.

"A destiny," continued Bernhard, "your mother foresaw with terrifying clarity." With that sort of solemnity reserved for rituals of great significance, he reached into his coat, retrieving a small, timeworn envelope, its seal bearing the familiar crest of maternal lineage. "Within, you shall find her last words, a revelation that concerns not only you, but the fate of the confederacy entire."

***

We shall, for the moment — and do indulge this dreadfully insistent author — step aside from our principal fellow and the enigmatic envelope's contents, to cast our lot with Bernhard. In light of the interrogative setbacks involving the Tatzelwurm agent, he took the reins of inquisition. As a new day unfolded, he sallied forth to the designated den where the knave was held in an iron embrace, resolved to storm the stronghold of silence once and for all.

In but an hour hence, the carriage rolled to a halt. Bernhard and his cohorts alighted before the Blatternspital Madhouse. Fronted with a façade of inviting elegance, this white stone edifice masked only the monstrous theatre within. Reader, brace yourself, and squint if you must. Herein lies a carnival of the demented, where the mind — not so much healed as held captive — is but a plaything for the depraved, even paraded as novelties to the vulgar public; much like the freakish curios at a country fair.

Upon reaching the ominous-looking tall dark-timbered doors, Bernhard announced their presence with an authoritative knock. This rapping appeared to summon naught but vile shrieks which seemed to claw their way through the doors' gaps. Verily did the eyes of our intrepid visitors dart hither and thither, trading glances of utmost consternation.

After a prodigious pause, a narrow aperture of darkness yawned open with a noise as jarring a coffin lid disturbed. The keeper of the threshold — a ghoul so cadaverous it defied belief — peered out from the abyss with orbs as soulless as hollow graves.

Gasping, gulping, and blanching, Bernhard's companions shrank from the wraithlike sentinel. But as for Bernhard himself: "We seek an audience with Dr Pernicious' patient," plainly stated he.

Only after appearing lost in a scrutiny as cold as his own deathly pallor did the porter relent. Bestowing a grin so ghastly it could at once freeze the blood in one's veins, he beckoned with a clawlike appendage for them to enter the maw of madness.

Inside the bowels of this asylum — this underworld — they proceeded along dark, cold corridors chequered like a chessboard of the damned; even their footfalls echoed amidst the morbid concert of screams and maniacal laughter that seemed to bleed from the very stones.

After passing dozens of visages, whose gazes were but tormented windows to afflicted souls, they halted before a door from which emanated the very essence of dread.

"You may repose here." The porter gave a phalangeal gesture to a row of chairs, evidently less for sitting and more for restraining.

"We'll stand, if it's all the same," came the collective retort as feet inched away from the sundry leather straps and iron clasps glinting ominously.

"As you wish," uttered the porter as he floated like a spectre, disappearing behind the door, leaving Bernhard and his men enveloped by a crescendoing symphony of despair and hair-raising shrieks.

Abruptly, a set of double-doors across from them swung open. A nurse bustled out with grim purpose and an expression as devoid of mercy as the syringes she carried were of comfort.

"What devilry is that?" Bernhard's men pointed at a tableau of horror revealed within: a patient screeching like a banshee was strapped to a wooden chair atop a metal disc being spun in the name of therapy! The poor soul was attended by nurses with countenances as compassionate as gargoyles, all under the watchful gaze of a doctor whose eyes only danced with sinister delight.

Bernhard's lips twisted into a smile. "Centrifuge therapy is what you behold. A most innovative approach to madness, wouldn't you agree?"

"I now understand your insistence on this place for our captive," answered one. "This institution is positively —"

Upon the already misery-infested atmosphere, there now erupted the reedy, depressive diapason of a church organ, dispensing the dismal strains of Toccata and Fugue in D minor.

"Mercy on us!" exclaimed another, crossing himself. "Is not this the very vestibule to Hell?! Who, in their sound mind, would summon such a dirge?!"

"Ah," quipped Bernhard, "'tis only Bach's finest for Bedlam's worst."

As if out of nowhere, and as though summoned by the organ's very notes, the porter materialised in their midst, causing Bernhard's men to flinch in fright.

"Dr Pernicious will join us momentarily." The porter gestured with a bony finger for them to proceed.

Down a stairwell dark and desolate as the music still vibrated through the walls, the porter led them to a basement corridor, where dim candle light fought a losing battle against the gloom. Each cell they passed was alive with its own nightmare. The patients — nay, prisoners — clanged wooden spoons against the bars in a hellish orchestra, their mutterings, sneers, laughter, and wailings adding to the woeful discordant din.

As if this were not eerie enough, the porter himself skipped about like a lunatic, arms waving like a conductor of the mad-men, while the mournful droning still thundered from above. But at last, "this one, here," said he.

The heavy rattle of keys ensued; the door creaked open to reveal a single light shaft entering a slit of a window, striking the gagged and bound captive. About the cheerless periphery, implements of torture leered from the shadows.

Dr Pernicious eventually made his entrance.

Never was there seen in any man the very embodiment of a spider entering its web. His presence seemed to suck from the space what little light braved to enter it. His visage, being so pallid, so spectral, was that of an ossuary; harrowing cheek bones, cavernous sockets, an excrescent proboscis formed the scaffolding draped with waxen flesh. And his eyes — oh, those eyes — exhibited the coldest passion of a monster who had dissected more souls than bodies.

The captive, now visibly trembling, was a perfect study in fear. His horror-filled orbs, sliding from the hideous doctor, now fixed upon the sinister implements presently held aloft and caressed with a lover's touch.

"This incessant din," enquired Bernhard, "does it ever wane?"

The doctor's orbs slowly slithered from his apparatus of torture. "Never." A minacious grin crept across his lineaments like a shadow in a crypt.

"Excellent." Bernhard turned to the prisoner. "You must unburden yourself of your secrets," said he, "or else dance with madness until death. Now, *who* leads you? How far do the Tatzelwurms extend into the courts? What is your plot against the confederacy, and was it you behind the funeral attack?"

***

Bern's underbelly called to Adolfus once more. That shadowed alleyway which housed whispered conspiracies and veiled transgressions. That same fetid tavern, whose dank walls and shadowy corners served as a fitting stage for the clandestine meeting that lay ahead.

Adolfus entered the secluded room. The space, again lit by naught but candlelight's weak protest, was as unchanged as the treacherous intentions that had brought him before. Again, Adolfus' men took their station, silent sentinels to the night's shadow-play. Again, a subtle disturbance announced the other party's arrival, their presence betrayed by the soft rustle of cloaks and the cautious tread of their boots beyond the decrepit tapestry.

Laden with the moment's gravity, a pause preceded the hatch's opening. Though the key players would again communicate through so narrow a slit — ensuring that neither would be able to discern the other's countenance — Adolfus' eyes narrowed; he strove to descry the man's features just beyond the candle's reach. "Your endeavours have indeed ripened into the discord I sought," said he. "The city murmurs with unrest. Your next move must be *decisive*."

From the other side, the voice, betraying neither excitement nor hesitation, met his words. "Tell me, then, of this move."

Aware that trust in this line of work was not to be met out incautiously, Adolfus leant closer to the tapestry. "You are to weave a narrative most devious," began he, his words slithering through the slit like a serpent's hiss. "Rumours must spread, implicating the mint master in schemes of *illicit* trade. This narrative needs not bear the fruit of truth, only the bitter seeds of doubt."

The mystery co-conspirator remained silent, doubtless absorbing the directive. "A whisper can indeed cut deeper than a blade if it finds the right ear," acknowledged he at last. "And is this *all* you require from me?"

"Owing to the recent thwarted trade deals, there is soon to be enforced a new tax levy," continued Adolfus. "Here you must also strike! You are to leak this information and sow fears and discord within the merchants' guild itself."

The other tilted his head; his eyes narrowed as his mind clearly drew conclusions. "With the mint master's position undermined by the very people he seeks to govern," said he, "you see opportunity in this vulnerability to control the city's economic strings?"

"Do not pry into what is not your concern! Now, there is one more thing." He pushed a rolled-up paper through the hatch. "That man must be captured and delivered. He is a catalyst for chaos, and his apprehension is crucial."

Paper thus unfurled, and 'tis at this juncture, dear reader, that we step over to the tapestry's other side to become privy to a revelation that these characters themselves have still to grasp.

Momentarily flinching, the man scanned the poster; his eyes flickered with the sparks of unmistakable alarm. For the truth, now shockingly unveiled to us, is that this man, meeting with Adolfus, is none other than Franz.

"Why is this man of such... *interest?*" said he.

"The reasons are *my own*," replied Adolfus. "But this man's capture will be handsomely recompensed. A bounty generous enough to fund your deepest coffers, *perhaps?* Gold enough to sate your *most ravenous* of desires, even?"

Though his countenance remained a fortress of impassivity, most truly did Franz's mind race. With such a fate laid bare before him in ink and paper, he stood at a crossroads of the soul. To betray Peter, to deliver him to an unknown doom, was to turn his back on a once kindred spirit — perchance an ally not yet known? However, to aid him, to shelter him from the unknown, was to forsake the very power and position that might lead Franz to the heart of a vendetta that had consumed his every waking moment these past decades — a quest for retribution against his father's unjust demise.

"Wealth," at length, answered Franz, "I am already possessed of...."

Adolfus was doubtless quick to grasp his meaning. "You seek a station to elevate you above the city dregs? A position of power, *perchance?*"

Franz remained silent. The weight of his decision was indeed heavier than both the silence that now filled the room and the gold it might bring. His thoughts exploded into countless threads; a tapestry of confusion and calculation. And as his hand hovered over Peter's image, the pull of destiny tugged at his very soul. Peter's face seemed to gaze back at him through the gloom, silently pleading for clemency in a world bereft of it. Yet, what of his own father's blood, crying out for justice from the unfeeling earth it had been spilt upon? Could he, Franz, forsake this chance to wield the dagger of revenge?

The room's suffocating air pressed upon him; its very atmosphere seemed to constrict around him. The wavering candlelight, stirred by a sudden breeze, cast monstrous shadows that danced upon the walls, mirroring the dark waltz of Franz's thoughts.

The tapestry swayed gently as Adolfus awaited a response; his impatience was manifest even through the fabric's barrier that separated them. "What say you?" pressed he, oblivious to the turmoil he had wrought. "Will you undertake this task?"

11 – 13 AUGUST 1792

We now enter the uneasy atmosphere which had enveloped the Bernese city, a pall under which further disaster seemed to loom. For missives from France had brought news; news that spread through the streets and council chambers like a wildfire; news of the Brunswick Manifesto — a blunt instrument of threat against the French revolutionaries. Whispers of war increased. Fears of invasion grew more certain by the day, until no citizen, whether of humble stock or lofty rank, could feel secure.

Yet while such ominous rumblings from abroad set the nerves of all a-jangle and saw our goodly citizens groaning under their uncertainties, another matter closer to home stepped forth to consume the city's gossip; that of the notorious fugitive — the schultheiss' own first-born, turned criminal!

Indeed, 'twas impossible to traverse a single corner of this midday sun burnt city without encountering the city's guards marching hourly — their synchronised steps reverberating — or the WANTED posters, each featuring the same man with determined eyes and a price on his head.

And it is into this scene, our band of Lucerne rogues, having at last gained entrance to the city's confines, rushed eagerly through its gates, determined to seize upon their prey.

Bearing the scars of that violent clash, they scanned every passing face with a mixture of professional scrutiny and personal vengeance. Their hunt for our hero had become more than a mission; it was a quest to heal their wounded pride. The traders, shopkeepers, and city folk, suffering the intensity of such study, cast wary glances at each other. The appearance of these harsh-countenanced men and their armour glinting in the blaring light only added to the blend of fear and fascination which held the city in its iron grip.

"Look here!" One of the guards abruptly stopped and slammed his hand against a notice board. "The menace himself!"

"There too!" Another pointed at a poster across the street. "And there also!" He indicated still several more, covering a weathered crier's box. "With his face plastered across the city, how are we even to secure our bounty?"

Their schemes and vendettas, seemingly thwarted, the guards fell into a most fierce contention, blaming each other. So engrossed they became in dissension they noticed not the clatter of an approaching carriage.

"Tell me," spoke a male, signalling his driver to stop. The carriage halted beside the guards; the fine horses snorted. "Why such vehemency among you over this man?" The glass slid down, and a gloved hand protruded forth, pointing at the poster. "Surely no bounty alone fuels such a boutade?"

Caught off guard by his presence, the men exchanged weary glances. But after hushed deliberation, their leader, a tall man with a scar tracing his jaw, approached the carriage to address the stranger. "We crossed swords with the villain. He left his mark on us. Our honour demands satisfaction."

From within the carriage's obscured confines, upon the man's lips, there could be seen a cunning smile. "Ah, *honour*," said he in a musing tone, "both a powerful ally and demanding master. Perhaps I can help you serve both? From your accent and insignia, I perceive you are of the Lucerne Guard?"

The leader eyed the shadowy figure and his offer with some suspicion. "*Who are you?* And *why* would you assist *us*?"

The man's face emerged from the shadows. "You may call me Adolfus. Let us just say I require men of your... *dedication*. Where are you staying?"

"We shall lodge at the Goldener Schlüssel."

"Expect me as the evening bell tolls. Consider it an investment in justice."

At that, with a nod that sealed the unspoken pact, Adolfus' self-satisfied visage vanished back into the shadowy interior, and the carriage rolled away.

***

Elsewhere, at Neues Schloss Bümpliz, under the dappled shade of trees, on a gravelled pathway bordered by pristinely squared hedges, we alight and join our hero and Bernhard as they walk side by side — the crunch underfoot puncturing their grave silence.

"Every method known to us has been exhausted," said Bernhard, finally speaking; his voice, soft but firm, mingled with the breeze and the rustling of leaves overhead. "The blackguard will not speak."

Peter's gaze was fixed ahead; his eyes purposelessly roamed the property's elegant white and taupe stone façade. His mind adrift with disappointment and burdened by the weight of his brother's unsolved death, he replied, "I wonder, is it his resolve or our imagination that is the deficiency here?"

As the sun continued to shed its sweltering heat on the environs, a maid began pulling the property's exterior shutters closed over the panelled windows.

"Are we, therefore, to be bested by the rogue's silence?" continued our hero. "There must be a crack in his armour? A chink you can yet exploit?"

That the captured Tatzelwurm member had remained obdurate in his silence — even after starvation, thirst, and various means of torture were inflicted against him — the situation appeared more hopeless by the hour.

Peter stopped abruptly at the walkway's end, causing a few small stones to scatter across the courtyard. "I must avenge my brother, Bernhard. I will have the truth, no matter the cost!"

This declaration was shattered by a crescendo of galloping hooves. A rider burst into the courtyard in a cloud of dust, as if carrying the very winds of fate. The steed — deep chestnut, its coat glimmering in the sunlight — skidded to a halt, sending gravel skittering in a spray beneath its hooves.

"I am come to report to Peter," proclaimed the messenger.

Our hero warily beckoned him over. "I am he..."

With urgency aflame in every motion, the man dismounted and approached with a leather-bound satchel. Chest heaving from exertion, he produced an envelope. "It relates," said he, "to Viktor's residence, sir."

"It *does*?" Peter tore it open. The following words leapt from the page:

> *The clock is missing. Please advise what we ought next to do.*

"Curse this affair!" muttered Peter.

"What news comes?" Bernhard leant in, attempting to peruse the lines.

"The one piece that might hold the answers. It's gone."

Probably sensing that his continued presence was unnecessary, the messenger enquired if Peter had any message to relay. Informed as he was to convey only thanks, the courier returned to his horse and set off in a hard gallop.

"There is no time for further delay." Peter's mind raced with plans. He turned to Bernhard. "Tomorrow, I shall make for Basel. Mayhap the billet there could be key to all this?"

***

And so, at dawn's first blush of muted gold and shadows, our hero stood ready in the courtyard. The early morning's cool air, though a respite from the days of sweltering heat, bit at his skin. The carriage awaited; the horses stamped as though as impatient as our hero to set off.

As he contemplated the journey ahead, he realised he had, for some time, not once thought of Elizabeth. *At last, the spell is broken...*

Just as he was about to mount the carriage, a rider emerged from the shadows. This breathless man brought word that one individual from among Ludwig's list had been traced to a neighbouring canton and was due to be apprehended this very day. The messenger handed over an envelope.

These words, though auspicious, dissuaded Peter not from his proposed journey. With a curt nod, he ordered that should the man be caught, one of his men should come to Bubendorf at once. At that, he stepped inside the carriage.

***

Yet, even as Peter set off, news arrived with the subtlety of a storm at the grand yet foreboding hall of Adolfus' schloss. A letter, its contents alarming enough to the quicken the pulse of many a worthless brigand, was pressed into his hands by a night courier.

The very fiend sought by our hero's agents — a mere pawn in this game of shadows — had learned of his pursuers and sought securer lodgings at an inn rather than hazard returning to his own abode. From there, the rascal penned a letter to Adolfus, seeking guidance and imploring assistance. His words, clearly scrawled in haste, were laced with dread; the ink had evidently barely dried before the message was pressed into the hands of a trusted courier.

Indeed, Adolfus was struck with the precariousness of this situation. Immediately, he saw in the threads of past apprehensions weaving through the present, the strings that connected to Vitus and led inexorably to our hero. The peril was clear: should Peter's agents capture this man, it would not be long before the trail would lead to Adolfus' own gilded door.

His mind as sharp as the quill he seized in hand, he wrote his response. His instructions were unequivocal: remain hidden; speak to no one; trust nothing. The despatch was hastily sealed, the familiar emblem pressed into its crimson wax with an unspoken warning.

Thrusting the note into the waiting messenger's hands, he bade the rascal deliver it with all due haste and to leave not the man's side for fear something should, by some cruel twist of fate, spirit so vital a charge away.

The rascally messenger thus hastened away, after which Adolfus summoned a cadre of men whose loyalty was as much to the glint of gold as to the cause.

"Redouble the city surveillance!" stated Adolfus. "Though it is all too likely that Valentin has already slipped the net, he must not evade our grasp a second time."

One advisor, hawk-like orbs and pinched of countenance, leant forward. "Shall we send men back to that inn where he stayed? They may still uncover some trail; some clue we have overlooked in our haste."

"Yes. Do that, and without delay. Leave no stone unturned; even if we must tear that inn apart brick by brick!"

***

For every stride Peter's horses made towards Bubendorf, the indefatigable Adolfus' machinations spread further into the shadows. These two men, separated by miles yet inextricably linked by fate, were engaged in a battle of wits and will. A high-stakes game of cat and mouse played out across the vast landscape, mile-stoning every intrepid hour that passed.

As the sun reached its zenith, Peter arrived at Schloss Wildenstein's familiar gate. Even as he crossed the threshold, an inexplicable sense of foreboding vibrated on the air — lifting the hairs on his neck. This feeling soon found its corroboration in his sudden meeting with Phillipina in the hallway.

Upon laying her eyes on him, she turned so startling a shade of white that one might have mistaken her for a ghost. She recoiled with such alacrity that an observer could be forgiven for thinking Peter was some sort of plague-ridden wretch; a pariah to be shunned at all costs.

Ere the words of a confused greeting could form upon Peter's lips, the woman unleashed a torrent of invectives, her words — poison-tipped daggers — branding him as the "scoundrel whose infamy knew no bounds" she had always believed him to be.

So stunned into silence was our hero that he could only stand motionless, as if he had been turned to stone by the force of such fury.

Drawn thither by Phillipina's fiery denunciations, Pier emerged; his own countenance mirrored his daughter's shock and unease. "Peter," stammered he, "what brings —"

"Has something happened?" interrupted Peter, at last finding his voice. He stepped forward, only to be met with the sight of father and daughter stepping back — Phillipina clinging onto her Pier's sleeve.

Such peculiar behaviour naturally served to deepen Peter's mystification. He would have probed the cause of their conduct were it not for the sound of hurried footsteps echoing through the open door, drawing his attention to the scene unfolding behind him.

Edmunda, with Emil, Hans, Harris, and Helene close on her heels, spilled through like a flash-flood, their collective distress palpable in every hurried step.

"Oh, heavens above!" shrilled Edmunda. "Our dear Lizzie has vanished!"

No sooner did her tear-filled eyes alight on our hero, than she nigh sucked all the air from the space with so horror-stricken a gasp that it seemed she might expire on the spot. Her clogs ground to a halt while her arms flung wide — forming a barricade into which her hapless entourage crashed with all the grace of a herd of startled cattle.

"You!" shrieked she; her eyes bulged so far from their sockets as to leave no doubt of her ire. "This calamity is all *your doing* I'll warrant!"

Forthwith, the hallway did erupt into a pandemonium as would have made bedlam appear no more than a tranquil tea party. From every which direction, accusatory fingers jabbed at our hero like swords wielded by an angry mob. Incriminations, each more vehement and vituperative than the last, flew through the air with all the fervour and frequency of flaming arrows loosed in the heat of battle — Edmunda reviling him as a villain of the blackest sort; Phillipina excoriating him as a venomous snake; Emil lamenting the day he had ever made his acquaintance; Hans arraigning him with all the self-righteous indignation of a convicting judge; Helene lambasting him with a fury as scorching as the flames of Hades itself; Harris, as silent as a mute, knowing not where to look. Pier stuttered and stammered, his tongue tied in knots.

Through this dissonant chorus of opprobrium, Peter gleaned, to his subsequent horror and the shadow which stretched across his conscience, the tragic fate that had befallen poor Ernest — a casualty of the very violence that had been intended for him. As awful as this circumstance was, leaving him breathless and reeling, and as deserving as he was of such condemnation, now was not the time to debate it. In an attempt to restore a semblance of order amidst the chaos, he raised his voice above the din. "*Where* and *when* was she last seen?"

These words, called with such authority, evoked a fleeting *tableau vivant* of bafflement. But then: "Liestal village; two days past," came the resounding reply, spoken with the fervour of a mob baying afresh for blood.

Of a sudden, footsteps resounded and one of Peter's agents — his clothing drenched in sweat and dust — burst through the wall of accusers. His eyes darted about, searching for his master amidst the sea of hostile faces. "We have him!" breathlessly exclaimed he, at last. "The man you seek!" He grasped Peter's wrist. "We've *captured* him!"

Natch, at this obscure revelation, did all widening eyes swing on our hero. Every expression, a study in contradiction, a mixture of horror and grim triumph, openly avowed the unshakeable conviction that Peter's increasing guilt had been confirmed beyond all doubt.

"Forgive me," uttered Peter as he cut through the stuttering gathering and led his agent outside into the courtyard's relative privacy. "Pray, tell me."

The agent struggled to catch his breath. "He's already spoken of a headquarters... a place where he and his fellow scoundrels convene monthly.

Tomorrow is the next meeting. I believe this is the breakthrough we've been seeking! Let us leave now."

Peter fell silent, torn between his quest for truth and the immediate plight of Lizzie's disappearance. The latter, undoubtedly connected to the incident in Lucerne, clawed at his breast, demanding action. Time, that cruel mistress, was once again conspiring against him. This agent brought perhaps the very answer our hero desperately sought; however, duty distracted his mind elsewhere.

Likely sensing his hesitation, the agent urged, "we must return to Bern now."

Presently, there spilled out from the schloss a crowd of bewildered on-lookers. Turning from them, Peter drew close to his fellow's ear and whispered into it. "There is something I need you to do..."

***

After many an hour spent scouring Liestal's streets and alleys, our hero, Emil, and Harris, found themselves at last in possession of a most vital clue. Having importuned every passerby and interrogated every shopkeeper, they chanced upon a tavern where Fortune, in a rare display of her kinder nature, had seen fit to smile upon their endeavours.

It so happened that, several nights prior, a band of unsavoury-looking rascals, accompanied by a sole female — her countenance and masculine garb in keeping with her company — dined at this very establishment. The tavern keeper, a man well versed in the disparity of talk, and whose nose for intrigue was as keen as his ears were sharp, had managed to snatch enough of their un-savoury discourse. Though they spoke in vague terms, his shrewd understanding deduced that they plotted to kidnap some unfortunate lass.

Pressed as we are, dear reader, both for page and time, let us dispense with the minutiae of the subsequent enquiries. Suffice it to say that, armed with new intelligence, our trio soon found an obscure property, whose very exterior reeked of the corruption lurking behind its walls. There, through means perhaps not entirely befitting a gentleman, they were able to extract a confession from one of the co-conspirators in this dastardly plot. Though the fiend claimed ignorance of the damsel's name, he knew enough to point them in the direction they must go to rescue her.

Dangerous as such a rescue might be, our hero dismissed Emil and Harris back to the schloss to comfort a fretting Edmunda. With the proverbial bean-spilling rogue in ropes, Peter hastened for the garrison to procure their aid.

The scene at the garrison was no less tense. Owing to Jago's zeal, Peter's face covered many walls and street posts in ink and bounty. 'Twas only after he entrusted the prisoner to the guards — and with much effort and many promises to surrender to their chains when the deed was done — that he persuaded them to assist him in his rescue.

Hence, with a small detachment in tow, our hero set off.

Within the frantic counting of but sixty minutes, the rescuers were on the approach to what they could perceive from the purpling dusk was a deteriorating chateau. All appeared silent. But the faint glow, as of a torch, appeared intermittently beyond a shuttered casement.

Having dismounted at a short distance, the party tied the horses and advanced. Doors soon gave way beneath their onslaught, the sound a thunderclap in the stillness. Within, the air was heavy with the dust of desolation. The rescuers moved with purpose, and to their no little wonder, finding their passage unimpeded and remarking a warm slit beneath a door, they burst in on a room where Peter stumbled upon a tableau most unexpected.

Among several startled countenances, a female stared back at him. Though not Elizabeth's face, it was still one familiar enough to give him poise.

"Du Pont?!" The woman's cry arrested his alert like a bell's toll. "What brings *you* here?"

'Twas in that moment, as the haze of uncertainty lifted from Peter's eyes, he recognised she was none other than Franz's own sister. "I ought to ask *you* the same!"

Meantime, in an inner room, our fair heroine, having heard this name and recognising Peter's voice, did naturally assume this to be his true appellation.

At any rate, the guards sprang into action. Lizzie was liberated. The captors were rounded up and herded outside into the cold embrace of iron and wood. Franz's sister, her eyes alight with hatred and betrayal, fixed upon Peter with unforgiving malice. But lo, as if this scene were not already filled with enough mystery and maligned marvel, the next staggering occurrence descended.

Barely had Lizzie been handed into the carriage when a group of around eight riders swiftly approached. 'Twas only as they came within reach of the flambeaux haze our hero observed the vanguard rider was Jago.

Peter's no little astonishment was instantly augmented when he remarked one of the men behind him was Franz himself. Indeed, both our hero and he beheld each other with some perceivable awe.

***

For but a brief moment, we must go back to the scene where Adolfus, within the decrepit confines of that dark room, had unwittingly employed Franz's services.

"What say you?" had pressed the former. "Will you undertake this task?"

Here — as the candle began to die, relinquishing its little light against the encroaching gloom, further enveloping the two men in deepening tenebrosity — we now learn the outcome to this request.

"Consider it done," said Franz. "Your man will be found."

Thus, with these words, an agreement was struck in the shadows, binding the two men in a web of intrigue — a Faustian pact, if you will, dear reader. Franz, like a chess master, moved his piece across the board in a most dangerous game; a game where the stakes are life and death, and the currency is the souls of men. And Adolfus, ever the opportunist, had rejoiced in seizing upon his greatest chance to furthering his own ends.

But will Franz remain true to his word, or will he contrive to outwit Adolfus, thus preserving both Peter and conscience...

***

Back inside the carriage — shadowed by the guards, the prison wagon, and Jago with his motley crew — as it now rattled along the uneven path, Peter, and Lizzie, sat opposite each other, abided the space between them in silence; a silence fraught with every uncertainty and unspoken words. The dim interior, lit intermittently by the moonbeams, held its passengers in a shadowy embrace. And in this cloistered world on wheels, truths on both sides begged for air.

Peter, though try he did, found not the courage to confront her for the past deceit she had practised upon him, nor the fortitude to canvas Ernest's tragic demise. Moreover, his mind, a battleground of present discomforts, was further besieged by the bewildering notion of Franz aligning with Jago, and the revelation of Franz's sister being one of Lizzie's captors.

Through a silvery slant, it could be seen that Lizzie's gaze was a storm of confusion. Her lips seemed to part as if to speak a hundred times, but no words came. However, after some time, a whisper finally broke the seal. "Why," uttered she, her eyes a reluctant consort to his, "do I again find myself both ensnared by and indebted to you?"

Peter met her gaze, his own conflict mirrored therein. "I begin to ask myself the same... you must *abhor* the dangers which, like shadows, continually lay siege upon you — shadows I fear are indirectly cast by my own hand."

Her eyes swiftly retreated to the window, where the world blurred by in the shades of night and moonlight. For some moments, she was silent.

"Indeed," now said she, "your hand may cast these shadows; nevertheless, it is also the same that pulls me from the blackness time and again."

The carriage turned, and for a moment, they were suspended in seeming weightlessness.

"An occasion," said Peter, "I would have before gladly rejoiced in. But now I consider it solely my duty. Were it not for your father..."

Though he disdained Elizabeth for her guile, our hero suffered the greatest conflict of agony. Ernest, innocent in her past schemes, had only ever offered Peter paternal affection as genuine as any blood-bound kin. In seeking Peter's soul, his sundry enemies had taken Ernest so unjustly. Thus, with the loss of his own dear father, the afflictions of grief were compounded.

Fate so blindly distributes its lashes upon the innocent. Yet, such is the order of the world. But again, as much as he resented Elizabeth, he knew not even she deserved such cruelty.

To temper his detestation, his pity rose up — even compassion.

Unbeknownst to our hero, his inner turmoil was a war between the swelling revulsion for her misdeeds and a lingering affection; a war still far from resolution.

"Besides," resumed he, "there are a myriad of circumstances, I trust, on both sides which will leaven the duty devoid of conciliatory accord and rather ferment the sentiments of disgust."

Though anxiety clearly arrested her countenance, Lizzie inclined her head; she braced her hand against the seat as if to steady herself against more than the carriage's movement. To query Peter's true identity, even under such extenuating circumstances, was for her to tacitly confess her own duplicity, to lay bare months of prolonged exploit. Her bottom lip curled inwards; her eyes exhibited vast perturbation. Truly, she contended with her own battle.

Peter sensed her dilemma and difficulty more eloquently than he would have cared to admit. 'Twas not an uneasiness he could behold with indifference. Oh, how he wished solely to loathe her; to revenge himself upon her; to triumph over her!

How curious is the human heart, swift to condemn in one beat — deeming a soul beyond redemption, unworthy even of our disdain — and in the next, upon the shift of fate's winds, our resolve may waver, succumbing to the pangs of self-doubt; even faltering on the precipice of forgiveness.

The carriage dipped into a rut, subsequently propelling Lizzie forward. Without conscious thought, Peter's arms shot out to steady her. Likewise, Lizzie sought their protection. In that fleeting caesura of motion, the barriers between them appeared to quiver. In this moment of shared vulnerability, the fragile thread of understanding dangled within their grasp.

The party soon reached Wildenstein.

Whilst the Liestal guards waited outside the gate — according to our hero's solemn promise to return as soon as he had settled Lizzie into a chamber — Peter rather drew Pier to one side. "I must impose upon your trust," said he as he reached inside his pocket. "Take this for now as surety." He handed to him his mother's diary.

Eyes fixed upon it, Pier visibly started. "How is it *you* have this?" He regarded Peter with manifest concern and confusion, indeed, confirming our hero's inkling of some connection between their families.

Peter clasped his hand. "I will explain all soon. But for now, be assured I am Valentin's friend, and I will bring to justice all behind his mother's demise."

At these words, Pier's countenance rippled with emotion. As if battling some internal violence, he looked away.

But time being against our hero, in point, Peter begged to be allowed passage through the property's rear door where, following the descent into the woods, he would, as earlier arranged with his agent, find a horse tied by the spring.

Still plainly moved by the sight of Vivienne's diary, Pier obliged, and our hero, escaping the irons and chains of the waiting Liestal guards, set off for Bern.

***

Meantime, at Adolfus schloss, his heels clicked loudly — a metronome to his mounting unease — and his cane clanked forcefully against the drawing room marble floors. The hours passed since he despatched the roguish messenger to guard his ward weighed heavier and heavier upon his peace.

Such apprehensions were not about to lighten, either.

The very rascal being returned, now entered; his face bore news that, before any utterance, chilled the blood in Adolfus' veins.

"The man, my lord," spluttered the courier, "he's been taken. He was seen being bundled into a wagon."

Indeed, Adolfus sought the support of a nearby bureau. "How could this...?" A snarl curled the corner of his lip. "For sure, this is Valentin's work!"

As the revelation settled like a leaden cloak upon his shoulders, he turned his horror-stricken gaze upon his lands beyond the window; a vista of control and dominion. But now, the chilling apparition of exposure loomed over him afresh. His empire, built upon the precarious pillar of secrets and shadows, might now topple in the light of Valentin's defiance.

"If that man confesses and reveals too much," exclaimed Adolfus, "all will be for *nothing*!"

Back to his escritoire, he stormed. His hand trembled as he scribbled a missive. "Fly with this now. Allow nothing to hinder your path."

Barely had this brigand departed when another arrived, bringing reports fresh and disturbing from France. Tuileries had been stormed. Around six-hundred Swiss Guards defending it massacred; a further blow — one entirely beyond Adolfus' sphere of control! Notwithstanding his own perilous uncertainties, such a report had potency enough even to disturb this sly schemer, Adolfus.

***

Before dawn's nascent light spread across the land, whispering promises of revelation over Bern, Peter, cloaked in triumph's prelude, stood before the captive — a treacherous cog in the grand conspiracy — who quivered under Fate's grip.

With a voice frayed with desperation, the man yielded not solely the location of the forgers' den and the corrupt scriveners' imminent convocation, but also the existence of a secret chamber. This chamber stored decades of iniquitous ledgers; a cache potent enough to shatter the edifice of Bern's elite — the very patricians entwined with the unmerited disgrace of our hero's mother.

"Do you speak the truth?" demanded an agitated Peter. His mother's visage flickered in his mind's eye as his heart anchored to a precipice of vindication. "There is evidence that can acquit my mother?"

The corrupt instantly bargained his knowledge for clemency and sanctuary, promising further secrets — keys that would also unlock our hero's exoneration.

Hence, a pact was struck, and with the accord sealed, Peter turned to marshal his contingent. The surrounding air crackled with the tension of impending justice as he departed for the forgers' sanctum.

***

Oh, but simultaneously, in a gloomy, nondescript room of a Bern city building, Adolfus' henchmen clustered around a frayed map of Lucerne city. Their faces, scored with urgency, they gazed upon the annotation, marking the forgers' headquarters. Their orders from Adolfus were clear: obliterate all evidence; leave no trace of the dark enterprise.

With the precision of a small army, the men furnished themselves with the tools of their grim task and moved to erase the truth Peter sought to unearth. Thus, whilst Peter, armoured in righteous fury, rallied his own forces, the race against time had begun.

***

For our hero, the journey to Lucerne was fraught with every sickening sensation conceivable. Every moment that passed, every beat of the hoof, drove deeper the anxious expectation of soon prevailing upon all who had disturbed the harmony and longevity of a family.

The city of Lucerne stood as an unwitting sentinel as Peter and his men at last reached what was to be the epicentre of their retribution. But upon nearing the ancient building whispered to be the forgers' lair, the air, once heavy with the promise of justice, was now choked by a billowing miasma, an acrid stench!

The heart of their quest — the lair itself — rose before them, being devoured by a flaming inferno. Against the blazing backdrop, silhouettes of fire marshals and townspeople dashed to and fro.

Once infused with the taste of victory, all now stood mute, each face corroded with the same horrified disbelief. The flames, lighting up the environs, painted our onlooking hero and his retinue with the hues of devastating defeat.

Overwrought with despair and desperate to salvage what he could from the ruins of his hopes, Peter dismounted to hasten into the fiery den. But his agents, seizing upon him, dragged him back.

"No!" shouted they, barely audible over the roaring flames. "It's too late!"

"No!" cried our hero, crumbling to the rough ground.

The structure, once the repository of damning evidence, now symbolised nothing more than the annihilation of Peter's aspirations. With each timber that succumbed — with a loud groaning noise — to the flames, joist-by-joist, piece-by-piece, Peter's resolve turned to cinders, the fire's heat searing the very marrow of his bones.

The shadows flung by the fire danced, as if mockingly, underscoring the futility of his crusade and the seemingly unquenchable power of his still unknown enemies. Having suffered so many setbacks, this loss was more than the mere destruction of evidence; it was an arduous journey resulting in but a bitter portrayal of fruitless endeavour, eviscerating his soul of absolution.

There, in the conflagration's wrath, lay the ashes of hope, the remnants of his campaign to clear his and his mother's sullied names.

Again, as with the scroll, the flames consumed all hope and futurity, leaving naught but the bitterest taste of defeat.

Most truly, in this black moment, the weight of months bearing the brand of guilt, and the sundry dangers and desperation he lived through, pressed upon our hero with renewed force.

Even the night sky seemed to close in around him; the stars themselves flickered out one by one until all that remained was the inky blackness of despair.

In this, in his darkest hour, Peter could not help but wonder if the universe itself had conspired against him; if the very fabric of fate had been woven to ensure his downfall.

How was he ever to return from this?

13 – 19 AUGUST 1792

Even as despair descended, the smallest ember of defiance would not be extinguished. Peter could not — *would* not — allow this tragedy to be the terminus of his plight.

Desperate as he was to salvage something — *anything*! — from the conflagration before him, its heat a searing wall, its tongues of flames licking the sky, demanded immediate action.

Ergo, rallying his comrades, together, they threw themselves into the lines of bucket brigades, joining the ranks of fire marshals, men, women, building workers, and soldiers from the garrison.

The air clamoured with shouts and cries, the hiss of water meeting flame, and the crackle of burning timbers. From hand to hand, buckets of water from the nearby Lake Lucerne were hauled; a desperate lifeline in the face of so palpable an inferno. Leather hoses, like great serpents, were strung up to surrounding pumps, their nozzles aimed at the heart of the blaze. Water-carts trundled through the chaos, bringing aid to the soon beleaguered firefighters.

Still, even as our hero and all others battled the flames, the fire seemed only to defy their efforts. Driven by upward air drafts, sparks danced and whirled across the sky, threatening to ignite the surrounding properties. The very air shimmered with heat; the smoke stung the eyes and choked the lungs of all who dared to face it.

In a desperate bid to contain the fire's spread, an adjoining, run-down dwelling became the firebreak. Its walls were torn down, the splintering of wood and crashing of masonry adding to the cacophonous symphony of destruction and desperation.

At last, after a day and night's laborious exertion, the mighty roar was reduced to a whisper of smouldering embers. Dawn broke upon the land; its pale light filtered through the haze of smoke. Peter and his men — faces blackened with soot — stood amid the charred aftermath: a tomb of ash and debris, collapsed chimneys, and joists jutting from the wreckage like the bones of some giant beast; a scene of utter devastation that seemed to mock their despair.

Our hero, his eyes still stinging from the acrid smoke and the heat which still clung to the air, with difficulty surveyed the scene; he searched for anything that might have survived the conflagration.

But alas, where once had stood tables and chairs, bookshelves and desks, there was now nothing more than a jumble of charred wood and melted metal. The very fabric of the building reduced to an indecipherable mess. Papers that might have held vital clues were now nothing more than flakes of ash; their secrets lost forever to the flames.

Of a sudden, the skeleton of a structure groaned.

Barely had our hero's men pulled him to safety when a roaring preluded the partial collapse of its weakened frame. From somewhere above — perchance, what must have once been an antechamber — with a metallic screech, a groaning of wood, and a burst of ash, a last-standing chimney breast toppled, dragging down several charred joists.

From amidst a cloud of choking dust and soot, a small wooden and iron box tumbled forth, its fall broken by the debris-strewn ground. The box, its wood almost entirely burnt, its metal scorched and dented, seemed to have defied the very flames that had sought to consume it.

Heart now racing more from mounting anticipation, Peter — his gloves barely shielding his hands from the residual heat — retrieved the object.

The lock's mechanisms, melted and useless, gave little resistance, revealing the partially burned contents within. A ledger; its edges charred and its pages fused by the heat. Peter flung the box to the floor — clattering like a gunshot through the wreckage — and leafed through the brittle pages.

The text danced indecipherable before his eyes. Here in his hands, did he hold a trove of fragmented secrets? His breath hitched. The implications swirled in his mind like the surrounding ash. This document, whatever secrets it held, was perhaps the slender thread from which Peter's quest now dangled.

***

The next day, at his desk in the privacy of his study, our hero carefully examined the ledger's fragile pages. With each sheet turned, he strove to decipher the faded script and incomplete entries — the damage making the task excruciatingly slow. Each fragment of information gleaned only led to confusion, disappointment, and questions. There were names listed that he did not even recognise and services paid for that baffled his comprehension.

A rap came on the door; the butler entered, saying Bernhard had arrived.

"Ah! Send him through at once."

A sober-looking Bernhard stepped inside.

"I can see from your face," said Peter, motioning to the chair on the desk's other side, "that you herald nothing that will lift my mood."

"Indeed." Bernhard sat down and glanced about the shelves of leather-bound tomes. "Our captive remains as tight-lipped as any clamped oyster. We have gleaned nothing."

Peter could only shake his head at this report. The enemies' enshrouding shadows only thickened and deepened the riddle. How were they ever to prevail over this enigmatic foe?

Bernhard's eyes fixed on the ledger. "So, this is the sole acquisition of the Lucerne endeavour you wrote me about. Does it at all answer to your questions?"

Peter gently slid it to him. "Alas, like the tight-lipped captive, it yields nothing to light the way." His gaze drifted to the window.

How long could they continue down this path, chasing shadows and dead ends? There had to be some strategy, some way of outmanoeuvring their opponents... His gaze wandered from the window, settling on the inkwell. It was in this moment the spark of inspiration ignited like flint to steel.

He turned full on Bernhard. "What if, rather than seeking information with blade or bribe..." — the gears of his mind turned with the mantel clock's chiming ten — "... we wield ink and implication?"

Bernhard's brow pinched together; his eyes narrowed. "Go on."

"A message..." — Peter rose from his chair with sudden vigour — "Yes! A poster... cryptic enough to stir their paranoia and draw them out."

For some time, Bernhard uttered nothing; from the expressions which flitted across his phiz, his thoughts clearly shifted from one possibility to the next. "Yes," replied he. "But for this to succeed, we must word such a thing without alerting the entire city of our intentions..."

13 – 19 August 1792

***

Within hours, a city printery became a hive of activity. Under Bernhard's management, posters were produced with feverish haste, each one emblazoned with symbols and phrases that, while appearing innocuous to the uninitiated, would, to those versed in the clandestine language, proclaim a message so clear: the captive was a pawn; his release hinged on the currency of information.

As night fell upon the city like a curtain, Bernhard despatched his network of agents. Their shadows slipped through the still locked-down streets to affix the posters to walls, alleyways, and noticeboards.

With dawn shedding its rays over Bern, the populace's murmurs soon began. The citizens pointed at and pondered over the strange posters. The myriad symbols — chief among them a cat-like faced dragon (the Tatzelwurm) coiled around a mountain peak — were perplexing; the text, indeed bemusing:

> Under the eye of the mountain dragon, the silent pawn awaits the Queen's gambit. When the moon hides its gaze, the board shall be set for a trade of whispers. Seek the crossroads where the Bear's gaze breaks the river's flow.

Still, amidst the perplexed throngs, whose whispers carried the twin sentiments of curiosity and confusion, there were found those whose eyes narrowed in recognition. The message, it seemed, had found its mark. The trap was set.

And so, our hero and Bernhard needed now to wait. In a mere two days hence, the captive would be conveyed to the Bärengraben — the bear pit. There the game of knowledge would, pray, see the captive bartered for the answers so pivotal to our hero's plight.

***

Once more, we step over into quaint Bubendorf, to the elegant Schloss

Ebenrain, where we find our supporting characters of this twisting and turning drama, each playing their unwitting role in the grand tapestry of our tale. Amongst these, two deserve our particular attention.

Volatile talk saturated the sweltering August air as Franz paced the library with an erratic rhythm; his footsteps echoed his heart's tumultuous beating; his hands clenched and unclenched as he grappled with the chains of his predicament.

"You must help my sister!" He rounded sharply on Jago, who, with an air of nonchalance, reclined into his late father's carved high-backed chair and now rather directed his attention to his late father's dalmatians. "You assured me it would be simple — abduct Elizabeth; play the hero; and besmirch that, that... rotten fellow, Peter."

Jago sat up rigidly and pushed the dogs away. "And so it would have been, had not that impudent man arrived with the Liestal guards and complicated matters! No one, I assure you, is more vexed by this turn of events than I."

"But what of my sister?" Franz balled his hands into fists. "You still have yet to devise a plan to extricate her, *and my men*, from the gaol!"

The fading light from the high windows cast a sombre hue over the room, deepening the furrows of worry scored into his brow.

"I am neither without sympathy for your sister," replied Jago, "nor exhaustion from the endless hours spent striving to conjure a mode in which we can extricate her — and your men! But this is hardly my fault!" One dalmatian pawed for his attention. "— There you go," said he to the dog, feeding into its mouth a titbit; an act which incited instant rivalry among the other three. "The garrison," resumed he, fixing his stony gaze on Franz, "is beyond my sphere of influence. Besides, they are more preoccupied with the pending wars."

The air crackled with the palpable energy of unspoken accusations and shared dread. Franz, cautious in all his dealings, had not yet revealed to Jago his prior relationship with Peter. And most truly, in this moment, the despair he felt for his sister only heightened his zeal to seize upon our hero and deliver him to the still-anonymous instigator from Bern.

For Jago, his own enmity towards our hero was not borne of simple rivalry, but rather the unpredictable nature of a man he could not control. And, as our fair reader may have already surmised, long before Peter arrived in Bubendorf, Jago had fixed his passions and desires upon our fair heroine; were it not for his father's prepotency, he would have already cast his future happiness at that altar and claimed her for his lover.

"My sister suffers in a cell because of your ambition," resumed Franz, half-pleading, half-demanding. "You *must* rectify this!"

***

'Twas now the next day's late afternoon, and we rejoin Adolfus. His carriage, a chariot of purpose, trundled along the winding cobbled streets, ferrying him towards the Bernese Rathaus, where he was set to convene with the Small Council. His agenda, as one might expect, was filled with matters of great import — addressing the escalating threats from abroad, establishing a date for Varus' formal appointment to the office of Bernese schultheiss, and the execution of his next scheme upon the mint master.

It so happened en route that his keen eyes caught sight of a crowd gathered before a wall; their attention fully consumed by a cryptic poster that had appeared overnight. Intrigued, Adolfus rapped upon his carriage's roof, and the driver halted. With the window pulled down, he called out to the assembled citizens and enquired into what had so captivated their interest.

Scarcely had the words left his lips when the voice of one of his personal guards rent the air. The man reined in his horse, a mighty black steed, with a flourish. "My lord," said he, "there is something you *must* see." With that, he held aloft a rolled-up, tatty-looking poster and presented it to the window.

Adolfus extended a hand, his rings glinting in the light as he grasped the poster. His gaze swept over the cryptic symbols, and his breath caught in his throat. There, before his eyes, sharing the page with the cryptic text, was the very emblem of Vitus' inner circle and the image of the Tatzelwurm. A cold prickle ran along his spine. The carriage walls seemed to press closer, as if with the weight of a thousand unseen eyes.

The guard being ordered to hasten to the Rathaus to inform the council that today's court would be re-adjourned, Adolfus then commanded the coachman to divert to the obscure inn where, from that upper room, he would send for and convene with his fellow rogues.

Having arrived there, Adolfus immediately sent word to his rascally brigands, and they at length arrived.

"Certainly, they have stumbled upon a connection," said Adolfus to them. "This" — he tapped on the emblem in ink — "is a sign of resurgence. Vitus' men stir from their slumber. We must know why."

Adolfus again snatched up the poster. "'... the silent pawns await the Queen's gambit... when the moon hides its gaze...'?" His features tightened as he stared about like one enraged with delirium. "What *could* this mean...?" 'Twas only when his eyes alighted upon the window and glimpsed the moon beyond, that his expression altered. He stalked to the glass; his eyes shot upwards, riveted to the waning moon. "'When the moon hides its gaze...'?"

Realisation struck him like a thunderbolt. "That's it!" He spun around. "Tomorrow is a new moon. They mean to trade something for intelligence...? — yes! They seek to discover what they can of Vitus' demise!" From the window, he stalked back to his desk and slammed the poster down. "'... Where the Bear's gaze breaks the river's flow... But which location is *this*?"

One of his agents proposed that this could be the bear pit.

"Yes!" Adolfus seized the rogue by his shoulder. "I think you must be right." He squeezed him with an uncustomary affinity. "I must lift the lockdown at once. If Valentin is indeed behind this, such freedom of movement must surely lure him in!" He scrawled a note and shoved it into the ruffian's hand. "Take this to the Goldener Schlüssel. I must meet with the Lucerne guards immediately."

We must again turn back the clock. Recall, if you will, that Adolfus was to meet with the Lucerne rogues some several nights ago. Well, we learn the treacherous lord, seated within his carriage's opulent brocade interior, pulled up outside the Goldener Schlüssel. There, the carriage door opened to reveal the scarred leader, flanked by two of his men. Beckoned forward, they climbed inside, and the carriage resumed its journey, swaying and jostling along the roads.

"Your grievances have not gone unheard," had said Adolfus, his gaze locked with the hardened eyes staring back at him. "The debt owed to you is long overdue, and indeed, the time for recompense is at hand."

The Lucerne rogues had exchanged glances, eager and grim, and the leader's deep voice rumbled in response. "We've been patient enough. But patience is a luxury for the rich."

Adolfus flashed a self-satisfied smile. "And rich you shall be, in power and coin, if you succeed in finding the one who has wronged us both."

Truly, the promise of vengeance fanned the flames in the men's eyes. Adolfus had them, and he knew it. With Franz's network of spies already on the hunt, and these additional hardened men now in his employ, the net was tightening around his enemy.

Adolfus leant forward, radiating untouchable authority. "To dismantle the roots of our indignation, we must track down all associates. These men are the key to finding the one whom we seek..."

From his cloak's folds, he withdrew a bundle of papers. Unfurling them, he revealed a series of meticulously sketched faces — hard eyes, sharp jaws, and wary expressions: the late Vitus' allies. "Study these faces; they are our map to our hunted."

The leader took a sketch and traced its lines. "How do you suppose we find them?"

"Tomorrow, you will visit the Bernese garrison archives. I will ensure you gain access. Here" — Adolfus passed a slip of paper to him — "are two names. Obtain their records; watch their homes, their families, their every move. They will guide you to our enemy's men, and, in time, to the man himself."

Now that we are caught up on that, around an hour later, Adolfus rolled up outside the inn and the leader climbed inside the carriage.

"Tomorrow," said Adolfus, "take your men to the Bärenpark. You are to linger near there, cloaked in darkness. You are to watch, to learn, and to follow. But do not engage, nor reveal yourselves. And *do not* disobey my command..."

***

Four-and-twenty hours hence — amidst twilight's darkening hues — a formidable group of twelve, comprising several of our hero's men and more of Bernhard's, approached the bear park with the captive in tow; the bargaining chip, his head hung low and hands bound behind him. Each marching footstep was muffled by the evening mists that crept in from the river. Every shadow appeared to elongate into phantasmal forms. Eyes darted around, the captors and captive alike on high alert for any sign of the Tatzelwurms.

Close by, concealed within the thick shrubbery's embrace, the Lucerne guards kept vigilant watch, their breaths measured as they lay in wait.

The bears, so accustomed to spectators during the day, had retreated to their dens, leaving the pit silent and empty while the air, stirred solely by the intermittent breeze, wound through the environing trees; a deceptive calm.

As the captors waited in the uneasy silence, without warning, the stillness shattered like glass under a hammer's blow.

From the park's shadowed fringes, figures cloaked in the darkness surged forward — their movements a blur of lethal intent.

Savage and efficient, these attackers descended like wraiths. With precision born of superlative training, their swords bit into the evening air, swiftly cutting through the ranks.

The battle was a raging tempest. The enemy pressed their advantage with relentless aggression, overwhelming the defenders, who fought back with the desperation of those who knew that defeat meant more than mere loss — it meant the unravelling of all they had worked so hard to achieve.

But for each strike they parried, the society's warriors responded with two of their own, their blades singing a song of impending doom.

Amidst the chaos, two enemies broke from the fray; their hands deftly freed the captive with swift movements.

As the liberated fiend was hurried away, the clash of steel intensified behind them, a deadly duel that held the fate of many in its ferocious grip.

Soon, the fight reached its bloody culmination — the air ladened with spilled blood's coppery scent and the cries of the wounded. Then, as quickly as it began, the battle tide waned, and the warriors, doubtless of the secret society, melted back into the shadows.

Once the last of the defeated ranks limped away, the Lucerne guards emerged from their cover. Their presence as imperceptible as the bears now watching from their dens, they hastened to collect their horses reined nearby and then followed the wounded on foot.

***

Now, dear reader, do put away your despairing gasps, for this humble narrator will share with you a secret. The afore-observed defeat of Peter and Bernhard's men was, in fact, entirely the reverse. For, merely several hours prior, the following discourse took place:

"An ambush is the most likely approach they shall take," said Peter, fixing his audience with a confident stare. "In light of their skills, which are indeed formidable, we ought to let ourselves appear as overpowered..."

Here, several men concurred with this notion, recounting the fierce battle they fought on the night of Vitus' murder.

"If we carefully conceal groups surrounding the park's access points," continued Peter, "and for some farther distance beyond, we will easily tail them back to their haunt. We can then better prepare for our mode of attack."

Indeed, it appears that our hero had quite outwitted Fortune on this occasion. Thus, the stage shall soon be set for him to storm the dragon's lair...

***

The Lucerne men trailed the injured across the Nydeggbrücke bridge and beyond the city walls. There, they observed the several carriages the men boarded. Mounting their own steeds, they followed them as they snaked along the outer streets and, at length, arrived at the courtyard of a secluded schloss to the west of the city.

Glances of silent agreement exchanged between them, the Lucerne guards, armed with the necessary intelligence, returned to their inn to write Adolfus and to await his visit.

Adolfus soon arrived. As before, he ushered the leader inside his carriage and then commanded the coachman to drive.

"So?" Adolfus was as much intrigued as impatient. "Report!"

With some satisfaction cleaved in his features, the man recounted the events. "But it was all so dark, and it all happened so fast, that we were unable to discern if Peter was among the men we tracked."

This detail only added to Adolfus' impatience. He instructed the coachman to return to the inn and ordered his co-conspirator to cautiously survey the schloss and to report to him, at once, the first sign of the prey.

***

Several days had now passed. At last, to the no little satisfaction of our hero and Adolfus alike, both found success in their respective surveillances. For Peter, his agents had spied out the premises where they followed the attackers to. Many unsavoury countenances, as well as various wealthy persons, came and went. But the former captive was yet to exit it. Thus, they determined this to be the society's lair. For Adolfus, the Lucerne men had confirmed seeing Peter leave the schloss. They followed him and his men to a property, which overlooked the above-mentioned lair, and from an adjacent room, they got to hear his plans. This, being material to our history and Adolfus' great schemes, beckons us to alight into the next scene medias res:

"You are certain your men heard correctly?" demanded Adolfus of the leader. "They intend on storming that premises this evening?"

"Yes. But why not have him apprehended this very moment at the schloss? My men and I, I am sure, with some comrades added to us, can easily prevail."

For some moments, Adolfus was silent. Indeed, this suggestion was sensible. However, a cunning stratagem crossed his mind; he perceived several advantages to delaying Peter's capture. "No. It is better we wait until our common enemy is on unfamiliar grounds, where he will be more vulnerable to an ambush. This is what you must do…"

***

Evening arrived. With his twenty agents in tow — and the additional support of Bernhard's men, all in the blues, whites, and reds of the Bernese Swiss Guard grenadiers' company — Peter, heart thrumming, stalked along the alleyway towards the otherwise unassuming, large wooden and brick building, stood in the suburbs beyond the city walls; the windows glowed with the false warmth of revelry within.

The plan to storm the building this night had been a last-minute concoction; a desperate bid born from patience fatigued.

"Are you ready, men?" Peter turned to the line of soldiers behind him.

Nods given, muskets and bayonets to the ready, they moved as one — their convergence silent, their prowling concealed by night's shadows and haze.

The spy, who earlier noted the coded knock and passwords during his clandestine observations, approached the property. Bearskin removed, he rapped on the door. The small viewing slot slid open, revealing the wary eyes of the doorkeeper within. A murmur of the magic word was all it took for the viewing slot to close and for the doorkeeper, suspecting not the tempest he was about to invite inside, to open the door.

Now it was that Peter and his allies charged forth, breaching the threshold — the cacophony of noise from within covering their thunderous intrusion.

Along a faintly lit corridor, the invaders hurtled and burst through a set of double doors onto a railed gallery, clouded with the stench of cigars and cheap ale, and scattered with painted hussies, velvet couches, and intoxicated clients.

Below, at the bottom of a wide staircase, a maelstrom of vice and indulgence unfolded in a large open space: the clamour of dice, the clinking of coins, the rhythmic shuffle of cards as they danced across felt tables, the whirring of roulette wheels spinning, the raucous laughter, shouts of triumph, and the murmurs of the inebriated and the desperate.

Countless candles flickered, casting their amber glow across the rough-hewn beams, and the myriad of anxious faces now turning towards the gallery, eyes wide with dawning horror.

In a flash, Peter's agents descended upon the masses below; Bernhard's men commandeered the gallery, at bayonet-point forcing the strumpets and their drunken gallants to the main floor.

"Everybody down!" Our hero's sword sliced through the air, compelling the last few defiant harlots and gamblers to cower. No longer would this place serve as a haven for the corrupt and murderous; it would stage their unmasking. "Now show your wrists!"

The punters, a motley array of fearful and indignant merchants and gentry alike, complied. They bared their arms as Peter's men fanned out among them. One after another, pale wrists were revealed, unmarked, however, by the sought-after telltale ink.

But amidst the palpable tension, a solitary figure crouched by a fireplace hesitated, his eyes wide with a betraying anxiousness, his hand seeming to edge towards his hilt.

"You there!" Peter advanced on him. "Show me your wrist!"

Several blades now swung at the man's throat; our hero, hand steady, reached for the man's sleeve. The suspect pulled away; but Peter seized upon him. The fabric being peeled back revealed the damning Tatzelwurm curled upon the man's wrist.

Just as the silence of realisation grew on the air, the doors above burst open anew.

Clad in their official regalia, the Lucerne guards — faces red with fury, swords gleaming with hostile intent — poured into the room, followed by a rag-tag band of brigands.

Anon steel clashed against steel; the gambling den instantly transmuted into a riotous pandemonium. Shouts and screams rent the air. With sickening cracking sounds, fists collided with jaws.

In the chaotic thundering of overturned tables, harlots and opportunists swiftly pounced upon the scattered bounty; they snatched up coins, jewels, and hastily discarded playing cards as fortunes changed hands during the tumult.

Chairs smashed over heads and crashed into the splintered walls. Cries of pain and groans of despair sliced through the din while blood mingled with spilled wine, flowing in rivulets across the stained floorboards.

Thrust into the thick of the fray, our hero's blade met the Tatzelwurm member's aggressive lunges. While parrying these attacks, he glanced behind just in time; the Lucerne leader sprang upon him.

With quick reflexes, duelling fore and aft, Peter simultaneously countered the downward strikes of both assailants — each more intense with each blow.

But even as our hero fought with the skill and fury of a warrior, the heavy, reverberating thud of reinforced boots boomed over the din.

The Bernese artillery — an added blur of blue touched with red and white — exploded from above and descended upon the scene with the implacable force of a tempest. Their orders were clear: to arrest all, irrespective of allegiance.

***

We pause the tumult momentarily to cast our gazes back to the previous night. After Adolfus directed the Lucerne guards to an ill-reputed inn where ample savages would be found to increase their numbers, he perceived the wisdom in betraying these equally expendable men; men who might yet prove problematic for his schemes. Additionally, Adolfus had recently learned that this underground gambling house was not solely a Tatzelwurm franchise (now a liability needing obliteration by hands other than his own) but was secretly run by one of the mint master's close affiliates. 'Twas here that Adolfus contrived his next design. A trusted intermediary was employed to convey a message to the patrician, stating that his presence was required to oversee an important transaction that very night. Indeed, with one fatal swoop, how possible it seemed that Adolfus might eliminate every variance to the disadvantage of his machinations.

***

Confusion reigned as the Lucerne guards realised the betrayal. Amidst the fracas, they began to scatter, heading for the doors in a desperate bid for escape. The tattooed assassin, sensing an opportunity in the chaos, slipped away through a hidden door in the wall as elusive as the shadowy society he served.

Peter's eyes darted back and forth. Even as his soul cried out to pursue his brother's murderers, Lizzie's image, steadfast and expectant, tugged at his conscience. Oh, how he deplored the hold she still had upon his will; the power she wielded over his every action!

With a heart near bursting with fury, he sent his most trusted agents to pursue the assassin, while he gathered the rest of his men and fought his way to the exit, determined to bring the escaped Lucerne rogues to justice.

Outside they burst into the night air. 'Twas a scene not less chaotic. The alleyways and cobblestone thoroughfares were awash with the fleeing forms of gamblers and harlots, their terrified screams echoing.

"Which way?" demanded our hero's men.

"You, that way!" Peter sent half his force one way. "The rest, follow me!"

Boots pummelling against the uneven stones, breath ragged, and hearts racing, our hero and his comrades charged forth into the labyrinthine streets.

For long minutes, there was no sign of their prey. But just as despair set in, a glimpse of swift movement was espied; a red-coat rounded a distant corner.

"There!" cried Peter.

As they gained the corner, they observed horses bearing the escaped rogues away. Thankfully, there, nestled nearby, the same small stable bore several more charges ripe for the taking.

Thus, Peter and his men mounted the steeds and took off in hot pursuit.

Through the tangled maze of streets and dirt tracks, they galloped, the sweltering air whipping at their faces as they rode

As they broke away from the outer suburbs — the city walls falling away behind them — the chase entered the surrounding woodlands, plunging them into a vast tenebrosity.

Deeper into the forest they rode; the branches whipped at their faces and the uneven ground threatened to unseat them at every turn. But unwavering, Peter and his men pushed on and soon began to close the distance.

The Lucerne men split ranks, and our hero, shouting a command at his own, likewise broke formation — each group tasked with running down a different band of rogues.

Furious was the pursuit; the enemies' escape well-nigh. Skilled and desperate, they wove through the trees and leapt over gullies with the reckless abandon of men who knew that capture would mean a fate worse than death.

But Peter and his men, equally determined, gained dominion inch by hard-fought inch.

The first bunch of rogues found themselves unhorsed; their mounts were taken out from under them by the expert shots of the late Vitus' best marksman. The villains were speedily subdued, bound, and left under guard, while the rest of the pursuers raced onward, their hearts thrashing with the thrill of the chase.

The second band of escapees met a similar fate, their horses driven to the point of exhaustion by the relentless pursuit. The fiends tumbled from their saddles, only to be set upon by Peter's men, who made short work of securing them.

Finally, the last group remained; the most stubborn and cunning of the lot. They led our hero and his residual men on a merry chase, doubling back, splitting up, laying false trails and using every trick in their nefarious arsenal to evade capture.

But Peter's resolve was unshakeable.

His heart drumming a war beat, his mind charging with prophetic intent, he with a final, supreme effort, spurred his horse onward.

The beast's hooves churned up the forest floor's loamy soil; the wind whipped through Peter's hair as he closed in on his quarry.

The ultimate confrontation, when it came, was as abrupt as it was brutal.

The rogues, cornered and desperate, turned to fight; their swords flashed in the silvery light as they furiously whipped the air, parrying the assault.

But they were no match for Peter and his battle-hardened company. They set upon them with a righteous fury that would not be denied, their own blades singing a deadly song of justice and retribution.

20 – 21 AUGUST 1792

What a triumph this was for our hero. The fiends had escaped the gambling house only to fall in the end. Peter, his chest heaving with exertion and his face streaked with sweat and grime, looked upon his vanquished foes with a mixture of vindication and exhaustion. Among them were several faces he recognised from Lucerne, including the leader of this rapacious pack, who stared back at him, eyes aflame with vengeful anger.

But even as our hero savoured this victory's sweet taste, his thoughts raced to the trials and tribulations that surely impended. The war against the secret society was still unresolved. The raid had not gone as planned. Whatever report would arrive from the men who pursued the Tatzelwurm, our hero was impatient to receive it.

With a weary sigh, and prisoners gathered, Peter bade his men lead them to an abandoned mill, pre-arranged the night before for their custody.

***

Our hero, having managed a few hours' sleep, was awoken by the butler rapping loudly on his door. Urgent news had arrived. Guessing at the import of the intelligence, Peter leapt out of bed and followed him to the drawing room. There, one of his agents wore a grim expression.

"We were too late," explained he. "The fiend vanished, and the tunnel system — nay, warren — had us lost in no time. Was naught but pitch black everywhere, and it took us several hours to find our way out; a storm drain on the Aare's bank."

"Storm drain...?" Peter recalled the tunnelled system Franz had led him through. "How bitterly disappointing those serpents got away!"

The man shook his head. "Did you apprehend those other rogues?"

"Yes."

"What will you do with them?"

"I shall march them to the Liestal garrison, where they will be trialled and, I hope, brought to justice for Ernest's death."

"But for your own safety, ought not you rather send them with your men?"

"This is the least I can do to make amends for the suffering inflicted on that family. Besides, we still have the other prisoner, do we not? He can yet testify to my innocence. I shall employ his counterfeiting skills to my advantage."

***

The Bernese jailhouse's heavy wooden entrance door swung upon, creaking ominously as it admitted Adolfus to the gloomy stone foyer. The jailer, a squat man with a nervous disposition, hurried to meet him. "Lord Adolfus, we weren't expecting you until —"

"Silence!" Adolfus' sharp and piercing eyes shot to the door that led to the jail's confines. "Take me to them. Now!"

Visibly swallowing his unease, the jailer hence led him through a maze of narrow hallways lit with torches that cast shadows eerie enough to scare the most hardened of criminals. At length, they stopped before several large cells, their iron bars thick and unwelcoming.

Adolfus' gaze swept the gloomy interiors filled with the many beaten, bruised, and bloodied gamblers and strumpets arrested the night before. Having expected to find our hero, his men, the Lucerne guards, and also the mint master's comrade shackled and defeated, what a shock he had when he noted only two of the latter.

"What is the meaning of this?" Again, Adolfus surveyed every wretched face which stared back at him. But lo, his eyes most certainly had not deceived him. He turned his now ferocious glare on the jailer. "Are these all the arrested?"

The man, plainly foreseeing the tempest about to be unleashed, gulped and backed away several steps. "All who were brought here last night to these very cells, as instructed."

"The buffoons!" Adolfus jousted the jailor with the tip of his new cane. "I expect every guard involved with last night's arrest to be brought here within the hour."

***

'Twas now around mid-afternoon, and we must cross over once again into Bubendorf. Within the stately setting of Pier's dining room, we find Lizzie, Edmunda, and Emil congregated with Pier, Phillipina — and Schatzi at their heels — partaking of a late luncheon and discoursing the recent events.

"Though the scoundrel retrieved you from the violent hands which again ventured to carry you off," said Phillipina, "the Folletto deserves no less than the retribution which will soon come crashing down on his head!"

Still fragile from the earlier abduction, and still torn in her regard for our hero, Lizzie made no comment.

Displeased to have met with silence, Phillipina turned her attack on Pier. "And Father, how could you not have kept your eye on him? Thanks to your negligent vigil, the vile fiend vanished into the night, when he ought to have been shackled away to some eternal hell."

Likewise, Pier made no comment. Notwithstanding every shred of evidence which looked so convincing to our hero's disfavour, it was the late Vivienne's diary, along with the promise of a full éclaircissement, that guided Pier's moral compass.

Edmunda had sat silent for some hours, but hearing the rotten scoundrel Peter's name, she found vigour enough to reprobate him too. Adding to this the account of the curious name Du Pont, a name so infamous it had even reached the gentle ears of many Bubendorf townsfolk, Edmunda was only the more convinced that our hero was nothing but an anti-hero; an antagonist of the worst kind. Verily, did she believe his amnesia was naught but a crafty contrivance to worm his way into their good graces; a scheme to hide from every huntsman who must, undoubtedly, be hunting the world for him.

Into this scene of vilification, a footman entered. He announced that an officer and two guards from the Liestal garrison asked for Miss Elizabeth and Master Emil.

Possessed of collective perplexity, Lizzie, Edmunda, Emil, Pier, and Phillipina exchanged sundry glances.

But at length: "Did they," said Lizzie, "explain why they are here?"

The footman answered in the negative.

Consequently, Lizzie and Emil followed him outside to the main gate, where the three men stood beside a fine carriage: deep green in hue with black and gold wheels.

The officer stepped forward. "Elizabeth, and Emil?" They nodded. "We are come to escort you to the garrison. We have in custody the men involved in your father's death."

"Heavens above!" Lizzie near tottered and sought Emil's support. "You are certain that it is they?"

"Only as soon as you can identify and confirm this being the case."

The journey was fraught with tension. Lizzie's mind raced with a thousand conjectures and questions, while Emil, his own mind reliving the terrible ordeal, was silent and grave.

They soon reached the garrison. Within a small chamber, beyond a large glass pane, a line of dishevelled bound men stood under heavy guard beneath a glaring skylight. Their faces a study in contrasts, some wore defiant glares, their eyes blazing with an unquenchable fire; others had downcast eyes, their spirits seemingly broken by the weight of their circumstances.

The sight of these men plunged terror into Lizzie's heart; its icy fibril gripped her very core. All ability for movement seemed to have fled her limbs, leaving her rooted to the spot. Emil, no less awe-struck, pointed with a trembling finger. "That's them; the five on the left," said he. "I'm sure of it. The others, I... I'm not so certain."

"And you?" calmly said the officer to Lizzie. "Do *you* recognise them?"

Beset by an inrush of violent emotions, she struggled to stay the tears and the violent trembling that seized her entire frame. Her words, at first, emerged as a mere breathy whisper. But gaining the mastery of herself, "yes," confirmed she. "All of them. They are unequivocally the men from Lucerne. Several of them I beheld fleeing my home on the day of..."

The tears came full. The grief and pain she could no longer contain. She had to withdraw to another room, seeking solace in solitude.

Amid the strident curses and bellows from the guilty as the Liestal guards hauled the identified miscreants away, Emil pursued his sister. Only after her emotions had abated did she enquire into what manner the men had been apprehended. The officer beckoned them to follow him into a nearby chamber. Verily, never has shock been so vividly stamped upon any visage as that of our heroine.

There stood Peter, his stance rigid, gazing out of a window.

The officer gestured at our gallant hero. "This is the man who has brought them here."

Upon hearing his voice, Peter turned to face them.

So overwhelmed by his appearance and the circumstances attendant to his presence, Lizzie's breath near forsook her. Again, she sought the support of her brother's arm.

"I perceive," said Peter as the officer took his leave, "that my presence has disquieted you." Cautiously, he approached her. "I am well aware that I can never restore your father to you, but I fervently hope, I implore" — he clasped her hand — "that bringing his assailants to justice shall, at the very least, mitigate the abhorrent injustice you have borne. I shall elucidate everything to you when the time is more fitting."

Perchance it was the blend of sorrow, despair, and loss; mayhap, the commingling of hope, relief, and gratitude. Or perhaps that their hands, so long sundered, found solace in each other's enclasp. But at any rate, as if oft the reverse, though our hero had resolved in Lizzie's absence to see her no more, now once more in her company, he promptly forgot all those vows. Our heroine, too, overcome by the whole, once more indebted to so enigmatic a man, found her sensibilities at once overtook her leading aversions. Each vilification to Peter's dishonour, each dubiety, flitted from her mind like a sparrow taking flight from a branch.

'Twas now she found her voice. "I thank you... This shall bring Mother much comfort."

Thus, the erstwhile lovers stood both silent and trembling; their hands locked together; Peter being unable to relinquish his hold; Lizzie being almost equally incapable of withdrawing her own.

Anyhow, this scene, having I trust, unfolded long enough to provide our esteemed readers with a sufficient indication of what might yet transpire, their carriage awaited.

20 – 21 August 1792

***

We momentarily bid adieu to our hero and heroine as they journey back to Wildenstein, for we must hasten ourselves to Ebenrain. Once more in the library, Franz paced with restless abandon as each day stretched interminably while his sister and comrades languished behind bars. Meanwhile, Jago — hunched over his desk strewn with letters and legal documents; a stark reminder of every failed endeavour to secure the prisoners' release — contended with the added burden of four dalmatians, whose spots and whimpers were as bothersome as every obstacle before him.

"Naught!" cried Franz. "Every effort, every plea, it's been all for naught!"

Jago looked up; his eyes were heavy from several days and nights spent in futile strategising and vain negotiations. "I have exhausted every possibility, Franz. No bribe has been substantial enough to sway the colonel! He is stiffer than any cadaver."

Franz slumped into a chair. "So, what now?"

Two of the dogs — doubtless sniffing out an opportunity for fussing and, perhaps, a morsel of food to alleviate their own melancholy — were soon at his feet, tails wagging.

"Shall we," continued Franz, "simply bide our time whilst they are led to the gallows? Nay! It is high time we seize control of our destiny!"

Jago's expression beseeched immediate clarification.

"I shall break them out myself!" flatly stated Franz.

"Have you taken leave of your senses? There is no conceivable way you shall emerge from there unscathed!"

"I can muster up an army if need be!"

Before Jago could reply, the library door groaned open, and a messenger hurried in, breathless. "Master," panted he, bowing and glancing warily at Franz, "the man you seek has returned to Bubendorf."

"He *has*?" Jago leapt up. The dogs also stood alert; their ears pricked up as if they, too, understood the significance of this development. "Where is he now?"

"Not long past arrived at Wildenstein, Master."

Jago thrust his high-backed chair aside. "I must hasten to the garrison!"

Franz's gaze was as sharp and calculating. "You must keep him here in Bubendorf, at all costs!" He rose from his seat. "I shall divulge all upon my return from Bern. There is someone there who might be able to help. If not, expect me with reinforcements."

***

Peter and Lizzie having arrived at Wildenstein, we find them now ensconced in the parlour, where a spirited gathering was in full swing. Present were Peter; Pier, the gracious host; Phillipina, the sceptical daughter; Edmunda, the softening matriarch; Elizabeth, our confused heroine; Emil and Helene, the blushing lovebirds; Hans, the suspicious kinsman; Harris, the eager-to-please fellow; and Ludwig — our hero's valet. To the gentle clink of fine chinaware, their discourse orbited around the recent events and the enigmatic figure at the epicentre of it all: our hero. Ah! Do forgive our narrator's remiss, for Schatzi was also in attendance, garnering admirable attention, savouring the sundry pets to his furry head and the sundry morsels siphoned off to his mouth.

"So, Peter — nay, Mr Du Pont," persisted Phillipina in her accustomary sarcasm, "or should I still address you simply as the Folletto...?" To this, she annexed her usual scowls. "Do be so kind as to enlighten us on your sudden metamorphosis from fugitive to hero?"

"Desist, my child," quietly interposed Pier, placing a hand atop hers and casting a sideways reproof in her direction.

Lizzie observed the exchange with a mixture of curiosity and apprehension. The revelation of Peter's involvement in capturing the Lucerne men had evoked a maelstrom of conflicting emotions. His actions appeared to contradict the accusations levelled against him, yet the past still cast a long shadow over her heart. However, with the official Bernese document, seemingly absolving him of all charges, she began to entertain the notion that she ought to extend to him not only her gratitude but her earnest conciliation — for there remained the matter of deceit she had hitherto practised upon him.

"I must say," said Edmund to Peter, "you bringing those rogues to justice has restored some peace to my heart; and, perhaps, softened my opinion of you."

Phillipina scoffed loudly. "Pray, good woman, be not so hasty in trusting this menace of Venice!" Her father did try to shush her, but she continued, "we are still to learn his true identity and discover his mysterious motives. This could all be part of some elaborate ruse."

"Aye!" echoed Hans. "What secrets ought there be between kith and kin? If you've naught to hide, then why not reveal your true self?"

Seated between such conjecture and interrogations, Peter endeavoured to deflect the whole. "I can assure you I am not Du Pont, and nor are my intentions dishonourable — even if I cannot yet reveal the truth or my past."

"Balderdash!" Hans slumped into his seat, arms crossed in an open display of his disbelief.

A servant now entered with replenishments of tea and a variety of victuals, and began arranging them upon the side table. 'Twas at this moment that Harris *and* Ludwig — the latter, his incognito, being that of an old friend — embarked upon a comedic yet earnest duel of attentiveness.

Privy to our hero's true identity, and no doubt eager to ingratiate himself into his favour, Harris hastened to refill Peter's tea just as Ludwig reached for the silver pot. Victorious on this score, Harris smiled as wide as the room and pronked like a stag across the carpets. With uncharacteristic servility, he bowed and proffered the beverage. "Master Peter..."

Defeated on the aforementioned score, Ludwig visibly grappled to dispel his ill-humour. But recomposing his countenance, he undertook to approach with a selection of cakes for all upon a tray.

"No, no, permit me." Harris snatched a plate. With a flourish, he placed it before our hero, careful even to ensure the plate's motif pointed south.

"He prefers the lemon tart!" countered Ludwig. "*Not* the chocolate cake!" He swapped the plates with a deft hand, careful to correct Harris' err by pointing the motif north.

Indeed, this spectacle of vying stole all attention. Some wore raised eyebrows; others asymmetrical frowns. But all looked back and forth at each other as though they beseeched some tacit explanation.

"Gentlemen." Peter feigned a chuckle before paying his valet a stern look. "I am more than capable of serving myself."

Hans and Phillipina exchanged severe glances and tutted. Emil and Helene, not without blushing and smiling at each other, stifled a giggle. Pier seemed to study the whole with profound curiosity. Edmunda leant in to Lizzie. "The way that Ludwig behaves, anybody'd think he was his servant."

"Indeed..." Lizzie shook her head, equally perplexed. To be sure, the mystery of Peter's past and his connection to Ludwig only deepened the enigma surrounding him.

A footman appeared, announcing Jago had arrived.

The room's focus shifted abruptly as Jago entered.

Despite the appearance of aplomb which he wore in his expression, our hero perceived a tempest brewing in his eyes.

"I am just now come from the Liestal garrison," said Jago, clearly affecting civility as his gaze pierced the crowd to fix on Peter. "I heard a most astonishing account. Pray, I must discover for myself these tales of heroics?"

It would take little imagination to enter into the air of affront with which Jago, though he strove to conceal it, heard the shocking account.

At any rate, as soon as it was completed, rather than join the party to celebrate Peter's liberty, he claimed pressing business took him back home.

Some hours later, our hero and Pier retired to the library to discourse the circumstances of the diary. The many questions our hero posed to the other were, to his no little bewilderment, answered only somewhat evasively. How Pier knew the late schultheissin was something Pier could not elaborate on; he only averred he was, at one time, intimately acquainted with that family. Regarding the memorial plaque, this, Pier admitted with visible discomfort that yes, the late great-uncle and -aunt had resided here at this schloss. Likewise, when Pier probed Peter's connection to the family, our hero answered with the same vagueness, reiterating that, for reasons of his own, he, too, could not divulge too much yet.

Thus, each piqued and intrigued by the other's circumventions, but bound to the same family for some righteous purpose, they shook hands, trusting to a future time the full disclosure.

The night closed in fast, and Peter bid Pier goodnight and retired with his late mother's diary to his room. Exhausted from all that had passed, but nonetheless relieved to be at last liberated from the ill-repute which overshadowed his character in this humble vicinity, he lay down to sleep.

Just then, a sudden recollection raced upon his mind: the mysterious billet, previously contained inside the timepiece's secret compartment.

It is not to be wondered at that upon breaking the honeybee seal and unfolding the paper, finding only a blank page, his perplexity was considerable. And what of the clock, still likely being in Lucerne? And the various conversations reported to him relating to his brother's timepiece and the enigmatic talk overheard pertaining to secret meetings yet to occur?

Tomorrow, at dawn, our hero would make for Lucerne to retrieve the timepiece and, he hoped, uncover what further mysteries lurked within its cogs.

***

During this interval, back in Bern, a hushed tension permeated the council chamber. Each council member, distinguished by their sombre garb and divergent expressions, sat around a grand oval table. At the helm, Adolfus presided with an air of imperious calm.

"I have summoned this assembly today," began he, "for with the period of mourning for our late Gustav being complete, we must finalise Varus' appointment. However, prior to that" — he paused, poised now to execute his stratagem upon the mint master — "there is another matter of equal import that entails our immediate consideration."

At this juncture, the Welsch Treasurer replied, "indeed, there is. And I beseech every council member here to lend due heed to these words." He cast a self-assured glance around the table. "It has come to my attention that Vitus is not, in fact, at his schloss convalescing — as Adolfus averred."

Sundry gasps went up.

"Moreover," continued the treasurer, "I am informed that Vitus has neither been seen nor heard of for several weeks. His private physician has most certainly not attended to him. This begs the question, wherefore is he and, if he indeed suffers from some peculiar ailment, who is tending to him? I harbour suspicions that our esteemed Adolfus conceals something. And if so, what?"

"Is this true?" echoed several council members as they turned from the Welsch Treasurer to Adolfus, their eyes wide, their brows floating high.

Where once the blood had receded from Adolfus' visage, the hue of self-satisfaction suffused his expression. He reclined with an air of sangfroid and, summoning an aide, bade the man fetch him his satchel.

In due course, extracting from the bag an opened missive, he tossed it across the table to the Welsch Treasurer. "This will quench your flame," said he; a sarcastic smile lurked around the corners of his mouth.

Indeed, 'twas now the Welsch Treasurer's complexion curdled into an off-white hue as he passed his eyes across the lines.

"My esteemed councillors," resumed Adolfus, rising from his seat to look down on all who had dared oppose his cunning and contrivances, "that letter is, in fact, penned by Vitus himself. Peruse it, if you will. But I can summarise the content and inform you he is abroad in Italy, basking in the sun and partaking of its vineyards, masquerades, and striving daily to dispel the sorrow that still consumes him every hour."

Mouth slanted wide, the treasurer turned his aggravated stare at Adolfus, who, noting the unmistakable defeat crawl over his visage, remarked, "that is Vitus' own hand, is it not? Ought not you have focused on addressing the mounting fiscal issues, rather than pursuing vain ends?"

Perceiving the man was quite incapable of formulating a response, Adolfus hastened to his delayed objective. He addressed the council with words relating to the failed trade deals, exponentially rising tax levies, and the guilds' protests to dismiss the mint master. "It has come to my attention that our esteemed Mint Master may not be as virtuous as his office demands."

As flickers of surprise and curiosity claimed every face, Adolfus produced from his satchel a weighty folder. Depositing it onto the table, he opened it with deliberate significance. "These," said he, withdrawing several documents and brandishing them aloft, "are records from a recent raid on a notorious gambling house. An establishment frequented by those of questionable repute; among whom apprehended was a man deeply connected to our Mint Master."

Murmurs filled the room as Adolfus distributed the documents. The papers appeared legitimate; they detailed accounts of the raid, replete with names and purported testimonies linking the arrested man to financial misdeeds allegedly masterminded by the mint master.

"Naturally, this council comprehends the gravity of such accusations," continued Adolfus, his tone a blend of regret and resolve. "It is our duty to investigate meticulously. Should these connections prove true, it would constitute a grievous breach of trust; one we cannot disregard."

***

Many a league yonder, Bernhard reclined in pensive solitude within his library's walls. His visage bore the indelible marks of profound contemplation as his gaze flitted over a message that had recently come into his possession.

What, pray tell, could have elicited such a grave phiz?

Even were our sage readers to lean in and peer over his shoulder for a fleeting moment, they would glimpse but a cryptic message, necessitating either a cypher or prior comprehension. Permit, therefore, this humble narrator to divulge that the text alluded to clandestine activities of an elusive secret society — yes, the Tatzelwurms — and their possible connection to the recent expiration of a list of powerful patricians from several cantons.

Unbeknownst to our hero, Bernhard had, for several years, been gathering intelligence on this society — an organisation some century old in legacy. Sparse though the message was, he recognised the need to sooner infiltrate and unravel their nefarious schemes.

He concealed the letter within a hidden compartment of his desk and then traversed the room to a segment of the towering, floor-to-ceiling bookshelves.

His fingers walked along a row of aged leather spines before settling upon a volume titled "The Art of War." With a deft motion, he tilted the volume, triggering a soft click. The book shelf groaned and slowly slid aside, unveiling a narrow passage shrouded in shadows.

Enveloped by musty air, he stepped through and descended a narrow staircase into a vast chamber lined with an arsenal of the extraordinary. The room, humming in the soft amber glow, housed an eclectic collection of tools: cipher machines, disguised weapons, and maps dotted with cryptic symbols. Each item whispered tales of espionage, clandestine operations, and secret alliances. Sprawling a large wall, a detailed map of Europe was pinned, marked with strategic locations and lines that formed a web of intrigue stretching across borders. Bernhard traced a route from Berlin to Vienna, and Vienna to Venice, murmuring to himself about the furtive movements of shadowy figures.

At the heart of the chamber stood an imposing, circular gilded table, encircled by twelve high-backed gilt chairs. Distributed around the table's perimeter, arranged with meticulous precision, were twelve sealed envelopes, each bearing the same inscription: The Sons of Tell Initiation.

Bernhard approached a section of the stone walls and pressed a hidden switch. Moments later, a trusted servant appeared.

"The time has come," declared Bernhard. "Gather the twelve."

***

Elsewhere, Franz hurried through the once more bustling Bernese streets, illumed by the pallid lunar glow. Arriving at the ominous façade nestled within a foreboding alleyway, he thus hastened again into the tapestry-divided room to meet a second time with Adolfus, who, having received urgent word, waited with heart-pounding expectation.

Once more, the slit was drawn aside, and these two men locked eyes.

"What could be so pressing that you summon me to this place at such an ungodly hour?" said Adolfus.

"The man you seek," replied Franz, "I know his current whereabouts."

Adolfus lurched forward. "Where?"

"Before I reveal this, there is something you must promise to do for me..."

***

The morn came and Peter, promising Pier he would return in ample time for the banquet, set off for Lucerne, along with Ludwig.

20 – 21 August 1792

Having waved him off, Pier and Phillipina ventured into Liestal to procure some items for the evening's festivities, where they happened to meet with Jago, who invited them to take some light refreshments with him.

Apprised as Jago was of Peter being gone out of the canton, and understanding that it would be some hours before Pier and Phillipina would return home, Jago — possessed of sudden cunning and noting their hands ladened with various appurtenances — feigned concern for their ease. He offered to convey their cargo to Wildenstein on their behalf. Some meagre exchange of polite refusal being passed, Jago prevailed.

Bidding them good day, he hastened away.

Leave being granted by the servants to enter the property, Jago proceeded to the parlour. After depositing the sundry festive accoutrements, he gave his fullest attention to the movement within the property. It now being the hour of lunch, and all the house staff being away to repast in the kitchens, Jago thus crept upstairs in search of Peter's room.

Instinct, that nagging feeling all mortals often experience when something was amiss, had plagued Jago the entire night through. Convinced that our hero still concealed secrets, he resolved to search Peter's effects for some indication of this.

Thus, as he deftly rifled through several draws in the room, he chanced upon a red coat. Recalling Peter had arrived in Bubendorf wearing regimentals, he snatched it up and passed his sedulous eyes over it. Not long did it take for something to catch his attention; sewn into the back of the collar were two initials: *P.B*

Jago's eyes stretched wide. "P.B?" He scrutinised the monogram — particularly its embroidering. For some moments, he was lost in a world of thought. "This cannot surely be...?" His eyes alighted upon the leather-bound diary, stuffed between other clothing in the same draw; he momentarily cast the coat aside, other curiosities taking precedence.

As he flicked through the pages, indeed, even more staggering to his senses was a certain small paper which fell to the floor.

Now, dear reader, this is not the late Vivienne's poem, but rather the verse wrongly attributed to our hero in our first tome.

"Good Lord! Impossible!" As one agitated at the sight of some apparition, he blanched and trembled. "How is this —?"

Alas, dear readers, an account for such strange behaviour must wait, for movement stirred along the corridor outside the room and brought him back into himself. Hastily, he returned the diary to its place, secreted the poem in his pocket and, collecting the red coat, folded it under his arm and quit the schloss with all possible haste.

***

Alas, our hero returned to Bubendorf empty-handed — for the horologist's store had been locked up. But urged by Pier to ready himself for the evening's event, he retreated to his chamber, donned attire befitting the soirée, and wore the mask of aplomb.

As the reds, purples, and ochres commanded the changing heavens, the courtyard's white marquee burgeoned with guests bedecked in their fineries; all of them were at ease, jovial, admiring the decor and table so exquisitely displayed for their delectation and delight.

Scarcely had the banquet commenced with the first course when Edmunda enquired after Jago's tardiness.

These words had but left her lips and the marquee's flaps were flung aside; Jago, still clad in his daywear and flanked by several familiar stern-faced Liestal guards, strode in.

"Jago?" Pier rose from his seat. "What is the meaning of this?"

Without a word, Jago marched forth and, in a most dramatic gesture, hurled the red coat onto the table.

Indeed, the confounded silence which interluded crackled.

"Arrest that criminal!" Jago levelled a condemnatory finger at our hero.

"*Criminal?*" echoed Peter — as did the rest of the assembly.

"Ladies and gentleman," continued Jago, his voice rising above the subsequent clamour, "the man before you is nothing more than an impostor and murderer!"

The crowd gasped uniformly. All eyes swivelled back to Peter, who, so taken aback by this accusation, found himself able neither to move nor answer.

"Jago, Jago," intervened Pier. "Pray, what is this all about?"

"Dearest Pier," replied he, "I regret to inform you, but should you inspect that coat's collar, you will discover the proof of your missing son's demise."

Pier dazedly shook his head and merely glanced at the coat. "My son?"

Phillipina rose from her seat and darted round the table to snatch up the coat. In point, as she investigated it, her widening eyes portended some horrid truth. "Father," uttered she, "this is indeed my brother's jacket. Here are his initials. I embroidered them in myself."

Once more, all eyes — now incredulous — swung round on our hero.

"But this is not all!" Jago produced from his pocket the folded paper. "This poem here," — he held it aloft — "penned by *your son*, he showed to me many months before he... *disappeared*..." Jago appeared to let the implication hang heavily upon the air.

"This *pretender*" — Jago levelled a finger once more at our hero — "cannot tell us who he really is, for he conceals a vile crime!"

Each guest's countenance fluctuated between outrage and fear; they demanded of Jago — they demanded of Peter some explanation. But unable our hero was to offer any words, for he had no inkling of what Jago was leading to.

Jago, observing his perplexed silence, continued, "these past months, I have conducted my own enquiries into my most cherished friend's whereabouts. It was yesterday that..." — he appeared to avail himself of the night's air — "that I learned of his fate..."

An eerie, chilling silence prevailed.

"I am truly so sorry, Pier, but your son... he... he is *dead*!"

Pier staggered backwards. "*Dead*?!"

Phillipina threw the red coat down and seized Jago's sleeve. "What do you mean, my brother is dead?"

Removing her grip, he took her hand in his. "I learned yesterday that he was murdered."

"*Murdered*?!" Phillipina let out a shriek and collapsed to the ground.

Oh, how the banquet erupted into chaos! Glasses overturned, chairs toppled as guests rose and collapsed in confusion. And Pier, poor Pier, clutching at his chest and uttering indiscernible mutterings, had to be ushered by several servants back to his seat.

Not yet done, Jago delivered his final blow. "And the villain who perpetrated this profane, monstrous act is none other than this beast here who now masquerades behind his possessions! Guards, arrest him!"

As the horror descended fully upon all gathered, the guards flew forward and, seizing upon our hero, dragged him away.

To be continued...

ABOUT THE AUTHOR

Justan Autor is a newcomer author to the world of novels, bringing a passion for the arts to historical fiction.

Throughout his youth and adulthood, Justan has been painting, landscape gardening, tailoring, playing the pianoforte, and composing classical music. It was only 5 years ago that he discovered his true calling in narrative and novel writing.

Inspired by a love of 18th and 19th century literature, Justan aims to bring seldom-told tales of the past to life. His second novel immerses readers in the sights, sounds, and struggles of 18th century Switzerland, employing evocative settings, multilayered characters, and dramatic storytelling — all with an element of the burlesque — that should, he hopes, resonate with readers, transporting them into a living past.

Justan's diverse artistic talents and passions come together to shape his unique voice and perspective in the realm of historical fiction.

Visit Justan's website at
www.justanautor.com

Visit Justan's Facebook page at
www.facebook.com/JustanAutor

Staten House

Printed in Dunstable, United Kingdom

63975527R00167